PRAISE FOR THE FRACTURED EUROPE SEQUENCE

"The Europe sequence is some of my favourite fiction this century, and *Europe in Winter* is no exception. Mind-bending, smart, human, with espionage thrills wrapped up in a reality-altering Europe, all told with sparkling prose and wit that should, if there was literary justice, catch the attention of prize after prize. I love these books. I want more. Now."

Patrick Ness on *Europe in Winter*

"As rich and as relevant as its predecessor. It's funny, fantastical, readable and remarkable regardless of your prior experience of the series. Which just goes to show that, no matter how well you think you know something – or someone, or somewhere, or somewhen – there's almost always more to the story."

Tor.com* on *Europe at Midnight

"*Europe in Autumn* is one of the most sophisticated science fiction novels of the decade: a tour-de-force debut, pacey, startlingly prescient, and possessed of a lively wit. When approaching its follow-up, I felt both nervous and excited. Would Hutchinson be able to pull off the same magic a second time? The answer is undoubtedly yes. *Europe at Midnight* is pitch-perfect, bursting with the same charisma and intricate world-building as its predecessor."

LA Review of Books* on *Europe at Midnight

"In a way, what is most striking about *Europe at Midnight* is not the hard edge of its politics, or even the casual brilliance of its science fictional reworking of the political thriller, but Hutchinson's thrillingly assured control of his material. He writes wonderfully, his prose animated not just by a keen eye for character, but by a blackly witty sense of humor."

Locus Magazine* on *Europe at Midnight

"The author's aut⋯⋯⋯⋯⋯⋯dge of eastern Europe, a⋯⋯⋯⋯⋯⋯mbine to crea⋯⋯⋯⋯⋯⋯ia."

"A well-constructed, tightly written thriller."
J Elmes on *Europe in Autumn*

"Hutchison brings to mind a pinch of Ken Macleod's politics, a few grains of Adam Roberts' fragmentary Europe from *New Model Army*, with an underlying base of China Mieville."
PG Harris on *Europe in Autumn*

"It's a pleasure from start to finish and back to the start again with idea after idea keeping you on your toes."
Dom Conlon on *Europe in Autumn*

"...on a helter-skelter journey across a fractured Europe, before taking an unexpected turn into stranger territory. Well written, hugely imaginative and with a wonderful Eastern European flavour."
A Warren on *Europe in Autumn*

"An evocative and nuanced book with slowly building tension and a perfectly realised cast of characters."
Lioc on *Europe in Autumn*

"Simply brilliant – a fascinating and believable tail of topographic quirky-ness."
S Laurie on *Europe in Autumn*

"This will appeal to fans of spy novels who are looking for something a bit different."
Kay Smillie on *Europe in Autumn*

"A well-written, slightly odd, slow burner that first intrigued, then gripped, and best of all delivered."
SDJ Forty on *Europe in Autumn*

"This is an extraordinary book. It weaves together more ideas than I think I've ever seen in a single book, and features a wide range of recognizable, interesting characters. The writing is clear, and often very funny; the plot is all over the show, but somehow arrives at a satisfying conclusion."
Nevillek on *Europe in Autumn*

"With seemingly effortless literary flair, Hutchinson reveals how the stories intersect in a complex, unsettling allegory of political manoeuvring, subterfuge and statecraft."

The Guardian on *Europe at Midnight*

"Not since 'The Man in the High Castle' have I read a novel and wondered halfway through if in fact it was reading me."

Andrew Wallace on *Europe at Midnight*

"This is an absorbing and unexpectedly intimate read exploring the hard yard of espionage, with parallel universes just one more way to give a spy a hard time."

imyril on *Europe at Midnight*

"Introspective, reflective, thought provoking... for me these were two delightful books that look forward in unusual ways while projecting an air of nostalgia and remembrance for ages past."

Lioc on *Europe at Midnight*

"*Europe at Midnight* is more a parallel than a sequel, appropriate for this gripping story of a parallel world and a shattered Europe."

Patrick McMurray on *Europe at Midnight*

"An excellent mix between Le Carré and Asimov's *Foundation*."

Geert Biermans on *Europe at Midnight*

"Taking the best from science fiction and cold war era spy thrillers, Dave Hutchison has created something uniquely his own. I cannot recommend this series highly enough. This is a smart, well executed ongoing story that delivers on multiple levels."

The Eloquent Page on *Europe at Midnight*

"The book unfolds slowly and grows on you: much of its charm is in the gentle way it builds things up...
Which isn't to say it lacks drama or action."

D Harris on *Europe at Midnight*

"Intriguing blend of spy, noir and SF."

A V McEwan on *Europe at Midnight*

"Merging together the very best of the thriller genre with the best of science fiction this book is just that damn entertaining and that damn good...
Buy it and relish a masterful storyteller at the top of his game."

The Eloquent Page on *Europe in Winter*

"The alternative Europe puts this book in the same sort of space as Peter Higgin's *Wolfhound Century* novels. Adam Roberts' *New Model Army* is similar in its fracturing of Europe. There is a strong parallel with the overlaid realities of China Mieville's *City and the City*. Outside the realms of speculative fiction, the tradecraft of the security services, the shifting alliances, dubious motives and complex plotting is strongly reminiscent of Le Carre, or Len Deighton."

PG Harris on *Europe in Winter*

"A very clever speculative spy thriller set in a near-future Europe where all is definitely not what it seems."

PeteMC on *Europe in Winter*

"Deliciously complex, humorous, twist and turns, gradual reveals, and the wonderfully superb climax to the book."

Highland Hellian on *Europe in Winter*

"It is very hard to describe, blending a 'realism' of a fragmented Europe of the nearish future with completely believable sci-if alternate but overlapping universes."

David Mason on *Europe in Winter*

"Frankly I could read this forever...
I just want to go on, seeing the layers peel away, shuffling the jigsaw pieces around, reading backwards and forwards to check details. Hutchinson's writing is almost interactive in the way it gives you an evolving problem to engage with."

D Harris on *Europe in Winter*

"The most fantastic twists and turns all tied up in breathtaking storytelling."

Paul H on *Europe in Winter*

"*Europe in Autumn* is the work of a consummate storyteller and combines great characters, a cracking central idea, and a plot that will keep you on the edge of your seat. Excellent."

Eric Brown on *Europe in Autumn*

"This awesome concoction of sci-fi and spies – picture John le Carre meets Christopher Priest – is an early favourite of the year for me."

Tor.com* on *Europe in Autumn

"The map of Europe has been redrawn, and its cartographers remain at work... the continent now exists as a patchwork of small nations and polities... for all that people want to carve out their own discrete realms, perhaps the greatest gift in Dave Hutchinson's future Europe is the ability to cross borders."

Strange Horizons* on *Europe in Autumn

"My best reads from the past year... [include] *Europe in Autumn*, by Dave Hutchinson, set in a future Europe fragmented into mini-states."

Derek Shearer, *Huffington Post* on *Europe in Autumn*

"One of the best novels I've read in a long time."

Adam Roberts, *The Guardian*, on *Europe in Autumn*

"With its understated stakes and imperturbable pace, its deliberate density and intellectual intensity... you have to work at it, but it's worth it, not least because what Hutchinson has to say about the world today is now more imperative that ever."

Niall Alexander, *Tor.com*, on *Europe in Winter*

"Hutchinson's entire Europe-series are wonderful: not quite science fiction, not quite crime, not quite current realism, but some of all."

***Benteh* on the Fractured Europe Sequence**

EUR
AT
DAW

OPE

DAVE
HUTCHINSON

N

First published 2018 by Solaris
an imprint of Rebellion Publishing Ltd,
Riverside House, Osney Mead,
Oxford, OX2 0ES, UK

www.solarisbooks.com

ISBN: 978 1 78108 609 4

Copyright © 2018 Dave Hutchinson

The right of the author to be identified as the author of this work
has been asserted in accordance with the Copyright, Designs
and Patents Act 1988.

This is a work of fiction. All the characters and events portrayed
in this book are fictional, and any resemblance to real people or
incidents is purely coincidental.

All rights reserved. No part of this publication may be
reproduced, stored in a retrieval system, or transmitted, in any
form or by any means, electronic, mechanical, photocopying,
recording or otherwise, without the prior permission of the
copyright owners.

10 9 8 7 6 5 4 3 2 1

A CIP catalogue record for this book is available from
the British Library.

Designed & typeset by Rebellion Publishing

Printed in Denmark by Nørhaven

The Fractured Europe Sequence

Europe in Autumn
Europe at Midnight
Europe in Winter
Europe at Dawn

PART ONE

FERNWEH

GRACE MERCY

EVERY COUPLE OF years, Pete and Angie did the whole of the Staffordshire and Worcestershire, from the Great Haywood junction with the Trent and Mersey to the staircase and lock that opened into the Severn. They'd been doing it ever since they bought *Grace Mercy*, almost thirty years ago now. Usually, they left it as late in the Summer as possible, after all the tourists had gone. Sometimes they did the trip with the kids, and latterly grandkids, but these days they mostly did it alone. It made a nice end to the season.

Grace Mercy was a fifty-footer, an old hauler Pete had first seen, derelict and rotting, tucked away in a corner of a basin in Bristol. He and Angie had only been married for a couple of years – he was working for a local engineering company and she was a nurse at the Frenchay Hospital – and they were struggling with the mortgage and the bills. He saw the old boat every day as he walked to and from work, and sometimes he just stood and looked at her for a few minutes, a half-formed idea somersaulting lazily through his head.

He was not an impulsive man, even when he was in his twenties. It had taken him almost five years to get up the momentum to ask Angie to marry him, and by then her parents had been warning her that there was something 'slow' about him. The looks on their faces at the wedding ceremony suggested that they hadn't changed their minds very much.

It took him a little over eighteen months to broach the subject of *Grace Mercy* with Angie. They were having dinner one evening at their flat in Bedminster and he looked at her and said, "Ange, how about we buy a boat?"

"A *what*?" she said.

"A boat," he said. "A narrow boat. We could do it up, take tourists for cruises."

"Are you crazy?" she said. "We can barely afford this place, let alone a boat."

"No," he said. "I mean sell the flat, live on the boat."

"You must think I'm as daft as you are," she said. "I'm not living on no boat."

And there the conversation lulled. But if Pete was not an impulsive man, he was also not a man to just drop an idea once it lodged in his mind. At lunchtimes, and late at night, he sat with a little paper notepad and a pencil and he worked out the figures. After work, he hung around the basin for a couple of hours, chatting to some of the old geezers who lived on the boats moored there. One of them, a little leathery chap named Arthur who claimed to have been born on the Kennet and Avon, gave him a tour of his boat. "And that there is the *counter*, and that over there is the *cratch cover*."

Arthur himself was dismissive of Pete's plan. "Don't know why anyone would want to take themselves off travelling," he said. "It's a fucking horrible life; I had a bellyfull of it." But he carried on his patient little tutorials, and Pete started to get an idea of what he would need and what he could get away with, and eventually the figures started to agree with each other.

Finally, he tracked down *Grace Mercy*'s owner, a solicitor who lived over in Redland, and asked to have a look at the old boat. The solicitor had inherited it from a cousin and she had no idea what to do with it, and no time even if she had. She was basically paying the mooring fees and half hoping the boat would either sink or be stolen; at least then she could claim on the insurance and be rid of it. The idea of anyone actually wanting to buy the old wreck had never occurred to her, and she was more than happy to let Pete have the keys for a couple of hours during his lunch break.

Some work had already been done to convert *Grace Mercy* for cruising, but it looked as if the solicitor's cousin had either run out of money or died before they could complete the job. The hull appeared sound. Inside, she was just dirty and a bit mouldy, lacking all but the most basic fixtures and fittings. Nothing a bit of elbow grease and a lick of paint wouldn't sort out. The engine was a monster, a Beta Greenline diesel rated for fifty brake horsepower, an engine for a much heavier boat. It was a ruin, but Pete knew engines and he knew he could fix it. He took the keys back to the solicitor at her office in the city centre and told her he was interested. He just had to have a chat to his wife.

This, of course, was the insurmountable barrier, the immoveable object. The figures worked out, just. They had some savings – a wedding present from his parents, only to be touched in the direst of emergencies but already being chipped away – and a bit of equity in the flat, but in order to buy *Grace Mercy* they would have to sell the flat first, then live onboard while they renovated the boat, and there was no way Angie would agree to that.

And then, one day, something so absurd happened that Pete could only liken it to winning the Lottery. He was poking disconsolately about below decks one lunchtime, the memory of yet another evening's argument still painfully sharp, when he heard someone calling from the quayside, and when he went up to look there was a plump, round man in an expensive suit standing there holding a briefcase.

"Are you the owner?" asked the plump man.

Pete shook his head regretfully, realising as he did so that he was finally letting his dream bob away. "I wish," he said.

"Do you know who the owner is?"

"Yeah. I was going to buy it off her, but there's no way I could afford it." Then he found himself qualifying it to this complete stranger with, "Well, I *could*, like. Just. But it's the wife."

The plump man gave him a long, level look that Pete found quite unsettling, even though there seemed no malice behind it. "Is it just the money?"

"Well, yeah. And the living on a boat, like."

The plump man seemed to come to a decision. "May I come aboard?" he asked, looking dubiously down at *Grace Mercy*.

"Knock yourself out. There's a ladder just along there."

With some difficulty, the plump man managed to negotiate the ladder without dropping his briefcase into the water. He was breathing heavily when he finally made it down to the cockpit, but he immediately put out a hand and said, "I'm Alan Strang. Would it be any help to you if you had a *sponsor?*"

"A what?" Angie asked that evening, when Pete told her of this turn of affairs.

"He won't say who it is. Just someone with a lot of money who wants to help out local folk. Like that charity that makes kiddies' dreams come true."

"Kiddies is right," she snorted.

"They'll give us the money to buy the boat and do her up," he said. "All they want in return is a trip on her every now and again, just to see how we're doing."

Angie looked unconvinced. "All sounds a bit rum to me," she said.

"It's just someone local who had a bit of luck and wants to spread it around," Pete said, almost literally beaming good thoughts at his wife. "Come on, Ange. We don't have to sell the flat. We can do the boat up at weekends and in spare minutes, and we can take her out on our holidays."

Angie shook her head. "You're the one with all the spare minutes, sunshine, not me." But he could see her starting to waver, and over the next couple of weeks she wavered more and more, and finally they were sitting in a rented office with Alan Strang, signing some papers. And a month or so later *Grace Mercy* was theirs.

It took him almost three years to renovate the boat, at weekends and after work, spare stolen moments tinkering with the diesel and replacing bits and pieces and painting and sanding and painting again. Arthur and some of the old geezers wandered over from time to time, to point out what he was doing wrong and generally make nuisances of themselves. Eventually, Angie started coming down to the basin when her shifts allowed – she'd taken one look at *Grace Mercy* the morning after he'd told her about Alan Strang's offer, and said, "Well, it's only someone else's money and your own time you're wasting" – and pottering about with the painting. Before long she was standing watching disapprovingly as he disassembled the diesel, which he had dubbed Behemoth, and not long after that she was helping out. After a few days she knew the abused old Greenline better than he did.

Together, they managed to get Behemoth working well enough to putter over to the basin's dry dock so Pete could inspect the hull properly and give it some coats of bitumen paint. One of the sacrificial anodes that helped protect the hull from corrosion was missing, probably the result of a collision with something, and Pete welded on a new one, but remarkably, apart from a few dents and scrapes, almost everything below the waterline was in good order.

They converted the fore cargo space into family accommodation, keeping the original after cabin for themselves. The fore cabin would be a bit cramped for more than three people, but that, reasoned Pete, was part of the experience. Tourism was belatedly starting to pick up again after the Xian Flu; people who had stayed at home were beginning to venture out, and if they were still not confident enough to travel to the Continent, or couldn't be bothered to negotiate the dizzying array of visa requirements that had sprung up as the European Union splintered, then they were happy enough to take a break at home.

And *Grace Mercy* was good to Pete and Angie, down the years. Families did book the boat, for weekend breaks or longer cruises. Eventually, the business was doing so well that they gave up their respective jobs, and they moved onto the water more or less full time, although they never did quite sell the flat. The kids were born and brought up on the boat.

They never saw Alan Strang again, although they exchanged cards at Christmas and a stipend from their *sponsor* continued to be paid into their account every month for the upkeep of the boat and a little extra left over. The sponsor themselves never showed up, as far as they knew, although Pete always suspected that they'd come on board incognito, as a paying guest, just to check things out.

A few times, he got emails from Alan Strang asking that he take the boat to this or that set of GPS coordinates and transport whoever was waiting there to another set of coordinates. Angie was suspicious of these jobs, but their passengers seemed, on the whole, perfectly blameless and innocent, and Pete considered them a harmless part of the deal they had struck in order to buy *Grace Mercy* in the first place.

Once, on the Kennet and Avon, he'd been asked to go to a certain place, and following the GPS he'd found the boat chugging along a stretch of canal he'd never seen before, opening out onto a big wide powerful river. He checked the coordinates and found the satnav had gone down, but there on the bank stood a woman, waving her arms above her head, so he brought the boat alongside and she hopped on board.

"Hi," she said, "I'm Hannelore." She looked as if she'd spent the night in a hedge, but she appeared cheerful and relaxed, even though there was what seemed to be gunfire in the distance.

"What's that?" asked Angie.

Hannelore looked towards the sound. "LARPers," she said.

"Whaters?" said Angie.

"Live Action Roleplayers," Hannelore said. "Corporate team-building weekend. Men playing Cowboys and Indians." She gave Angie a long-suffering look that Angie understood very well. "Muppets." She beamed at them. "Still, exciting though, eh? A bit like Dunkirk."

Pete looked around him at the river, the wooded banks. He realised he didn't know this stretch of water at all. "Well, not really," he said.

Hannelore shook her head. "No, not really. We'd best be on our way, Captain," she told Pete. "If they find us here they'll just be tiresome for a while and I've had about enough of men being tiresome."

This was not a problem; Behemoth could shift the boat at a surprising speed, if need be, but Pete found himself momentarily at a loss. "GPS has gone down," he said.

Hannelore just grinned and shook her head. "Nah, it's okay, Captain," she said. "I know the way. I'll show you."

And so she did, and Pete soon found himself back on familiar waters, and shortly after that they dropped Hannelore off at Swineford Lock and watched her walk off down the towpath as if she didn't have a care in the world, although Pete thought he detected a certain determination in her body language.

Angie gave him a hard look, and he winced.

"Suppose she's on the run from the police or something?" she said.

"She'd have to be bloody desperate to make a getaway on a narrow boat, love," he said.

That, at any rate, seemed to be the last of what Angie called 'the bloody weird jobs' for quite a long while. Years passed and the only people to set foot on *Grace Mercy* were tourists. Sometimes things went wrong, but more often they went right, and Pete thought that wasn't such a bad way for everything to work out.

BALTIC
APOCALYPSE

1.

THE BIG FILM that year was, improbably, a Polish-Estonian coproduction, a blockbuster featuring much gunfire and many explosions and a body-count roughly equal to that of the Thirty Years' War. Rob opined that it had the stupidest title he had ever seen, and refused to watch it.

Much of the film had been shot in Tallinn, with some location work out in Lahemaa. It had had its world premiere at Kino Sõprus, the oldest cinema in the country, and because the director was from Prestwick it had fallen to Alice to liaise with the film company and the cinema organisers, and to arrange a reception at the Ambassador's residence afterward. And that, Rob *had* been interested in, sticking to her like a limpet, demanding to know who was who, wanting to be introduced to people who caught his eye, crashing conversations she tried to have, and sucking up to Nicky, the Ambassador, who couldn't have cared less because she genuinely despised the English in general and Rob in particular. At one point, orbiting genially back through the party after a visit to the loo, Alice had seen him across the room, pressing a printed copy of his latest self-published collection into the hands of one of the producers.

The thing with Nicky and Rob had actually become a Thing, had threatened Alice's posting here for a while until Rob had announced he was going to report Nicky for racial discrimination. Alice, terminally embarrassed by the whole shouting match, had attempted to keep her head down while Rob and HR exchanged angry emails and angrier phone calls. Rob had accused her of not giving him sufficient emotional support, which was something he did a lot.

Eventually, the whole thing blew over. Alice never really heard the full story, but she got the impression that word had been sent from Holyrood that the business was starting to attract media attention and that everyone involved should have a quiet word with themselves and shut the fuck up.

"Big Mo threatened to come over and shake some people by the ears," Selina confided over lunch one day. Big Mo was Scotland's First Minister, and the mere prospect of a visit from her was enough to put the fear of god into the entire Embassy.

Alice didn't really want to talk about it – would rather it all went away or a hole appeared in which she could bury herself, or something – but curiosity got the better of her and she said, "What happened?"

Selina shrugged. "Politics." And she held her hand up beside her ear and wiggled her fingers – her shorthand for the kind of bollocks which no rational person would take seriously, but which ruled the lives of the Embassy staff.

"Am I going to be sent to London?" Alice asked. Of all Scotland's infant Embassies, London was generally agreed to be the worst; hamstrung by astronomical property prices, it was quartered in a small rented semi-detached house in Lewisham, the laughing stock of the diplomatic community. The English press periodically ran photos of it, accompanied by satirical captions.

Selina guffawed. "Ach no! Someone on Nicky's staff'll get called back for a quiet chat. Probably wee Jake; he's expendable. Then we'll all just carry on trundling along."

And carry on trundling they did. In time, Nicky and Rob learned to tolerate each other's presence. Rob would even attempt to schmooze her – he liked to schmooze – although she drew the line at that.

Alice never quite recovered, though. She ^adored Tallinn, but the incident had someh^ experience of the place. It was as if someo^ over her perceptions of the city, or maybe remo^ tell. She found herself noticing stuff she wouldn't ^ finding patterns and conjunctions she would have glosse^

"You're becoming paranoid," Selina scoffed.

Alice snorted. "It's a miracle I'm not on crack." But she ne^ mentioned it again.

Two months on, and she was still seeing posters for the film stuck on walls, peeling and torn and bleached by the weather, that peculiarly-designed and utterly baffling exclamation mark standing out on a background of invading Russian armour crashing through a burning forest. It had not gone down well with Moscow, and even less well with Estonia's ethnic Russian minority, who had staged disruptions on the location shoots, vigorously boycotted the cinemas where it had been showing, and staged an abortive cyber-attack on the preparations for the premiere. The posters were a tattered and defaced reminder of a whirlwind which had raged through eighteen months of her life. They also reminded her of Polsloe. Seeing them made her feel angry and slightly giddy at the same time. Tattered and defaced.

For their Embassy in Tallinn, the Scottish Government had taken a longish lease on the top five floors of a building around the corner from the Hotell Palace. The ground floor was occupied by a supermarket and a boutique, and the basement by a club which occasionally hosted all-night raves for those of a nostalgic turn of mind and a taste for MDMA. It was not unusual for Alice to come into work on a Saturday morning and discover groups of ravers, still festooned with strings of glowsticks and carrying big plastic cups of beer, waiting unsteadily for the tram. It was hardly an auspicious location for an Embassy – they looked with some envy at the Irish Embassy, perched high above them in the Upper Town – but she liked it. It was only a five-minute walk into the Old Town, and traffic crossing the tram tracks which ran down the middle of the road outside the Palace sounded, momentarily, like galloping horses. When a lot of cars and vans were released at once by the traffic lights, it was like a stampede, and she found the sound soothing.

ont door had once had a thumbprint lock, a little box smaller packet of cigarettes mounted on the wall. For reasons which lost in the mists of drink and party drugs, this blameless device enraged the ravers, who had rendered it useless by smearing the ader with epoxy glue. The Embassy had chalked it up to youthful iigh spirits, complained to the club owners, and replaced the box. A few days later, the new reader was coated with solidified glue.

The Embassy sighed and tutted and complained to the club and replaced the reader again, and once more, the following weekend the reader was vandalised. This time the ravers had upped the ante by pouring quick-setting plastic over the box, and it was encased in a fist-sized lump of acrylic from which sharp, clear stalactites had dripped and puddled on the pavement below.

This was obviously unacceptable, and this time the Embassy provided the police with grabs from the security cameras which showed masked, hooded figures skulking around the front door. The police were sympathetic but had to admit that the images did not provide sufficient identification evidence to justify an arrest, let alone a prosecution.

The Embassy hired a private security firm to patrol the street at night, and replaced the lock. Two days later it was pried completely off the wall, placed on the doorstep, doused with petrol, and set alight. The security guards saw nothing.

By this time, the matter had reached Holyrood. Big Mo called the Estonian Ambassador in for a cup of tea and a chat, and the Ambassador was respectfully unable to offer very much in the way of a solution. An application to close the club would take time, and would only inflame passions further, he argued. He was, however, complimentary about the scones he was offered.

In the end, the Embassy had bowed to the inevitable. The thumbprint lock was removed permanently and replaced with a simple bell-push. A chair and a small desk were placed in the narrow entrance hall, together with a monitor linked to the security camera over the door, and behind the desk were installed Paavo, Saamuel, Mart and Aigar, four colossal security men, basically meat icebergs dressed in three-piece suits and armed with tasers and tear gas and riot guns.

This level of inconvenience seemed, finally, to satisfy the Faceless Enemies of the Thumbprint Reader, and the vandalism ceased, save for a single incident of graffiti when someone stencilled a rather fancifully-endowed cock and balls on the wall outside.

There was still a pale patch on the wall, where the offending genitalia had been high-pressure-cleaned off the stonework. Alice had stopped noticing it. She pressed the button by the door, held up her pass and smiled for the camera, and the lock buzzed. She put her shoulder to the door and pushed hard against the springs before the lock could close again.

The security men worked in pairs, one at the front desk at all times with the other as backup for breaks and emergencies. Today, it was Mart sitting under a daylight-emulation lamp in the slightly dingy entranceway. It wasn't much more than a corridor leading to the lifts and the stairs to the upper floors, and the security desk very nearly blocked it entirely. Mart and Paavo tended to work as a team; Mart was solemn and gracious, Paavo a little flirtatious, but apart from that they were more or less indistinguishable, vast and neckless and shaven-headed, a steroid-powered Tweedledum and Tweedledee.

"Good morning, Mart," she said, approaching the desk and handing over her pass.

Mart slotted the card into a little reader on the desk in front of him. "Morning, Ms." He called all the female staff 'Ms', regardless of their marital status.

Alice put her thumb on the plate of a fingerprint scanner on the desk beside the card reader. Mart consulted his screen, nodded slightly, gave back her ID. Nicky had handed down a fiat, via Meg, the Embassy's head of security. Security procedures had to be followed to the letter, on pain of dismissal. No one was to be nodded through, no matter how well the security men knew them.

The Embassy's Cultural Section was housed in two rooms on the first floor, and numbered three staff. In descending order of seniority they were Tim the Attaché, Selina, and Alice. Tim was a vague presence, most often to be found elsewhere in the city enjoying various cultural freebies; Alice and Selina, a tall willowy Aberdonian with the cheekbones of a supermodel and the vocabulary of a stevedore, did most of the day-to-day work not involving attending parties and gallery openings and exhibitions.

"They've invited Mr Octopus again," Selina told her when she'd hung her coat up and sat at her desk.

"Oh, *that's* grand," she said. The concern at the moment was a little literary festival, which last year had been attended by a couple of poets from Tayside and Jimmy Cox, the author of a series of tough-guy novels set in Glasgow around the time of Independence. Cox had groped her drunkenly and rather apologetically at an evening reception at the Town Hall. "How'd he manage to sleaze his way back in?"

"He's smart and he's funny and his books are popular here. Anyway, the wee cunt hasn't sleazed his way back yet. We can still veto his invitation."

"Can we?"

"We can tell the organisers we'll withdraw our support if they don't withdraw his invite."

Alice snorted. "*That'll* have them shaking in their boots."

"You'd be surprised; we've still got a lot of goodwill after the movie."

"The movie. Pft."

"Seriously. Want me to draft a memo to the Festival? Won't take five minutes, Tim'll sign it without bothering to read it, and The Cox will be persona non grata in Tallinn."

Alice thought about it. Cox's last visit had ended with an Ambassadorial dressing down for him and a very uncomfortable interview with HR for her. Trying to get his invitation revoked would only start the whole thing up again.

"Come on," Selina said. "That was fucking sexual assault. Nicky and the cunts upstairs really fucking messed things up; Cox should have been arrested."

And he would have been, if HR hadn't suggested that it was best to keep the whole thing quiet and in-house. No need for fuss and bad publicity, Alice. We'll deal with this ourselves. And then she'd imagined how Rob would have reacted to it going to court and all of a sudden she'd just wanted the whole thing to go away. She shook her head. "Let the little twat have his holiday," she said. "But I'm not doing the Festival. It's your turn, anyway."

"Alice."

"Leave it, Sel. Okay? I just want to forget he exists."

Selina sighed. "He touches *my* tits, I'll feed him his tiny little bollocks."

"Attagirl," Alice said. The Festival was still months away. She had some leave saved up; maybe she could arrange to be out of the city while Cox was here. There were less than threequarters of a million people in Tallinn; it was surprising how often you bumped into people you didn't want to see. "What else is going on?"

Selina consulted her pad. "Jim Ryan's private view at that new gallery in Pirita tonight. Tim's got dibs on that; there's a buffet. The folkies arrive tomorrow. You know, this keeping your head down and not making a fuss thing is going to cause you all sorts of trouble one day. He *attacked* you."

"Enough, Sel. Subject closed. Okay? What else?"

Selina put the pad down on her desk. "That's it."

Alice looked at her. "What are we doing here?"

"I don't fucking know. Lunch?"

Alice checked the time on her phone. "It's only twenty past nine."

"Ah, fuck this." Selina stood up and grabbed her bag. "Get your coat. Fact-finding."

FACT FINDING WAS Selina's euphemism for 'exploring the cultural heritage of Tallinn while looking for new restaurants to try out.' The only rules were that they walked everywhere, to offset the calories, and that cultural heritage took second place to a good meal. They'd managed to clock up an impressive number of kilometres and lunches in the three years since Alice had taken up her posting, and the wonderful thing was that there were always new restaurants.

Today was a recently-opened vegan place just off Raekoja plats. It was two doors down from a studio which produced amber carvings, which qualified it as Cultural. It was also very quiet. Estonians – particularly Tallinners – were pretty hip, as these things went, but veganism had yet to sweep the country to any great degree.

And Alice didn't think this place would be here very long,

anyway. The owners had taken what she thought was the lazy route and basically turned it into a vegetable curry house. The food was hearty and tasty but pedestrian.

"Well, this is fucking grim," Selina noted, poking at her chickpea curry.

Desperate not to have curry for brunch, Alice had managed to find a mushroom and lentil hotpot lurking near the bottom of the menu. "Hm."

"Have you seen the new spook yet?"

"Sorry? Spook?"

"Malcolm's replacement. Arrived last week."

"Has Malcolm left?" Alice's contact with the sole official representative of Scotland's Foreign Intelligence Service had been limited. She couldn't, now she thought about it, remember the last time she'd seen the dour, stork-like figure of Malcolm Smith at the Embassy.

Selina sat back and gave her a long-suffering look. "There was a leaving party."

"I didn't get the memo." Alice forked some hotpot into her mouth. "Who's the replacement?"

"Name of Harry. Looks about fourteen. Meg's got a wide-on for him."

Not for the first time, Alice wondered how all this gossip managed to pass her by. Perhaps it all wound up in the same place the news of Malcolm's leaving do had. Having said that, she did vaguely remember seeing an unfamiliar young man in Meg's company a few days ago. "Is that him? I thought he was the new post-boy."

Selina guffawed. "Work experience."

"Did Malcolm fuck up?" Beneath all the day-to-day concerns of life at the Embassy, there was the ever-present fear of Fucking Up. Scotland's Diplomatic Service was still in its infancy, and the potential for embarrassment was without bounds. The entire staff of the Paris Embassy had been replaced after it was discovered that the Russians had, more as a thought experiment than anything else, managed to suborn every single one of them. The English press, Scotland's most faithful nemesis, was still running op-ed pieces about that particular catastrophe.

Selina shrugged. "Not that I heard. Just got posted somewhere else. Someone said Madrid."

"That'll have pleased him." In her very few interactions with him, Malcolm had always struck her as a Northern Europe sort of man. He looked as if his skin would burn and peel off if he stood under a hundred watt bulb for twenty minutes.

"Aye, I know what you mean," Selina said. "How was your weekend?"

"It was fine. Why?"

"Just asking. You've got the look."

"What look?"

"*That* look."

"I've got no idea what you're talking about, Sel. What look?"

Selina cocked an eyebrow at her.

Alice sighed. "It was fine. Really."

Selina shook her head. "I tell you, this keeping your head down and not making a fuss will get you in trouble one day."

"Maybe. But not today."

"It's only ten past eleven," Selina noted. "Still plenty of time."

Alice gave up on the hotpot, pushed it to one side. "How was *your* weekend?"

"We went to Helsinki."

"Ooh. Exciting."

"Had a bit of a row. I got a memo from HR a couple of weeks ago; Holyrood wants us to get married."

"Oh, Sel."

Selina shrugged. "Sue's not keen. Neither am I, for that matter, but she's fucking incandescent about it."

"Is it Holyrood who wants you to get married, or Nicky?"

"Doesn't matter, really. Of course, they can't say it's because they think a couple of tweedy old dykes living in sin makes them look bad; they quoted Section 237, Para 5 at me."

Alice shook her head. The terms of her contract with the Scottish Diplomatic Service ran to well over a thousand pages; she'd never bothered to read it properly.

"It's the one that says all staff must be married," Selina said.

"That's bollocks. Nicky's not married. Well, she is, but..."

"Yeah." Mr Nicky was reputed to be living in Nassau with a former swimsuit model, something Alice found so exotic that it was hard to connect it with anyone she knew. "Anyway, Sue wants us to leave."

"What, Estonia?"

"The Service."

Alice sat back in her chair. "Oh. Oh, Sel. I'm sorry."

"Oh, I'm not fucking going to. Hence the row. Put a bit of a dampener on the weekend."

"Why didn't you say something?"

Selina deadpanned her and blinked slowly.

All right. Fair enough. "What are you going to do?"

"We're sleeping on it, for now. I'll see how long it takes HR to decide to poke me again."

"It's stupid. Why do we all have to be married?"

Selina made a rude noise. "PR. We're all one big happy family, right?"

Alice, whose own family was certainly large, but far from happy, sighed. "Isn't there someone you could complain to?"

"Oh, sure. There's always someone willing to take up the fucking cudgels. Sue won't have it, though. She's not wired like that. She's like you, in a lot of ways. Head down, don't make a fuss."

Alice sensed one side of the weekend's argument being rerun for her. She said, "If there's anything I can do..."

"Thanks." Selina looked at her curry and sighed. "Let's go for a burger, eh?"

WHEN THEY GOT back to the Embassy they found that Tim had made an appearance, left a stack of paperwork behind, and vanished again. Very little of the paperwork was immediately urgent, but Alice was so relieved to have something to do that she happily ploughed into it.

It was gone six when she finally got home. The flat was two changes of trams and a bus ride across the city from the Embassy, but it came with the job so it seemed a bit rude to complain. It was a nice flat, the area wasn't bad, and she got on with the neighbours.

Things could have been worse.

She walked from the bus stop, past her building, to the shop on the corner, where she spent ten minutes pottering about buying groceries and chatting to the girl on the checkout. Then she carried on round the corner, along the block, turned left, and walked along the street parallel to hers. Halfway along, she took the grocery receipt from her pocket, crumpled it, and dropped it in a litter bin. At the far corner, she turned left again, and another left, until she was walking past her building again. She went around the block three more times, her footsteps becoming more and more weary each time, until she finally approached the front door, waved her phone over the lock sensor, and went inside.

Up on the fourth floor, the door of the flat opened on to a short corridor lined with cupboards and coathooks. She took off her coat and shoes, put on a pair of slippers, hung her coat, and continued into the living room.

Where the door to the spare bedroom – Rob's study – was opening and he was coming out, dressed in a sweatshirt and jogging bottoms, his feet bare on the wood floor of the living room, grinning his old piratical grin.

"Hallo, sweetheart," he said, giving her a hug that she returned limply. "Get anything nice?"

Alice held out the carrier bag, and Rob looked inside. He started taking things out and looking at them, arranging them on the kitchen counter at one side of the living room. "We've got a jar of peanut butter, haven't we?" he said, looking at one item.

"I couldn't remember if we did or not." She shrugged. "I was in the shop; I thought I might as well."

"I don't think it's even been opened," he said. He went over to one of the kitchen cupboards, looked inside, and took out a jar. He unscrewed the lid and held it up to show her the intact seal. "See?"

"Yes," she said. She folded the bag and put it on the worktop. "How was your day?"

"Fine," he said. "Did a lot of work. How was yours?"

Work, for Rob, mostly involved sitting at his shitty old laptop and spamming people with emails and posts about his books. Every now and again – usually when Alice needed him for something, which was increasingly rarely – he locked himself in his study, professing himself busy with a new poem.

She embarked on a recitation of the salient parts of her day while he looked at the groceries she'd bought. He picked up the folded carrier bag, unfolded it casually, glanced inside, folded it again, and she knew he was looking for the receipt with its time stamp which would have exposed the half hour of peace she'd given herself between leaving the shop and coming home.

He put the bag back on the counter – he hadn't really been listening to her telling him about her day; the point was that she should do it – and said, "I thought maybe we could have those pork chops for dinner."

"Okay," she said. "Just let me wash my hands."

He grinned again. "Sure, sure. Whenever you're ready." And he gave her another little hug and went back into his room and closed the door.

Alice went into the kitchen. Breakfast mugs and plates were still piled in the sink, along with whatever cookware and crockery Rob had used to make his lunch. There was a new, crusted stain on the hob and a couple of empty milk cartons on the worktop. She looked at all these things and counted to ten without being consciously aware of doing it.

2.

WHEN SHE LOOKED in the mirror, she saw a slightly dumpy woman in her late thirties, with a bland, easily forgettable face, long brown hair, and tired eyes. She favoured slightly old-fashioned dresses – Rob liked them – and flat shoes. Sometimes she wore makeup, but not very often. *Bovine* was the word that came to her mind. She drifted through her life with all the insane enthusiasm of a contented farm animal and there was nothing at all she could do about it.

She'd worked hard to get where she was, which was quite funny until she thought about it. She'd worked hard to lose her Govan accent – she now sounded a little like Maggie Smith in

The Prime of Miss Jean Brodie – worked hard at school, worked hard studying European Politics at Nottingham, worked hard on her MA in International Relations at Tallinn University. She was in her final year when Independence finally, and rather suddenly, overtook Scotland in a neurotic spasm of civil unrest which only worsened when Westminster tried to restore order. Her father, an SNP streetfighter down to his mitochondrial DNA, professed it to be the best time of his life; the rest of her family advised her to stay put until things settled down.

That took care of itself, in the end. She was already dating Rob, he had more or less moved in with her, and between them – it seemed that way, at the time – they decided to marry in Tallinn. After that, it was just a question of finding a job.

She'd never really left Estonia. She was working two days a week for a little international relations think-tank in Tartu when the infant state opened its Estonian Embassy, and a couple of years later a paper she presented at a conference in Edinburgh caught someone's attention and she was called to Holyrood for an interview.

"You're no goana work for they cunts, are you?" said her father, who had by this time experienced something of an ideological schism with the new government regarding his state pension.

"Sure," she said. "Why not?"

Well, *why not* turned out to be three years of babysitting various visiting Scottish artists. Rob had been all for it at first, imagining all sorts of useful new contacts, but after insisting on meeting the first half dozen or so visitors he gave up, externalising his disappointment in a poem about a wife who hated her husband.

For Alice, it had all been rather fun. New faces every few days, new experiences – she was still in contact with some of them – but in terms of career advancement it was a bit of a bust. She was thinking about casting around for another posting when Tim came into the office one morning and solemnly informed her and Selina that a *movie* was going to be made in Estonia. He made this sound so unusual that Alice was moved to mention that numerous films had *already* been made there. In fact, *Darkness in Tallinn* was one of the reasons she'd wanted to study here in the first place. Tim blinked as the title went entirely over his head.

"It's to be called," he told them, "*Baltic Apocalypse*. With an exclamation mark."

"Oh?" Selina said, nodding sagely. "An *exclamation mark*, is it?"

Tim looked at them both. His lack of self-awareness was legendary in the Diplomatic Service. "The director's from Prestwick," he said. "So we're to offer them every facility. No job too large, no job too small. That's from the First Minister's office, via Nicky."

Selina and Alice looked at each other, then looked at Tim again, suitably impressed expressions on their faces.

"From *Prestwick*, is it?" Selina said thoughtfully.

The airport was only ten minutes' drive from the Old Town – you could walk it easily in an hour or so, if the weather was nice and you were that way inclined – but Alice took a cab on the office account because a) it was professional, and b) Selina had once actually managed to lose an airport pickup on public transport, a poet who styled himself The McGregor of McGregor. They'd been chatting on the bus into town, the bus was crowded, Selina's attention had been distracted for a moment while it was at a stop, and when she turned back The McGregor was gone.

He turned up five weeks later in a commune on Saaremaa, married to a woman who called herself Ehaema and claiming political asylum from what he described as 'the fascist regime of Holyrood'. The whole thing had been kicked upstairs – Alice and Selina, and indeed Tim, did not occupy the correct pay grade to deal with matters like this – and in the end it was agreed that it was less trouble to just leave The McGregor where he was. The commune on Saaremaa worshipped a meteorite which had supposedly landed on the island several thousand years earlier. If The McGregor wanted to do that, fine.

In the end, the marriage of The McGregor and Ehaema – the name meant 'Mother Twilight', which ought to have given him *some* sort of hint – proved problematical, and he had decamped alone to Vienna, where he took to publishing enormous political rants against the Scottish government under his real name. It turned out he wasn't even a real McGregor.

Anyway, a memo had come down from Nicky and now all airport – and more rarely railway and harbour pickups – were to be accomplished by taxi, so here she was, in the middle of a nice bright morning, standing in Arrivals holding a piece of card on which the word *BODFISH* had been printed in Comic Sans. "Fuck 'em if they can't take a joke," Selina had said the first time she'd used that particular font, and it had become their Thing, one of a host of little Things they had erected against the stultifying effects of the job.

For some reason which had never been explained to her, flights from Scotland to Tallinn were always at absurd times of the day, either fuck-off early in the morning or late at night. Alice didn't mind the early flights, particularly. They were fine so long as you got plenty of sleep the night before and didn't spend a busy couple of hours in the bar at the airport waiting to board.

The two dishevelled figures emerging from the arrivals gate, burdened with guitar cases and rucksacks, had done way too little of one and way too much of the other, judging by the way they were trying very hard to walk in a straight line towards her. One was short and thin, the other tall and verging on corpulent. Both had impressive beards and were dressed entirely in denim. As they reached Alice, a miasma of whisky settled over her.

"I'm Luke," said the tall one as they shook hands. "This is Wally." Wally looked more or less asleep on his feet.

Alice said, "I'm Alice May, from the Embassy. Welcome to Tallinn."

"Aye," said Wally without quite focusing on her. "Can we go now?"

Bodfish were a folk duo from Pitlochry with, she understood from her background reading, quite a following. Alice didn't get folk; she'd listened to Bodfish's new album, *Songs The Lords Taught Us*, and found it somehow baffling and atonal and twee all at once. Also, she hated the title.

She conveyed none of this, either in words or body language, on the short drive into town. Wally fell asleep. Luke blinked out of the window at the strange new city passing by outside. They were still something of an unknown quantity as far as Alice was concerned, so she'd booked them into the Palace, where she could keep an eye on them.

At the hotel, she handled check-in for them – Wally was still basically unconscious – handed over envelopes with two hundred kroons apiece for incidental expenses – the Estonians, like practically everyone else, having fled currency union at the first opportunity – and made sure they got to their rooms. Then she went round the corner to the Embassy.

"The Bodfish has landed," she said, settling herself at her desk.

"Hm? Good." Selina was reading something on her tablet. "What are they like?"

"I'll let you know when they've had a sleep and sobered up."

"Not Tim's cup of tea, then."

"Gods no. Why?"

"He was asking about them earlier. Said he was thinking about going to the gig."

The thought of Tim being a folkie was faintly absurd. "It's only a pub gig. No free nosh or anything."

Selina shrugged.

"You okay?" asked Alice.

Selina nodded without looking up from the tablet.

Alice put her phone on the desk, and it buzzed. She poked at it and saw she had received a message via an app which she somehow had not been able to gather the momentum to delete. The message said, *waves* and she felt the world grey out a little, even now.

AT LUNCHTIME, SELINA went out on some unspecified errands. Alice sat for a while looking out of the window. The day had started to cloud over, and a freshening breeze blew spots of rain onto the glass.

Eventually she reached into her bag and took out a hardback book, an old Estonian-language copy of *Oliver Twist* she'd picked up in a secondhand shop. She had a small library of books like this, and she rotated them every couple of weeks, even though she never read them. They were all hardbacks, and they were all Dickens, because Rob hated Dickens.

She opened the book near the middle so the spine flexed open, and shook it gently over the desk. A little package wrapped in clingfilm, no larger than her index fingernail, fell out. Inside was a SIM card. She took the back off her phone, swapped its card with the one from the book, and switched it on.

There were only three things on the new card – a messaging app, a folder bulging with messages, and a contacts folder with only one number. She put her fingertip on the little icon for the app, and there was a knock on the door.

She was doing nothing against the rules, but her heart pounded and she reacted without thinking, defaulting to a childish pantomime. She crumpled the clingfilm along with the original SIM in her fist, held the phone to her ear, and said, "Yes?"

The door opened and someone she vaguely recognised popped their head into the office. "Hi," he said.

"Hello," said Alice.

"I didn't mean to interrupt..."

"Oh. Oh, it's okay," she said to the phone. "Yes, let's do that. Talk to you tonight. Yes. Bye." And she pantomimed hanging up and smiled at... Harry, she remembered now. The new spook.

He came into the office and approached the desk holding out his hand. "It's nothing important," he told her. "Harry Gardener. I'm new here."

His handshake was firm and confident but not threatening. "Alice May," she said. "I've seen you about."

"I'm just going around introducing myself," he said. "Junior commercial attaché." And he rolled his eyes a little, making a joke of the obvious cover in a way that she found rather engaging.

"Junior cultural attaché," she said, waving at the office. "Welcome to my world."

"I'm sorry I interrupted your call," he said. "I'd have moved on if I'd heard you talking."

First rule of lying: don't offer any information. "No need to apologise. Are you settling in okay?"

"Yeah." He gestured at the visitor chair in the corner. "May I?"

"Of course."

He pulled the chair over to the desk and sat. Now Alice had a good look at him, she could see that he wasn't fourteen years old at all. But if he was thirty he was wearing really well. You know you're getting old when the spies are younger than you are.

"This is my first posting, actually," he said.

Alice raised an eyebrow. "Straight out of spy school?"

Harry chuckled. "We try not to use the 's' word. Gives people all sorts of wrong ideas."

"'School'?"

He laughed. He was averagely tall, well-built, quite good-looking, but catastrophically untidy. Alice had an irrational urge to comb his hair. "I haven't seen the Attaché about much; I really should introduce myself to him."

"Estonia's a small country, but it's *really* cultural," she said. "Mr Rivington's always busy."

"And your colleagues..."

"I'll tell them you popped by. Give them your regards."

They sat there looking at each other for a few moments. Then he said, "Well, as I say, I'm sorry for interrupting you."

"Not at all. In fact, I'm done now for the next couple of hours. Fancy a bite of lunch somewhere?"

He blinked at her, and for a moment she thought she'd wrongfooted him. In fact, for a fraction of a second he seemed about to blush. *Still got it, girl.*

Then he recovered himself. "No, thanks." He got up. "Things to do. Maybe another day." He put his hand out again. "Good to meet you, Alice."

She shook his hand. "Likewise."

After he'd gone, she sat looking at the door for some moments, wondering what the hell all that had been about. She didn't think spies just went around introducing themselves to people. Malcolm certainly hadn't; she'd seen him occasionally wandering around the Embassy for almost a year before she asked Selina who he was.

She realised she was still clutching the SIM and the twist of clingfilm in her fist. She put them on the desk beside her phone and looked at them. Woke the phone up, tapped the app icon, looked at the message. Sighed a little, inside, where nobody would ever hear it.

POLSLOE HAD COME into her life as a series of emails from the film's director, almost two years ago now. She'd kept all of them, all the way back to the one where he wrote, 'I'm just going to copy my assistant Andy Polsloe in on this,' and Polsloe had responded with **waves**.

He was living in Los Angeles back then, but he was from New Zealand originally, his childhood home demolished by the most recent great earthquake to shake Christchurch. At first, they just talked business – the endless nitpicking detail of setting up a long location shoot in Estonia – and he was witty and charming and very very smart, and he never talked down to her. He took her seriously, valued her advice, asked good questions.

They started to talk more and more about things outside business. After threatening for longer than anyone could remember, California was trying to follow the lead of Texas in seceding from the Union, and they discussed that, comparing things there with the piecemeal atomisation of what had once been the European Union. She started to look forward to seeing a new email in her inbox.

Personal things began to creep in. Polsloe's girlfriend, Selma, was a poet and a big drinker. He mentioned, in passing, an argument they'd had. Alice mentioned Rob. They joked about setting Rob and Selma up, two poets together.

By now, they had taken their personal exchanges onto a messaging service. She began to live for their chats about life in Tallinn and LA. One night, she confessed to a particularly trying day and he asked what had happened, and almost without quite meaning to she found herself unburdening her soul.

She told him everything, stuff she'd never even told her parents, about Rob, the way he'd treated her, the way he continued to treat her. When she'd sent the message there was a long pause, and she was certain she'd offended him somehow, or scared him off. And then he sent, *holds your hand*.

THE VENUE WAS called, for reasons lost in the mists of alcoholic memory, The Butt-Shaped Cat. It was just the other side of Raekoja plats, the Town Hall Square, but at that time of the evening the traffic was appalling so it was quicker for her to just walk Luke and Wally there from the Palace through the crowds of shoppers and tourists and people going home from work or out for a meal. Bodfish had slept and showered and put on a change of denim, but they were no more voluble than they had been this morning.

"The city's doing a lot of maintenance on the roads around the square," she explained as they walked. "Being Estonian, they've decided to do it all at once, so there's only about an hour a day when it's quicker to drive. It's not far to walk, anyway."

Luke grunted. Wally made no sign that he was even listening. Alice gave up. Ordinarily, she would have been doing the tourist thing, pointing out this and that, explaining little bits of history and folklore, but it had been an unsettling day, Selina hadn't made a reappearance, and if Bodfish weren't interested she couldn't be bothered.

She'd tried calling Selina, but her phone had cut to voicemail. Same with Selina's partner. Lost for what to do, she'd busied herself with paperwork all afternoon. At one point she'd swapped SIMs in her phone and looked at the latest message again, then swapped the SIMs back. Tim had wandered in around half four, nosed about for a bit, then left again without asking where Selina was, which at least saved Alice from thinking up a story to tell him.

In spite of its name, The Butt-Shaped Cat was actually a rather sweet old-fashioned folkie pub, a basement operation down a set of stone steps beside a little folklore bookshop. It was basically two big, vaulted rooms, the larger lined with the kind of big wooden picnic tables you found in parks. It sold a basic menu of food and a somewhat larger menu of beers, and when Alice and Bodfish arrived it was packed.

"Well, this is hopeful," she said. Wally and Luke just looked around the bar.

Alice spotted Mari on the other side of the room, and waved her hand over her head to attract her attention.

"Wally, Luke, this is Mari," she said when Mari reached them. "She owns the pub. Mari, this is Bodfish."

Mari was tall and ash-blonde and wearing jeans and an ancient Young 'Uns teeshirt. "Really great to meet you," she said, shaking hands with Bodfish. "I've been a fan for ages; welcome to Tallinn."

Luke grunted something. Wally looked at her.

There was an awkward moment of silence while Mari processed this. Then she recovered and said, "There's a room in the back where you can leave your stuff. In the meantime, can I get you something to drink?"

Wally and Luke blinked slowly at her in unison.

"Okay," Mari said, signalling a little desperately to one of her staff. "So Frances will show you to the green room and I'll be there in a moment for a chat. Yes?"

Bodfish gave no sign that they understood a single word.

When they'd gone, Mari turned to Alice and raised her eyebrows.

"Don't," said Alice. "I know."

"Are they ill or something?"

Alice shrugged. ".Maybe it's jetlag."

"Yes," said Mari. "All those timezones between here and Edinburgh." She shook her head. "They're really good, too. Their last album was extraordinary." She saw the look on Alice's face. "Okay, you're not a fan. Take my word, they're good. Thanks for setting this up for us."

"Oh, you're welcome. It was no trouble; their management was really keen for them to come."

"Probably wanted to get them out of the way for a few days. I've booked a table at Tambourine for after the gig; Eloise is keeping the kitchen open for us."

Alice flashed on what it would be like to spend an entire meal with Bodfish, pushed the thought away. "Thanks. We'll put it on the Embassy's card." She felt her phone buzz in her pocket, took it out, saw the ID, and felt her heart sink. "Sorry, Mari, I'll have to take this."

"Sure. I'll go talk to the boys. Are you okay?"

The phone stopped buzzing. Then it started again. "Me? Yes, I'm fine, thanks."

She let Mari go, then she thumbed the answer icon and said, "Hello, Rob."

"Where are you?" he said. "I've been worried sick."

"I'm at The Butt-Shaped Cat."

"Why?"

"The Bodfish gig. The folkies."

"Why didn't you tell me about it?"

"I did."

"No you didn't."

"I told you about it weeks ago."

"No you didn't."

"I did, Rob. I said they were coming over and that I would be nannying them."

"You didn't. I would have remembered."

She sighed. "Fine. Okay. I didn't."

"Don't be like that."

"Like what?"

"You always get fucking sarcastic when you're caught out."

"Rob, I *told* you."

"When are you going to be back?"

"Not for a while. The gig hasn't started, then I have to make sure they get back to the hotel."

"What are we going to do about dinner?"

"Mari and I are taking them out for a meal after the gig. You'll have to sort something out for yourself."

There was a silence at the other end of the line. When he spoke again he was whinier but still combative. "There's nothing in the fridge and if I take something out of the freezer it'll be gone midnight before it defrosts."

"Well, get a takeaway, Rob. Phone for a pizza or something."

More silence.

"Put it on the Embassy tab, Rob. There's a list of the takeaways we have an account with in the kitchen drawer with all the teatowels."

"Why did you put it in there? How was I supposed to find it in there?"

"Jesus, Rob, it's been there for three years. How could you not have noticed?"

"What time will you be back? Approximately?"

She sighed. "The gig runs for about ninety minutes, then we're going to Tambourine, then I have to deliver them back to the Palace. I'll get a cab back from there. I don't know. Twelvish?"

Some more silence. "Okay. But you should have told me."

As ever, there was no point in arguing. "Yes. Okay."

"Okay. I'll see you later."

"Yes, fine."

Rob hung up, and she stood there for a few moments, looking around the bar, phone in hand, counting to ten. "I *did* tell you," she said under her breath.

She put the phone back in her pocket and walked through the bar to the far room. This was a little smaller than the main room. At the far end, a little stage had been constructed using garden decking. Low tables and comfy chairs were scattered around the rest of the room, most of them occupied by people who were drinking and chatting quietly. Alice wandered around the room, looking for somewhere to sit. She nodded hello to Nikolai, who was running the sound and the lights from a battered old laptop at a table in a corner.

"Long time, no see," he said as she sat down on a stool beside him.

"Been a while, yes," she said. "How've you been?"

He made a rude noise. "Lot of comrades *very* unhappy with you." Nikolai's chief pastime was the politics of Estonia's ethnic Russian community, of which the best thing that could be said was that it lacked tedium.

She had to do a momentary inventory of all the things she might have done to annoy the Russians, before coming up with the obvious one. "I didn't write the fucking film," she said with more feeling than she intended. "I wasn't the only one *enabling* it. Tell your friends to fuck off."

He minutely adjusted something on the laptop's screen, then raised his hands in surrender. "Not my circus, not my monkeys."

It was a Polish expression, but that didn't matter. "It is too your circus, you horrible man."

"One would have thought," he said precisely, "that *someone somewhere* would have mentioned to *someone somewhere* that making a film about a failed Russian invasion of Estonia *in Estonia* was not the smartest idea anyone ever had."

"I had a discussion to that effect with the director."

"I know." He smiled and reached out and patted her hand.

"So why are the comrades still so annoyed?"

He shrugged. "Habit. They like to keep limbered up. I hear you have a new *Rezident*."

He meant young Harry, the spook. "How did you know about that? I only found out about it yesterday."

"I had a chat with Malcolm Smith last week."

This was, somehow, not even a surprise. "How is Malcolm?"

"Sunburned."

"Give him my regards, next time you have a chat."

Nikolai nodded. "Will do. How are you keeping?"

Alice shrugged. "Same old same old. Have you seen Selina about? She's gone AWOL."

He shook his head. "I've been in the Motherland; only got back a couple of hours ago."

"Reporting to Moscow Centre?"

He chuckled. "Nah. Been visiting the old man. He's sick."

"Oh, Nik," she said, suddenly horrified at having been so flippant. "I'm sorry."

"He's on the mend," he told her. "Gave us all a bit of a scare, is all."

Nikolai's father was widely agreed to have been one of the greatest of all Estonia's newspaper editors, barred from the very top of the tree by dint of enthusiastically employing his talents in support of an ethnic Russian homeland within Estonia's borders. On retirement, he had thrown his hands up in disgust at the land of his birth and gone to live in St Petersburg.

"Does your mum know?"

Nikolai nodded. "I messaged her. She wouldn't come." Nikolai's mother, appalled at the prospect of a move to Russia, had divorced her husband and taken herself off to Paris, where, the last Alice had heard, she was living with a repackager of out-of-copyright erotic novels. "It's okay. He'll be all right."

Alice had met Nikolai at the University, where he had been funding his PhD by teaching classes on Russo-Estonian relations. They'd had a very brief fling, the year before she met Rob, but it had run its natural course long before she'd got a chance to meet his family. He was stocky and amiable and very smart, and quite often she found herself wondering where her life would be now if they'd stayed together.

"Let me know if there's anything I can do. Please."

He smiled and patted her hand again. "It's good to see you," he said.

She turned her hand palm up and took his hand in hers. "You too, Nik."

He gave her hand a squeeze and let go and typed some commands into the laptop. A couple of the little spotlights set into the ceiling changed colour, then changed back. "You got a good crowd in tonight."

"Yeah." She looked around the room again. "They're good, apparently."

"Botfish?"

"*Bod*fish."

"Whatever."

"Mari asked if I could see if they fancied a gig here," she said. "Their management was really keen. Keener than they are, by the looks of them."

"You don't sound like you're a fan."

She snorted. "Me and folk music."

He laughed. "Yes. You and folk music." He glanced at her. "You look tired. You okay?"

Only two people in the whole world knew about Rob. She'd never told Nikolai because, as well as being sweet and kind and gentle, he knew some genuinely dangerous people. She was afraid that if she told him, some slumbering beast of chivalry would awaken in his breast and a couple of days later a hit team of Ukrainian ex-pats would arrive in town, tooled-up with chainsaws.

"Just busy," she told him.

He looked at her a moment longer, then nodded. "Okay," he said. "You say so."

"Is there a boat in?" she asked, surveying the room again. There seemed to be a lot of people here tonight who did not necessarily present as Estonian. Near the stage, a tall woman with shortish brown hair and an older man whose face reminded Alice of the presidents' faces carved into that mountain in America were talking. Or rather she was doing all the talking. She was resting a hand on his forearm, but their body language was not that of lovers. Or what Alice thought of as the body language of lovers, anyway.

"Baltic cruise," Nikolai grunted, busying himself with the laptop and changing the colours of the lights again. "Gdansk, Stockholm, Helsinki, Tallinn, Riga, Klaipda, back to Gdansk for the flight home. Fourteen days and all the folklore you can stand."

"I always fancied one of those cruises," she said.

"Yes, I remember. Well, they can fuck off." He squinted at the clock in the corner of the laptop's screen. "This is running late."

In Alice's admittedly limited experience of the folk scene, Folk Time was not quite the same as Time anywhere else. "They'll get round to it."

"You don't have a drink."

"I'm okay, thanks."

He shrugged. "Good. You're okay, I'm okay. Okay."

"Oh, shut up." She punched him goodnaturedly on the forearm.

He howled theatrically and rubbed his arm. "Ow! Now I'm not okay."

"Showtime," she said, pointing across the room to where Bodfish, accompanied by Mari, were picking their way between the seats and tables towards the stage. "Hey," she added, something just occurring to her. "Don't you need to do a soundcheck or something?"

Nikolai blew a raspberry. "They didn't want to. I'll wing it. It's folk; who cares if nobody can hear it?"

Alice watched the musicians step up onto the stage and stand there, guitar cases in hand, looking out into the room as if it was the first time they had ever seen an audience and they were not overly impressed with the concept. "They really are very strange people," she said.

"Artists," Nikolai muttered scornfully, typing.

Mari said a few words of introduction while Bodfish fiddled about with their guitars, there was a polite round of applause from the audience, and when that died down Wally and Luke stepped up to their mikes and without any preamble launched into a song.

And they were okay, really. Wally had a nice voice. The song was about someone on a whaling ship; it wasn't earth-shattering but it was all right. Alice felt her shoulders start to relax and her mind wandered.

They were both desperate, in their way. Polsloe's girlfriend Selma could become violent when she drank, which was often. Polsloe was torn between wanting to take care of her and a simple human need to flee for his life. Rob had never hit Alice, but she could feel her life with him slowly crushing her to death. She couldn't afford to leave, though. Her salary was tiny, not enough to set up on her own. She needed some seniority at the Embassy – any Embassy, really, anywhere – and to get that she had to stay where she was, play the good little wife, not make waves, hang on. She wasn't just waiting for a step up on the career ladder, it was a ladder to freedom.

It was a ladder which, increasingly, led to Polsloe. Some of their messages were so frankly intimate that, reading them back even now, after everything, she found herself getting hot. The first time they videoconferenced, in a room at the Embassy with Tim and a dozen or so other interested parties, it was all she could do to stop herself walking down to the front and pressing herself against the screen.

All of a sudden, she became aware of a silence in the room. She looked at the stage, and Bodfish had stopped playing in mid-song. They were just standing there, looking out at the audience, which in turn was looking at them, baffled. Was this part of the act? The beginning of a medical emergency? Alice stared.

Later, when she tried to put things together in her head, it seemed to Alice that Nikolai actually moved first. He was out of his seat and moving through the audience, but he wasn't quick enough. Quite calmly, Luke handed his guitar to Wally, stepped off the stage, walked up to one of the tables, and punched a member of the audience in the face, and then Alice couldn't see what was happening because the room was suddenly full of shouting people.

AT SOME POINT, someone came by and gave her a plastic cup of black coffee. It was unsweetened, but she drank it anyway and then sat with her hands in her lap, holding the empty cup, staring at the blank wall across the corridor. From time to time, police officers and civilian staff walked by, but no one paid her any attention. She took out her phone and checked the time, put it back in her pocket.

This was not the first time she had visited the new police station off the Town Hall Square. Scotland lacked a Consulate in Estonia; visiting Scottish citizens occasionally misbehaved, or were the victims of misbehaviour, and it fell to the Embassy to represent them in their dealings with the authorities and offer them any aid they needed. Most often, this involved bailing unruly stag parties out of the cells and making sure they were on the first available flight home, which was onerous on a number of levels, so there was a rota.

HR had worked on the rota for weeks to make sure it was scrupulously fair and that no one did any more days on tourist duty than anyone else, and when it was posted on the Embassy intranet all the senior staff's duty days fell during their holidays, which was obviously regrettable but unavoidable. In the end, the junior staff had sat down in the canteen one day and sorted something out among themselves.

The police station had been built behind the façade of several original buildings. From the outside, if you ignored the discreet sign by the front door, you could easily miss it among the rest of the Hanseatic architecture on the street. Inside, it was a place built for a siege, a series of cubes within cubes connected by blast doors, extending several floors below ground level. The Global War On Terror had finally arrived in Estonia five years ago with a colossal truck bomb in Tartu, and ever since, the police and Security Services, already on a hair-trigger due to constant Russian provocations, had adopted a bunker mentality. The police station had been open for seven weeks, and in that time it had dealt with drunks and rowdy stag parties and pickpockets and one murderer. It had, so far, seen nothing like the cavalcade which arrived in the wake of the abortive Bodfish gig.

Someone stopped and stood in front of her. She looked up and found Meg, the Embassy's head of Security, and Antonia, who did HR, looking down at her. They both looked grumpy.

"What happened?" said Meg.

"I don't know," Alice said. "They were only halfway through their first song and one of them just got down off the stage and thumped this guy."

"Was he heckling?" asked Antonia.

"Not that I noticed, no."

"Were they drunk?" Meg said. "The band?"

"There's only two of them. I don't know. They were fairly well bevvied-up when they got off the plane this morning. Yesterday morning." She rubbed her face. "But they were no trouble. I got them to the Palace and as far as I know they spent all day sleeping it off.

They seemed all right in the evening." She blinked at them. "What are you doing here?"

"Someone at the pub phoned the Embassy," said Antonia.

"But I'm here," Alice said. "I'm dealing with it."

"Where are they?" Meg asked.

"In the cells."

"We had a word with the duty sergeant," Antonia told her. "The victim isn't going to press charges. The police are still in two minds, but we think they'll settle for immediate deportation and a ban on Bodfish ever coming here again."

Alice felt she had managed quite a good grip on things this evening, but she sensed events starting to slip away from her now. It was not immediately apparent why senior staff were here; last year she had cleared up the aftermath of a near-riot between tourists and locals on the other side of the city and she'd had to do that entirely alone. "There was no need for you to come," she said. "I had it under control."

"I want this written up and on my desk by lunchtime," Meg said. "Copies to Antonia and Nicky. Go home; the police will put the wee gobshites on the morning flight and somebody will meet them at the other end."

"What? No. I mean, I can do that. It's my responsibility."

"Not any more," said Antonia. "It's late. Go home."

Alice got to her feet, picked up her bag and slung it over her shoulder. "What's going on? Am I in some kind of trouble?"

"Nothing's going on, and you're not in trouble," Antonia said. "Just go home."

"And don't forget that report," Meg told her.

It seemed like a long walk down the quiet corridors to the front door. On the way, Alice passed a little seating area. The couple she'd seen in the pub were sitting there, side by side, the tall woman and the man with the hard face, who was, apparently, a Norwegian citizen. He had a black eye. In the chaos at The Butt-Shaped Cat she hadn't been able to speak to them, and later the police had kept them apart. She agonised over whether to go over and apologise, but in the end she kept going and they gave no sign of having noticed she was even there.

*   *   *

"Do YOU KNOW what time it is?" Rob asked before she had even closed the door behind her.

"Yes, I do, actually," she said.

"Where the hell have you been?"

She pushed the door shut, put her bag down at her feet, and took her coat off. "There was a fight," she said, hanging it up on the hook behind the door. "One of the folkies punched someone. I've been at the police station trying to sort it out."

"Liar."

"Oh, not tonight, Rob," she sighed, carrying her bag into the living room and dumping it on a chair. "I've had a fucking awful day."

"You said you'd be back at midnight. It's almost three in the morning. Where have you been?"

"I've spent the past five and a half hours at Raekoja plats police station trying to defuse a diplomatic incident between Scotland and Norway," she snapped. "I've had nothing to eat since lunchtime and I am *really fucking unhappy* right now, so stop it."

"I don't believe you."

"Here," she said, taking her phone from her pocket and holding it out to him. "Here. Phone the police. Ask them. They're on speed dial. Press seven."

He didn't even bother looking at the phone. He just stared at her, a cynical smile on his face. "Well *I've* had nothing to eat either."

"What?"

He nodded in a self-satisfied way. "I couldn't find your list."

It was important to remain calm, not to shriek. She walked into the kitchen and opened the drawer. The list of takeaways had sat on top of the teatowels almost since they'd moved into the flat, but it wasn't there now. Alice lifted the teatowels out of the drawer, but the list was gone.

"So I've been sitting here all night worrying about you and I haven't had anything to eat," said Rob, triumph in his voice. "And you were out with your mates and couldn't be fucking bothered to call me."

"I was not out with my mates," she said, sitting on her anger with an effort. It was not beyond Rob to have moved the list in order to provoke a row. "I told you. I've been at Raekoja plats police station almost all night. I have *not* been having a good time." She didn't mention the unsettling presence of Meg and Antonia. It was pointless trying to explain that to Rob; she was going to have to process it herself. "And if you were so fucking hungry you could have made yourself a fucking sandwich."

He was suddenly on the defensive. "Hey, don't be so twitchy."

"I'm not being twitchy," she said.

"Yes you are."

"I'm really not."

"You really are."

"Well, I am *now*."

"Oh, come on, Shmoo," he said, putting an arm around her shoulders.

She pulled away. "Don't call me that." At one time she'd thought it was cute, until she looked it up, and then it had become just one more signpost on the nightmare road.

"Hey." He put on his hurt little boy's face, the one he'd used to break her heart when they were courting. "If you don't want to talk, fine."

She looked at him, out of words. She was a monster, clearly. Out all night, abandoning her husband to starve on his own, then picking an argument with him when she came back. It was a miracle he'd stayed with her this long. Rob World was back in its accustomed orbit.

She felt her shoulders slump. "I'm going to bed."

"You should have something to eat."

"It's too late, Rob." And she went into the bedroom.

LATER, LYING AWAKE listening to Rob snoring beside her, she had a horrified realisation that she had swapped the SIMs in her phone so often today that she couldn't remember whether the one in it when she'd offered it to Rob was her normal, blameless one or the secret Polsloe one.

THE SUDDEN NATIONHOOD
OF AEGEA

1.

THIS MONTH, HE was Greek. Being Greek was worthless, but it was
better than nothing. Being Greek at least entitled you to coupons for
food and clothing, and if you had enough of those you could sell
them for other things.

Over the past eight years, he had been, variously, Turkish,
Albanian, Italian, Libyan – once, and only once; nobody wanted
to be Libyan – Croatian and Macedonian. The nationalities of
the North remained, for him as for everyone else across the great
stateless basin of the Mediterranean, as far beyond reach as the
spiral galaxy M31 in Andromeda.

Changing nationalities was a mere formality. Men in summer
clothing periodically came to the island, guarded by UN soldiers,
and set up lines of folding tables on the crumbling quayside. The
people of the island queued up, presented their most recent papers,
and received in exchange a fresh set, and all of a sudden they had a
new homeland. It was that easy.

The whole thing had bemused Benno at first, but his friend Stav
had explained it as a handing-over of responsibility. "No one can
afford to feed us," he said. "Not for long, anyway. So they take
turns. If we're Greek the Greeks feed us; if we're Albanian the

Albanians feed us, the gods help them. And round and round it goes."

Stav was two years older than Benno, a tall, whip-thin sixteen-year-old with the solemn face of an Abyssinian king and a startling Afro, from which protruded the handles of a pair of stainless steel combs. He habitually wore a threadbare and stained pair of black UNHCR coveralls, and when the weather grew cold and stormy he had a much-scuffed leather aviator's jacket, restitched many times with a kaleidoscope of different types and colours of thread.

Neither of them could have said, with any great certainty, where their people had come from, and the nations their families had set out from no longer existed anyway, fragmented and swallowed and fragmented again and absorbed by the chaos of nations and polities and caliphates and tyrannies and utopias and kingdoms and empires that covered half of Africa and the Middle East in the wake of the climate catastrophe in the Sahel. It didn't matter. They were all citizens of the Mediterranean now, cycling through temporary nationalities in order to receive aid, patiently waiting for a weakness to appear in the wall which barred the North from them.

Benno's parents hadn't even made it this far. They'd died in an epidemic somewhere along the North African coast when he was four. He could barely remember them. Stav was luckier; his family – mother, father, sister and grandmother – were, as far as anyone knew, still alive somewhere, on one of the other islands, or on a boat, or clinging desperately to the mainland for a while before being washed back out to sea. That was all any of them did; drift back and forth across the Med in a huge, slow, ragged tide. Some of them had been doing it for decades.

The terms of each nationality varied. Greeks distributed books of coupons every week, to be redeemed with the traders who visited the island in a small flotilla of boats bearing various useful items such as food. Italians and Turks set up kitchens and handed out scannable wristbands to make sure no one took more than their ration. The Albanians...well, the Albanians did their best. What none of these temporary and deeply conditional nationalities conferred was the right to travel onward.

The island had no name; it was just a rock sticking out of the

Aegean, covered in old shipping containers and fringed by a bobbing orange halo of discarded lifejackets. You could walk round it in a couple of hours, reach the summit of its modest central peak in forty minutes. It had been Benno's home for three years now.

Like everything else here, the shipping containers were surplus to requirements, acquired cheaply by the Greeks using a UN grant and arranged in haphazard rows on the lower slopes. They'd been intended as a temporary measure, something to give shelter to the tide of refugees while the government tried to work out what to do next, but decades on, the government was still trying to work out what to do and the containers were still here, their paint mostly scoured off by years of Mediterranean summers and winters, lines and lines of rusting metal boxes full of people. The majority were what the men in lightweight suits described as 'living units', although that phrase hid a multitude of sins, but others had been converted into schools and mosques, workshops for tailors and metalworkers, a couple of bakeries, and a church for the tiny community of Copts who, to their own bemusement, had been here longer than almost anyone else. The island's population waxed and waned, making it impossible for the UN to hold an accurate census, so they had settled on saying that 'several thousand' lived there. 'Several' was good PR because it allowed the peoples of mainland Europe to kid themselves that it was perhaps two or three thousand, rather than more than ten thousand, which was probably a more accurate figure. Two or three thousand was manageable. It was barely a problem at all.

Stav was scornful of the UN, Europe, Humanity in general. "This has been going on for fucking years," he said. "If they were serious about doing something about it, don't you think they'd have done something already?"

Benno shrugged. "We'd starve without them," he said. "Probably."

"Yeah, right. And that would look bad on the news." Although it was quite some time since any news crews had visited the island, The Crisis having given way to The Ongoing Situation, which was not nearly as sexy. "Nah. They won't let us into Europe, we can't go back, and they can't let us starve. So they do just enough to keep us alive." He snorted. "Homeopathy." Benno had no idea what he meant. Stav was always using words like 'homeopathy'; it made him sound wiser than his years.

They were sitting on a couple of upturned crates down by the harbour, squinting into the noonday glare off the sea. Far away, so far that they almost seemed like hallucinations, great white ships passed back and forth, quartering the Aegean and the Mediterranean with their cargoes of aged white rich people. Benno had seen one of the huge cruise liners up close once, while taking passage from one island to another. He was with about a hundred other people in an ancient rigid inflatable boat, driven along by a pair of puttering outboards which had already been old before The Crisis began, when the liner caught up with them. They'd been watching it half the day, slowly growing larger and larger, unwilling to deviate from their own course because they were perilously low on fuel, but confident the liner would turn aside when it spotted them.

But it didn't. It didn't even sound its sirens. It just kept coming and rode their boat down, scattering bodies and possessions into the sea. Benno, who had managed with a few of the others to swim clear of the huge boat's bow wave and wash, bobbed in the water and watched it sail serenely off into the distance as if nothing had happened. He remembered seeing an elderly fat man in a T-shirt and bermuda shorts leaning against the rail on one of the decks, smoking a pipe and looking out towards the horizon. Not once did he look down at the desperate people in the water below. More than half the people from the boat had drowned; the survivors clung to the wreckage until a patrol boat came along and gave them a tow to the nearest speck of land and then departed again without bothering to help further.

"Ringo's given me a job," Stav said.

Benno scowled. Ringo was the unofficial chieftain of the island. He had an ad hoc compound of a dozen containers further up the slopes of the mountain, patrolled by enforcers who carried clubs and machetes. Officially, the Greeks were the law on the island, but no one could remember the last time a Greek policeman had set foot on the place.

"You want a piece of it?" asked Stav.

"No, and neither should you, if you want my advice."

Stav did not. "You could do worse than have a word with him."

Benno struggled to come up with anything worse than being mixed up with Ringo. "He hasn't made you an enforcer, has he?"

"Nah. This is different. This is special."

Well, of course it was. Ringo got what he wanted by a combination of charm and terror; Benno had invested quite a lot of time and effort into making himself so insignificant that he was invisible to the island's ruler, the way he and the others had been invisible to that cruise ship. If he had nothing Ringo wanted, Ringo could want nothing from him.

"I thought you had more brains that that," he said.

"Do you really want to spend the rest of your life on this rock?"

"Of course I don't. But I don't want to spend the rest of my life watching Ringo's back for him and shaking down everyone else for their coupons and food either."

"That's what life is. Either you win or you die."

This was so obviously one of Ringo's sayings that Benno burst out laughing. "That's a quote from *Game of Thrones*, you idiot."

"What?" Stav affected to understand popular culture, but he had no time for decades-old television series. "Fuck you, Benno," he said, getting up and kicking his crate across the broken stones of the quay. "I can't help you if you don't want to be helped." And he stomped off.

Benno sat where he was for a while. Contrails crossed the great empty blue vault of the sky, carrying people who might as well have been the representatives of alien cultures to places which might as well have been from fantasy novels, for all the connection they had to him. He wondered if they looked down as they crossed the Aegean, on their way to Spain or France or Hungary or even further afield, and saw this tiny speck of an island. It would be hard, he thought, to see any people down here from that altitude. The whole Mediterranean basin must look calm and clean, if you flew high enough.

Finally, he got up and started to walk up the slope of the island. The concentric rows of containers were *streets*, and they were numbered. The radial thoroughfares between them which led down from the peak to the shore were *avenues*, and they were lettered. The little group of containers which comprised Benno's neighbourhood was at the corner of Twelfth Street and Avenue K. There were signs painted on the containers in several languages – and retouched every now and again when they began to fade – to help newcomers navigate about, but Benno had long ceased to need them.

He walked back for a while through the Fourteenth Street market, a double line of old folding picnic tables, planks balanced on crates, blankets spread on the ground, where people bartered their meagre possessions for food or water or clothes or vouchers. It wasn't much – Ringo and his men taxed new arrivals and anything of any use or value made its way up to his containers at First and B – but the market was still crowded. You never knew when there might be a bargain.

Further along, there were tables with fish displayed upon them. The island was almost bare of vegetation and agriculture of any kind – although that didn't stop people trying to grow stuff – and the few goats which had somehow subsisted here had not long survived the first wave of refugees, but the surrounding waters were full of fish, many of them as ugly and alien, to Benno's eyes, as creatures from another galaxy. Ringo had tried to corner the trade in fish, but it was impossible to stop people throwing makeshift nets into the sea from the rocks to feed their own families, and his one attempt to take them from the market had been met with an uncharacteristic undercurrent of grumbling which he had wisely paid attention to.

In truth, there were worse places to be. The international aid effort was chaotic and ill-funded, and the island was run by a despot, but at least it was not North Africa or the Middle East. No one wanted to be in those places. And if you ever became downhearted, you could always climb to the top of the mountain and look to the northwest and see a dark line on the horizon and remind yourself why you were doing this, why you risked your life again and again in boats nobody in their right mind would take on a calm lake, the dark line that was the Greek mainland, and beyond it Europe, land of fable.

Benno shared a container with three other families, the interior subdivided by blankets hung from string stretched from one side to the other. Because he was alone, he had one of the rear corners to himself, a nest of old clothes and cushions and bits of cloth he could curl up in, it was really quite cosy. The other family at the rear of the container, a middle-aged couple who self-identified as Somali even though Somalia had ceased to exist as a geopolitical entity almost two decades ago, had sort of half-adopted him. They thought it was a sin that an orphan boy should be all alone in this place, although Benno was more than capable of taking care of himself – more so than they were, in fact; he'd lately found himself bringing home scavenged bits and pieces of food and clothing for them and he was slowly gearing himself up to moving out before they became dependent. It really was only a matter of time. Stav said there was a space in his container, but after today's conversation Benno wasn't sure he wanted to live with Stav.

The Somali couple – he didn't even know their names – were out when he got home. The family who occupied the front third of the container were Moroccan, he thought – a mother and several children, he had never counted them. In the middle were a very quiet man and woman and their son, who was five or six. They kept their space neat and tidy and rarely spoke to anyone. Benno thought they might be escapees from Damascus, he'd seen that same look of bafflement before.

"Someone was asking for you," the Moroccan woman said when he stepped through the door of the container.

"Oh?"

"A man. UN." That could be anyone who looked remotely European and dressed neatly.

"He knew my name?"

"No, but he described you."

This seemed unlikely; the island was awash with boys of about Benno's age and description.

"He said he had some news for you, about your family," the woman's husband put in.

"It's not me he's looking for, then," Benno told them. "I have no family."

"He seemed pretty sure he had the right place," the woman said. "He said he had to go back to the mainland tonight, but he'd be back tomorrow."

"Then we'll see what he wants tomorrow," said Benno, and he pushed his way through the hanging sheets to the back of the container.

He'd rigged some sheets around his little living space, for privacy, and he made sure they were secure before settling down in his nest. He waited a few moments to make sure he wasn't going to be disturbed, then he dug his hand down into the tangle of cloth and cushions and pulled out a small package wrapped in bubble-plastic. He picked with his nails at the tape securing it, unrolled it, and the phone dropped into his lap. He looked at it for a while, then wrapped it up and hid it again, thinking of the single text message he'd seen the day he'd found it.

2.

LIKE ALMOST EVERYONE and everything, the dead man had come to the island by sea.

One of the chief pursuits of the island's inhabitants was to scour the shoreline for potentially useful flotsam and jetsam. The Aegean was a vast dustbin; objects thrown over the side of boats or washed off the decks of ships during storms drifted and clumped and drifted again on the currents and tides. Much of it was discarded fishing gear, nets and floats, but some of it was more esoteric. Someone had once found an entire case of bottled peaches wedged among the rocks on the south side of the island – Ringo had taxed that, when he heard about it – and once, almost everyone had come down to the beach on the west side and watched a shipping container drift by, tantalisingly out of reach. There was no way to get to it – they were not allowed boats lest they decide to carry on to the mainland under their own steam – and even if there had been, it would have been nearly impossible to tow it into the ruined little harbour. Even so, some of the wilder young men braved the savage currents which rushed around the island and tried to swim out to it. Almost all of them turned back, but one made it and managed to haul himself up onto the corrugated steel roof. Where he stood, suddenly completely at a loss for what to do next, waving foolishly while the women on the shoreline shouted obscene suggestions and the old men just watched and shook their heads sadly. Eventually he dived back into the sea and finally returned to the beach half dead with exhaustion.

So the container had bobbed, hour by hour, away into the distance, its contents unknown and unknowable, like the flyby of an alien space probe. That evening, sitting on a rock a little way up the mountain, Benno had thought he could just see it, drifting serenely towards the horizon on the very edge of visibility, but when he blinked it was gone.

And there were always the life jackets, discarded by arrivals on the island or brought here by the wind and currents from other landfalls or the sad, nameless survivals of capsizes far out at sea. The island was surrounded by them; from the air it looked like a crusted grey pustule rising from a ring of inflamed skin. The authorities periodically cleared them and dumped them on the shore in great mouldy orange and red middens, where they bleached in the sun.

Fishing gear was a better bet. Nets could be repaired, and quite often they were tangled with lines of hooks, which had become an unofficial currency among the inhabitants of the island. Sometimes, if they were bored, Benno and Stav would wander out to the lesser-frequented coves and inlets to see what the sea had brought them.

One day, scrambling over the rocks, Benno found a plastic crate rising and falling in the surge of a pool. He waded out to it before it could be washed over the lip of the pool and back out to sea. Waist-deep in the water, he manhandled the crate over to the side and managed to shoulder it up onto a rock, and he was examining its fastenings when a shadow fell across him and he looked up and Stav was standing there looking grave.

"I found something you ought to see," he said quietly.

"Me too," said Benno, indicating the crate.

"No," said Stav. "You *really* ought to see this."

Benno suddenly realised there was something wrong with his friend's body language. Most of Stav's attitude had gone, and he looked like a frightened sixteen-year-old, which was quite scary.

"What's wrong? What is it?"

"Just come and look, Benno," Stav said quietly.

Benno clambered out of the pool, made sure the crate wasn't about to topple back into the water, and followed Stav from rock to rock until they came to a little inlet about twenty metres away, and there, rocking back and forth in the surging surf, was the dead man.

He was not the first dead man the two boys had ever seen. He was not the first dead man they had seen that week. At another time, in another place, they might have been afraid, but death was as much a part of their lives as breathing. But this dead man was different.

"He has a gun," Stav said quietly.

He had been in the water for quite some time; his body was putrid and grotesquely swollen and blackened. Fish had fed on him. His face was a landscape of exposed bone and teeth, and his right leg was missing above the knee where something larger had taken a bite from him. He was still wearing a tattered pair of jeans, stretched tight by bloat, but whatever shirt he had once had was entirely missing, rotted away, exposing a distended belly. He was, though, wearing a harness of some more durable material, and on one side, just below his armpit, there was a holster, from which protruded the unmistakeable handgrip of a pistol.

Guns were forbidden on the island, for obvious reasons. It was a prohibition that was relatively easy to police; every new boatload of arrivals was searched by the authorities and any firearms – and sometimes explosives – were confiscated and their owners taken away for rigorous questioning; most of the time they were never seen again, and the accepted wisdom was that they had been given a fast-track return to their place of origin. If their place of origin could not be established, then it was a boat-ride to the North African coast and a forced disembarkation on the first available beach, no matter which temporary nation it was in at the time. Machetes, fortunately for Ringo and his crew, were classified as tools.

Benno and Stav stood looking at the body for quite some time. It had become wedged sitting almost upright between two rocks, and the smell that wafted up from the inlet with each swell of the waves was quite remarkable.

"What do you suppose happened to him?" said Stav.

Benno shrugged. Given the state of the body, it was unlikely they would ever be able to tell.

They stood there another minute or so. Stav looked about to see if anyone was watching, then he started to strip out of his jumpsuit.

"You're not serious," Benno said.

"Do you want Ringo to have it?" said Stav.

Well, no, but equally Benno didn't want Stav to have it either. "If anyone finds out you've got it they'll send you back," he said.

Stav folded the jumpsuit and carefully laid it on the rocks. When he straightened up, Benno could see his ribs and the bony prominences of his hips. Everyone on the island – with the exception of the UN people and Ringo and his enforcers – was suffering from borderline malnutrition. "To where?"

Benno pointed south across the sea.

Stav looked where Benno was pointing, then said, "Nah," and jumped into the inlet.

The smell near the body must have been even worse, because Stav took two wading steps through the waist-high water and vomited. Then he vomited again, but he kept going until he reached the dead man. There was some kind of strap securing the pistol in its holster, and its time in the water and Stav's eagerness to get out of there made it tricky to undo. His fingers kept slipping and he kept retching and muttering and the surge of the waves coming into the inlet kept shoving him against the body. It was all rather absurd and disgusting. Abruptly, he seemed to lose his footing and his head disappeared beneath the surface and didn't come up again.

Benno watched for a few moments. He scanned the area, but there was nobody about, and finally, swearing in a loud voice, he peeled off his T-shirt and shorts and jumped in after his friend.

The smell down here was terrible, but he managed to keep his stomach contents down, bending over and submerging his head as he searched with outstretched arms. His fingers brushed Stav's back and he stepped forward, got his hands under Stav's shoulders, and hauled upward. They both surfaced snorting and spitting water.

"Idiot!" Benno yelled. "I should have let you drown."

"Why didn't you, then?" Stav said, wiping his face and stepping forward again to fiddle with the straps on the dead man's chest.

"Because there's already too many dead people in this pool, you prick." Benno shifted his feet as the surf surged again, and he felt something smooth under his toes. He ducked down, searched briefly, came up holding, miracle of miracles, a mobile phone.

It went without saying that the people of the island had no phones. Ringo taxed any that arrived, and there was no coverage anyway. And the sea water would have rendered it useless. But even a useless phone was valuable; the components could be used to make jewellery. If he could hang on to it for long enough he could exchange it for... well, there were many things he could exchange it for, he'd have to give it some thought. But first he had to get it to safety.

Stav still had his back turned, trying to undo the strap securing the pistol. Benno said, "If you don't need rescuing again, I'm going. I don't want any more part of this stupidity."

"Fine, fine," Stav said without turning round. "You go, little baby. Let the adults take care of things."

Benno snorted, "Adults," and climbed up the rocks to where he had left his clothes. The stench of the rotting body clung to his skin and his hair so he walked naked a few hundred metres along the shoreline until he came to a sheltered cove. He left the phone wrapped up in his clothes and, first making sure no one was around to steal his things, waded into the clean water and scrubbed himself with his hands. Afterward, he could still smell putrefaction on himself, but it was at least faint enough that he could put his clothes on without having to burn them afterward.

He walked away from the shore, the phone in his pocket, until he came to a line of low cliffs, not more than a handful of metres high. Checking again to make sure he wasn't being observed, he climbed up the steep slope until he found a crevice, and into this he placed the phone, sealing it in with a small rock. Then he climbed down again and went to find some soap. When he came back to look for the crate he had originally found, it had, of course, been taken away by someone else.

He didn't see Stav again all day, or all the next day, or the day after that. One evening, just as the light was beginning to fail, he went down to the cliffs again, scrambled up, and retrieved the phone. He shoved it into a bag full of recovered netting, slung it over his shoulder, went home, and buried the phone deep in his nest.

A couple of days later – still no Stav; he'd gone back to the inlet, just in case, but it was deserted and the body was gone, either removed for burial or simply washed back out to sea by the tide – all the other residents of his container were out at the same time, and he was able to take out the phone, sit by the doors where there was some light, and cautiously examine it.

Benno might have been a child of migration, he might have been an orphan drifting from island to island, but he was also a child of his century and he was not a savage. This was one of the many mistakes the peoples of the North made when they considered the tide of refugees coming from the South. They saw only indigent cargo, barely even human, certainly not intelligent unless it was in a sly animal kind of way. They would have been at first surprised and then disbelieving if anyone told them that the Moroccan woman in Benno's container had once lectured in economics, or that the Somalis had – or claimed they had, anyway – been ministers in the last Somali government worthy of the name. Benno himself could read and write and he spoke four languages, with varying degrees of fluency. So no, a mobile phone held no great mystery for him.

If one had been sitting in a café in Hamburg or on a train between Amsterdam and Paris, this phone would have appeared disappointingly cheap and mass-produced and ordinary, a couple of years out of date and a bit battered – although that was to be expected, considering what it had been through. Benno turned it over and over in his hands. The screen was a little scratched, but it was intact, which was good; with care the glass of a phone screen could be knapped into blades sharp enough for surgery, and he knew a doctor on the other side of the island who was always complaining that his medical supplies were insufficient. He prised the back off and looked inside. The battery would be useless, of course; it contained valuable metals and chemicals but in too small a quantity to make recovery worthwhile. But the circuit boards inside could be broken up and turned into pleasing earrings and bangles, and he knew someone who could do that. All he had to do now was decide what to ask in return.

He snapped the back onto the phone and ran his thumb over the little buttons on the side. Still thinking about what price to put on the phone's components, he idly pressed the power stud, and almost dropped it as the screen lit up.

He scrambled hurriedly through the hanging curtains to the back of the container, draped a sheet over himself so the light wouldn't show, and watched the phone wake up. This was unusual, a cheap phone ruggedised enough to withstand prolonged immersion in salt water and still boot up on the first try. Even more unusual, he saw, the user – presumably it had fallen from the pocket of the dead man Stav had found – had not closed down properly, as if he had been interrupted while he was using it. This was poor security, of course, but continually typing in your password or going through the thumbprint recognition procedure was a chore if the phone had only gone to sleep for a few moments while you were otherwise occupied. The dead man in the inlet had expected to return to whatever he had been doing with the phone, and had left it wide open to anyone who came along and switched on the power.

Although it was hard to see what he had been doing. Swiping through the phone's memory, Benno discovered that it was all but empty. There were no numbers in its contacts folder, no notes, no downloads, no calls. Apart from the factory standard apps there were, in fact, only two things on the phone. A single text had been received from an anonymised number, and according to the banking app it was loaded with seventeen and a half thousand Swiss Francs.

3.

BENNO HAD FEW visitors, and no one who asked for him by name or description – if Stav turned up looking for him he'd just stooge around for a while chatting up the eldest of the Moroccan couple's daughters – so the presence of an apparently UN person looking for him was problematical. On the whole, the UN preferred to deal with the people of the island en masse rather than as individuals. When the time came to get a new wristband to give them access to aid, the refugees were called down to the harbour in groups several hundred strong and made to parade past folding tables at which officials with pads and boxes of wristbands sat. The bands had simple barcodes which allowed the authorities to keep a log of who had received food or clothing – they used old hand-scanners when giving out aid – and little RFID chips which detected whether the band had been removed and given to someone else. Last year, some enterprising lad had managed to steal one of the official pads and hack the wristband logs so that everyone was allowed unlimited food. This had meant that the food had run out in half the usual time and there had been a small riot, and later tear gas and rubber bullets, followed by repatriations – the UN's euphemism for loading a hundred or so people at random onto a coastguard boat and taking them back to North Africa.

The wristbands, though, had no individual identification data, just barcoded serial numbers. They didn't 'belong' to you, and when the Italians or the Turks handed over responsibility for food aid to the next nation everyone just cut them off and threw them away.

Nationality papers were something else – little laminated cards with their name and photograph and current nationality. Once upon a time, the cards had included date of birth and place of origin, but for the people of the island, as for everyone else wandering the Aegean and Mediterranean, these things were becoming vague and misty. The routine for changing nationalities was the same as the one for receiving the wristbands; long lines of refugees queuing up down at the harbour at irregular intervals. It was unheard of for the UN to make housecalls.

So, what? Someone presenting as a UN official wandering around asking after him. And not by name, either, just by description, which was suggestive. No. This was about the gun.

"Why?" said Stav.

"Because someone saw me with you that day and you've done something stupid and now they're looking for me."

"Don't be ridiculous," Stav told him. "Nobody's looking for *me* and I'm the one who's got the thing."

"They don't know which of us has it," Benno said. "And how do you know nobody's looking for you?"

"I've not heard anything." But Stav sounded doubtful. "Anyway, I haven't done anything stupid. All I did was stash it. You're the only one who knows I've got it."

"Are you sure you haven't done something stupid?" Benno had seen Stav that morning, talking to some of Ringo's enforcers, and he'd felt a great dread settle on his heart.

"Don't start that again," Stav sighed. "I'm not in the mood." They were sitting down by the harbour, eating grilled fish from one of the pop-up cafés which lasted about as long as the day's catch. Stav picked a bone from between his teeth and flicked it away. The day was overcast but between the ranks of containers the air was hot and motionless; at least down here there was a breeze off the sea.

"What does he want you to do?" asked Benno.

"What?"

"You said he had a job for you. Ringo."

Stav shook his head. "I can't tell you if you don't want a piece of it."

"Dickhead."

"Seriously. If you want to be part of it I'll tell you everything you want to know. Otherwise, forget it."

"Okay. I'm in."

"Really?" Stav looked him in the eye. "No. Asshole."

Worth a try. Benno said, "Did you hear anything about the dead guy?"

Stav shook his head. "He's gone, though. I went back and checked."

"Me too."

"Not like anyone cares about one more dead guy, anyway."

"Dead *white* guy," Benno reminded him.

"Hard to tell *what* colour he was. Sort of greenish-black."

"He had a gun. That makes him a dead white guy, whatever colour he was."

Stav acknowledged the point with a wave of the hand. "Anyway, no one's talking about him, not even the UN people. I'm guessing he just washed back out to sea with the next tide. We were lucky to find him when we did."

Benno wasn't so sure about that, but he didn't say anything. He took a last bite of fish and threw the remains onto the quayside, where about a dozen gulls immediately disposed of them. The refugees had tried eating the birds but not even extreme starvation would make them palatable.

"What are you going to do about it?" said Stav.

Well, that was the question, wasn't it. Benno had left his container early this morning, in case the UN man turned up, and spent several hours sitting at the entrance to a cave near the peak of the mountain, watching cruise liners scribing white lines across the sea. He had a vague notion that if he stayed vigilant and kept moving, the UN man would eventually give up and go away. He figured that he would be hard to find in the crowds; the island may have lacked adequate accommodation, sanitation, food, medical care and educational facilities, but it was not short of unaccompanied boys matching his general description.

Stav got up and brushed bits of fish off the front of his jumpsuit. "I have to go," he said.

Benno sat where he was and looked up at him. "Off to play with your new friends?"

"I think perhaps you could do with some friends yourself," Stav said, and he walked away.

HE SPENT THE rest of the day wandering about the island trying to blend in and look inconspicuous. This was something he would normally have done without even bothering to think about it; he basically lived in an environment where to become conspicuous was to invite unwanted attention, and unwanted attention was always bad. The thing to do, he thought, was not to obsess about the UN man, not to spend all the time looking over his shoulder. That would only have looked suspicious. Best thing to do was just act like everyone else, trying to get through the day without succumbing to desperation.

There was a UN compound on the island, but most of the officials lived aboard a ship moored offshore. The ship, like most large vessels in the Aegean and Mediterranean these days, had railguns mounted fore and aft and midships, to take out any approaching fast boats. Eighteen months or so ago a motley group styling themselves 'pirates' had taken over one of the smaller cruise liners, coming in fast under cover of night in boats almost too small to show up on radar and using grappling hooks to get on board. At which point their plan had simply evaporated. Basically, the entire extent of the plan had been to get on board the liner; they had no clear idea what to do after they had achieved that, so they settled for penning up the crew and passengers in one of the ship's cinemas and broadcasting increasingly unhinged ransom demands. When these demands were not met – they included safe passage to the United States, a billion dollars in uncut diamonds and the return to power of several unseated African political strongmen – they shot several of the passengers and posted the video online. At which point Italian Special Forces had HALOed onto the ship one night and retaken it, killing all the pirates and a large percentage of the passengers in the process. Ever since, the cruise lines had been arming their ships.

Piracy, these days, was a foolish trade anyway. Most ships were fitted with beacons and tracking devices, so you couldn't actually *take* them anywhere without the owners and the authorities knowing where they were. Stealing the cargo was out of the question; most of it couldn't be offloaded without dockside freight handling machinery. The best you could do was hit a liner fast and hard, rob the passengers, ransack the kitchens, and leave again before the authorities arrived. Which was a high-risk, low-return sort of operation. Those railguns tilted the playing field in favour of the people on the liners.

The UN ship was a decommissioned Spanish Navy destroyer, most of its armaments removed, painted white with the letters UNHCR on the sides, and renamed *Angelica Newbon*. Nobody on the island knew what the name signified; the vessel was just an ever-present reminder of their plight. It had a pad at the stern to allow small VTOL aircraft to land; you always knew when high mucky-mucks had arrived because you could hear the howl of the engines for tens of kilometres all around. Benno couldn't recall having heard aircraft recently, which made him wonder about the UN man's claim, relayed by the Moroccan woman, that he had returned to the mainland last night. The mainland – the *Greek* mainland, anyway – was too far away to do the trip by boat in one evening. It seemed such a fundamental lie that Benno wondered why the UN man had bothered to say it at all; it seemed kind of insulting. *You are a refugee and it doesn't matter what I tell you.*

He made his way back to his container, but as he neared the intersection he saw someone standing outside speaking with one of the Somalis. From a distance, the figure did indeed present as a representative of the UN, in as much as anyone who was not wearing near-rags presented as a representative of the UN. He was well-fed, for a start, wearing a white shirt and tan chinos and a Panama hat, and he had a leather satchel slung over one shoulder. He had his back to the street so Benno could not see his face, but his body language suggested he was perfectly at ease in a place where some UN officials refused to go without an armed bodyguard. In fact, his body language was completely atypical; there was none of the gruff officiousness, the stiffness, of the usual aid officials, and as Benno watched he saw the Somali man break into a warm, beaming smile, which was something of a miracle in itself. Benno had never, to his recollection, ever seen any of the Somalis so much as grin in all the months they had been living in his container.

And then the man in the Panama hat did something even more astonishing. He put out his hand, and the Somali reached out and shook it, still smiling. The UN usually only touched the islanders during medical procedures or arrests.

There was something so very wrong about this scene that Benno backed away through the crowds of refugees until he could no longer see the UN man and the Somali, and then he turned and ran.

THERE WAS NO way that anyone in their right mind could describe life on the island as 'normal', but it had developed its own rhythms and routines and hierarchies, things that were hard to explain but easy to sense if you spent any great length of time there, and today, today something was *not right*.

It wasn't just the presence of the UN man, he thought. It was something larger, a great powerful undertow. You could see it on the faces of the islanders, the way they spoke with each other, the way they moved through the narrow streets and avenues between the little town of containers perched precariously just above the surface of the sea. It was there in the arguments which broke out between groups of people, the way vendors at the market avoided eye contact, the way Ringo marched down into his domain at the head of a large group of enforcers.

Legend had it that Ringo was not a refugee at all, that he had Italian nationality via his father, that he was only on the island because elsewhere he would have been a nobody but here he was a king. Certainly he was paler-skinned than many of the other islanders, but Benno had spoken to an old man who had been one of the island's earliest inhabitants, and he said that Ringo had come here as a child from Tripoli, one of the few survivors to make it ashore after a surplus US Army drone bought by the Greek government rocketed their boat.

There were thirty or so enforcers, dressed in the usual motley of shorts and threadbare shirts and jeans and 'do rags, some of them barefoot, some of them wearing flipflops fashioned from bits of old lifejackets. Many of them were carrying machetes; the ones who were not had clubs. Ringo himself was unarmed. He was wearing a spotless white shirt and sawn-off jeans, and on his head was a straw hat with a wide floppy brim which shaded his face but did not hide his broad white grin.

"What's happening?" someone in the crowd behind Benno said.

"He wants us all down at the harbour," said someone else.

"He can fuck off," said a third voice.

"You want to watch your mouth, friend," a fourth voice said.

"Ah, fuck him," the third voice said. "My life's bad enough without that prick thinking he runs it."

"We can't *all* go down to the harbour," the first voice said reasonably. "There isn't room."

Watching the enforcers parade past, Benno caught sight of a tall bushy afro with a pair of steel combs winking in the sunlight, and he began to move.

The harbour was built around a little natural amphitheatre, something patiently carved out of the island by the sea over many millennia. Benno had no idea why it was there; he had never seen any sign of prior inhabitation. Even in the days of Homer this place must have been next to worthless. Stav thought the harbour itself might have originally been Roman, maybe a staging post for shipping across the Aegean and Mediterranean, a place of rest and shelter on the way to and from the coast of Asia. Benno wasn't too sure; he had a feeling it might have been the remains of German occupation during the Second World War.

Whatever its provenance, the place was a ruin now. The stones of the quayside were broken and tumbled, the harbour itself full of silt and sand dumped there by storms and currents. The UN had dredged a narrow channel through which smaller boats could pass to offload food and relief supplies, but it was more or less useless for anything else.

When Benno got down there, the natural sloping curve that almost enclosed the harbour was crowded, although it was hard to know whether all these people had come in response to Ringo's summons, because they wanted to see what the fuck was going on, or because they were simply bored. Down on the quay, the enforcers – Stav among them – were building a pile of rocks, while off to one side armed contractors hired by the UN watched silently. Benno shouldered through the crowds a little way up the hillside until he was looking down on the scene, marvelling on a certain level that Stav was actually doing physical work.

The pile of rocks complete, the enforcers stepped away and Ringo came forward, climbed carefully to the top of the pile, and took off his hat. He gazed out and up at the wall of faces, and he smiled.

"My friends!" he said in a loud voice. The harbour was far from acoustically-perfect, but Ringo's was a voice that carried. "This is a great day for our home!"

He was speaking English; the island was a babel of languages, but most people here spoke English well enough to follow what he was saying. Even so, there was a wave of muttering through the crowd as English-speakers interpreted for those who were not and everyone else reacted with some cynicism to the phrase 'our home'.

Ringo let it die down, then he said, "For years we have been invisible. For years we have been no one, sitting on an island that is nowhere. But today, all that changes. Today, we seize our own destinies again. The days when the nations of the North dictated our lives are over."

More translating, more muttering, more heads shaken in puzzlement.

"For the past six months, I have been negotiating on your behalf with the United Nations," Ringo said, to the evident bafflement of the crowd, none of whom could recall ever giving him permission to do that. "Today, we reached an agreement that this island, our home, will become an independent sovereign nation."

More translating. Then total silence.

"From today, this island is to be known as the Independent Republic of Aegea, and we are all its citizens!" Ringo shouted.

Benno, who by now was watching the crowd rather than Ringo, saw people turning to each other with nonplussed expressions on their faces.

This obviously displeased Ringo, who had clearly been expecting somewhat more enthusiasm for the news that the island had hauled its way up the ladder and become a Third World country. He said, "Our new status means that Aegea now qualifies for UN aid."

"And most of it will wind up in your pocket, you cunt," someone behind Benno muttered quietly. "Just like it does now."

"It also means that we will have our own sovereign passports and visa rights," Ringo went on.

Some people – not very many – cheered at this, but most of the islanders had a knowledge of passports and visa rights which would have astounded a consular official, and they knew these were empty gifts. Visa rights to where? Unless Ringo had suddenly discovered a vast reservoir of oil or a motherlode of uranium beneath the island, nobody would want to know them.

There was no oil, no uranium, but the island was rich in apathy. Everyone was just too tired, too hot, too hungry, to become excited about Ringo's news, which in all honesty might as well have been about some faraway realm for all the practical use it was. The crowd began to drift off, in ones and twos at first, then in greater numbers. Benno attached himself to one of the larger groups and wandered off with them, keeping his head down. The last he saw of Ringo, he was still standing on his little pile of rocks, a hard look on his face and a little band of enforcers beside him looking confused.

* * *

4.

THE ISLAND'S NEW status – assuming Ringo had even been telling the truth and it wasn't some cruel trick to tax even more of the people's meagre possessions – had little or no visible effect. It was still hot, there was still not enough food. The Council, the ad hoc group of old men to whom everyone complained about everything, met with representatives of the UN and returned with the news that yes, absurd though it patently was, there was indeed a new country named Aegea, and they were living in it. Anything else would take time; according to the UN these things ground slowly, and until then things would continue as before.

If the people of the island were used to anything, it was things continuing as before, and any immediate changes were cosmetic. Word went round that the enforcers were now the Army of Aegea, but they were still denied firearms and presumably their uniforms were still being made, so it was easy to forget about that.

Less easy to forget was Ringo's simmering displeasure at the cool reception for his declaration of independence. In the following days there was an increase in tax raids. Enforcers descended en masse on the lower slopes of the island and marched through the ranks of containers, taking whatever they wanted. Food, clothing, personal possessions, all went back up the mountain to where the King brooded on the ungratefulness of his subjects.

Benno kept moving. There was nowhere on the island that was safe to stash the phone for more than a couple of days; people were continuously wandering around scavenging, checking out nooks and crannies for hidden stuff. This wasn't considered stealing, particularly; if something wasn't actually in your physical possession it didn't belong to you. The people of the island had survived by scavenging for so long that anything was fair game.

He saw Stav a couple of times, from a distance. Stav appeared to be doing well as a member of Ringo's army; at least, he looked well-fed. Benno wondered what he had done with the gun; keeping it on his person would have been absurdly dangerous so he must be moving it periodically from one place to another, the way Benno was moving the phone.

The island may have been ridiculously crowded, but in the end it was still only a small island. He saw the man in the Panama hat from time to time, from a distance, moving easily through the crowds of refugees, smiling and chatting. Benno's strategy had been to keep out of his way until he gave up and went back where he had come from, but he showed no sign of giving up any time soon. They were going to play this absurd game of hide and seek, it seemed, for the foreseeable future.

The one thing in his favour was that the man in the Panama hat had not enlisted the aid of the authorities, and he found that interesting in itself. Usually if the UN wanted to find someone they did it by brute force, sweeping across the island in great numbers and questioning everyone until they located their target. This happened every couple of months. But it wasn't happening here. The man in the Panama hat was going about his business calmly and methodically, with the minimum of fuss and, apparently, with a great deal of good humour.

One afternoon, he spotted the familiar Panama hat among the crowds at the Seventh Street market, next to an even more familiar afro, and that evening he sought out Stav.

"He wanted to know if I'd seen you," his friend said. "Which I haven't, so I didn't even have to lie to him. Where have you been?"

"Did he say what he wanted me for?" Benno asked.

Stav shook his head. "He didn't seem angry or anything, the way they usually are. Just asked if I'd seen you."

"He knows my name?"

"Of course he knows your name. He said you're not in any trouble, if that means anything."

Well, the people of the island learned fairly early not to fall for *that* one. Everyone was in some kind of trouble, the refugees more than most.

"Ringo's noticed, though," Stav added. "UN man wandering around the island asking for a certain person, eventually word was always going to get back to him. He's curious about what makes you so interesting."

That was all Benno needed. If he was of some sort of value to the UN, he had become of value to Ringo too, and there was no way that could be a good thing.

"He's busy with this country thing," Stav told him. "But he's told the boys to keep an eye out for you. You know what he's like. Hates to feel left out."

That was an understatement. "Don't tell anyone you've seen me," Benno said. "Please."

Stav gave his friend a long, level look. "What have you got yourself mixed up with?"

"I don't *know*. Really, I don't."

Stav gave it some thought. "You want the gun?"

"What? *No*." Whatever trouble he was in, a firearm could only make it worse, not better. "Are you crazy?"

Stav shrugged. "A bit of protection never hurts."

Benno punched him in the shoulder. "Idiot. I'm being chased around this fucking island by the UN *and* Ringo, and you want me to carry a gun as well?"

"It's only a matter of time before someone hands you in, you know."

This was true enough. Ringo might not have been uniformly popular on the island, but there were enough people who wanted to curry favour with him in return for some small luxury. He thought he could stay one step ahead of the man in the Panama hat for quite a long time, but not the enforcers and the rest of the islanders. At some point in the next few days, or even hours, he was just going to bump into the wrong person and that would be it.

"I need to get out of here," he said. "Off the island."

Stav blinked at him. "And go where?"

Anywhere, at this precise moment. "I don't know."

"There's only four ways off this place," Stav said. "And all of them will get you caught."

The only boats on the island belonged to either the UN or the aid agencies which brought food. They were all heavily guarded and tagged with locator beacons. Stealing one was out of the question. The idea of somehow getting onto the *Angelica Newbon* and stowing away on one of the aircraft which came and went was so ridiculous that he didn't even consider it. Deliberately getting himself repatriated to Africa wasn't going to work, either; all he'd be doing would be putting himself in the UN's hands. And there was the final, misty, mythical route off the island – a relative who had somehow managed to make it to Europe finding you a job and a residents' visa and sending for you. This last had never, to Benno's knowledge, happened to anyone.

Benno looked out across the sea. They were sitting in a secluded cove, not far from where they had found the dead man. Along the beach, a family was walking the sand, looking for things cast up by the tide. From time to time, people tried to leave the island by constructing rafts from bits of rubbish and discarded lifejackets. The currents around the island were strong, and if you could get beyond the surf they would sweep you out to sea. The only drawback with that was it was almost certain death, from thirst or starvation or drowning. Even if you were spotted and picked up by a patrol boat, there was a good chance that you would just be brought back here for processing. It was an exercise so utterly pointless that only the truly desperate would attempt it.

"What's the date?" he asked.

Stav told him. "Why?"

Benno thought about it. Four days. All he had to do was keep going for another four days. "I have an idea," he said.

5.

The arrival of food aid brought a carnival atmosphere to the island, albeit a carnival taking place on a virtually barren rock in the middle of the ocean, administered by men with guns and accompanied by the sound of helicopters flying overhead and patrol boats endlessly circling.

No one actually wanted to take responsibility for the refugees. The Mediterranean and Aegean were mostly fringed with countries which had been driven to their knees by multiple economic collapses even before the Xian Flu had raged through them, nations and kingdoms and republics and polities which were barely able to care for their own populations, let alone the vast numbers of the stateless. Humanitarianism, they all agreed, was a noble thing, but it actually began at home.

It was axiomatic that the nations of the North loathed and feared the refugees, and had done so for a very long time. The preferred option was to stop them coming at all, and for decades various programmes of nationbuilding had been going on in North Africa and the Middle East. These inevitably served to make things worse, but were so lucrative for the private firms and corporations to whom the enterprises were outsourced that they were deemed impossible to shut down.

While governments washed their hands and private enterprise looked the other way, it fell to a bewildering landscape of aid agencies and charities and NGOs to prevent what would have been a catastrophe of biblical proportions in the Mediterranean. No one agency could possibly hope to carry the weight of so much aid, so an informally-rotating timetable had evolved. It had not escaped Benno's notice that none of these agencies came from the North, unless you counted the UN, which was everywhere and could barely cope.

This month, it was Albania's turn. The Albanian operation was ramshackle and amateurish, but the people of the island – those who were actually aware of the existence of Albania – agreed it was something of a miracle that they were here at all. They arrived in a converted trawler, a factory ship leased from the Russian fleet moored in Crimea, and transferred their aid to the island via a small fleet of inflatables.

Back in the early days of the island, the lure of the aid drops had proved irresistible to many who had seen them as, if not a route to the North, at least a route to the mainland. Italy, Spain, Albania, even Croatia, were at least a start, a foothold on the continent. Consequently there had been many attempted stowaways. The majority of these had been unsuccessful, but a few had made it as far as the aid ships before being discovered, and one, the legendary Suleiman, had actually reached the mainland. The people of the island knew this because Suleiman returned three years later, having foundered on Hungary's impenetrable border and been deported to Tunisia to start all over again.

Benno had some doubts about the existence of Suleiman – although some of the older islanders swore that they had known him – but the sheer implacable number of escape attempts had led to a massive crackdown in security surrounding the aid visits. The number of failed attempts rose to a hundred percent, and eventually the urge to escape by that route was simply conditioned out of the islanders. No one had tried to get aboard the aid ships since long before Benno had arrived on the island.

The Albanians habitually arrived in the middle of the night; the sound of the factory ship's engines as it approached the island and dropped anchor thundered out across the sea and echoed up the slope of the mountain, and there it was when the sun rose, huge and bright red a couple of kilometres or so away.

What happened next was a period of administration. Representatives from the Albanian aid agency visited *Angelica Newbon* to process paperwork and agree a timetable. This could take anything from several hours to all day, while the islanders gathered along the shoreline and looked out at the enormous cornucopia which had come to visit them.

The next stage was the setting up of tables and pop-up kitchens along the quayside, watched over by UN troops carrying rifles and tasers, and a crowd of mostly newer islanders who had not yet learned that the existence of tables and kitchens did not necessarily mean the imminent arrival of food. When it became clear that food was not forthcoming, most of the people stayed to watch anyway, just because it was something different. Aegea could have cornered the world's export market in boredom.

Setting up could take all day, what with having to transport all the equipment and supplies, so the actual food drop usually didn't place until the day after that, and by this time most of the islanders were starting to get twitchy and restive and the UN guards were tense and bad-tempered.

Approaches to aid differed, from organisation to organisation. For some it was a simple drop, hundreds of bags of rice and other supplies handed out for the islanders to do with what they wished. Others just brought clothing and medicine. The Albanians took a mixed-media approach – there was a disbursement of dry goods such as rice and salt and sugar and clothing and medicines, but there was also hot food, and on the morning of the third day an almost orgasmic smell of cooking drifted up from the harbour and seemed to envelop the whole island, and people began to gather on the quayside in large numbers.

This was always a fraught time for the guards, and the entire UN contingent turned out to keep order, decked out in riot suits and carrying weapons both lethal and not.

"Look at them," Stav muttered, surveying the crowd. "Like sheep. We are the descendants of warriors, and look at us now."

Benno, who was fairly certain that his own lineage contained no warriors, scanned the area, uncomfortably hot in his uniform and visored helmet. The only weapon he was carrying was a holstered baton, but otherwise he was indistinguishable from the guards. Stav had told him the uniform came from a stash Ringo had been keeping for several years, for what purpose Stav could only guess. "When you get yourself caught, and you will, just don't tell anyone where the gear came from," he'd told Benno. "This is the stupidest idea anyone on this rock ever had, and that's a pretty fucking high bar to clear."

Benno had not confided the entirety of his plan to Stav, because if he had his friend would not have agreed to help. The uniform had been something of a surprise in itself. He knew that somewhere in his compound near the top of the town Ringo had stocks of decent Western clothing, and that would have been sufficient for his needs.

"Right," Stav said, "I'm going. I'd wish you good luck, but it's pointless. You'll either be back here or in Libya or dead, and they're all pretty much the same thing."

"What was the job?" Benno asked.

"What?"

"The job you were going to do for Ringo. Please tell me it wasn't just joining up as an enforcer."

Stav looked sly and tapped the side of his nose. "Too late now, brother," he said. "I told you; you should have come in with me when you had the chance."

"Dickhead," Benno muttered, his voice sounding weird and dull inside the helmet.

"Hey," Stav said. "I'm not the one wearing a fucking monkey suit." And with that he sauntered away towards the crowd on the quayside.

Benno watched him go, feeling the first stirrings of panic. There was probably still time to change his mind, but then what was he going to do? He'd spent the past four days moving from place to place, avoiding contact with anyone. He couldn't do that for ever.

The uniform helped. People tended to shy away from it. The important thing, though, was not the uniform, it was the *attitude*. The UN guards all had a peculiar sort of weary swagger, as if worn out by arrogance. Benno joined a group of guards keeping an eye on the line of islanders which by now snaked all the way around the harbour and up the hillside. One of the guards nodded to him, but otherwise no one remarked on his presence.

A security gate had been erected on the quayside to scan for weapons, and the line was passing through that. On the other side were a couple of dozen tables at which sat men and women in summer clothing. Here, the islanders presented their documents and were issued with a new, temporary Albanian citizenship before going on to the kitchens for a meal and then to collect their aid packages. It was a long, inefficient, drawn-out process seemingly designed to annoy as much as help, and as the day grew hotter and the smell of cooking began to make people restless there was some jostling. Benno and the other guards patrolled up and down the line; often it was enough for the islanders to see their body language, but sometimes it was necessary to use sharp words, or occasionally to grip someone by the arm and shake them. Benno remembered the last time the Albanians had been here, a near-riot when some bureaucratic hitch had left the islanders queuing almost all day and then being told to return to their containers.

The first day of an aid visit was always a little chaotic, anyway, no matter how efficient the agency. People were impatient to get their food and other gifts, the enforcers were hanging about waiting to tax whatever they received, the guards got tired and irritable, the aid workers were always on edge. Even on the best of days there was some tension.

Benno and the little group of guards he was by now an unquestioned part of were sent down to the quayside to relieve the guards watching over the security gate. It was not a terribly onerous task – nobody wanted to lose their rations because they'd failed the security scan – but looking back from here Benno could see that the line of islanders now ran off out of sight. The aid drop was so poorly organised that it was going to take days. Why anyone would do this so ineptly was beyond him.

Being near the security gate meant he was also near the quayside, where numerous boats belonging to the Albanian ship and the UN were moored. These were also being guarded, by patrolling UN personnel and members of the ship's company, but no one was expecting anybody to try to steal one because it was assumed the islanders had simply given up on that particular escape route.

The immediate vicinity was busy with people, easy to separate out by the way they dressed. The UN were all in riot suits and helmets. The aid people were in neat, clean summer clothing. The islanders were mostly in rags. Everything beyond the gate seemed quite orderly, with islanders proceeding down the line of tables and the aid people processing their documents and handing out new citizenships. It was a hot, cloudless day again, and far off in the distance the Albanian ship seemed to levitate above the surface of a sea that was almost too bright to look at.

There was still time to change his mind…

Benno took a deep breath and stepped forward. An old man with a long white beard was about to step through the security gate. Benno grasped him by the upper arm and pulled him roughly out of the line. "Now then, uncle," he said loudly, "what are you playing at?"

The old man looked outraged and began shouting at him in Pashto, jerking his body to try to break free. There was muttering in the line of islanders, but not nearly enough. Benno was aware what he must look like to the old man; a monster in a black armoured costume, his face hidden behind a featureless bubble of one-way plastic, and he felt sick as he drew back his hand and slapped his captive across the face.

More muttering, and this time a few shouts from the line, but still not the effect Benno had wanted. And now one of the other guards was coming over to him.

"Oi!" shouted the other guard. "What the *hell* is going on?"

Benno let go of the old man, who fell to his knees sobbing. "He was…"

"He was *what*?" The other guard reached him and leaned forward until their visors touched. "You do *not* hit the residents!" he yelled.

This was not Benno's experience, but he looked back up the line and saw that everyone seemed to be calming down again. The hoped-for disturbance had not materialised. Fucking islanders; too apathetic to even riot.

"What's your name?" the other guard demanded. "Who's your squad commander?"

These were not questions for which Benno had prepared answers; he'd been expecting the island to be in chaos by now. He opened his mouth to say something – anything – and at that moment a shot rang out in the crowd further back up the slope.

The islanders came from many cultures, spoke many languages, worshipped more than one aspect of God, but one thing they all had in common was a deep and intuitive familiarity with gunfire. The ones closest to the shot fled, suddenly leaving a tall figure with a splendid afro standing all alone, hand raised over its head. The figure's hand jerked once, twice, and there were two more shots. Behind his visor, Benno gaped and shook his head.

The tall figure dropped its arm, clasped its hands together in front of it, and pointed its fists at the nearest guard. There was another shot and the guard stumbled backward and fell, and then everyone was running and shouting and screaming.

"Help the Albanians!" the guard who had been shouting at Benno yelled. "Get them to the ship!"

Benno glanced round. The aid workers were doing a fairly good job of making themselves scarce on their own as it was, but he didn't argue. He turned to run along the quayside, and as he did he saw Stav crumple to the ground twitching, tasered by at least two of the UN people.

Then he didn't have any time to think about it. He moved along the quayside, chivvying the panicking aid workers towards their boats, looking for an opportunity.

He found it near the other end of the harbour. There was a nearly-empty boat, half a dozen Albanians climbing down into it, and a couple of UN guards joining them. Benno looked back along the quayside. It was almost deserted now, a wasteland of scattered overturned tables and comms gear. Further away, a huge boiling crowd was shouting and fighting. Benno heard more gunshots, then he was scrambling down a rusted ladder stapled to the wall of the quay. One of the staples pulled loose and the ladder peeled alarmingly away from the rotten concrete and he dropped the final metre or so into the boat below.

It was obvious nobody else in the boat knew what to do. The guards were standing nervously, weapons drawn; the Albanians were sitting down, clearly terrified. Benno took a deep breath, tried to load his body language with authority, and said to the nearest guard, "Get this thing moving; we have to get these people back to the ship."

Clearly relieved that *someone* had a plan, one of the guards went to the back of the boat and started the motor; the other cast the boat adrift by the simple expedient of cutting the mooring ropes with a knife, and they turned away from the island towards the Albanian ship.

"What the *fuck*'s going on?" the guard who had cast off asked.

"Don't know," Benno said. "We just have to get these people to safety and then come back and help regain order." This apparently sounded competent enough to satisfy everyone else in the boat, although it was clear the guards were not entirely enthusiastic about the going-back-and-helping-to-regain-order part. Benno looked back towards the island and saw that the quayside was crowded with people, apparently all fighting. Further back on the slopes of the mountain, smoke was rising in several places, sucked up into the rotors of circling helicopters. It was chaos, as he had hoped, even if it wasn't *his* chaos. He thought of Stav, lying on the ground being tasered over and over again. How many times could you be tasered before it was fatal?

The journey out to the ship only took a few minutes, but it seemed longer, and they had to stooge about for a while to let boats which had left the island ahead of them disembark, but finally Benno found himself climbing a steep set of steps hanging over the side and then he was standing in a landscape of metal and clutter. The deck of the Albanian ship seemed to stretch forever in all directions, piled with crates and boxes and pieces of equipment. People were running everywhere.

Benno ducked down behind a row of crates and shrugged out of his riot suit. Underneath, somewhat sweaty and crumpled now, he was wearing chinos and a polo shirt, the standard uniform of the aid worker, courtesy of Stav from Ringo's stash. He stuffed the riot suit between two crates and walked away.

The important thing was to look as if one belonged, as if one knew where one was going and what one was doing. He moved confidently across the deck until he reached an open door, took a quick glance inside, then stepped through and went down the metal stairway beyond.

The ship was just too big to search all in one go. Benno went down corridors and companionways and stairs and ladders and across one enormous hold stacked with aid supplies, and finally he found what he was looking for, a small storeroom tucked out of the way in what appeared to be a seldom-visited part of the vessel. He checked he was alone, then opened the door, stepped inside, and closed the door behind him.

"Very good," said a voice. "Nicely done."

Benno turned. There, sitting on a crate, his Panama hat in his hands, was the UN man. It was like the conclusion of some long and particularly involved magic trick. Benno balanced his weight on the balls of his feet, preparing himself to rush the man, but he seemed perfectly relaxed and at ease.

"I'm not going to hurt you," he said. "I'm not going to turn you in to the authorities. In fact, I'm probably going to offer you a job, if you want it."

Benno just stared at him.

"My name's Strang, by the way." Up close, he was quite tubby, but to the inhabitants of the island everyone in the outside world looked tubby. "That was quite an impressive bit of business back there, causing a riot to cover your getaway. Thick-ear stuff, but not bad for a piece of improvisation."

"I had help," Benno said.

"Your friend with the gun?" Strang looked sad. "Well, no. I'd like to say he sacrificed himself to save you, but he didn't."

"What?"

Strang laid his hat on the crate beside him and clasped his hands.

"You weren't the only one using the disturbance to cover his actions. Ringo has taken control of the island."

"Ringo already controls the island."

"Ringo works for the UNHCR," said Strang. "He's an instrument of control; they control him, he controls the island. They don't even have to pay him or expend resources, just let him get on with it and threaten to take away his toys if he steps out of line. But his little bid for nationhood shifted the landscape somewhat. All of a sudden the UN were dealing with a head of state rather than a petty warlord, so they were about to have him removed. Ringo decided to move first; he's already rounding up the UN personnel on the island, presumably to use as hostages."

Benno stood where he was.

"Let's face it," Strang said. "Aegea was never going to fly as an independent state. It's worthless. The only natural resource it has is refugees, and nobody wants *them*."

Benno thought of Stav again. Was that the 'job' Ringo had given him? Spark a riot so he could seize complete control?

"That's the stupidest thing I ever heard," he said, preparing to turn and leave.

"No one ever said Ringo was smart," said Strang. "He was just a pliable bully. Now the UN and the Greek authorities and whoever else they can talk into joining in are going to clear the island by force. And yes, Aegea is a sovereign nation *pro tem* and yes, it will be an act of war, but it will be a short war and Ringo will lose and nobody will care very much."

"Why were you looking for me?"

"You have something that belongs to me," Strang said. He saw the look on Benno's face and added, "Please don't insult my intelligence by denying it."

The phone in his back pocket was only a few millimetres thick, but all of a sudden it weighed more than Jupiter. "What if I do?"

"I don't want it back. I don't even want the money – you can keep that, with my blessing, because you're going to need it. There should be a text file, and all I want is to know what it says."

Benno thought about it. "And then what?"

"Well, you can't go back to the island, obviously; in a week or so there won't be anything there to go back to. I can get you papers for any nation in Europe, anywhere you want to go – although I'd suggest you think quite seriously about working for me. You seem to have some talent."

"And if I don't, you'll send me back anyway."

Strang sighed. "This is not a life-and-death situation. I don't need that contact string *right now*. I can wait. Eventually I'll have the phone and you'll be back in Africa or the Middle East or wherever the UN decides to dump you and you'll be no better off."

Benno looked at him for a long time. "A job," he said.

"I think you'd find it interesting. There'll be a lot of travel."

Benno thought about it some more, then he took the phone from his pocket and woke it up and thumbed through to the text file so he could get it right.

"'I used to date the Rokeby Venus'," he read.

BRING ME THE HEAD OF ST MAGNUS MARTYR

1.

SHE LEFT EARLY, just stuck a change of clothes in a bag and headed into the centre of town. She showered at the Embassy and put on the fresh clothes, and was sitting at her desk writing her report of the Bodfish disaster before eight o'clock. For the first half hour or so, her phone kept buzzing; Rob, no doubt wanting to know where she was, what she was doing, and why she hadn't cooked his breakfast for him before she left. She ignored the calls and kept typing, pausing only to take bites from a canteen chicken salad sandwich. He'd make her suffer later, but fuck him.

The report was mostly finished by the time Selina put in an appearance. She hung her coat up, sat at her desk, checked her phone briefly, then took her pad from the drawer and started scrolling through her emails.

"Hello," said Alice.

Selina looked up. "Hi," she said.

"Are you okay?"

"Sure."

"Really?"

Selina nodded. "Yup."

"Lunch later?"

Selina went back to looking at her pad. "Um, I've got some stuff I need to do, Al. Sorry."

Alice looked at her a few moments longer. "Okay."

"How were the folkies last night?"

Alice thought about it, but Selina didn't seem particularly interested. "Lively," she said finally.

"Good-oh." Selina put her pad back in the drawer, locked it, and stood up. "Don't know when I'll be back." And she grabbed her bag and coat and was gone.

"Bye, Selina," Alice said to the door. On the desk, her phone buzzed again and its screen lit up with Rob's ID. "Oh, fuck *off*," she said and went back to spellchecking her report. Antonia was a demon for typos.

LUNCHTIME CAME AND went with no response to her report, or even a sign that it had been received. She called Meg and Antonia, but their phones cut to voicemail. She phoned the Palace and was told by the front desk that Bodfish had, indeed, left the building that morning. "Someone from your Embassy handled it," the receptionist told her.

Around one, she put on her coat and grabbed her bag and went downstairs, desperate to get out of the Embassy for an hour or so. There was a little restaurant in the Upper Town which she and Selina had been planning to check out together, but if Selina couldn't be bothered to be around, it was her loss.

The corridor leading to the front door was crowded. Mart was sitting at his desk, and two men were standing in front of him. Alice went and stood beside him, waiting until he'd dealt with the visitors so he could sign her out, but he turned and beamed at her. "Ah, Ms," he said. "These gentlemen are asking to see the Cultural Attaché."

Alice looked at the two men. They were both of indeterminate middle age and of less than average height. One was sort of weaselly-looking, in a vaguely handsome sort of way, his blond hair slicked back from his forehead, dressed in jeans and a chunky sweater and a combat jacket. He was holding a plastic carrier bag. The other, improbably, was in full goth getup; long pomegranate-coloured hair, pale skin, black eyeliner, a long black coat and leather trousers. Even more improbably, she had the weirdest feeling that she knew him from somewhere.

This was an awkward situation. Tim was out of the office – she had no concrete evidence of this, but Tim was almost always out of the office so it was a reasonable assumption. Selina was nowhere to be found. Alice wanted to be out of the office too, and there was an enormous temptation to just play dumb and make a break for the outdoors as a simple expression of rebellion, but Mart knew who she was, she still didn't know how much trouble she was in after last night, and anyway it was bad form to just turn people away.

So she put on her professional smile and said, "Of course." She turned to the men. "I'm Alice May," she said. "How can I help you?"

The weasely one held up his carrier bag. It appeared to contain a largish box. "We have an object which may be of interest to you," he said in Estonian-accented English.

"Okay. What is it?"

The weasel pouted and did not quite look at Mart. "It is a matter of some delicacy," he suggested. Mart did not quite glower at him.

Alice mentally said goodbye to lunch. "Well," she said, switching to Estonian. "We'd better take this upstairs, then. Mart, would you sign them through, please? I think Interview Room Two is free; we'll be in there."

In the lift up to the second floor, there was an awkward silence. She didn't feel inclined to make smalltalk, and neither did the Estonians. The goth stood ever so slightly too close to her, though.

She led them down the corridor to the smallest of the three rooms they used for press interviews. It had windows looking out onto the street and a table and three chairs. Alice took off her coat and hung it on the hook beside the door, and when she turned back the Estonians were sitting side by side on the other side of the table, watching her.

She took her pad, and a notebook and pen, from her bag, arranged them on the table, and sat down opposite the Estonians. She called up the pad's voice recorder and set it running. "So," she said, smiling. "Perhaps we could start with you telling me your names?"

"We would prefer to remain anonymous," the weasel told her.

"I can always check the names you gave when you signed in," she suggested, trying to read the visitor's badge clipped to the lapel of his jacket.

"They're not our names," said the goth.

Alice looked at the two men and geared herself up to bring the interview to a premature end. "This is highly irregular..." she began.

The weasel cut her off. "Indulge us, miss," he said. "Just for a moment. Please?"

Alice allowed herself a long, deep, mental sigh. "Okay." She made a note in her notebook. There was a hidden camera in the ceiling, and a panic button under the edge of the table on her side. Just in case. "Well, how can I help you, gentlemen?"

"We have a proposal for the Government of Scotland," said the weasel.

She kept her smile professionally bright and perky. "Oh yes?"

"We are in possession of a cultural artifact which we wish to return to its rightful place." He reached down and picked up the carrier bag, placed it on the table, and took out the cardboard box. She glanced at the goth, who was watching her just the merest touch too intently for it to be comfortable.

The weasel had lifted the flaps of the box and was lifting out a roughly football-sized mass of cloth, which he placed on the table and proceeded to unwrap. There were many layers of cloth – bits of old blankets and T-shirts, and what looked to have once been part of a truly frightful pair of curtains. The weasel folded each one neatly and put it in a pile on the table before moving on to the next one. The pile kept growing; the mass of cloth kept shrinking. The goth kept looking at her. She had a sudden image of the weasel finally removing the final layer of cloth and there being nothing there, at which point a camera crew would burst in and congratulate her for being a jolly good sport. For some reason, this made her angry, down in a place where she had not felt anger for a very long time.

But the bundle was not empty. The weasel unfolded a last layer and then sat back and tipped his head to one side.

"Oh my," said Alice.

Sitting on the table in front of her was a human skull, apparently of some great age. It had been extravagantly decorated with pearls and semiprecious stones and gold wire, and remnants of gold leaf still clung to the bone. There was a large pair of faceted carnelians in its eye-sockets, which gave it a spooky orange-eyed appearance, as if it was gazing into a distant and very powerful sunset. There was a big jagged hole in its left temple. Alice looked at the two Estonians, utterly bemused.

"This," said the weasel, "is the skull of St Magnus Martyr of Kirkwall on the island of Orkney." The goth nodded solemnly.

With an enormous effort, Alice managed not to sigh. "I was under the impression that the skull of St Magnus was at Kirkwall Cathedral," she said. "Are you telling me it's been stolen?"

"They've got the wrong one," said the goth.

"The wrong one," Alice repeated.

The weasel glanced at his colleague, and Alice got an impression of annoyance. He looked at her and said, "The people of Orkland, I regret to say, have been the victims of a cruel hoax."

The very name was enough to provoke a discreet wince. Orkney had embraced the spirit of Scottish Independence with such passion that it had been lobbying with enormous vigour for its own secession.

"It seems more likely to me," Alice said carefully, "that *this* is something of a cruel hoax."

"We have *provenance*," said the goth, somehow managing to make the word sound deeply salacious.

"A journal detailing the theft of the skull, shortly after its discovery in 1919," said the weasel, "and its replacement with a skull dug up from a local graveyard."

She looked at the weasel, then at the goth, then back again. She had a sinking sense that this situation was the answer to the question 'How can we make Alice's life even more surreal?'

She said. "And your role in this matter is...?"

"Middlemen," said the goth.

The weasel sighed. "Facilitators," he said. "We represent an heir of the person who originally stole the skull. They wish to return it to its rightful place, to make things right again."

"They'd rather the authorities weren't involved," added the goth.

"Why not just *post* it to Kirkwall?" Alice asked. "Along with the *provenance*?"

"This is not the sort of thing one would entrust to the mail service," the weasel suggested reasonably. "Particularly these days."

This much was at least true; posting stuff from one side of Europe to the other, across borders which could appear and disappear overnight, was a tricky proposition.

"And it would prove embarrassing if the party we represent was to be searched on entry into Scotland and the skull found in their possession," the goth put in.

This week, Alice realised, felt a little like the time when she was a little girl and her parents had taken her on a day-trip to Largs. She'd had a brand-new bathing suit, and while her mother and father were distracted by yet another argument she'd waded out into the Firth of Clyde until all of a sudden she realised she couldn't feel the slippery shingle beneath her feet and she was bobbing along on the waves.

Her father had noticed, eventually, that she was missing, and had come shouting and splashing into the water to grab her, but that wasn't going to happen this time. No one was coming to rescue her; she was going to drift off towards the horizon and she would be lucky if anyone even realised she was gone.

"Are we boring you?" asked the weasel.

She blinked. "Sorry," she said. "I was just trying to think of an easier way to do this than walking into the Scottish Embassy in Tallinn."

He regarded her levelly. "This is hardly a standard situation. It requires nonstandard procedures."

She looked at the skull, and those eerie orange eyes looked back at her. She said, "What's in it for you?"

"We would of course expect some kind of recompense," said the weasel. "I have a wife and children to support."

"Well, *children*, anyway," said the goth, and Alice suddenly knew where she'd seen him before.

"You're him," she said. "The rocker."

The goth beamed in a rather sleazy manner. The weasel looked annoyed. Alice said to him, "If you're trying to remain anonymous, it might not have been the best idea to bring with you someone who was on the news last week."

"Was I?" said the goth. "Why?"

"The Falt Skreen Teevies are reforming. There was some archive footage."

The goth narrowed his eyes. "The Falt Skreen Teevies or The *Bendi* Falt Skreen Teevies?"

Alice narrowed her eyes back at him. She found herself simultaneously remembering that the band had split into two competing and highly litigious units, and wondering why her mind collected bullshit like this. "I can't remember."

The goth pulled a sour face. "Fuckers," he muttered, from which Alice surmised he had not been invited to take part in the reunion. It didn't matter which iteration of the band; they were essentially indistinguishable, musically speaking. It was a distinction so small that only a quantum physicist could recognise it.

"Can we get back to the matter at hand?" asked the weasel.

Alice looked at the skull again. It seemed somehow creepy and innocent at the same time, almost childishly garish until you remembered that there had once been a living, thinking human person in there. She found herself wondering what they had looked like.

"Well," she said, "I can't make any decision on my own, you understand. This will have to be referred to our Cultural Attaché."

"Are you not the Cultural Attaché?" asked the weasel. "We asked to see the Cultural Attaché."

"Mr Rivington is unavailable at the moment," she told him.

He lifted the skull off the tabletop and put it back in the box. "Perhaps we should wait until Mr Rivington *is* available," he said.

"That sounds like a good idea," she said. Tim would be pissed off about having to deal with this, even if he just wound up throwing the two Estonians out, but at least it wouldn't be her problem any more.

"Just a moment," the goth said calmly, putting a hand on his friend's forearm. "Let's not be so hasty."

The weasel and Alice both looked at him.

"We've come a long way," the goth reasoned.

Well, not unless they'd come from somewhere else in Europe; you could drive from one end of the country to the other, from Tallinn to the Latvian border at Valga, in about three hours. Alice watched the weasel's face, and her heart started to sink.

"Let's not have a fiasco, hm?" said the goth. "This young lady is dealing with the situation perfectly well." He beamed at her. "Aren't you?"

So far, all she had done was hear them out and try to palm the whole thing off on Tim. Some rusty circuit of professionalism closed within her, and she heard herself say, "We would need to do tests. You appreciate we can't just take your word for the provenance of the... um..."

"Skull," said the goth helpfully.

"Yes," she said. "The skull."

"That sounds reasonable," said the goth. "Tests." He looked at his friend. "Doesn't it?"

The weasel thought about it. "It doesn't leave our sight," he said.

"That may not be practical," Alice said. "The tests might take some days." In truth, she had no idea, beyond what she'd gleaned from crime novels, where forensic tests took as long as the plot demanded.

"What's to stop you just taking it and denying we were ever here?"

"The gentleman on the ground floor will remember you. As will the person in Reception. You've been recorded on our security system." He snorted. She went on, "It shouldn't be beyond our legal department to produce some kind of receipt acceptable to everyone."

"We'd want *our* legal department to inspect this receipt first." The goth looked at him, and Alice suddenly knew all she needed to know about their 'legal department'.

"This has all suddenly become unnecessarily complicated," she said. "Could you not, you know, just sort of *trust* me?"

"We're not signing anything," he told her.

"She knows *my* name already," the goth said.

"I don't, actually," she said, and she saw his smile dim. "But it would only take a moment to look you up," she added.

The two Estonians exchanged glances. "All right," said the

weasel. "Carry out your tests. We'll come back on Monday. If you haven't done your tests by then, or if you try to pretend this meeting never occurred, we'll return with our lawyers."

"Of course."

He thought about it some more. "Very well," he said. He popped the top back on the box and slid it across the table to her. "We'll see you on Monday."

"I DIDN'T EVEN want the fucking thing," she said wonderingly. "What am I going to do with someone's head?"

"What *have* you done with it, out of interest?" Selina asked.

"Put it in a cupboard in the office."

"Sorry about that, by the way."

"About what?"

"Yesterday. There was no way I was going to make it as far as the tram, never mind work."

Alice shrugged it off. "Doesn't matter. Is everything okay, Sel?"

Selina looked at her. "Me and Sue," she said, and she shrugged.

"The getting married thing?"

Selina nodded. "The getting married thing. Aye."

"You seem... happier today."

"Aye, well, everything's relative."

They were at Troika. Rain was lashing the city and nobody wanted to sit outside under the umbrellas on the veranda, so it was hot and crowded in here, the waitresses in their folk costume having to walk carefully between the tables in case they tripped over an umbrella or knocked something off a table. There was some kind of row going on in the kitchen; Alice could hear pots and pans crashing about and a man shouting very loudly in Russian. Her Russian was pretty good – it had to be, if you wanted to do any serious business in Estonia – but she wasn't fluent in cursing, which was what she presumed this was. There was a commotion and the door to the kitchen flew open and a young man – a boy, actually, not much more than sixteen – stepped backward out into the restaurant and stood there breathing heavily for a moment. Then he took a deep breath, set his shoulders, and went back into the kitchen, and the shouting started again.

"Never a dull moment," Selina said. "What happened with the folkies, by the way?"

Alice shrugged. "I filed a report, haven't heard anything back yet."

"You won't. It wasn't your fault."

"I was supposed to be in charge."

"It's not your fault if some beered-up folkie decides to thump a punter, Al. What were you supposed to do, wrestle him to the floor?"

"Probably."

Selina looked around the restaurant. "Tim would have just thrown them out on their ears, you know," she said. "The guys with your head."

"Yes. I know."

"Couple of locals coming in like that; it's obviously a shakedown. That's even before you take into account what they're trying to sell. Have you been in touch with the Cathedral?"

"What?" Alice shuddered. "No. Jesus, Selina. Can you imagine getting *them* involved?"

"You'll have to, if it turns out to be kosher."

Alice stared at her friend, and Selina shook her head and drank some of her beer.

"You're right," she said. "What are the chances of it being the real thing?"

"Exactly. All I have to do now is find someone who can prove it's not."

Selina sat back and smiled as one of the waitresses brought their meal, wild boar stewed in red wine. They ate for a while in silence, then Selina said, "I might know someone who could help you. With your head."

"Ach, the head can go fuck itself," Alice said, suddenly deciding. "I'll just give it back to them on Monday and tell them it's a fake. Fuck it."

"Suppose it's not, though."

"Oh, don't start." Alice stirred through her green salad with her fork.

"But think about it." Selina rested her elbow on the tabletop and leaned her chin on her hand. "Suppose you tell them it's a fake and they sod off and get it tested by someone else and it turns out to really be the skull of St Magnus?"

"I thought we'd established that it isn't."

Selina was looking at her with devilment in her eyes. "But what if it *is*, and you miss it?"

Alice sighed. "Who is he?"

"Who?"

"This chappie who's going to help with my head."

Selina smiled contentedly at her lunch. "Name of Sepp," she said. "Forensic anthropologist at the University."

"Sepp."

"Sepp. Good bloke."

"I wish you'd stop doing that."

"Doing what?"

"Setting me up with every male you bump into who's got a heartbeat."

"Who? Me?" Selina put on a show of outrage. "Never."

Alice made a rude noise. Improbably, Scottish artifacts did occasionally turn up, although the gods only knew how they wound up in Estonia in the first place. The Embassy kept a rather grumpy professor of antiquities on a small retainer to assess them, but she was reluctant to get him involved, partly because she didn't like him, but mostly because that would make the whole thing official and she had a sense that this was something best kept quiet until the authenticity of the skull was established. After the Bodfish thing, she felt happier not to make any waves until absolutely necessary.

"Okay," she said. "What's his number?"

IT WAS AN interesting time to be involved with the political sciences. Some years ago, around the time of the Xian Flu, it had been epidemiology and microbiology, but the Xian Flu was yesterday; today was... well, no one had yet come up with a name for it. The EU had fragmented into its component parts, more or less, and the resulting wave of nationalism had driven first one, then two, then dozens of smaller national groups to fly off like bits of rubber from a blown-out tyre. Border wire was very moreish. The map of Europe these days looked like one of those insanely-complicated jigsaws one brings as a present for the long-term bedridden, except that it was still evolving. New countries popped up seemingly overnight, and were gone by the next morning. Others staggered on for a few weeks or months before realising that being a nation took a lot more than simple enthusiasm. Some reached a sort of stable point beyond which you could more or less bet that they would survive. Hindenberg, the ethnic German state pared carefully away from Poland, seemed, to the Poles' displeasure, to have reached this point.

Alice was doing her thesis on the development of Hindenberg when she met Rob at a faculty party. Mostly it was people she knew, variously gossiping and discussing the continuing crisis – or whether it could even properly be termed a crisis – but a few outsiders had drifted in, friends-of-friends. He came over to her and they started chatting. It was her first night out since splitting up with Nikolai, Rob was bright and smart and charming and funny, and one thing led to another. In her memory of those days, it seemed to her that she stepped out of that party and straight into their marital home. She supposed she had been happy back then.

It was a while since she'd been back to the University, even though it was an easy walk from work. The place looked familiar and unfamiliar at the same time, as if she'd only ever seen it in photographs before. All the students looked ridiculously young and optimistic, and she found it hard to believe that she had ever been like that. Now she felt tired and old and she was carrying someone's head in a plastic bag and life really hadn't worked out the way she had hoped.

The Department of Forensic Archaeology was in a new building. She pressed the buzzer by the door and the security man inside let her in and gave her directions to the room she was looking for. It was quite a walk down the corridor. When she reached the door she checked twice to make sure it was the right one, then she knocked.

"It's open!" called a voice from inside.

Alice opened the door and stepped through, found herself in a big bright airy workroom, its walls lined with shelves and pieces of equipment she couldn't recognise. There was a large high table in the middle of the room, and sitting there on a stool was a tall man in his early thirties with black curly hair and a wide grin.

"Ms May?" he asked, getting off the stool and approaching her with his hand out. "Sepp Weisz." His handshake was firm and confident.

"Thanks for agreeing to see me at such short notice, Professor," she said.

He waved it away. "It's always fun to do something a little different. You said you had something you wanted me to look at?" He was wearing jeans and a newish university hoodie.

Alice held up the bag. "You must tell me if this is an imposition," she said. "I can see you're busy." Although if she was going to be honest with herself he didn't seem all that busy at all.

He grinned at her. "I live a life of utter boredom, Ms May."

"Alice," she said.

He nodded. "I am Sepp. May I...?"

He took the bag from her, and together they went over to the table, where he removed the box, lifted the lid, and peeked inside. "Are people in the habit of bringing archaeological items to the Scottish Embassy?" he asked, lifting out the ball of rags and placing it gently on the table in front of him.

"You'd be surprised what people bring us."

He laughed. "I don't doubt." He perched himself on his stool and started delicately unwrapping the skull. "Ah." He reached across the table and pulled a small lamp over to where he was sitting, switched it on, and angled it so it shone on the skull. "Very nice."

"Is it?"

"Oh yes," he said, turning the skull back and forth under the light. "I haven't seen an example like this in quite a long time."

"Is it real?"

Sepp sat back and regarded the skull, hands folded in his lap. "Well, the skull is real, and the decoration – although that's a later addition of course. How much later, I won't know until we run some tests. Do you have any provenance?"

"There is, apparently, but I haven't seen it."

Sepp nodded. "It's nice," he said again. "It should be in a museum, not in a box." He turned the skull again and angled the lamp so the light shone obliquely on a pattern of scratches on the back. Alice hadn't noticed them before. Sepp got down from the stool and went over to a little coffeemaker that sat on a workbench on the other side of the room. "Coffee?"

Alice shook her head. "No, thanks. I've got to give it back on Monday."

Sepp poured himself a mug of coffee, carried it back to the table. "We can take samples, analyse them at our leisure," he said, perching on the stool again. "I'd like a colleague of mine to image it as well, just so we have a record."

All of a sudden, she felt the way the weaselly Estonian must have felt. She didn't want to let the skull out of her sight.

He noticed her indecision. "We wouldn't need to take much material, and we can take it from the inside of the cranium," he said. "Remove one of the teeth, drill a core, put it back. No one will know we've done anything. Forensic science has come on in leaps and bounds; you'd be surprised."

"I'll bet." She thought about it. "Okay. How long would you need to keep it?"

He shrugged. "The sampling won't take any time at all. The imaging? Not much longer. I can let you have it back on Monday morning."

"That's really quite fast," she said, thinking of how long it took to get anything done at the Embassy.

"Most of that will be taken up by office politics," he said. "I doubt the work itself will take much more than a couple of hours."

"It won't cause you any trouble, will it?"

"Nah." He grinned. "It's all interdepartmental diplomacy. Bullshit paperwork. Gets in the way of doing anything, but anyone with half a brain and a good heart can get round it. I love doing stuff like this. Breaks up the routine."

"Thank you. I owe you dinner, at the very least."

He grinned. "You don't owe me anything at all. But dinner would be lovely."

Polsloe had, if nothing else, taught her recklessness. "Are you busy this evening?"

He thought about it, but not for very long. "Nope."

"Good." She found herself smiling a genuine, warm, happy smile. "Any preferences?"

Sepp shook his head. "Your choice. I've only been here a few months and I haven't had much of a chance to check out the local restaurants. Educate me."

Wednesday was Rob's poker night with his mates from the Poets' Club, but she'd still have to be careful. "How about I meet you here, about six?"

IF YOU ADDED up the time they had actually spent together, the thing with Polsloe – it was becoming increasingly hard for her to think of it as an *affair* – had lasted a little over a week. He was busy with the film, she was busy at the Embassy; it was difficult for both of them to slip away from their various encumbrances. It had been fun and exciting and… well, *nice* to be in the company of a man who didn't bully her, but the opportunities were frustratingly fleeting and rare.

Poker Nights were good, though. Rob usually went out early in the evening with a bunch of mates who all styled themselves – with varying degrees of accuracy – as poets, and didn't return until well after midnight. According to him, they just sat around in one or other's apartment and had a few beers and played cards, although he'd once come back much drunker than usual and she'd thought that she could smell perfume on him when he came to bed. It was so faint as to be almost undetectable, and the next morning it had been overwhelmed by the smell of alcohol coming off his skin. Maybe she'd imagined it.

One of the best things about Poker Night was that Rob never phoned her when he was out with his chums. Any other time, he would call her incessantly, wanting to know how she was, where she was, what she was doing. From a stranger, or even a boyfriend, it would have been stalky behaviour, but Rob defended it by saying he was worried about her, and wasn't that the kind of a thing a husband should do? Once, just for the sake of devilment, she had called *him*, on the pretext of checking something or other – she couldn't even remember what it was, now. There had been the sound of music in the background, and men talking, and Rob had been annoyed.

Later, when he got home, he had accused her of checking up on him, then segued into a rant about how hard he worked and how he never left the flat and he deserved a night out every now and again. He had then flounced off and slept on the living room sofa, and for a couple of days afterward the atmosphere at home had been more strained than usual. She never called him again.

Anyway, on a couple of occasions she and Polsloe had managed to arrange their schedules to take advantage of Poker Night. Polsloe had rented an apartment just outside Tallinn, and they met there and so long as she was careful about arriving and leaving, and she was back home by eleven, everything was fine. The first time had been rather wonderful in a mad sort of way, a sense of throwing themselves off a cliff edge together. The second time had been... well, that was also rather wonderful, but she'd left with the impression that Polsloe's heart was somehow no longer in it, as if he had what he wanted now and some of the fun had gone out of the whole thing. She asked him about it and he denied there was anything wrong, but she knew. It was one thing to talk to, to sympathise with, someone whose husband was a monstrous manipulative bully. It was quite another thing to try and have a relationship with someone like that, sneaking about, having to steal odd moments or odd evenings, not being in control. She told herself it was a difficult situation for both of them, that it wouldn't be surprising if he grew frustrated, but somehow there was more to it than that. "I wouldn't blame you if you just buggered off, you know," she told him, but later she did.

THEY WENT TO NOA, which was about as far out of Tallinn as it was possible to be and still be in the city. The old restaurant had recently undergone a refurbishment, but it still had the huge windows looking out across the Bay to the Old Town skyline. Sepp was impressed, or performed a reasonable facsimile thereof; Polsloe had taught her recklessness, but he had also taught her that if something seemed too good to be true it most likely was not.

"That's really something," he said, settling into his seat and craning his neck to take in the view. "I had no idea this place was here."

She'd never come here with Polsloe; their restaurant nights – the few they'd managed – had taken place in other towns, where there was only a tiny fraction of a chance of being seen by someone either of them knew. With hindsight, she was rather glad; it would have been a waste of a view and a nice memory.

"Haven't been here in ages," she said, smiling and looking out over the water at the lights of Tallinn.

A waiter arrived with the drinks menu. Sepp chose beer; Alice, automatically defaulting to Polsloe Mode – no alcohol, in case Rob smelled it on her breath and embarked on an extended debriefing about where she'd been, who she'd been there with, what they'd done, what they'd talked about – asked for mineral water.

"So," he said, when their drinks had arrived. "Work at your Embassy sounds very unusual."

"Really?"

"People walking in with the heads of saints. That sort of thing."

"Oh." She laughed. "No, this is a first. It's really very dull, usually. Mostly sorting out stag parties who've got themselves arrested."

"You don't have to do that, do you? As a cultural attaché?"

"It's not a big staff; we have to double up sometimes."

The food menus arrived. Sepp looked at his and said, "You know, I have no idea about any of this. Can you recommend anything?"

"I had the lamb last time I was here; that was pretty good. They've got a new chef, though, so it's all a bit of an adventure."

"How about starters?"

"I was going to skip them, but you go ahead."

He shook his head and said, "Nah. I need to watch my weight as it is." He scanned the menu one last time. "Lamb sounds good," he said to the waiter.

"Make that two," said Alice.

The waiter left, and there was one of those moments of awkwardness when you want to make conversation but can't think of anything to say.

Finally Sepp said, "How long have you been in Tallinn?"

"Quite a long time. I was at university here; I never really left."

"Like it?"

She smiled. "Oh yeah. It's a good country. The Estonians are great."

"So why aren't you happy?"

"That's a very... *personal* question, if you don't mind my saying."

Sepp tried his beer. "I'm sorry," he said. "I didn't mean to be rude."

"You weren't, it's just..." She let the sentence trail off, uncertain what she had been going to say next. "Things have been busy; I've been a bit distracted recently."

"Forgive me," he said. "I don't get out much."

She laughed. "I find that hard to believe."

He smiled at her. "New country, lots of work to do. I never seem to get round to it."

"I expect it'll settle down eventually."

"One would obviously hope." Sepp took another drink of his beer. "This is very good, you know."

"Estonians are great brewers. I read somewhere that there are more microbreweries per head of population here than anywhere else in Europe."

He grinned. "Then I really must make time to do some exploring. Perhaps you could make some recommendations?"

"I'd be delighted."

The food arrived, and to Alice's relief it was as good as she remembered. "So," she said, "how do you know Selina?"

Sepp looked up. "Pardon me?"

"Selina Brooks. From the Embassy. She suggested I come to see you."

"Oh!" His eyes widened fractionally. "Yes, Ms Brooks. One of my colleagues did some work for her last month. Perhaps he dropped my name; I don't know her personally."

Alice sighed inwardly. Had Selina's determination to pair her off with someone finally reached the point where she was recommending people she'd only *heard* about? She couldn't recall a situation last month which might have merited calling in an expert from the University, but she was beginning to suspect that whatever was happening in Selina's private life was driving her ever so slightly off the rails.

She said, "She spoke very highly of you."

He chuckled. "That was very kind of her."

"Hm." She and Selina were going to have to have a long, quiet chat soon.

She'd never told Selina about Polsloe because by then she had been deep in matters of operational security, and operational security dictated that *no one* knew, it was the only way to feel even remotely safe.

And then the film was finished and there was the premiere and he was gone again, back to Los Angeles. They'd messaged each other intensely for weeks afterward, but then the messages grew fewer and fewer and eventually he gave up trying to communicate with her for weeks at a time, and by then she was coming to terms with the probability that she had simply been a convenient shag. These days, they exchanged stiff, formal communications, like two deep-cover agents who had offended each other.

He was with another poet now, a Russian emigrée named Karla. And what the fuck was it with these poets anyway? Alice had actually met her at a poetry festival a couple of years ago, declaiming in a loud voice about Estonian oppression. They'd followed each other on social media but barely communicated until Karla took up with Polsloe, at which point every now and again there would be a post which, on the face of it, was perfectly innocuous and even quite funny but which somehow – deniably – addressed something deeply personal in Alice's life. Karla was clearly playing a game – look at me, I am younger, better-looking, in bed with him right now, and you are a dried-up old bitch and I won – but no matter how much it hurt, and it hurt very much, Alice could never quite bring herself to engage. There was always the possibility, at the back of her mind, that Polsloe was complicit in these posts, that the two of them were sitting side by side and sniggering at her. Polsloe always came back, anyway, when he wanted something. Friends; always there when they need you.

Alice wondered how Selina – whose response to being told about Rob had been to try and find another man for her – would react if she ever found out about Polsloe. Would she be disappointed not to have been let in on the secret? Happy that Alice had actually done something proactive with her life for a change? She was certainly going to be disappointed with Alice's response to Sepp; he was a nice enough man, and good company for an evening out, but he was not what she was looking for, not any more, and when the meal was over they shook hands and parted and that was that.

2.

SHE WAS OUT bright and early on Monday morning and back at the University around ten. There was a different guard on duty at the Department of Forensic Archaeology, but he buzzed her through and she walked down the long corridor and knocked at Sepp's door and opened it without waiting for a reply.

"Oh," she said.

A little old man with white hair and a kindly face was sitting at the big table in the middle of the room, squinting at something on a monitor display. He looked at her over the top of the monitor and raised bushy eyebrows.

"Sorry," Alice said. "I was looking for Professor Weisz."

"Yes?" the little old man said genially.

"Professor *Sepp* Weisz?"

"Yes?" the little old man said again, this time a little puzzled.

"He was here last week," she said, ploughing on through a growing sense of unease. "Thirtyish, black hair, grey eyes. About so tall." She indicated a spot about six feet off the floor.

"I am Weisz," said the little old man. He took off the ID card hanging on a lanyard round his neck and held it out. "Look."

She took the card. Looked at the name and photo on the front. Looked at the little old man. "I had dinner with him," she said. She looked at the photo again. Looked at Weisz. "I gave him something important."

Weisz's eyes widened fractionally.

"No," she said. "No. Not like that. An... object. An artifact. It's not mine; he said he was going to test it for me."

"I think," Weisz told her, taking back his ID, "that you have been the victim of a practical joke. Who are you, please?"

"Alice May," she said. "I'm with the Scottish Embassy." And without thinking, she put her hand out.

Weisz looked at her for a few moments, then shook her hand. "Let's try to work out what happened, Ms May, shall we? What was the object you brought for testing?"

For a few moments, her mind was perfectly blank. She couldn't remember what the object was. She couldn't remember who he was, who she was, where she was, or why she was here. All she could do was stare at him.

Weisz tipped his head to one side. "I can't help if you don't tell me, Ms May," he said mildly.

Things snapped back into place, but they didn't do it all at once, and she had a worrying sense that they weren't all snapping back into the right places. "It was a skull," she said. "A decorated skull."

He looked at her a moment longer, then he took out his phone. "Well, that shouldn't be too hard to check." He speed-dialled a number. "Markus? Hi. I'm fine, thanks. How are you?" He listened for a moment. "Excellent. And Krista? Good. Listen, we have a little problem up here. Something seems to have gone astray; we think it was sent to you for testing..." He raised an eyebrow at Alice.

"Last week," she said. "Wednesday."

"Wednesday, or possibly later," said Weisz. "A decorated skull, I surmise First or Second Century." He chuckled. "Yes, I know. Well, *I* did, apparently. Or someone claiming to be me. Would you? Very kind." He took the phone from his ear and said, "I presume this person said he was going to order the usual suite of tests? Carbon dating? DNA?"

Alice shrugged helplessly, and Weisz scowled fractionally. Alice said, "I'm so sorry for all this. I'm sure there's a simple explanation."

Weisz put the phone back to his ear. "Yes, I'm here, Markus." He watched Alice while he listened. Finally, he said, "Interesting. Yes, it is, isn't it. Ah well. Many thanks, Markus. Yes, we must. Perhaps next week? Excellent. Regards to Krista." He hung up and raised his eyebrows.

"Fucksake," Alice said faintly.

*　　*　　*

"I WAS ON holiday last week," Weisz said as they walked between buildings. "Well, a bit of a working holiday, actually. A dig at a Romano-British site in Sussex. Do you know Sussex?"

Alice shook her head, not trusting herself to speak.

"It rained the whole time. Anyway, the point is that I was not in Estonia last week, and my lab was locked. Theoretically, it can only be unlocked with one of these," he lifted up his ID and dangled it from its lanyard, "and the University's security system logs every use. In addition, there are the usual surveillance cameras everywhere, including in the lab."

"So the man I spoke to should have been recorded."

Weisz nodded. "One would think so." He glanced at her. "You don't seem to be crazy or to have bad intent, so I'm assuming some sort of crime has taken place. The University will want to know about that."

Alice felt her heart shrink. "It's good of them to help," she said.

"Oh, they couldn't care less about your skull," he told her, leading her up to a small brick building and holding the door open for her. "But they will be worried about the insurance."

Inside, most of the ground floor was an open-plan office, divided into workstations by shoulder-high partitions. It was quiet and clean and the air conditioning was the tiniest bit too fierce. All the workstations, she noticed, were occupied by men, and as she looked around the room she saw Mart, the security man from the Embassy. He glanced up from whatever he was doing, their eyes met, then he quickly looked down again.

Alice didn't have time to wonder what Mart was doing here. A tall man wearing a rather unpleasant suit was coming across the office towards them.

"This is Mr Ivanov," Weisz told her. "Head of Security."

Ivanov had the over-firm handshake of a man who liked to be in charge. "Professor Weisz said on the phone that you have been a victim of crime," he said in perfect English.

"I don't know what I've been the victim of, to be honest," Alice said. "I don't know what's going on."

"We'd like to review the security camera footage from my lab last Wednesday," Weisz said. "Also the key logs."

"This is quite irregular, you understand," Ivanov told them. "There is the matter of data protection."

"It's footage from my lab, Sergei," Weisz told him. "I waive my rights. As I presume does Ms May..."

"Absolutely," said Alice, utterly lost at sea.

Ivanov thought about it. Alice realised belatedly that he was wearing a hairpiece which did not quite match the colour or texture of his natural hair, and suddenly she could look at nothing else.

"You will have to sign a declaration indemnifying myself, my staff, and the University from any and all legal proceedings arising from access to data stored by this office," Ivanov said.

Weisz sighed and clapped Ivanov on the shoulder. "Sergei, my friend," he said. "Don't be a dick. Show us the movies."

Ivanov gave him a sour look. "Come with me," he said.

Ivanov's office was austere to the point of ridiculousness, which made the large plush chimpanzee sitting on a chair in the corner even more out of place.

"For my granddaughter," he said without bothering to look at the toy. "It's her birthday tomorrow. There's no room in their flat to hide the damn thing."

Weisz regarded the chimpanzee soberly. "Why not keep it at yours?" he mused.

Ivanov scowled, took a remote from his desk, and pointed it at a large screen mounted on the wall. The screen lit up, divided into hundreds of tiny tiles each showing a different view indoors and outdoors. Ivanov tapped in a string of digits and one of the tiles expanded until it crowded all the others out of the way. Alice recognised Weisz's workroom, the table where she and the fake Sepp had sat chatting last week. It looked as if the camera was up in a corner of the ceiling at the back of the room. At the bottom of the screen was today's date, and beside it the time, counting up second by second.

"Which day was it?" asked Ivanov.

"Last Thursday," Alice said. "Around lunchtime. Say one o'clock."

Ivanov punched some more numbers and the image on the screen blinked. The viewpoint was the same, but all of a sudden the table in the middle of the room was empty, the tall stools lined up neatly. The figures in the bottom corner were showing last Thursday's date, just ticking past noon.

They watched for a while, but nothing happened. Ivanov touched another button and the clock on the screen sped up. The light in the room on the screen began to fade and brighten noticeably as clouds passed across the sun outside. The room remained empty of people. Ivanov and Weisz looked at her, but she couldn't take her eyes off the clock. One o'clock, half past, two o'clock...

"No," she said. "No. I was there. *He* was there. Are you sure this is the right day?"

Ivanov blinked at her. "Madam," he said. "Please."

Alice walked right up to the screen. The date was correct, the time... flicking past four o'clock in the afternoon, long after she had left. "This is wrong," she said.

Weisz turned to Ivanov. "Perhaps we could check the door logs, Sergei...?" Ivanov started to say something, but Weisz added, "The young lady is clearly distressed. We ought to help her, if we can."

Actually, distress was the least of what Alice was feeling. She turned to look at the two men. "I'm not lying and I'm not mistaken," she told them. She pointed at the screen. "I was here on Thursday. And so was someone who said he was you." She pointed at Weisz. "I gave him something and in a few hours the people who gave it to *me* are going to be coming to get it back. If I don't have it by then, I'm going to send them to talk to *you.*"

Weisz and Ivanov watched her for a few moments, as if waiting to see if she would start screaming. When she did not, Ivanov went back to his desk and tapped a few commands on his keyboard. "The door was unlocked on Wednesday evening," he said, reading something from the monitor. "The key used is registered to the cleaning contractors. That's perfectly normal – occupied offices are cleaned every evening, unoccupied ones get two visits a week. It wasn't unlocked again until Professor Weisz came into work this morning." He read some more, and sucked his teeth and shook his head.

"What is it?" asked Weisz.

"The cleaners didn't bother to lock your laboratory on Wednesday night. They're always doing it; I've lost count of the number of memos I've sent about this."

"It was locked this morning," Weisz said.

Ivanov nodded. "They locked it after doing the cleaning on Friday night. I apologise, Professor."

Weisz sighed. "*Could* the video be wrong?"

"Absolutely not."

"Well, I don't believe Ms May is lying or insane or mistaken. Clearly *something* has happened to her."

Ivanov looked at him, then at Alice, then back at Weisz. "Is she sure this is the correct office?" he asked.

"Oi," Alice snapped. "Don't you *dare* talk about me as if I'm not here. And yes, I'm sure it's the correct office."

Ivanov and Weisz exchanged glances. "Well then," Ivanov said to Alice, "you will need to file a report, Madam."

An hour later, after recording a statement and filing an official complaint, Alice stormed out of the security building. As she left, she glanced around the open-plan office, but Mart was nowhere to be seen.

THE ANGER CARRIED her most of the way back to the Embassy, but by the time she got to the office it was gone and all she could think about was the skull and what she was going to say to the two Estonians when they arrived to collect it.

There was, of course, no sign that either Selina or Tim had been in the office recently. In fact the whole Embassy seemed unusually quiet, as if everyone was dozing after a long lunch. Normally, she would have welcomed the peace, but today it all seemed rather sinister.

She dialled Selina's number but the call cut to voicemail. "Sel," she said, "call me right now. I don't care where you are or what you're doing. Your pet professor's stolen the fucking head."

She sat at her desk wondering who to tell about the missing skull. That she was going to have to tell *someone* was inescapable – the complaint she'd filed at the University would eventually find its way back here – but actually reporting what had happened seemed quite beyond her right now. *I took the skull to be tested and I gave it to someone who was pretending to be someone else and now he's gone and so is the skull*. Somehow, she didn't think that would work.

Telling Rob was entirely out of the question. He would basically firewall himself from the whole thing, but it would be another black mark he would roll out any time he wanted to demonstrate how rubbish she was. *You can't be trusted with anything. Look at that thing with the skull; you completely fucked that up. What were you thinking?* The prospect that this, on top of the Bodfish fiasco, might be enough to get her sent home was just too vast and far-reaching to contemplate right now. It was impossible to compute.

The thought of contacting Polsloe briefly crossed her mind – she could really use a hug right now, however virtual – but this was none of his business. If he replied – as he had done in the past when she'd needed a shoulder to cry on – *Sorry. In a meeting*, it would most likely break her.

She took out her phone and put it on the desk and watched the little numbers of its clock tick impassively upward, her mind perfectly blank. Five minutes passed. Ten. Fifteen. She called Selina again, was rewarded with the voicemail beep.

Finally, she took a deep breath and stood up. She pocketed the phone and, with what was for her an act of considerable courage, took the lift two floors up into Senior Country.

Visiting senior staff was always a little like entering a parallel dimension. Their offices were bigger and better-furnished, the place smelled of new carpet, there were cheerful paintings by local artists on the walls. Everything was cleaner. It was warmer in winter and cooler in summer. The lavatories were antiseptically-maintained and featured dispensers of expensive designer handwashes and moisturisers.

It was also, today, quite deserted. She knocked on Antonia's door and got no reply. She tried the handle but it was locked. Same story at Meg's office. She stood in the corridor and looked up at the ceiling. The floor above her was where Harry the Spook had his suite of secure offices, and the one above that was Nicky's realm. These were places a person of her pay-grade only visited by invitation, even in the direst of circumstances.

"Hello?" she said out loud. She said it again, a little louder, hoping that there would at least be a secretary about to hear her and tell her what was going on. But nobody opened a door and looked out into the corridor. It was as if the entire staff had gone off on a day trip and not bothered to tell her. Which was not entirely beyond the realm of possibility.

She went down to the first floor, where a seemingly unending series of local interns had sat behind the reception desk until boredom and lack of salary drove them off to pastures new. The most recent one – Alice didn't even know her name, they just nodded hello to each other from time to time – was a pretty, auburn-haired girl who favoured enormous hoop earrings. She looked up from whatever she was doing and smiled as Alice approached.

"Hi," Alice said as brightly as she could. "I'm Alice May. I'm with the Cultural Section."

"Kaarin," said the girl, extending a hand over her desk for Alice to shake.

"Kaarin," Alice said. "Do you know where Ms Whitson and Ms Colman are?"

Kaarin consulted her pad, checking Meg and Antonia's diaries. She shook her head. "They have no official meetings today." She looked up at Alice. "Perhaps they're at lunch?"

Well, of course that was always a possibility. "How about Mr Rivington and Ms Brooks?"

If Kaarin felt any surprise at Alice's failure to keep track of her own colleagues, she made no sign. She checked her pad again. "Ms Brooks called in sick this morning," she read. "Mr Rivington is in Riga."

Despite the veneer of calm she was desperately trying to maintain, this made Alice raise an eyebrow. "Riga?"

Kaarin read from the pad. "Dundee City Of Culture."

The Dundee roadshow had been making its unhurried way along the northern coast of Europe for the past three months, but it wasn't due in Tallinn for weeks. She and Selina had barely done anything about it so far, beyond some light liaison with the exhibition centre. Was Tim factfinding? Had he managed to detect a free lunch even at this distance?

She said casually, "I bet the Ambassador's gone missing too."

Kaarin narrowed her eyes fractionally and looked down at her pad. "The Ambassador is in Holyrood for a meeting," she said. She pronounced it like 'Hollywood'. "She's not due back until this evening."

This at least was not unusual; Nicky was always going back and forth between Tallinn and Edinburgh for debriefs and hothousing sessions. Scotland's diplomatic footprint was still perilously small and tentative and the Service was in a continuous state of refinement. As Ambassador, Nicky had at her disposal a small and aged executive jet which the government had bought second-hand from a bankrupt charter firm. It was narrow and cramped, and the one time Alice had been in the cabin it had smelled ever so faintly of sick, but it meant Nicky didn't have to travel late at night or stupidly early in the morning.

Kaarin was looking at her, a faint but friendly smile on her face. "Okay," Alice said. "Thank you." And then, for no reason she could have explained, she added, "Nice to meet you finally."

Kaarin beamed. "You too! Have a nice day."

Back in the office, Alice sat watching the clock for another hour. At some point, she realised she hadn't had anything to eat since breakfast, and she went down to the almost-deserted canteen and sat staring at a bowl of chips until they went cold.

She was sitting at her desk at three, staring into space and trying not to hyperventilate. She was still doing that at four. And at five.

At half past five she called the front desk and asked if anyone had come in to see her. Kaarin cheerfully informed her that the only people to visit the Embassy that afternoon were a couple of Estonian students making enquiries about visas, and a delivery driver with a new chair for Nicky's office.

At six, Alice surged to her feet and put on her coat.

SELINA AND SUE lived quite a distance outside the city, in a block in a new suburban development. Alice took a cab and told the driver to wait for her while she leaned on the button on the entryphone. There was no answer, but one of the other residents in the block arrived back with two bags full of shopping and when she waved her phone at the lock to open it Alice held the door open and slipped inside after her.

Up on the second floor, she banged on Selina's door and rang the bell until the noise brought out one of the neighbours, an old man with a florid face and a nose which had been squashed out of shape by some long-ago accident and never properly reset.

"You're wasting your time," he said. "They're gone."

She found herself almost shouting at the old man. "What do you mean gone? Gone where? When?"

He shrugged. "Moved out Friday night, saw them with their luggage. Don't know where they went."

"*Moved out*?" It was an effort not to shriek at the top of her voice.

"Looked like it. They had a lot of stuff with them. Are you all right?"

No, I am not all right. She took a long, deep breath. "Yes, I'm fine, thanks. Sorry to bother you."

Back downstairs, she pushed through the door and stood outside staring at the cab for so long that the driver started to open his door to see what was wrong. *Calm. Stay calm. Try to think.* She took out her phone and speed-dialled a number.

"CONCEPTUALLY, WHAT WOULD happen if I was to say you're over-reacting to perfectly explicable events?" Nikolai asked.

"I'd punch your face out through the back of your head," Alice mused. "Conceptually."

"Hm." Nikolai drank some of his beer, returned the glass precisely to the ring of moisture it had left on the tabletop. "Best not say that, then."

"Probably best," she agreed.

"Have you eaten today? You look awful."

"Oh, cheers, Nik."

Nikolai sighed and seemed to attract a waiter by force of will alone. He ordered a couple of burgers and a side order of fries to share, and when the waiter had gone again he said, "You're sure one of them was the bass player with the Teevees?"

"Positive. He was chuffed I'd recognised him."

"Shouldn't be *that* hard to find him, then."

"I called their management. You remember they split up?"

Nikolai nodded and said, "Uh-oh."

"Their manager refuses to even admit he exists, let alone give me an address for him."

"Pretty lively, that split," Nikolai agreed. "Record company?"

"He owes them money; if they knew where he was they'd be talking to him themselves."

Nikolai shook his head and muttered, "*Musicians.*"

"I finally sweet-talked an address out of one of the manager's secretaries. He's not there, hasn't been there for months; he owes the landlord money."

"And yet a week ago he was happily walking around town with a head in a bag." Nikolai took another drink. "Well, the head has disappeared and so have the people who brought it to you. I'd say the two cancel each other out. Fuck 'em; forget about it."

Alice looked at him and wondered precisely when her life had come loose from its moorings. "I can't just forget about it, Nik. *Something* happened. Eventually the University will be in touch with Tim about the complaint I made, Tim will boot it upstairs, and all kinds of shit will take off."

Nikolai thought about it. "I don't see that you've done anything wrong," he said finally. "You followed procedure, no?"

"You think that's going to matter?" she said. "I don't have the skull, I don't have the guys who gave it to me, but I *do* have an official complaint which I made to the University. How the hell is that going to look?"

"Maybe they couldn't make it today," Nikolai mused. "Maybe they'll turn up tomorrow looking for their head."

"They didn't strike me as the sort of guys who leave a jewelled skull with someone and then just *forget* about collecting it, Nik."

"I didn't say they'd forgotten. Maybe they were... *inconvenienced.*"

"Oh, I hope they were," she muttered. "I hope they were inconvenienced with extreme fucking prejudice."

He looked at her. "Go to the police, Alice," he said.

She shook her head. "That'll only make things worse. The whole purpose of the Embassy is to avoid embarrassment; you remember what happened with Cox?"

"I remember offering to do something about that."

"Yes, so do I." And the image of Cox returning to his flat in Troon or wherever the hell it was without his kneecaps had been her one comfort in the whole sorry mess. "Why the fuck did we split up, Nik?"

If he was surprised by the question, he didn't let it show. Very little surprised Nikolai. "It was your idea, if I recall correctly," he said eventually.

"Yeah." She sighed. "Sounds about right."

Their burgers arrived, and Alice discovered that she was actually starving. She wolfed her meal down and ate most of the fries, too, but Nikolai didn't complain.

"I can put some feelers out," he suggested. "If you want."

"About the skull?"

"I was thinking more along the lines of the rocker, but I can see if anyone knows something about a skull."

She thought about it. "That would be great, Nik. Thanks."

"It might at least help give you an idea of what's going on," he said. "And if I'm honest, I would like to know what this story is about too."

Alice took a big swallow of beer and sat back and looked around the bar of The Butt-Shaped Cat. The Bodfish gig seemed like a very, very long time ago, but to be honest this *morning* seemed like a very very long time ago. Waiting for Nikolai to turn up, she had tried every contact number in her phone and got no reply on any of them. It was as if the entire Embassy had simply dried up and blown away. She was seriously considering the nuclear option, calling Holyrood, even if it turned out to be a career-ending move. She was entirely out of ideas.

"The thing with Selina is interesting, though," Nikolai mused.

"She was butting heads with HR," Alice said. "Something about them wanting her to marry her partner." Nikolai pouted at her, but she went on, "She was talking about leaving Tallinn, but I didn't think she was serious."

"She'd have told you she was planning to go, surely."

"She's been a bit *distant* the past few days."

"Not so *distant* that she couldn't suggest you consulted with this false professor."

Alice kept coming back to that point, and dismissing it, and coming back to it again. She drank some more beer and looked at her phone again. There were two dozen missed calls and fifteen messages from Rob. She'd stopped reading the messages after the first two or three. It was interesting, in a detached, academic sort of way, how quickly the wheels could come off a person's life.

"It would be nice," she said to no one in particular, "if I could go to sleep tonight and wake up tomorrow and find out that the past couple of weeks have just been a particularly mad dream."

Nikolai grunted. "I hope not," he said. "I spent the weekend with a French air stewardess."

She punched him in the shoulder, even though she suspected it wasn't true. "Fucking caveman," she said.

Nikolai rubbed his shoulder. "This is why we split up," he said. "You wouldn't stop hitting me. I remember now."

"And you're just a fragile little butterfly."

"A flower," he said. "A fragile little flower. Like a daisy."

She looked at him. "I should go," she said finally. "Rob will be wondering what's happened to me."

If Nikolai had noted that she hadn't contacted Rob to let him know what was going on, he didn't say anything. "Okay," he said. "You know where I am though."

Alice got up, put her coat on, slung her bag over her shoulder, and went round the table to kiss him on the cheek. "Thank you, Nik."

"For allowing myself to be punched? You're welcome, I'm sure." He squeezed her hand. "I don't know what you've become mixed up in, but take care, okay?"

She managed a smile. "Do my best."

Things To Do In Moravia
When You're Dead

THE INSTRUCTIONS FOR the pickup were perfectly straightforward. Go to the Starbucks on Freedom Square, buy two lattes and a Danish, and wait to be contacted. He'd had Situations which had been much, much weirder.

Freedom Square was not actually square; it was as if someone had taken hold of opposing corners of a square and pulled gently but for quite a long time. A set of tracks crossed from one side to another, carrying the city's red and white trams, with which he had become much taken in the days since his arrival.

Everything was still – just – new enough to be slightly wondrous to him. Flying in to Brno at the weekend, the city had looked like a scatter of pastel Lego bricks cast across fields and forests and hills and the short flight from Cologne had not been seriously spoiled by a mediocre cup of coffee and a genuinely horrific sandwich.

Checking the time on his phone, he saw that he had been sitting here, in the little umbrella-shaded seating area outside the Starbucks, for almost an hour. Both the lattes were cold and the Danish was beginning to look a little stale on the surface, but he was in no hurry. This was a good place to sit and watch and absorb little details. Everyone here seemed content and well-fed, no one appeared to be in a hurry. The previous night he had eaten at a restaurant not far from here, and the sight of the piles of meat and sausage and dumplings and potatoes and pickled cabbage everyone was tucking into was still a little shocking.

He was a quick study, but he found the history of Europe confusing. What he had once thought of as the *North* was not actually the North; it was the nations fringing the Mediterranean. The real North, the true North, was France and the Low Countries and Greater Germany and the Baltics and Poland and England, to an extent. It was a landscape of shifting borders and changing names stretching back many hundreds of years. During its history, Brno had been known as Brünn, Brin, Bruna and Brunn. It had once been in Czechoslovakia, then in the Czech Republic, then in Czechia, then in the Czech Republic again. Now it was the administrative centre of a loose coalition of little polities and statelets which styled itself the Moravian Federation, whose size and membership waxed and waned to no formula he could determine; it might as well have been influenced by the phases of the Moon for all he could tell. And that was just one city; Europe was awash with places like this, more every year. To his outsider's eye it seemed as if the Continent was continually shaking itself apart and reconfiguring itself like one of those old children's toys that were a car or a robot, depending on what one wanted to play with at any particular time.

Someone sat down opposite him, a tall woman with brown hair and hazel eyes, the collar of her jacket turned up against the breeze. She smiled at him and rested her elbows on the tabletop. The stones of the square were not quite level under the table's feet, and it tilted under the pressure. Cold latte slopped out of the cups.

"Oops," the woman said.

Ben looked levelly at her.

"Do you know how that thing works?" she asked, nodding at the gherkin-shaped black obelisk of the city's astronomical clock which stood at one side of the square.

He shook his head. "I've been here a week and I still haven't worked it out."

The contact string completed, the woman nodded. "There's been a bit of a change of plan," she said. She was speaking English, but with a faint accent he hadn't encountered before. "The pickup's been moved."

This was not even a surprise. The organisation he had been inducted into that day on the Albanian aid ship was deeply informal and improvisational, as if constantly reshaping itself to fit Europe's changing borders. Over the past few years he had learned that things went wrong, plans were changed or dropped altogether. You never questioned, just rolled with it.

"Moved to where?" he asked politely.

"Place called Mikulov," she said. "Down by the Austrian border. I was there a few years ago. It's nice."

Ben didn't doubt it, but it was irrelevant to him. The fact that the message had been passed on to him personally, rather than by a text or a posting on an anonymised board or someone simply slipping a note under the door of his hotel room, spoke of some screwup somewhere along the line. But again, you just rolled with it.

The woman looked at him and tipped her head to one side in a way he found vaguely disquieting. He didn't like people memorising his face. "There's a café on the town square," she said. "It has a couple of guest rooms in the back; one of them's reserved for you in the name of Anderson. Check in there and you'll be contacted."

He nodded. "Okay." He watched coffee dripping off the edge of the table.

She looked at him a moment longer. "I'm to say you're doing really well," she said. "Everyone's very happy with you."

"Oh?" This was the first indication he'd had that there was an organising intelligence – let alone an organisation – behind what he had been doing for the past few years.

"Yes," she said, standing up. "You're going to come in quite handy, I think." She looked at the table. "Sorry about the mess." And with a final smile, she walked away and was lost in the crowds of people crossing the square.

He looked at the pool of coffee on the tabletop and wondered whether he should go and get some napkins and mop it up. Finally, he just left it.

THERE HAD BEEN, briefly, a trainer, a grumpy little Spaniard named Luis. In a cramped and stuffy flat in Turin, Luis had passed on to him the basics of *tradecraft*, which had seemed to Ben to consist chiefly of children's games. Hide and seek, find the parcel. Later, he had thought of it as a test he was required to pass in order to move further northward. There had been steady work since then, a series of border crossings carrying various Packages, the contents of which he was never allowed to know. He did the jobs and money appeared in his accounts, but apart from Strang, Luis had been the only person he had met who appeared to represent the higher echelons of what they called *Les Coureurs des Bois*, the only sense that he was actually working for some kind of larger structure. The woman in the square seemed to have been little more than a local representative, a messenger; what he had been taught to think of as a *stringer*. Some of the work he had done, in the early days, had been the work of a stringer, a dull round of admin and theatre, helping to backstop legends.On the other hand, he was actually on the European mainland and he had a job and money, things he had dreamed of but had never hoped in his heart would come to pass. It seemed ungrateful to ponder too deeply about the source of these wonders.

The bus journey to Mikulov was a little over an hour, an unhurried drive down side roads and through little villages. Autumn was falling over the fields and wooded hills, the colours still startling to him after a life which in memory had been unremitting beige. Bare rock poked from the sides of some of the hills, and on others he saw the square, dome-roofed silhouettes of little chapels perched high above the countryside.

One enormous hill, seemingly several kilometres long, rose beyond the trees a considerable distance away. The road angled away from it, back again, along a causeway across a big lake, and then all of a sudden the bus was puttering along the base of the hill beneath great crags. Craning his neck, Ben could see a considerable structure or structures atop the hill, and a few moments later they were picking their way through the traffic on the outskirts of Mikulov.

The town square, which was pretty in a sort of chocolate box central European way, sat about halfway up the hill, below the castle which he had seen from the road. He checked into the guest house, and found himself standing in a neat but small and slightly chintzy room with an excellent bathroom but no entertainment set and no coffeemaking facilities.

Fortunately, the café downstairs was more than equal to the task of satisfying his coffee needs, and also providing a slice of very nice chocolate torte. He sat at a table in the window and watched tourists wandering past in the square – which again seemed not to be square but more of a distorted rectangle. It was a nice sunny day but there was a chill in the air, and everyone was wearing jackets and warm clothing.

Around one o'clock, he ventured out, noting the restaurants and beer houses. There was an imposing-looking church around the corner of the square, and beyond that the cobbled street that mounted up in a series of curves and doglegs through formal gardens to the castle itself. From several vantage points he found himself looking down on the red-tiled roofs of the town, and beyond them out across the southern Moravian countryside. In the distance, a major road was choked with cars and coaches and lorries waiting to cross the border into Austria. The northbound crossing was a few kilometres to the west, on another major road, but he couldn't see it from here. Austria had hardened its borders decades ago against the first great tide of refugees from the South. Its southern borders were all but impenetrable, deeply fenced and heavily patrolled, but the northern edge was more permeable. Vienna was only a couple of hours' drive from here. There was something deeply satisfying about standing here looking at Austria's northern border.

As he turned away from the view, someone bumped into him. He saw a middle-aged couple in jeans and boots and matching red windcheaters walking away from the viewpoint hand in hand, rucksacks slung over their shoulders. The woman half-turned and waved and mimed what he assumed was an apology.

He wandered on, took a tour inside the castle. It wasn't what he thought of as a *castle* – he had an image in his head of brooding stone fortresses with crenellated walls and slit windows from which one could pour boiling oil down onto besieging troops, and this castle was more of a huge country house built on a crag overlooking the Moravian borderlands – but it was very pleasant. In one of the huge cellars he stared at what he was informed was the second-largest wooden barrel in Europe, with a capacity of a hundred thousand litres. The guide told the little tour group, "When everyone thinks of the Czech Republic they think of beer, but beer is rubbish. Beer is made; wine is *grown*." And he proceeded to distribute small plastic cups of the local white wine, which was sharp and fruity and very nice. There were printed leaflets about the region's wine industry. Ben took one and slipped it into his jacket pocket, and as he did so his fingers brushed a folded slip of paper which was already there.

Later, sitting in an Italian restaurant on the square and tucking into a roasted lamb shank with potatoes and cabbage, he took out the slip of paper and unfolded it. A date and time were printed on it in very small letters, and an address in Berlin. He refolded the paper, put it back in his pocket, and sighed.

He took his time returning to the guest house, visiting the tourist information office on the square and collecting an impressive wad of maps and leaflets about churches and castles and sites of particular interest. He dawdled in a shop which sold high-end watches and ornaments, window-shopped unhurriedly until he was as sure as he could be that he hadn't picked up a tail.

Back in his room, he opened the wardrobe and found on its lowest shelf a square white box about two feet on a side. It was surprisingly heavy; whatever was inside gave it quite a heft. It was completely sealed – he couldn't see any way to open it – and featureless, and its sides felt ever so slightly too cool. He put it back on the shelf and stood looking at it for a while, thinking, before closing the door again.

It was still, he found, easiest to think of it as a children's game, a thought experiment. *Here* was a thing, and it had to be *there*. How would you do that?

The obvious way would be to go back to Brno and simply fly to Berlin, but if it were that easy the box would not have been entrusted to him in the first place. Sending it through the mail or via more conventional courier services was clearly also out of the question.

Ben sat on the bed and sorted through the sheaf of leaflets he'd taken from the tourist office. Among the leaflets for castles and wineries and historic chapels were bus and train timetables. He studied these for a while. The maps were not terribly detailed, but they served to give an idea of the relative positions of places and roads. He was around six hundred kilometres from the box's destination, and he had to cross two borders with it. The first, between the Moravian Federation and the Czech Republic, was nothing more than a formality. The Czechs and Moravians were on good terms and their border was more of an administrative division than an actual frontier. The one between the Czech Republic and Greater Germany was going to be trickier, and he spent a few minutes going through different options. The trick was not to think about his own job, but those of the people charged with securing the borders; not planning how he would get the box to Berlin, but how he would *stop* the box getting to Berlin. Luis had described it as a kind of Zen. *Do not cross the border;* be *the border*.

He showered and then slept for a while, woke around three in the morning, put the box in the bottom of his rucksack, stuffed his clothes in on top of it, and left the room. There was a little garden behind the café, and at the end was a high wall with a gate. He unlocked the gate, stepped through, closed it behind him and pitched the keys through the bars where the owner of the guesthouse could find them tomorrow. The gate opened onto a narrow little street behind the square. He followed it to the end, turned down another side street that switchbacked down the hill, and was gone.

THE DIRECT ROUTE to Berlin was a six-hour drive. Ben did it in seven days, taking anonymous local buses from village to village, sleeping in hostels. The Czech countryside began to take on the atmosphere of a dream, sinking towards the end of the year, a long poem of village names and rivers and hills and forests while he dozed and woke and got off the bus at a random stop and began all over again. He judged that, if he was being followed, by the fourth day he would have driven his pursuers to such a peak of frustration that they would have arrested him out of sheer spite. When no arrest came, he got on another bus, and in this way he came to Hrádek nad Nisou.

The border here was interesting. Half a kilometre from the

town the Czech, German and Polish borders met in a T-junction of frontiers, a *tripoint*. The country here was farmland and woods and deserted little campsites, closed down by the border authorities. The point where the borders met was formed by the confluence of a little stream and a larger river, the Lusatian Neisse. For quite a distance, the Neisse formed the border between Poland and Greater Germany; further downstream it was a wide, slow, powerful river, but here, not far from its source, one could easily have swum it in a couple of minutes.

Not that there would have been any point. High fences ran along the banks and off into the distance. On one bank of the stream there was a Czech flag, on the other the Polish flag, and on the far side of the Neisse was the Greater German flag. At the centre of the confluence, where the watercourses met, an old European Union flag dangled limp and tattered and apparently forgotten from a rusted flagpole. It was not a place lacking in satire.

Dressed in hiking gear, Ben joined a little group of sightseers who had come to visit this place where three nations collided. They took photographs of the border wire, each other, the Polish and German guards patrolling beyond the fences. Some children took it in turns to dare each other to run up and touch the Czech fence and then run away again. It began to rain.

It was all plainly absurd. This was not the Czech Republic or Poland or Germany; it was all the same place. A little way back from the tripoint, there was what Ben thought might have been the remains of a little bridge over the stream that separated Poland and the Czech Republic, a place where once one might have simply walked from one country to the next, no more than half a dozen steps. He found it offensive.

It was also ideal for his purposes. In the way of border guards the world over, the Czechs and Poles and Germans had, more from boredom than any great sense of anger, begun of late to taunt each other through the wire. It had started with rude gestures exchanged by patrols, then rude words, then the occasional thrown rock. Presumably their respective superiors, awake to the possibility of an international incident, had issued various memos and edicts, but they had missed the fact that the border men were actually having fun. They all knew each other – a decade or so ago their extended families had probably all lived in the little villages scattered around here, irrespective of what side of the border they were on. One winter there had been a massed snowball fight between the representatives of the three nations which actually made the news, which was where Ben had found it, Googling away the endless kilometres on the bus, and seen possibility.

Gossip in town suggested that the situation had now escalated to practical jokes. The Germans had actually slung a donkey under a small hot-air balloon and flown it over the fence into Poland, much to the delight of the Polish guards – who named the donkey 'Herman' and immediately adopted it as a mascot – and the ire of their superiors. Not to be outdone, the Czechs had mocked-up a model submarine – not much more than a conning tower on a submerged platform – and floated it down the river bearing the flag of the *Kriegsmarine*, swastika and all, an act of such breathtaking bad taste that it was actually widely admired. There were so many 'incidents' at the border now that hardly anyone outside the area paid them any attention. The most recent had involved the Poles releasing several hundred Chinese lanterns in the fields on their side of the border. Charmingly illuminated, the lanterns had bobbed and drifted on a night breeze into Czech and German airspace before their candles guttered out and they fell to the ground, smashing glass vials attached to them which contained a particularly foul-smelling substance cooked up in someone's shed. The stink was so bad that the following morning the three groups of guards had to patrol wearing gas masks. They regarded each other, from their respective countries, and then they simultaneously turned, dropped their trousers, and mooned each other.

It was anarchy, and it was wonderful. The border might as well not be there at all.

LATE ONE NIGHT, Ben returned to the river. Observation of the guards' routine suggested that he had about forty minutes before the Czech guards patrolled this stretch of the wire, and over an hour before the Germans and Poles came this way.

A trip to Liberec the previous day had provided most of the things he needed, and he moved back and forth along the river bank, carefully digging holes and burying reinforced cardboard tubes and setting igniters. Then he walked a kilometre or so back down the nearby road to where he had parked a hire car.

The border station between the Czech Republic and Poland was a little scatter of buildings around a small petrol station and restaurant. When Ben got there a big truck and a tour coach were parked in one of the waiting areas, being checked by border guards. Several cars were waiting a little further down the road, where a simple metal pole blocked the way. He joined the queue and waited.

Most of the cars waiting to cross must have been local, because the guards waved them through with only a cursory document check. Ben waited until there was only one vehicle between him and the barrier, dialled a number on his phone, and pressed *call*. A couple of hundred metres away at the tripoint, the little sequencer he had hung in a tree woke up and started to scan through its contact list.

Ahead, the barrier rose and the car in front moved forward towards the Polish side of the border. Ben drove up to the waiting guard, lowered his window, and offered his passport and papers. As the Czech took them, there was a sound like a giant coughing and a great white sun rose into the sky above the trees. Everyone at the border post turned to watch, and then the fireball turned into an expanding shell of violet sparks.

Beside the car, the guard sighed. "They're at it again!" someone called from an open doorway in one of the buildings beside the checkpoint.

"Yes," said the guard, watching as another starburst exploded below the first one. And another. And another. "So I see."

"Should I call the Lieutenant?"

"Oh," the guard said, half to himself, "I think he probably knows already." He suddenly seemed to remember the documents he was holding. He glanced at them, at Ben, then handed the papers back and signalled for the barrier to be raised.

"What's going on?" Ben asked.

The guard looked at him again. "Party time," he said. "Go on; get a move on."

The barrier was raised, and Ben drove the twenty metres or so to where two Polish guards – who looked as if they could be the Czech guard's younger brothers – were standing at another barrier, watching the fireworks boom and flare above the trees.

"Bloke back there said you guys were having a party," Ben said when he handed his documents over.

"Not us," one of the guards said, barely sparing the passport a glance. He looked at his companion. "Is it?"

The other guard shrugged. "Nobody told me if it is."

Ben turned in his seat and looked out through the rear window as a particularly splendid chrysanthemum burst rose like a dome into the night sky. The shells were the size of cherry tomatoes, fifteen of them loaded into each tube. The man at the shop in Liberec had told him there were enough for a twenty-minute display. He wondered which would happen first, the fireworks running out or the Czechs finding the sequencer that was triggering the igniters. "Bit early in the morning for fireworks, isn't it?" he said.

The guard looked at him and gave his papers back, clearly more interested in going down to the Neisse and seeing what the fuck was going on. "Welcome to Poland," he said.

"Thank you," said Ben.

Less than half a kilometre along the road the guard at the German border didn't even bother to look at his passport, just raised the pole blocking the way and waved him through. As Ben drove into Zittau there was one last almighty flash of light and colour behind him, and then darkness closed over this little corner of Europe again.

IT WAS THE first time he'd visited Berlin, and it was quite a thing, a place of forests and boulevards and towering buildings of steel and glass and composite compounds and cars, cars, cars. He'd only travelled seven hundred kilometres or so but there was a real chill in the air, as if he had climbed halfway to the top of the world. This was the place his people – inasmuch as he *had* a people – had dreamed of. The True North, a cosmopolitan and more than slightly anarchic metropolis in a nation which was throwing off progressively smaller and more wacky countries. The sheer *vibrancy* of the place, after the sleepy quiet of the Moravian and Bohemian countryside, was almost intoxicating.

He left the car at the Hertz concession at Tegel, took a bus into town, and bought himself a warmer jacket at a hiking store. He also bought himself a hat, a rather fetching fedora with a brim he could tip down to hide his face. Everyone in Berlin seemed to be wearing a hat.

He went to Berlin-Zoo S-bahn station, found the left-luggage lockers, and put his rucksack in one, clothes and all. Dropped a five-mark coin into the slot and retrieved the key-card, and went shopping.

A few hours later, equipped with a new travelling bag full of fresh clothes, he was sitting in a café on Potsdamer Platz – which again was not, strictly speaking, square – drinking a latte and leafing through a printed copy of *Süddeutsche Zeitung*. He didn't read German – he strongly suspected that some of the words had been made up by someone striking a keyboard with their fists – but that didn't matter.

At one point, he got up to use the lavatory, and when he got back the newspaper he had left on his table, and the luggage locker key-card which had been tucked inside it, were gone.

He finished his coffee, picked up his bag, and went to do some sightseeing. As he left the café, it began to snow.

THE WRITERS' HOUSE

ROB DIDN'T SAY anything about her being late when she got back, which should have been a red flag but she was too preoccupied to notice. He stayed in his room while she prepared dinner – the reheated remains of last night's cottage pie, it was all she could manage to concentrate on – and he was quieter than usual while they ate, for which she was grateful.

As she was rinsing the plates and putting them in the dishwasher, he said conversationally, "Where did you say you were the other night?"

Partly it was the casual tone of his voice, partly it was the day's events still pinballing through her head, but still the alarm bells didn't ring. She said, "What night was that?"

"Thursday?"

It took a real effort to remember that far back, and then to remember what she had actually told him. "Planning meeting with Selina and Tim," she said.

"Yeah? How did that go?"

She closed the door of the dishwasher and straightened up, looked across the breakfast bar. Rob was still sitting at the dining table, fiddling with his phone. Alice turned to the sink and rinsed her hands. "It was okay," she said, drying her hands on a dishtowel. "Why do you ask?"

"Oh," he said, "I just wondered how you managed to fit that in and find time for this as well." He held up the phone. There was a photo on the screen, but she was too far away to make it out. A chill of panic went up her back.

"What's that, then?" she said.

He shrugged. "You tell me."

She went around the end of the bar and walked over to the table, peered at the screen. The photo wasn't a particularly good one – the ambient light was too low – but it was good enough to recognise herself and the Fake Sepp sitting at the table in NOA.

"Where did you get this?" she said.

"Never mind where I got it," he said tightly. "Who is this?"

"A consultant from the University," she said. "Rob, I need this photo and I need to talk to whoever took it." Here it was, photographic evidence of the existence of the Fake Sepp. Something to take to the police.

"What?" This obviously wasn't the response Rob had been expecting, and it made him angry. "Who is this?" he said again.

"I told you. He's a consultant. He was looking at... Rob, I need this photo."

"You're fucking kidding, right?" he said, curling his hand protectively round the phone. "You *lied* to me. You're *always* lying to me."

"This is really important."

"You're telling me it is." His face was starting to grow red. "You go out on a *date* with some random bloke and you *lie* to me about where you were."

"I wasn't on a date. It was work."

"Oh, don't," he sneered, getting up and kicking his chair back so that it fell over. He came over to her, still clutching the phone in his fist. "Just look at yourself."

Alice took a breath and tried to stay calm. "Rob, he *stole* something from me."

"What, while you were fucking?"

For a moment, everything went grey. Everything – the Bodfish catastrophe, the business with the skull, Selina's sudden midnight flit – everything seemed to surge up through her from somewhere around her feet, and when it had passed Rob was standing there with a stunned look on his face and his hand over his nose. As Alice watched, blood started to seep between his fingers and drip onto the carpet.

They might, if one of them had had the sense to back down, have managed to stop it then, but Rob turned and stormed into his room and slammed the door, leaving Alice breathing hard in the middle of the living room, completely bemused.

The doorbell rang. It might already have rung several times, Alice had no idea. She walked over to the door and opened it and found Antonia standing outside in the corridor, flanked by two security men Alice only vaguely recognised.

"Get your coat," Antonia said.

"What?"

"Get your coat, we're going to the Embassy." Antonia seemed on the edge of fury.

"What?"

"Don't just stand there saying *what*, you stupid bitch. Nicky wants to talk to you right now. You can either come with us willingly or we'll carry you to the fucking car."

Alice wondered if she was experiencing some kind of collapse. "I spent *hours* looking for you today," she said.

"Well, I'm here now. Last warning. Get your coat."

Alice turned and looked at the door of Rob's room. She couldn't hear any sound from inside, which was to be expected; he wouldn't smash up his own stuff.

"Fine," she said. At least it would get her out of here for a while. She grabbed her coat from the hook, stepped out into the corridor, and closed the door behind her.

IT WAS ALMOST ten o'clock when they reached the Embassy. Antonia sat beside the driver, Alice in the back with the security men and their industrial-strength aftershave. She tried to ask a couple of times what was going on, but nobody seemed to want to talk now she was actually in the car so she gave up and watched the night-time city pass by outside. It was a city she knew very well, a city she loved, and right now it seemed completely unfamiliar. At one point she looked at her hand. One of her fingers was starting to swell up. Had she actually *hit* Rob? After all this time?

She kept trying to picture the dining room at NOA, trying to remember the faces of the other people there. She'd scanned the room when she and Sepp arrived – an old reflex from her Polsloe days – but she hadn't seen anyone she knew. Had she missed someone? Someone Rob knew but she'd only met once in passing? Had Rob had someone *following* her?

It was easier, somehow, to concentrate on these things than think about what was going on around her. Rob was familiar; she knew the landscape because she had constructed much of it herself. This other thing, this late-night trip to the Embassy with a furious Antonia and a couple of security men, was completely unknown and she didn't know what to say or do.

They pulled up outside the front door and got out of the car, Antonia leading the way onto the pavement. Someone buzzed open the door even before she reached it, and they made their way down the corridor, past the security desk – manned by yet another guard Alice didn't quite recognise – to the lifts. It was a tight fit – the lift was just about big enough for four people, but not if two of them were tall body-builder types. Alice held her breath.

On the fifth floor, Antonia marched them along the corridor to Nicky's office and opened the door without knocking. Alice had a moment to consider that Antonia's behaviour was not what she would have expected from someone in Human Resources, then she was ushered inside by the security men.

It was a nice office, big but not too big. Along one side, the windows were concealed by thick dark blue curtains; along the other was a wall of bookshelves packed with those meaningless titles interior designers use to make whoever's office it is look well-read. At a big desk at the far end sat Nicky, presumably in the new chair that had been delivered earlier. Nearer the door there was a little seating group – a sofa and a couple of armchairs. Meg was sitting in one of the armchairs.

Nicky was wearing a red dress that left her arms bare, and her expensive-looking hairdo and makeup suggested an interrupted evening out. She was holding a pad and scrolling through something on the screen and the hard stare she gave Alice when she walked into the office was calculated to reduce her to a charred circle of carpet.

"Right," Nicky said, laying the tablet on the desk. "What have you got to say for yourself?"

"I don't know what this is about," Alice said.

Nicky glanced at Antonia, then looked at Alice again. "What this is about, you stupid little bitch, is the end of your career in the Diplomatic Service."

Alice stared, but a tiny rational corner of her mind told her that if that was all it was, she wouldn't be having this conversation. She'd be sitting in Antonia's office.

"I've lost count of the number of times you've fucked up in the past few days," Nicky went on. "You caused a near-riot in that folk pub, I've got some twat from the University yelling in my ear about a theft investigation, and now this."

"Now what?" Alice said.

"Here." Nicky held out the tablet. "Here."

Alice took the tablet and looked at the screen and found herself looking at a message she had sent to Polsloe. Scrolled down and saw more. Felt herself falling, falling.

"These are private," she heard herself say from a great distance. "How did you get them?"

Meg and Antonia exchanged glances that were just a fraction from edging over critical mass into smirks.

"This is a gross breach of my data protection rights," her voice said, as if from another room altogether.

"You are a member of the Scottish diplomatic service," said Nicky. "You have no data protection rights. Particularly with regard to unsanctioned extramarital relationships with foreign nationals."

A little corner of her mind examined that statement, pondering *sanctioned* extramarital relationships. She opened her mouth to say something, but no words came out. The room somehow seemed simultaneously stiflingly cramped and far too large. Still falling.

"You're suspended without pay, pending an investigation of your actions," Nicky said. She stared at Alice, thinking. "Actually, no," she said. "I don't have time for this. You're fired." She turned to

Meg. "Put her on the first flight back to Edinburgh tomorrow. Holyrood can sort her out."

"Yes, Madam Ambassador," said Meg.

"Get her out of my sight."

The two security men moved smoothly to envelop her in the fallout from their aftershave again, but she didn't move. She just stood staring at Nicky.

"She's still here," Nicky said.

The security men grasped Alice's upper arms and began to urge her back from the desk, but she planted her feet. "Red makes you look fat," she said.

Nicky sighed and waved her away. The security men pulled harder, and this time Alice let them turn her and walk her to the door and into the outer office and along the corridor to the lift, Meg trailing in their wake pulling on her coat.

In the cab, the security men sat with her in the back, Meg up front giving directions in quiet, fast Estonian to the driver, who became visibly more and more irritated.

"I do know the way," he muttered. "Only been doing this job fifteen years."

"Next left," Meg told him.

At the flats, the security men stayed with the cab while Meg rode up to the apartment with Alice, remaining well within her personal space until the door was closed behind them.

"Well, that went just fine," she said.

Alice stood in the middle of the living room, looking around the apartment. She'd been hoping Rob would still be here, because Rob's anger tended to go off in all directions and she would have liked to see Meg experience it. But the place was deserted.

"For what it's worth, red does make her look fat," said Meg.

Alice turned to her. "Fuck off out of my home."

Meg unbuttoned her coat and wandered over to sit on the sofa. "Well, not precisely *yours*, is it. Not *yours* at all, now you've been fired."

Rob's departure had been hurried and furious; the bedroom looked as if a firm of interior decorators had used it to stage a cage fight. "Fuck off."

Meg showed no sign of moving. "Nicky's angry, right now," she said. "You've embarrassed her. Those little love notes you and the Kiwi sent each other found their way to the local press."

Alice came out of the bedroom and stood looking down at her.

"Not us," Meg said, holding her hands up in innocent surrender. "Not *me*, anyway."

"Get out of here, or I swear to the gods I will kill you. I've got nothing left to lose."

"Well, actually, you *do*."

"What?"

"I'm on pretty good terms with the editor of the paper that's got your sexts. I've talked him into holding back on publication."

"Why?"

"Because they make us all look a laughing stock. Nicky, mainly."

"You don't give a flying fuck about Nicky's feelings."

"No. True. Except as far as I have to factor them in to things which I do give a flying fuck about."

"Like what?"

Meg looked at her and waved exasperatedly at one of the armchairs. "Sit down, for fuck's sake. You're trying to loom, and frankly you're not very good at it."

Alice stayed where she was.

Meg sighed. "There was a theft a month ago, from a museum in Tartu. A religious relic. The Estonians are really fucking cut up about it."

Alice felt herself starting to fall again. "So?"

"They want it back."

"What's that got to do with you?"

Meg shrugged. "Well, they want the relic back, but *I* want to talk to the people who brought it to you. Let's call it a professional interest."

"It was stolen," Alice said. "I don't know where it is. And I don't know who they are."

"It's really weird, you see," Meg said. "It's a pretty piss-poor Embassy, but the security system is top of the line, the best money can buy. And there's not a fraction of a second of footage of them anywhere." She sat back and draped an arm along the back of the sofa. "And that really is quite hard to do, without leaving some trace. Someone very very clever did that. And it's the same with the police cameras on the street outside, and the shop cameras, and the cameras on the trams and in the taxis. Estonia's very good at e-stuff, and they're absolute stars at surveillance. Not a sniff of anyone out of the ordinary entering or leaving or even walking in the direction of the Embassy."

"I don't understand."

"Well, of course you don't. Why should you? Sit down."

Alice sat.

"We got the wee girl in Reception to do us an e-fit and it was useless. According to her, one of them was some middle-aged rock star."

Alice carefully kept her expression neutrally confused. "What about the security man?"

"Ah, now, *he* seems to have gone AWOL. The firm we hired him from claims not to have heard from him. The other security men say they assumed he was kosher."

Alice flashed on Mart sitting in the security office at the University. "That's a shame," she deadpanned.

"You could probably give us a better artist's impression, considering the amount of time you spent with them," Meg went on as if she hadn't heard, "but I'm figuring you have a contact protocol for them."

"A what?"

"A phone number. A place and a time to meet. A message placed in the want-ads of a local paper. A chalk mark on a wall near the airport. Come on, Alice. They must have had some way to get in touch."

"They were going to come back to the Embassy. Today. But they never turned up."

Meg looked at her, a disappointed expression on her face. "This editor friend of mine's going to publish tomorrow. Once that stuff's out there, it'll never go away. It'll trot along in your footsteps for the rest of your life. It'll be waiting for you every time you apply for a job, no matter how small. It'll be a bad smell you can't ever wash off or hide with deodorant."

"But you can make it go away."

Meg smiled grimly. "You're not so stupid, you know. I'd have enjoyed working with you, under other circumstances."

"Why do you want these people?"

"Ah, now, that is way *way* beyond your pay grade. Even if you had a pay grade, which you don't any longer. Help me find them, Alice. I can't save your post here, but I can make sure you stay in the diplomatic service. Maybe even find you a little promotion somewhere."

"London."

"A promotion's a promotion."

"Fuck yourself."

Meg took out her phone and checked the time. "The story's going to go live in six and a half hours," she said. "That's how long you have to see sense."

"I don't know where they are. I don't know *who* they are." Which at least was eighty percent true.

Meg put her phone in her coat pocket and stood up. "Have a think," she said. "You can call me any time, but I'll be in touch in the morning whatever. Don't get up; I'll see myself out."

After she'd gone, Alice sat where she was for a while, staring into space, willing herself to catch up with events and failing. It finally occurred to her to curse Selina, who seemed to be the author of all her woes. Eventually, she got up and went over to the cupboard where they kept the drinks. There were several empty spaces on the shelves. Rob had taken all the Scotch and most of the vodka, apart from half a bottle of żubrówka she'd brought back from a trip to Warsaw, which he refused to drink because he said it tasted like perfume.

Truth be told, she wasn't all that wild about it herself, but alcohol was alcohol. She took the bottle and reached onto the shelf above it for a glass, and as she did so she noticed a little slip of paper in one of the other glasses. She took it out and saw printed on it the words YOUR FLAT IS UNDER VIDEO AND AUDIO SURVEILLANCE. GO TO THE KITCHEN AND MAKE A SANDWICH.

She read this several times, recognising all the words but unable to make sense of the sentences. She poured herself a drink, crumpled the note, closed the cupboard door, and went through into the kitchen.

Putting her glass on the worktop, she opened a cupboard and took out a plate, then lifted the lid of the breadbin and took out the loaf. Underneath was a small matt-black box with a red button on the top. Beside it was a note which said DON'T TOUCH ME YET.

Okay. What was most remarkable, she thought, putting the loaf on the worktop beside her glass and going over to the fridge, was how none of this seemed in the least out of the ordinary. It was perfectly normal to find notes in the drinks cabinet, mysterious little devices in the breadbin, and, she saw, a note on top of the package of sliced ham in the fridge. LOOK IN THE KNIFE DRAWER, it said. PRESS THE RED BUTTON. TAKE THE PHONE. LEAVE IMMEDIATELY. DON'T WAIT. DON'T PACK. LEAVE YOUR OWN PHONE BEHIND. USE THE EMERGENCY STAIRS.

She palmed the note and put it in her pocket with the other one, took the ham and the butter from the fridge, and put them beside the loaf. She went over to the knife drawer, where she found a phone she had never seen before. She took a knife out, went back to the worktop, took the breadknife from the block and cut a couple of slices of bread. Put them on the plate and buttered them, then slapped four slices of ham on one and put the other slice of bread on top of it. She cut the sandwich in half with the breadknife, took a big drink of vodka, carried the loaf back to the breadbin, and as she put it inside she pressed the red button on the little box.

And then she was moving, scooping the phone out of the knife drawer, walking fast through the living room, opening the front door. Pausing. Taking her own phone from her pocket and tossing it back into the apartment. Closing the door. Walking along the corridor to the door at the end which led to the emergency stairs.

About halfway down, the knife drawer phone buzzed in her hand. She looked at it, saw an anonymous caller ID. Thumbed *connect*.

"Hello," said a woman's voice in English. "Don't speak. Congratulations on following instructions. The little widget in your breadbin has scrambled all the surveillance devices in the building but you only have a two-minute window. Go down to the basement and along the service tunnel to the next building. The door's unlocked. Close it behind you. Go up to apartment 21 and wait." And the connection was cut.

Sure. Why not? Her life was basically over. Why not do what a voice on the phone told her to do?

Her apartment – what had *been* her apartment – was in a building which was one of three, side by side. Actually, they were all one complex, connected below ground by a warren of utility tunnels and communal storage rooms full of furniture for which the occupants had no space upstairs. The building manager had shown her round when they first moved in – Rob couldn't be bothered to go with her – but she hadn't been down to the basement since then.

The stairs ended in a corridor which ran off into dimness, just a line of emergency lights on the ceiling. She went along it at a fast walk, ears straining for any sounds behind her. About halfway along, a heavy door stood ajar. She stepped through, turned, put her shoulder against it and pushed it shut. Heard the lock click.

So now she was in the building next to hers. At the end of the corridor were more emergency stairs. She went up them to the second floor, opened the door on the landing, and looked cautiously out. A corridor with doors, just like hers. Nobody about.

She walked down the corridor until she came to apartment number 21, held the phone against the lock plate, heard the bolt withdraw. She pushed the door open, stepped into the apartment, closed the door behind her.

The phone buzzed again. Another anonymous ID. "Well done," said the woman's voice. She had a very faint West Country accent. "This phone is encrypted, so nobody can eavesdrop, but don't speak just now. My name is Victoria and I want to help you. You're safe now, so you can relax, but please don't leave the flat until I tell you, and don't go near the windows. You can watch television, but don't access the internet. Other than that, rest. Get some sleep, if you can. I'll call you in the morning." And she hung up.

Alice felt for the touchpad beside the door, brushed her fingers across it, and a double line of muted lights came on along the ceiling. She saw a living room not unlike the one she had closed the door on a few minutes ago. Different furniture – a long L-shaped sofa in one corner, a recliner in the middle of the floor in front of an entertainment centre – but the same layout. Door to the bedroom over there, second bedroom – Rob's study in her flat – over there. Kitchen. Bathroom.

All of a sudden, her legs went numb and her mouth flooded with saliva. She managed to stagger to the bathroom, but she didn't make it to the toilet. She threw up in the washbasin. And then she threw up again. And again. And again.

IT WAS A nice flat, even if it did remind her uncomfortably of the one she'd shared with Rob. But it wasn't intended for long-term confinement, which was what this was.

"All you have to do is be patient," Victoria told her over the phone the next morning. "I know it's not very nice, but it's better than the alternative. They're still looking for you. They were watching your building but nobody saw you come out, so they'll assume someone was inattentive or that you're a lot smarter than they're giving you credit for."

"That's hard to believe," Alice said glumly.

"People always overestimate their adversaries. That's how amateurs get away with it so often."

"Get away with what?"

"Ah, stuff."

"Who *are* you?"

"I'm the closest thing you have to a friend right now, I'm afraid."

"What do you want?"

"From you? Nothing, really. You've wound up in a bad situation through no fault of your own, because a bunch of muppets are squabbling over something."

"The skull?"

Victoria made a rude noise, at the other end of the encrypted link. "The skull's part of it, but really it's just an excuse for them to wave their cocks at each other and see who can bark loudest."

Alice sighed and looked round the flat. "How long will I have to stay here?"

"I don't know. Sorry. They're still watching your building, and they'll do that for another few days, although Christ only knows why. They probably think it's the *professional* thing to do."

"Aren't they professional?"

"They're behaving the way they think professionals behave.

That whole thing at the Embassy yesterday was a play put on for your benefit. You've been stampeded, put in a position where they thought you'd have no choice but to cooperate. It was clumsy, the kind of thing people who read too many spy novels come up with."

"I can't go back, can I."

"I'm afraid not. Although I'd have to wonder why you'd want to."

"Because it was my life?" Alice suggested.

She heard Victoria sniff faintly.

"If that thing was a *play*, what's to stop me going back and calling their bluff?"

"Oh, they weren't bluffing," Victoria said. "They obviously have the material they claim to have, and they'll use it. They won't even think twice."

"So what?"

"Beg pardon?"

"So what if they do? My life's over anyway. I'll never find another job in the Diplomatic Service; I'll be lucky if I can find *any* job. Let them release that stuff. What have I got to lose?"

Victoria thought about that. "You're actually very brave, you know, even if a lot of it right now is anger," she said. "But you're wrong if you think you have nothing to lose. Everyone has something to lose." A pause. "Let me help you, Alice. Don't do anything silly; just sit tight until it's safe to leave, then I'll get you out of the country."

"And then what?"

"The situation's still developing. I'll think of something."

"How do I know I can trust *you*? I don't know who you are. I don't even know what you look like."

"Well, of course you don't know you can trust me." Victoria sighed. "Look, you're not a prisoner. You can walk out of there any time you want. I'd advise you not to, because at the moment you have no resources of your own, but nobody will try to stop you."

Alice took the phone from her ear and looked at it. It was cheap, mass-produced, anonymous, most of its functions disabled or missing altogether. The contacts folder was empty and it seemed unable to recognise the number, or numbers, that Victoria was calling from, or indeed that anyone had called at all. Maybe she was imagining the whole thing. Maybe she'd wake up soon.

Victoria was speaking again. Alice put the phone to her ear and said, "Sorry, bad line."

Victoria sighed. "Look," she said. "Just stay where you are, okay? You're safe now and I'll help you."

Alice thought about it. "Okay."

BUT IT WASN'T. It was so far from okay that 'okay' might as well have been on the Moon. With nothing else to do but drift around the flat watching the news or trying to concentrate on a film, she found herself going over and over the events of the past few days, trying to make them fit together and finding that she had too many pieces. No matter how many different ways she arranged things, there was always something left over. If she accepted Victoria's story on face value, she had become the innocent dupe in some mad scheme between two or more unknown groups, but that left the problem of Selina, who she had known for her entire time at the Embassy, who knew all her secrets and who had now, at the height of the chaos, apparently fled the scene. Why would Selina – why would anyone, really, when it came down to it – want to wreck her life so comprehensively? She hadn't, to her knowledge, hurt anyone, and even if she had and this was an act of revenge, surely it was overkill? Karla briefly crossed her mind, but surely this whole thing was too *baroque*, even for her?

On the other hand, what had *actually* happened to her? She'd been present at a bar fight, she'd had something stolen from her, and she'd been outed as having had an affair. With the exception of Polsloe, she was blameless. Granted, none of these things reflected particularly well on her professional capabilities, but was any of this a reason to be fired? She suspected any half-competent employment lawyer would take her case into a tribunal and leave nothing but scorched earth behind.

So why was she hiding?

This thought kept coming back to her over the next couple of days. What had she actually done *wrong*?

There was a sense of *theatre* about all this. She had been... how had Victoria put it? *Stampeded?* But stampeded by whom? Someone had gone into her flat and planted the encrypted phone and the frequency jammer and all those notes. Someone had set up the escape route into the building next door, and prepped the safe flat. And they had somehow done it between her leaving that morning and coming back with Meg, which implied that they had known what was coming. Was she being stampeded in different directions, or the same one? Did it even matter? Her life had been burned down to the ground, but wasn't that what she had wanted all along? Wasn't that, when all was said and done, what Polsloe had really been all about?

On the morning of the third day, she found herself sitting in the living room, the phone in front of her on the coffee table. There was no way to call Victoria – the phone seemed to think it had never been connected to another mobile. She picked it up and turned it over in her hands, thinking. Remembering the notes about her flat being bugged, she carried the phone into the bathroom and turned on the shower and the taps. Then, before she lost her nerve, she dialled a number.

"Hello?" said a voice.

"Nik," she said. "I need your help."

There was a pause, then Nikolai said, "Why can I not see the number you're calling from?"

"It's a long story. Nik, I need your help," she said again.

"Why are you in the shower?"

"Nik, concentrate, please."

"Okay," he said amiably. "What's up?"

"I've been fired. And I've left Rob." And the sheer relief as she said those words was almost enough to drive her to tears.

Another pause, this time longer. "Okay," he said again. "Where are you?"

"I can't tell you that."

"This is hardly a good start to my helping you," he mused.

"I'm sorry," she said, "but I can't. We'll have to work around it."

"Right," he said doubtfully. "Okay. What do you need?"

"I need somewhere to go, somewhere safe where I can think, and I need transport."

"That's hardly a stretch," he said. "When do you need these things?"

"As soon as possible."

"Okay. Well, since I don't have a number to call you back on, call me in an hour."

"Thank you, Nik," she said. "I owe you one."

"I think you probably do," he said.

"And please, don't tell anyone you've spoken to me or what this is about."

He was silent a long time. Eventually, he said, "You'll forgive me, but this sounds a little more serious than losing your job and leaving Rob. Serious though those things undoubtedly are."

"I'll tell you when I see you. I promise. Talk to you later. And thank you again, Nik." She hung up and sat where she was on the toilet, trying to put her thoughts in order while the bathroom filled with steam.

THE WARDROBES AND cupboards were full of women's clothes, and disturbingly they were the kind of clothes she would normally have worn, but she managed to assemble an outfit which she thought might be different enough to at least briefly confuse someone who was looking for her. There was a big denim rucksack in one of the wardrobes, and into this she stuffed a couple of changes of underwear and T-shirts and jeans and a sweater, along with a bottle of water and a packet of cereal bars she'd found in the kitchen.

There was an ankle-length brown duster coat hanging in the hallway, and at nine o'clock in the evening she put this on, turned up the collar, slung the rucksack over her shoulder, and stood by the door looking around the flat. There was still time to change her mind.

She turned and opened the door a fraction, looked out into the corridor, saw no one. She slipped outside, pulled the door closed behind her, and with the click of the lock knew she was committed.

She went along the corridor and down the stairs to the basement, moving smartly but not hurrying so much that she would attract attention. When she got to the service tunnel she took a moment to orient herself – it wouldn't do to go in the wrong direction – and then walked along to the door halfway along. This was closed, but there was a handle, and when she pushed it down and pulled the door opened smoothly and she was able to step through into the tunnel beyond, closing the door behind her.

Up the stairs again, and she was in the third apartment building in the row, the one furthest from her own. The lobby was deserted, and instead of going out the front door she turned and walked down a short corridor to a door at the back. Here, she paused with her hand on the handle, trying to gather what courage she had left. Either this was going to work, or she was just making things a hundred times worse. She turned the handle and pushed the door open and stepped confidently out into the night as if she didn't have a care in the world.

At the rear of the buildings there was a long communal area with bushes and seats and a handful of picnic tables. It was mostly used by local drunks who gathered out here on summer nights annoying the residents until someone called the police to move them on. It seemed deserted at the moment, but there were altogether too many shadows out here for her taste and the thought of all the windows looking down on her made her shoulderblades itch.

Beyond the communal area there was an unbroken line of much older blocks, shabby and decaying, which ran along the street paralleling her own. These all had rear entrances, and usually one or other of them was wedged open whatever the weather. Tonight was no exception; she saw two doors open and made for the nearest one, expecting with every step that there would be sudden sounds of pursuit behind her.

But nothing happened. She stepped through the entryway and into a dark hallway that smelled of mould and piss, illuminated only by the streetlights picking their way through gaps in the front door. She opened the door, stepped out, turned right.

A few metres along the street, she crossed over and made her way between two buildings and across another scrubby communal area to an alleyway which led out onto the main road. Here, it was still early enough to be busy, and she put her head down and willed herself to submerge in the stream of pedestrians moving along the pavement.

A little way along the road, there was a line of parked cars. Alice slowed slightly as she approached, looking in the rear windows until she saw, neatly folded on the back shelf of a dark blue Simca, a claret and blue scarf. Nikolai had been deliberately vague about how she would recognise the car; all he'd said was, "You'll know when you see it," and she did. His inexplicable but quixotic support of West Ham had been a running joke during their time together. She took out the phone and held it against the door, and the keycode he had texted her engaged with the car's security system.

In the driver's seat, she sat for a few moments. A wave of giddiness passed over her, and with it a wave of panic. *Not now. Don't faint now, you stupid cow.* She imagined herself slumped behind the wheel until some kind soul noticed and called the police and the ambulance. But it passed. Her head cleared. She rolled down the window, dropped the phone into the gutter, started the car, and drove off.

AN HOUR LATER, on the outskirts of the city, she pulled into a quiet side street and let out a long, shaky breath. It took something of an effort to make her hands let go of the steering wheel. It had been some time since she had driven, and these were not the best circumstances in which to start again.

In the glove compartment there was another phone, this one apparently more conventional than the last. Nikolai had cautioned her against calling him while she was in flight, but the banking app showed a balance of several hundred kroons, and the GPS was loaded with a set of coordinates. She put the phone on the console between the driver's seat and the passenger's seat and set off again, carefully. It wouldn't do to have an accident tonight.

ESTONIA WAS NOT very large, and not very populous. It was not very a lot of things, apart from having a Baltic coastline, which had made it quite a strategic prize down the years. It was mostly flat – the summit of Big Egg Hill, the highest point in the entire country, was only about three hundred metres above sea level – and more than half of it was wooded. Once you got out of Tallinn the roads ran through great areas of aspens and pines and alders and ash, growing in such unmanaged profusion that it was impossible to run between them. It was not like the Forestry Commission plantations Alice remembered visiting on school botany trips, where the trees were planted in straight lines with wide gaps between them. Here trees grew wherever they wanted to, and she liked that.

There was talk of building a tram route all the way out to Lahemaa, and you really had to be Estonian to understand *that* joke. For the first time, though, it looked as if some kind of work was actually going on. She saw vans parked, every few kilometres, along the broad grassy central reservation of the E20, and people in hi-vis jackets with laser theodolites and measuring sticks and other, less explicable, measuring equipment, even at this time of night. Under the white glare of portable lights they seemed to be performing some peculiar ritual, an act of geomancy.

Following the GPS, she turned off the main road near Liiapeksi, but by then she didn't need the cheerful woman's voice to tell her where she was going. She already had a shrewd idea.

She was calmer now she was in motion, although there was still a corner of her mind which had not stopped screaming since she stepped into Nicky's office. She felt as if she was following the beams of the car's headlights into a new life, the old one discarded in tatters behind her. She still had no idea what she was going to do next, but she'd at least taken charge of her life, was no longer in the hands of faceless people at the other end of phone connections.

The Estonian Writers' Union kept a house in a small village in the Lahemaa national park, a place writers could stay when they felt in need of seclusion for that difficult second novel. She and Nikolai – who was of course a member of the Union – had visited the village while they were together and she'd rather liked it. It straggled along the shore of Käsmu Bay – Estonians liked to know their neighbours were there but in general didn't necessarily want to see them every day – and it was probably as close to being the last place anyone would think to look for her as Nikolai had been able to come up with at short notice.

In the end, as she approached the village, she turned the GPS off. The roads became progressively less and less well-maintained, and finally she was bumping along a narrow track that opened out suddenly on one side to a view of the beach and the little maritime museum. It was almost midnight, but there were still a couple of lights in the windows of the museum. Headlights off, she drove slowly by, following the track past a couple of holiday homes all locked and shuttered for the season. At the far end, the track widened into a turning circle ringed by scrubby, hardy bushes. She backed the car into these as much as she was able without waking the entire village, then turned off the engine and sat quietly waiting. She waited five minutes, ten, fifteen, but no one else came down the track. She got out of the car and stood beside it, listening. The world was blanketed by a great silence, broken only by the soft sound of the Bay lapping at the beach. She smelled woodsmoke on the sharp cold air, damp earth, sand, salt water. There were no footsteps. She might as well have been the last person on Earth, standing at the edge of the world, and for some reason this was hugely comforting. Her life had become impossibly, unsupportably complex over the past couple of weeks. Now it had become simple again; now it had all boiled away and she was standing here alone in the dark.

Turning up the collar of her coat, she walked back the way she had come until she reached a big white-boarded house set back from the track. Its many windows were in darkness, and she slipped through the gate and walked around to the back door. On tiptoes, she reached up and felt along the lintel until her fingers encountered a big old-fashioned key.

Inside, the house was cold and smelled musty, as if it hadn't been aired for a while. Alice walked carefully down the corridor from the back door, passing the kitchen and a formal dining room and a glass-walled conservatory built onto the side of the house. Beyond the glass, in the darkness, she could just make out the shapes of trees and bushes in the sloping garden.

She kept moving, looking in the front rooms, their furniture sitting under white dust sheets. Upstairs, she checked all the bedrooms and the study. The bathroom was jarringly modern, a stone-tiled wet-room with a huge mirror over a sink that looked like a small horse-trough. Nikolai had not implied that he would be here to meet her –

indeed that anyone at all would be here. All she could hear were the creak of the floorboards under her feet and her pulse hammering in her ears.

Back downstairs, she stood in the doorway of the conservatory. There was another smell in here, stronger than the general mustiness of the rest of the house. She looked at the dark shapes on the pale wooden floor and willed them to become rugs. When they did not, she took the phone from her pocket, held it out in front of her, and switched it on so the light from the screen would illuminate the room, and then she must have gone away for a little while because the next thing she remembered was a woman's voice saying, "You see what happens? I told you to stay put and you wouldn't listen, and now look."

Alice blinked. She was sitting at the table in the dining room. Sitting across from her was a tall woman with long brown hair and a look of annoyance on her face.

"Did you touch anything?" the woman said, and when Alice just stared at her she said again, "Did you touch anything?"

"Sorry," Alice said. "I know your voice from somewhere, but I can't place it." She looked around her. "This is…"

"Alice," the woman said. "Focus. I need to know if you've touched anything."

Alice looked at her. "Victoria?"

The woman pursed her lips. "Girl wins a prize," she said.

"I *know* you…"

"Yes, I was the one trying to avoid all this, remember?"

Alice shook her head. "No, I *know* you. I don't…" There were footsteps in the hallway and she turned her head as a figure appeared at the door, a man with a hard, unforgiving face.

"It's no good," he said. "She'll have left forensics everywhere." It was the man from The Butt-Shaped Cat, the man Bodfish had attacked. And Victoria was the woman who had been with him that night. Alice's eyes widened.

"So have we," Victoria pointed out.

"Yes, but nobody's looking for *us*." They were both dressed like special forces soldiers on a night exercise; dark overalls, boots, gloves. The man was wearing a knitted cap pulled down over his ears.

Victoria said, "Alice, this is Kaunas. Kaunas, this is Alice." Kaunas nodded hello; Alice just stared.

"What are you doing here?" she said. "How did you find me?" But she already knew. *Oh, Nik...*

"That doesn't matter right now," Victoria said.

"Oh, I think it fucking does."

Victoria stood. "Up," she said. "Get up."

They went back to the conservatory. For Alice, every step lasted a lifetime, but eventually they were standing in the doorway. There was a small standard lamp in one corner, and someone had switched it on. Thick curtains had been drawn across the windows, and blinds across the roof, and for a moment Alice concentrated on the fact that she had never seen curtains in a conservatory before; they seemed to defeat the whole point of *having* a conservatory. Nice curtains, though.

Kaunas stepped between them and out into the room, carefully walking around the bodies. Alice didn't know the first one; it was a stocky, middle-aged man wearing a good-quality business suit. He lay beside the sofa, the front of his shirt soaked with blood. One of his shoes had come off, revealing an argyll sock of quite startling ugliness.

Harry the spook was crumpled on the floor behind a small nest of tables, as untidy in death as he had been in life. He was in jeans and hiking boots and a big thick black sweater with several ragged, scorched-looking holes in the back.

On the sofa, Rob was sprawled in a posture which was familiar to her. It was the way he'd used to zonk out at home after dinner and a couple of beers. He was still wearing the clothes he'd been wearing the last time she saw him. Alice half-expected him to snort himself awake as his sleep apnoea kicked in, but his face was puffy and discoloured and his T-shirt was stiff and rusty with dried blood.

Nothing about this scene made any sense at all. It was impossible to process.

Kaunas squatted down beside Rob's body. "This one was killed somewhere else and then brought here," he said after a few moments. "The other one..." he waved towards where Harry lay. "Shot here." He got up and walked over to the third body, squatted again, delicately lifted first one side of its jacket, then the other, carefully examining the inside pockets. He gently massaged the trouser pockets. "This one, no idea. No ID, no phone, no weapon."

"What's wrong with this picture," said Victoria.

"Indeed." He stood again, put his hands in his trouser pockets, looked slowly round the room. "There are altogether too many people involved in this," he said.

Victoria snorted. "You think?"

Kaunas looked at Alice. "Do you know that one?" He pointed at the third body, the man in the suit.

Alice found herself standing outside with no clear memory of having left the house. Victoria was standing in front of her, pointing a torch at the ground near her feet so it wouldn't blind her. "None of this was your fault," she said.

"I do wish you'd stop saying that."

"You need to come back inside."

Alice shook her head. "No, I don't," she said, but apparently she did, because all of a sudden she was sitting in the dining room again, hands folded in her lap, and Victoria had pulled a chair round and was sitting beside her.

"We're leaving soon," Victoria told her. "Kaunas is just scoping out the perimeter and if all's clear we'll be going. I need you compos mentis enough to do that. Okay?"

Alice looked blankly at her.

"You're in shock," Victoria said.

"Oh? Really?"

"Well," said Victoria. "Sarcasm is a promising sign."

Alice turned her head away and looked out of the window at the darkened garden beyond. The worst thing was not that Rob was dead; it was that she didn't care. She wasn't happy, she wasn't sad. She just didn't care. She felt more for Harry, on his first overseas posting and dead in a house on the shores of the Gulf of Finland.

"What happened?" she said. "Why is everyone dead?"

"I don't know, and we won't find out by staying here. I suspect you were meant to find those bodies, but I don't know."

Alice looked at her. "Who *are* you?"

Victoria thought about this for some time. Finally, she said, "We're *Les Coureurs des Bois*. How would you like a job?"

PART TWO

RÜCKENFIGUREN

CATACOMB SAINTS

THE OPENING CEREMONY was in its tenth hour – and the parade of nations was barely halfway completed – when Tomás said, "Why are we watching this rubbish?"

"I'm not watching it," Rudi said from one of the beds.

Tomás turned from the room's entertainment centre. "Is there always so much waiting involved?" he asked.

"Mostly." Rudi opened his eyes and looked at the cracked plaster of the ceiling for a few moments before sitting up. "What time is it?"

Tomás glanced at the clock in the bottom right-hand corner of the entertainment centre's screen. "Half past six."

Rudi sighed and regarded the little Portuguese sadly. "This is ridiculous," he said. "I've never had good luck in this city."

"You've been here before?"

"A few years ago." That time, he had been doing a favour for Wesoły Ptak, the organised crime gang to which the restaurant where he worked in Kraków paid protection money. This time at least he was involved in a proper Situation.

"How did that go?" asked Tomás.

Rudi considered the question. That Situation had eventually lasted a few days short of seventeen months and had involved half the mobsters in Europe pursuing him. He still had no clear idea how it had ended; people had simply stopped trying to abduct him and he had long since ceased to expect an apology for the mess. Normally, he wouldn't pass on operational information, but the whole business had left a sour taste that he was still trying to rid himself of.

"It was a fiasco," he said.

Tomás waited to see if more information was forthcoming. When there was not, he got up from the threadbare sofa and padded barefoot over to the window. He was wearing cargo shorts and a thin white linen shirt, and a tiny gold cross on a thin chain tangled with the curly black hair on his chest. He lifted back the thin net curtain and looked down into the street. He didn't seem remotely nervous or apprehensive, which was good. Rather, he appeared mildly puzzled about what he was doing here. Which made two of them.

"Still there," he said.

Rudi got off the bed and went over to stand beside Tomás. The hotel was in a narrow little street some distance from the city centre; if one opened the window and stepped out onto the balcony and craned one's neck, one could just catch a glimpse, peeking over the roof of a credit union a few doors down, the cranes still surrounding of one of the spires of the Sagrada Familia.

The street itself was choked with pedestrians and cars and those annoying little electric scooters which seemed unique to the city – Rudi had never seen them anywhere else, which he thought was a blessing. On one of the buildings across from the hotel was a huge billboard for a blockbuster film called *Texan Apocalypse*, which was a remake of an Estonian film Rudi remembered from his childhood. The billboard featured burning vehicles and distant explosions and shadowy figures carrying ill-defined weapons. Below the billboard were several floors of balconies, each of them occupied by its own little garden of pot plants and herbs and trailing vines. And below those, at street level, was a brightly-striped canopy shading the tables of an outdoor café. At one of these tables, for some hours now, a man wearing chinos, a grey cotton jacket, and a Panama hat, had been sitting using a pad to read a newspaper.

Rudi had made him the moment he saw him, some vague sixth sense suggesting that here was someone to be noted, to be observed.

"It's the hat," Tomás had said. "Who on earth wears a Panama hat these days?"

For Rudi, it was more a matter of body language than anything else, but he had to agree that a Panama hat was something of an anachronism, and that made its wearer interesting. *I do not care if I stand out from the crowd*, the hat said, *I want you to know I am here*.

"Backup?" Tomás hazarded.

Rudi had shaken his head. There was no provision in his instructions for backup, although that didn't mean anything, particularly. If he'd learned anything over the past several years travelling hither and yon at the behest of Coureur Central, it was that everyone was continually winging it and half the time no one knew what anyone else was up to. It made, he supposed, for a suitably confusing environment for opposing forces, although it was hardly an optimal atmosphere in which to operate.

But he thought this was not the case here. The man in the Panama hat was not, he was certain, backup. He might, conceivably, be part of someone else's operation, nothing to do with them, but Rudi had long since given up believing in coincidence. Coincidence was for fools and optimists.

No, the man in the Panama hat – Rudi couldn't see his face from this angle but he thought he might be of a certain age – was there for them, and he was not backup. The easiest explanation was that he represented one part of the transaction for which they were waiting, ensuring that the Coureur was in place and ready to receive the Package. Which was unusual, in Rudi's experience, but not unheard-of.

"If he drinks any more coffee his heart's going to start dancing the Macarena," said Tomás.

"Hm," said Rudi. Maybe the man in the Panama hat was waiting for him to go out and say hello? Maybe the Situation would not move forward until they had made contact? He had no code phrases or contact strings for that eventuality, but the temptation was growing stronger. "Ah, fuck this. Let's have something to eat."

* * *

ORGANISING AN OLYMPIAD, in these Autumnal post-European days, was commonly regarded as something of a game of Russian Roulette. Quite apart from the cost, which could be ruinous, there was the ever-present question of whether a city, having been awarded the right to host the Games, would even be in the same nation four or eight years later to stage them.

This had led the International Olympic Committee to issue an edict that only nations which had been in existence for more than a decade – and there were those who felt that even this was perilously brief – would be allowed to bid for the Games. Catalunya, still opening its eyes and shaking itself a little at the suddenness of its independence, had just barely qualified, and Barcelona had put in a hosting bid more as a statement of nationhood than anything else.

Fortunately – or unfortunately, depending on how you looked at it – the only other bids that year had come from Dushanbe, Doha, and Pyongyang. The North Korean bid had been generally regarded as satirical in nature, although it was never easy to be sure when it came to North Korea. The other two bids – Doha was basically bankrupt and Dushanbe was... well – were never going to fly, despite slick presentations, and so Barcelona had found itself facing its second Olympics.

This had amused the international community in general and Spain in particular, which had been waiting for Catalunya to fail and come creeping back into the national fold. The cost of the Olympics had driven more than one city and several small countries to the wall. But Catalunya had been ticking along quite nicely; it hired a smart, aggressive organising committee, brought the Games in ahead of schedule and under budget, and branded them The Independence Games, which wiped the smile off the Cortes.

None of which was obvious to Rudi, walking down Carrer de Roger de Flor not far from Gaudi's cathedral. The streets were full of people dressed in various items of national costume, Olympic kit and football shirts, singing and waving flags and posing for selfies in the middle of the road, to the fury of local drivers. It was a dull and overcast day, with occasional spits of rain, but it didn't seem to be dampening anyone's spirits. Rudi supposed he ought to be charitable and feel pleased that they were having a good time.

He'd always liked the city, anyway. There was a peculiar density to it which he found somehow comforting, even if that density had been supersaturated by the invading army of sports fans of all nations.

The influx of people, and their megatonnes of hard currency, was also good news for the still-infant state. It was less good news for someone like Rudi, who had a list of restaurants he wanted to visit while he was here and was finding every single one packed to overflowing with diners of all nations.

They finally found a place on Carrer de Sicília, a bright, airy space with, for some reason which was not immediately apparent, several ancient and eye-hurtingly-polished Hispano Suizas parked among the tables. The maître d' led them to a table deep in the restaurant, in a corner which would have been secluded if the place hadn't been full of laughing, shouting, singing Olympic tourists wearing T-shirts emblazoned with the English flag.

"The Cross of St George," Tomás noted after they had been seated. "St George was either Greek or Roman, and he was born in Syria. I'll never understand the English."

"Hm," Rudi said, deep in contemplation of the menu. He looked up. "I had a terrific meal the last time I was here, but I was barely in town long enough to enjoy it."

"What, here? In this restaurant?"

"No, somewhere else."

"Perhaps we should have gone there?"

"We couldn't afford it; we've barely got enough operational funds for this meal as it is. Whatever the hell is going on, it's not being run by people who like to spend their money."

This last was so pointedly directed at Tomás that he sat back in his chair. "I'm sorry," he said. "I have been presuming that you were properly briefed."

"That would be a first."

Tomás was a former priest, a Jesuit defrocked for some transgression which he acknowledged but was unwilling to specify. He was in his late thirties or early forties, a lithe and attentive man with a sense of amused stillness about him, as if he was patiently awaiting the punchline to a particularly involving joke. He had been introduced to Rudi yesterday as a Consultant, someone who would assess the validity of the Package before Rudi took delivery of it. This had never happened to Rudi before, and he was justifying it to himself as yet another strange little wrinkle of Coureur business.

Les Coureurs des Bois, for whom Rudi did occasional work when he wasn't cheffing in Kraków, carried items of mail across the continually-reconfiguring borders of Europe's many new states and polities and countries and principalities. Sometimes, the items were illegal at their point of origin or their point of destination, or somewhere inbetween, but mostly they were mundane and blameless. One thing they all had in common, however, was that the Coureur carrying them did not know what they were. Opening the Package either before or during transit was strictly anathema.

"I'm an expert in antiquities," Tomás said. "Specifically, religious relics. The people I represent want me to assess the bona fides of the item in question before it's transported."

"And that couldn't have been done before?"

"Apparently not. The vendors are being awkward; they refused to make the item available for examination until the handover was ready to take place. A very large sum of money is involved."

"Of course there is." Rudi looked at the menu again. "And the item is a religious relic?"

"Well, that's for me to judge. The vendors claim it is."

Rudi glanced around the restaurant. A young woman in formal dress was sitting at a grand piano, playing something for the diners, but she was fighting a losing battle against the singing of the English tourists. "You seem as surprised to be doing this as I am."

Tomás shrugged. "I do this all the time, but it's usually for museums and churches and religious groups. Quite often for private collectors. This is a new situation for me."

"Every day," Rudi told him, "is a new Situation."

The meal, it turned out, was excellent. Rudi had the loin of lamb in a thyme crust, Tomás monkfish tempura. Dusk was beginning to fall on the city as they stepped out of the restaurant. The air was humid, and there was a light drizzle. A little further down the street, blue lights were strobing.

As they drew closer, they could see ambulances and police cars pulled up along the kerb. A motorcycle cop in ballistic armour and a heads-up helmet was taking statements from a group of people standing outside a café, and a little further down the street was taped off. Rudi could see one car apparently parked in a cavalier fashion, its bonnet crumpled against the front of an apartment building. A few metres away, a small white delivery van had come to a complete stop in the middle of the street, the lights and indicators of its rear nearside entirely sheared off in a bouquet of carbon composites.

Closer by, at the side of the road, was the detritus of paramedics, bloodied dressings, torn medical packaging, discarded surgical gloves.

Rudi stood and regarded the scene for some little while. Then he said, "We are going to walk. We are not going to run. We are going to catch the bus back to our hotel and we are going to check out. Then we are going to find somewhere else to stay."

Tomás looked surprised. "We are? Is something wrong?"

"I have no idea," said Rudi, "but I think it would be prudent." He nodded towards the gutter, where a white Panama hat lay torn and dirty.

OF COURSE, FINDING somewhere else to stay in a city that was hosting the Olympic Games was not a straightforward matter; they'd been lucky to find rooms in the first place. They wound up in a large, anonymous motel right on the edge of town, almost in L'Hospitalet, where a convention of extremely grumpy businessmen appeared to be taking place. Their room was on the ground floor, tucked away down a corridor which ended in the loading bay for the kitchens. It had a single bed and a sofa and all the generic amenities familiar to the international business traveller. It was hardly luxurious, but Rudi did not plan on staying there for long.

While Tomás stood at the window gazing out at the disappointing view of the car park, Rudi made a crash call to an emergency contact number to apprise the vendors of the change of venue. The number cut straight to voicemail. He left a message.

An hour or so later, his phone received a text acknowledging his message and telling him that the vendors were on their way, and an hour after that there was a discreet knock on the door.

There were two of them, a man and a woman. Both middle-aged, both well-dressed. She was stout and annoyed-looking. He was tall and grey-haired and bearded and had the look of an academic. They didn't bother to introduce themselves, just completed the word-string recognition protocol. They both had Basque accents, and Rudi braced for trouble. This whole thing suddenly smelled of Politics; there had been a lot of upheaval in the Basque country lately.

"Why did you move?" asked the woman.

"I had a bad feeling," Rudi told her. "We were being watched. Was that you?"

The Basques shook their heads.

"Well," he said, "someone was keeping an eye on us, and they wound up as a casualty. You're lucky I didn't pull the whole thing and start again. Do you have the Package?"

The man was carrying a large plastic shopping bag printed with the name of a high-end fashion chain. Inside was a striped hatbox. He took it out and handed it to Rudi, who handed it in turn to Tomás, who was sitting on the sofa. Tomás's luggage consisted of an overnight bag and a fat attaché case. From the case, he took a large grey velvet cloth, which he spread on the room's coffee table. He also took from the case a pad and a pair of white cotton gloves, which he put on before lifting the lid of the hatbox and reaching inside.

The object in the box was wrapped in a layer of bubble-plastic, then a layer of wrapping paper, then several layers of cloth, which Tomás unwrapped carefully, setting each layer aside before starting on the next one.

This obviously annoyed the Basques. The woman said, "Will this take long?"

"It will take," Tomás said, "as long as it takes. You wouldn't want me to make a mistake, would you?"

The woman snorted.

Rudi had been expecting an ikon, or perhaps a statue, but what emerged as Tomás removed the final layer of cloth was a human skull, elaborately decorated with gold and what looked like precious stones. There were two large faceted carnelians in its eye sockets and a line of pearls along its jaw. Tomás held it up and turned it this way and that, and then he put it down on the velvet cloth and sat looking at it. Someone had obviously taken a great deal of time and effort with it; it had once been gilded, but it had worn away in places. From where he stood beside the Basques, Rudi could see a large jagged hole in the skull's left temple.

Tomás took from his case a small battery-powered reading lamp. He placed it on the table and switched it on and looked at the skull some more. He took photographs of it with his phone. He seemed particularly interested in some marks on the back, and he took several photos of those.

"The skull of St Magnus Martyr, of Kirkwall," the Basque man said to break the silence.

Tomás picked the skull up again. "In 1578, vineyard workers in Italy discovered a catacomb containing a huge trove of skeletal remains," he said conversationally as he tipped it this way and that under the light. "There was, of course, no way back then to ascertain how old they were. It was assumed that they dated back to the early years of Christianity, and the obvious assumption was that at least some – perhaps all – of them had been martyred." He put the skull back down on the velvet cloth and sat looking at it, his hands in his lap. "This discovery was wonderful news for the Church. The rise of Protestantism had meant many Catholic churches were looted of their holy relics, and the Church has always found great strength in relics. And here was a new resource from which to restock them."

Rudi glanced at the two Basques, who had suddenly become quite impassive.

"So THE CATACOMB was ransacked," Tomás went on. "A lot of the remains wound up in churches in Southern Germany, where nuns would adorn them with jewels, and they would be put on display, and the congregation could worship in the knowledge that they were in close proximity to a saint." He picked up the skull again and smiled apologetically across the room. "This is not the skull of Saint Magnus," he told them. "I would suggest that it came from the catacomb on the Via Salaria. It may belong to an early Christian martyr, it may not. But what I can tell you with some assurance is that it is the skull of a woman."

The Basques didn't move a muscle.

Tomás carefully rewrapped the skull, put it back into the hatbox, and replaced the lid. "My principals will not pay for this," he told them. "You have had a wasted journey."

The woman said, "How can you be certain this is the skull of a woman, just by looking at it for five minutes?"

Tomás sighed and took off his gloves. "In a previous life, the Church chose to send me to examine miracles," he said. "Back in the Sixteenth Century, one could say pretty much anything was a miracle and no one would disbelieve you, but these days the standard of proof is somewhat higher. Rome has to be careful. I've seen more of these –" he tapped the box with a knuckle " – than I can quite remember, and I have learned to tell the skull of a woman from that of a man. It's actually quite straightforward. But I can run a genetic profile in a few minutes – I have the equipment with me – if you need scientific proof."

Some nonverbal communication seemed to pass between the Basques. The woman said, "We're not taking it back."

"Oh, now wait a minute," Rudi said. "This happened to me before and I spent almost a year and a half running around Europe with a piece of stolen merchandise. I'm not doing that again. Take this thing back where it came from and tell whoever gave it you that it's not what they think it is."

"No," said the man.

"Fine," said Rudi. "Fine. We can just leave it right here and let Housekeeping clear it up. I'm not taking it anywhere."

There was an awkward silence which lasted quite a long time.

Finally, the man said, "We are in a difficult position."

"Oh, for fuck's sake," Rudi said. "You stole it."

The Basques glanced at each other.

"No," said Rudi. "No, we are not getting involved in this. The skull isn't what you say it is and frankly you must be out of your minds to try a scam like this. What on earth were you thinking?"

"Do you think," the man asked Tomás, "*anyone* would buy it?"

Tomás shrugged. "I couldn't begin to answer that. I can only speak for my principals, and they will not."

"It belongs to someone very powerful," the woman said.

"Then the best thing you can do is return it to them and hope they're in a forgiving mood," Rudi told them.

There was another long, awkward silence.

"No," Rudi said. "Absolutely not."

"FRANKLY, I'M AMAZED they thought they could get away with it," said Tomás.

"Some people are too stupid to be criminals," Rudi said. "Most people."

"This is the problem with the Church," Tomás said. "People – non-believers – think faith is the same as gullibility."

"I'd have thought that was axiomatic."

"You'd be surprised. Who are we waiting for?"

"I consulted with *my* principals," said Rudi. "They're sending a firefighter."

"Beg pardon?"

"I can't get involved in this thing," Rudi told him. "I was contracted to come here with you, assess the Package, and if it proved kosher, jump it to its final destination. What we're doing now is outside my remit; it needs another level of management."

Tomás raised an eyebrow. "Your boss is coming?"

"No. But someone with authority to resolve the situation is."

They were sitting on the grass in front of the Fundació Joan Miro, beside a rather jolly sculpture of red metal petals. Rudi had bought a bottle of Catalan pinot noir and some bread and cheese and they were watching the world go by.

"Do you think they'll be able to?" Tomás asked. "Resolve it?"

Rudi shrugged. "Not my problem."

"Is this your friend?" Tomás said, nodding at a tall woman who was walking in their direction.

"I don't know. Let's see."

The woman walked right up to where they were sitting and looked down at them, smiling sunnily. "Is that the local pinot?" she asked in English, pointing at the bottle of wine.

"Yes, it is," said Rudi, going along with the contact string.

She nodded. "Any good?"

"No, it's awful. Would you like a glass?"

The woman beamed. "I'd love one; I'm parched. Hi, I'm Victoria." She sat down opposite them and crossed her legs.

Rudi poured wine into a plastic cup and offered it to her. "Nice to meet you."

Victoria had long brown hair and hazel eyes. She tasted the wine. "Nice," she said. "I'll have to get myself a couple of bottles." She had a very, very faint West Country accent. "So, you have a problem."

"No," said Rudi "But someone we know does."

She shrugged. "Walk away from it. We're not a charity. Fuck 'em."

"May I say something?" asked Tomás.

"Absolutely," she told him. "We're all friends here."

Tomás took a moment to gather his thoughts. He said, "All this time, everyone has been treating the... Package as just a piece of merchandise, and I find that offensive. It may not be what my principals were told it was, but it was once a human being like you and me."

Victoria grunted. "Second Century Roman Christian martyr," she said. "Not *quite* like you and me."

"She may have been a martyr, she may not," he told her. "I seriously doubt whether we'll ever know. But she *was* a person, not a parcel to be passed from hand to hand like something in a children's party game."

Victoria nodded. "What's that cheese like?" she asked.

"Pretty good," said Rudi. "Help yourself." He handed the paper plate to her, and she cut herself a slice.

"Do you know those conversations that begin *I'm not a religious person?*" Tomás asked. "Well, I *am* a religious person. I believe in the sanctity of life and I believe everyone deserves dignity."

"Your principals obviously don't think that way," she pointed out, nibbling at the slice of cheese.

"It's not the first time we've had a difference of opinion," he said, and she chuckled. "My point," he went on, "is that in all probability, if we don't do something to take charge of this situation, the... *Package* is going to wind up thrown in a river or dumped in a garbage bin. I don't know who it originally belonged to, but if we can possibly return it, we should."

"Suppose it originally belonged to a sect of baby-eating Satanists?" she asked.

"Did it?"

"No, but suppose it did. Suppose it was being used in awful rites to bring about the ascendancy of the Devil on Earth – you do believe in the Devil, I suppose?"

"I believe in evil," Tomás said carefully.

"How about good? Do you believe in good?"

"Now that," he told her, "is a harder thing."

Victoria popped the last of the cheese into her mouth and chewed thoughtfully. "This *is* pretty good, you know. I like it here; everything I've eaten so far has been brilliant. The Pozna thing," she said to Rudi. "That was you, right?"

The Pozna thing had been a Situation which had gone so badly wrong that Rudi had wound up being tortured, until Central had intervened to extract him. He still had nightmares about it.

"We're sorry that happened," she said.

"So I was told," he said.

"You're not bad at what you do," she went on. "You've got pretty good judgement. What do *you* think we should do about this thing?"

"Me?" he said, surprised.

"Sure. Do we return the thing to the baby-eating Satanists and let them establish the dominion of their lord Lucifer? Or do we let the thieving scumbags run away and chuck it in a bin?"

"You'll excuse me if I tell you that this conversation is not going quite as I anticipated," Rudi said.

Victoria laughed and cut another chunk of cheese. "I presume the thieving scumbags still have the thing?"

"They were very keen to give it to us, but I didn't think that was a good idea," said Rudi.

"Dead right. You'd never have seen them again and it would be your problem. Which it is anyway." She looked at them. "We'll arrange for a dead-drop. The original owners can pick it up themselves. The thieving scumbags would be best advised to make themselves scarce and not trouble anyone else for the rest of their lives. How does that sound?"

"And you can facilitate this?" asked Tomás.

"Piece of piss," Victoria said cheerfully. "Nothing easier. You just have to know the right people to talk to, that's all."

Rudi suspected it wasn't quite that simple, but sometimes diplomacy had to be carried on at levels invisible to the footsoldiers. He said, "Someone died."

"Not died," Victoria told him. "He's in hospital. He'll be okay."

"What was that all about?"

"Ah," she said, reaching out for the bottle and pouring herself some more wine. "Now, that's the interesting thing about this business. On the face of it, you have a couple of thieving scumbags who stole something they couldn't sell and now they want to give it back in return for their miserable lives. But it turns out that someone else is interested in the Package too."

"Who?"

"Don't know. The chap who was keeping an eye on you is an independent contractor; he was hired by an anonymous party. Looks to us as if someone *else* tried to take him out, for reasons unknown."

Rudi stared at her.

"Anyway, don't tell the thieving scumbags. They have no idea just how fucking lucky they are to be getting out of this alive."

Tomás said, "We should, really..."

"As soon as they don't have the Package any more, they cease to be important," she told him. "Snatching someone and torturing them and killing them, that's a lot of effort. People would rather not do it if they don't have to."

"Well," Rudi demurred, "quite often an example has to be made. *Pour decourageur les autres.*"

Victoria waved it away. "We're not talking about some tuppeny-ha'penny street gang here," she said. "These people have class; they don't suffer from penis issues."

"And what about us?" Tomás asked. "Are we in any danger?"

Victoria guffawed. "Christ no, Father. You two just witnessed a car crash and went to help. Nobody's upset with *you.*"

Tomás thought about it. "May I ask," he said, "who the Package originally belonged to?"

Victoria grinned at him. "Well, you can *ask*." And she laughed. When she realised no one else was laughing, she said, "No, I can't tell you. Best not to know."

This was good enough for Rudi, although the man in the Panama hat was going to niggle at him for a long time. "When shall we do it?"

"No time like the present," she said.

THE BASQUES HAD obviously been arguing between themselves while they waited at the motel, but they were contrite, not wanting to meet anyone's eye, even when Victoria lectured them and called them 'muppets'.

"Idiot people," she told them. "Have you any idea how much trouble you've caused? And for what? You're no better off. Jesus fucking Christ on a fucking bike. Where is it?"

The Basque woman nodded at the coffee table, on which sat the box.

"Fine." Victoria went over and picked up the box. "Well, fortunately for you, *adults* are going to take over now and tidy up after you." She glared at the couple. "Now fuck off and don't fucking do it again." And she actually waited for the Basques to realise they'd been dismissed and shuffle out of the room.

In the silence that followed, Rudi and Tomás looked at each other and wondered quite what they had witnessed. It was a little like, Rudi thought, seeing an angel of the Lord descending from Heaven with a flaming sword, but possibly he'd been spending too much time lately thinking about saints and faith.

When the Basques had gone, Victoria turned to them and smiled like the sun rising over a distant range of mountains. "Boys," she said, "go home. You did good. I'll take it from here."

HAD THEY NOT actually had to go there, Rudi would have counselled avoiding the bus station entirely. It was a Babel of thousands of people, all trying to get to various Olympic events around the city and elsewhere in Catalunya, overwhelming the red-T-shirted stewards who were there to help everyone get where they wanted to go. The place looked like a riot. On the other hand, from an operational standpoint, it was a golden opportunity. Chaos was the great camouflager. He and Tomás were just two more bodies in a great sea of confused people. And even when they had made their way to the stands where the international coaches departed they were perfectly anonymous. In Coureur operational lore, busy bus stations were ideal arenas for all manner of transactions.

They walked for a while, looking for the gate where Tomás's coach to Toulouse left from, and when they found it they stood there, gazing around at the surrounding madness. Rudi strongly suspected that Toulouse was not Tomás's final destination, and he did the little man the professional courtesy of not asking.

"Well," Tomás said, "that was a peculiar couple of days."

"I've had worse," Rudi told him, and meant it.

"The Pozna thing?"

"That was different. But yes."

Tomás shook his head. "You're still young. Things will settle."

Rudi thought that, on previous experience, this was unlikely. He said, "You would be doing me a considerable favour if you would explain some of what happened here."

Tomás laughed. "We're doomed to understand perhaps ten percent of what goes on around us; perhaps it's better that we get used to that as quickly as possible and not worry about the other ninety percent."

"Someone else said something like that to me once," said Rudi.

Tomás put his bags down beside his feet. "You understand that this business was about holy relics," he said.

"Yes."

"Relics are a tricky thing," Tomás said. "A damaged skull and some bones were found in a box hidden in a cavity in a column at St Magnus Cathedral in Kirkwall in 1919. According to the story of Magnus' death, he was executed by being struck on the head with an axe, and for the past century and a bit the bones found at the Cathedral have been believed to be his. It would annoy the people of Orkney quite a lot if a rival skull turned up all of a sudden in

Barcelona, but I expect they would survive. The Scottish are no longer a particularly pious people. The publicity might even bring some more tourists into the area."

"So?" said Rudi.

"My principals, the people to whom I report, take this sort of thing *very* seriously. It's a matter of... of *heritage*, of the legitimacy of history. The bones at Kirkwall link the place back to the time when Magnus Erlendsson was Earl of Orkney. It's said he was so pious that he refused to fight. At one battle he stayed on board his ship and sang psalms."

"He sounds extremely annoying," Rudi mused.

"The point being," Tomás went on, "that if the relics at Kirkwall are not those of St Magnus, if they are not a physical link to him, then all the stories about him are simply myths. He might as well be Robin Hood or King Arthur."

This sounded uncomfortably like the kind of angels-dancing-on-the-head-of-a-pin discussion Rudi had spent most of his life trying to avoid, but he made the effort. "So whoever has the *real* skull has a certain amount of leverage."

"With my principals, yes. History is a strange thing; it keeps being written and rewritten and overwritten and rewritten again. They're looking for concrete evidence, historical markers. *This* man was *here*. He did *this*. *This* thing proves it. Do you understand?"

"It sounds as if your *principals* have chosen a thankless task for themselves."

"That's not for me to say. All I do is go where I'm sent and do as I'm told."

"And someone is trying to prevent them doing that?" Rudi asked, thinking about the man in the Panama hat. "Someone wants to stop them verifying history?"

"I imagine there are those for whom it would be better left unverified," Tomás mused. "For one reason or another. I don't know who they are."

"One would be inclined to suspect your former employers."

Tomás sniffed.

"This all sounds very Dan Brown, you know," said Rudi. "No offence."

"If it makes you feel better to think of it like that, go ahead."

"Is that why you left the Church? Because they didn't like you doing this?" He saw the look on the little man's face and instantly regretted opening his mouth. "Please," he said. "You don't have to answer that. Forgive me for asking."

Tomás shook his head, and for a moment Rudi thought he wasn't going to say anything at all. He picked up his bag and looked down the echoing length of the bus station. "For years I investigated charlatans and unmasked conmen," he said. "And that was good. It was important work. And one day I discovered a real miracle and the Church declared it a Heresy. So we had a problem, the Church and I."

"A real miracle?"

"Better you don't know," said Tomás. He smiled at Rudi. "Seriously, my friend. The world is not as you believe, and I pray you never discover just how *much* it is not as you believe." He put out his hand. "And now I must catch my bus. It has been a pleasure."

Rudi shook his hand. "Likewise. Will you be okay?"

"Me?" Tomás looked surprised. "Yes, of course. I did my job, everyone is happy. Why should I not be okay?"

Rudi had thought he'd seen a flash of anger in the little man's eyes when he talked about his miracle, something fathomless and unresolved, the sort of anger which could easily break a person if they let it. "Just take care, Tomás, okay?"

"Sure." Tomás grinned at him. "You too." And he turned and walked away towards his bus.

A YEAR OR so later he was back in the kitchen at Restauracja Max. He'd more or less forgotten about the Situation in Barcelona; if he thought about it at all, it was as one more of the low-level snafus which seemed to characterise his Coureur life. Shortly after returning from Catalunya, he'd seen reports on the news of a series of truck bombings in the Basque country, and he'd wondered idly whether the skull had been offered for sale to raise money for those. Coureur Central tried its best to remain apolitical, but it was always hard to know exactly what cause the proceeds of a transaction were going to. He had done a search for the skull, but it seemed to have dropped entirely out of history, and as far as he was concerned it could stay that way for as long as it wanted.

One evening, the mafioso Dariusz turned up at the restaurant just after service, while the staff were cleaning up and Rudi was having a quiet postmortem chat about the night's events with the kitchen crew. Dariusz was a representative of Wesoły Ptak, the man to whom Max, the restaurant's owner, paid his monthly protection money. He was also, by means never quite explained, Rudi's primary contact with Coureur Central.

"There's a job for you, if you want it," Dariusz told him later over a glass of vodka, while Max's Filipina cleaning ladies hoovered. "Obviously you don't have to do it, but you were asked for by name. You must have impressed someone."

"May I ask whom?" Rudi said.

Dariusz chortled. "Well, you can *ask*," he said, and Rudi remembered someone else saying that, he couldn't remember quite who.

"Where is it?" he asked.

"Potsdam, in a week or so," Dariusz replied. "Better dress warmly; they're forecasting blizzards."

SPOOKYTOWN

1.

In June, Dortmund sweltered under some freak temperature inversion or other caused by global warming or a once-in-a-century weather event or witchcraft, all these things were mentioned on the local discussion shows. Whatever the cause, the city suffered week after week of heat and humidity and the basement bars and brewhouses all smelled unbearably of sweat. A series of shattering thunderstorms did nothing to relieve the enormous damp weight of the atmosphere; afterward the place was like an outdoor sauna.

Late at night, boys in quarter-of-a-million D-Mark supercars raced each other from traffic light to traffic light around the ring road that circled the town centre, roofs folded back, music pounding, drunken girls in the back seats shrieking with delight and waving bottles of cheap champagne.

There was no violence, no social disorder, but the potential hung heavy on the air, Alice had felt it the moment she stepped out onto the little plaza in front of the hauptbahnhof a week ago, towing her suitcase behind her and trying to appear invisible to the gangs of youths hanging around outside the burger franchises. Invisibility, she had learned, was less a physical thing than a state of mind. One of her trainers had likened it to zen, but by then she had grown tired of the trainers and their endless recitations of long-lost tradecraft mined from Twentieth Century spy fiction. *Do not think like a rock*, she had told herself, that first night. *Be the rock*.

Standing on her balcony at the Esplanade watching the noonday traffic going by four floors below, she felt the damp wet heat weighing on her. She'd spent the first few days trying to get a handle on the city, get a sense of its rhythms and its sense of itself, and the best thing she had been able to come up with was that Dortmund was... ordinary. There was a certain kind of central/northern European municipal architecture, you saw it everywhere, and it was here too. If you squinted your eyes and tuned out obvious signifiers like the street signs, the view she was looking at could have been parts of Copenhagen or one of the stubbornly Soviet era bits of Tallinn, or – if the place had been given a thorough clean-up – Upper Silesia. It did not immediately present as part of Greater Germany, which of course it was about to cease to be.

There was a knock at the door, and when Alice went to open it she found him standing outside in the corridor. The boy. Ben, Victoria had called him. "We'd feel a little better if you had some backup on this one," she'd said. "It's an evolving situation and there's no way to predict exactly which way it'll evolve."

"I can look after myself," Alice told her.

"I know; it's more for my peace of mind than yours, really. His name's Ben. You'll like him."

Except she didn't, not really. He looked about twenty, handsome and vaguely North African and unnervingly self-contained. *A killer*, she'd thought when he was introduced to her. Not that she'd ever met a killer, at least not knowingly, but his body language was very spooky, to her eyes. Victoria had volunteered no information about him other than his name, and he was barely more forthcoming. He wasn't staying at the hotel, but Alice had no idea where he was. He just came and went for time to time, checking in, making sure she had everything she needed, calm and courteous and, she thought, constantly on the verge of some quite appalling acceleration.

"Anything?" he asked, glancing towards the room's entertainment set, where the regional assembly of North Rhine-Westphalia was just dragging itself into its fourth straight week of speeches and deliberations and votes and vetoes, enlivened by the occasional violent protest. At first she'd sat entranced by the whole thing, but now she kept the channel on more as white noise.

"Still talking," she said.

"Is it always like this?"

"Some are quicker than others."

He nodded. "Is there anything you need?"

She was booked into the hotel as a representative of an English firm selling medical tech – portable MRI scanners, mostly – and in fact she had taken meetings with the comptrollers of several local hospitals, to whom she had sold quite a lot of equipment. She had no idea whether the orders would ever be fulfilled but she'd begun to think that if the wheels ever came off her new life – and she was constantly aware of the possibility of wheels coming off, these days – at least she could find herself a reasonable living as a commercial traveller. Anyway, the cover meant that she could receive visitors without attracting attention, and the hotel had given her the use of one of their shielded and security-scanned meeting rooms for the purpose, although she had respectfully declined because it almost went without saying that the hotel would be bugging the room themselves.

"I'm good," she told him. "Are you getting bored?"

"Not at all." Although he looked restless, eager to take off in some unthinkable direction and do something Alice didn't want to think about too much.

She made a decision and said, "I have a meeting in an hour. Do you want to babysit?"

This was something of a departure from tradecraft; he was supposed to be firewalled from the prospective assets she was interviewing, although she had a suspicion that he was shadowing her most of the time anyway, otherwise what was the point of him being here at all? It was not something which gave her much joy, if she was going to be honest with herself.

"Sure," he said evenly.

"You may call me Fram," said the prissy little man on the other side of the table, and he sat back and waited for her to congratulate him on his choice of name, or to ask him to explain it, either would have suited him. Alice knew all about Fritjof Nansen and his ship but she wasn't going to give the German the satisfaction. She found this kind of thing wearisome; a lot of people who wanted to be involved in espionage seemed to be complete dicks.

"I'm Lucy," she said, and they raised their phones and exchanged fake business cards – at least, hers was a fake, and she hoped his was too, although it was by no means a certainty. A lot of people who wanted to be involved in espionage also seemed to be utterly clueless about even the most basic operational security. She'd met with one asset at a flat over on the other side of the city, and during the course of their chat her eye had wandered to a bunch of framed photos hanging on the wall, all of which featured the asset and a woman and two small children, and she'd realised with a dreadful cold sinking sensation that the asset was holding this covert meeting *in his own home*. She'd mentally crossed him off the list, waited for an opportune moment, and made her excuses and left.

Fram was still an unknown quantity. He was dressed casually but expensively – Alice had seen those polo shirts going for a hundred D-Marks a pop at a shop elsewhere in the town centre. His head was almost perfectly round, like a seal's, and he had a fringe of short ginger hair around his scalp. His pale skin was red from the sun and the heat, and his Panama hat, its band darkened with sweat, was sitting on the table at his elbow. *The Poundland Harry Lime*, she thought, and then wondered if that made her the Poundland James Bond.

"Shall we order?" he asked.

"Yes," Alice said. "Let's." She took out her spectacles and scanned the menu.

They were in a steakhouse on Willy-Brandt-Platz, by the Cathedral. It was busy enough for casual conversation to be lost in the background noise, but not so busy that she couldn't make a run for it if necessary. The uniformed police in Dortmund were starting to look twitchy, and if they were getting twitchy so were the plain-clothes boys. Alice was technically doing nothing wrong at this precise moment, but being picked up by counterespionage would be embarrassing; she had some professional pride left, even if she was now in the wrong profession.

She glanced across the restaurant to where Ben, who had arrived fifteen minutes earlier, was sitting alone at a table and regarding a veal schnitzel as if it had never occurred to him that people would do this to meat. He seemed to be simultaneously quite at ease and vibrating with energy, and somehow the waiters had picked up on this because no one went near his table to ask if his meal was satisfactory or he wanted another drink. Alice wondered whether, instead of this endless round of excitable bureaucrats and disaffected citizens, she wouldn't be spending her time more wisely by recruiting the city's waiters. At least they seemed to have some situational awareness.

In the end, she decided to have a ribeye and fried potatoes with a green salad. Fram settled on a burger, and, without bothering to ask her, ordered for both of them. Alice narrowed her eyes fractionally at him.

"And two beers," he told the waiter. "Wheat beer."

"Just water for me," she said. "Tap water's fine. With ice. Bring a jug."

Fram looked crestfallen, but he recovered quickly and when the waiter had departed he said, "So, you have considered my proposal."

Fram was a walk-in, a volunteer. Walk-ins were tricky. Sometimes they were kosher, more often not. One had to ask oneself *why* was this person eager to betray his or her country? There were always gripes, but did they seem reasonable? Did they seem *credible*? Was this entrapment? Were the security services playing a long game? It was, more than anything, an act of faith in the end.

She said, "My employers have," and she watched Fram become a little more crestfallen. He'd been expecting the real thing, a *case officer*, someone who carried a set of one-time pads printed on a silk handkerchief sewn into the lining of her jacket and a frequency-agile phone in the heel of her shoe. Alice also found this wearisome. People who wanted to be involved in espionage seemed, in general, to have read too much spy fiction for their own good, or anyone else's.

"But they were interested enough to send you," he pointed out.

"I don't have any authority," she told him. "I was just sent to do a face-to-face and write a report. Someone else will make the assessment."

"Based on your report."

"Partly, but not wholly." She had no idea whether this was true or not. She hoped not. She leaned forward and lowered her voice a fraction. "You'll appreciate that this is not like applying to drive a tram."

He looked at her for a few moments, then to her horror he put his hand on the table and pushed it towards her and when he took it away a little flash-drive was sitting on the tablecloth. "I've brought you some bona fides," he said.

ALICE HAD TO physically fight the urge to look around and see if they were being watched. She said, "If this is what I think it is, I absolutely cannot take it."

He just sat there looking at her.

"Take it back," she said. "Right now, or I'm going to get up and walk out and that's us done."

He looked at her for a moment or two longer, then he reached out and palmed the drive. "I only want to help," he said in a sulky voice.

"And my employers appreciate that." Alice realised her heart was pounding. "But there is a time and a place for this kind of thing, and this is not that time or place."

Their meals arrived. Alice's steak was large and thick and there was a pat of herb butter melting on top of it. Fram's burger was a stack of beef patties and slices of bacon and salad and cheese almost six inches tall, with a wooden skewer through it and a little metal bucket of fries. Neither of them paid any attention to the waiter or the food.

When the waiter, somewhat miffed by the lack of a reaction, had departed again, Fram said, "I thought this was what you wanted."

"My employers haven't decided yet what they want from you," she told him, finally back in control of herself. "Depending on how things go, you may not hear from them again for quite some time."

"That's not what I was told."

Alice had no idea what Fram did for a living. She pictured him in an office somewhere, slaving away year after year, being passed over for promotion, becoming more and more resentful. Someone had scented that resentment, seen how it could be put to use, but it wasn't for her to decide how.

She said, "I don't know what you were told, but that's how it's going to be, and passing me secrets –" *or what you think are secrets, anyway, and you'd be surprised how often they really aren't* " – isn't going to change things." She decided to take a gentler, more confessional tack. "This business is all about waiting, most of the time." There you go, Fram. A little operational doctrine, straight from the horse's mouth.

Fram was unwilling to concede the point. "I was told I would be useful."

"Well, we're *all* useful, one way or another, aren't we?" When this seemed to bounce right off him, she picked up her knife and fork and planted her elbows on the table. "I know all this seems counterintuitive to you – it did to me, at first – but you're not letting yourself in for a life of action and adventure. What my employers do is really very dull, for the most part, but it does require patience. If you can't demonstrate that, you're of no use to us."

Fram sat back in his chair and regarded his burger. When he looked at her again, she thought some of the dickishness had gone out of him. He said. "So why are you here?" What he meant was 'so why am *I* here'.

"I told you. To do a face-to-face. Get to know you a little better." She raised the hand holding her fork. "And no, I do not want to know your name, the name of your partner, or the name of your dog. When the time comes for that, someone else will be in touch. Someone *operational*. So, let's have a nice lunch and a nice chat about stuff and we can go on our ways, eh?"

Fram considered this. Then he nodded and picked up his knife and fork and tried to decide how to tackle the frankly insane edifice of beef, salad, bacon and toasted brioche before him.

Alice cut a slice off her steak and tried it. It was very good, but she'd lost her appetite.

LATER, SHE MET Ben at a café a tram-ride and a bus journey away from the town centre. He arrived first, despite having left after her to make sure she wasn't tailed, and he was sitting at a corner table with an Americano in front of him and a chai latte waiting for her. When she got there, he was looking at his phone.

"So," he said when she sat down.

"So," said Alice. All of a sudden she felt very tired.

"How did it go?"

She shrugged. Fram had been toast the moment he'd tried to pass her that memory stick. He'd go back to his crappy little flat and his crappy little job and his one expensive shirt and he'd wait for someone to contact him, and no one ever would, and if one day he told someone about his brush with the secret world they wouldn't believe him because everyone knew he was a dick.

"This is like selling double glazing," she said.

Ben tipped his head to one side.

"Double glazing," she said. "You know, with the two panes of…" She held her hands up, palms an inch apart.

"I know what double glazing is," he said calmly.

"You know how it's sold, though, right?"

"Indulge me," he said, and he took a sip of coffee and glanced at his phone again.

She looked at him for a moment, then said, "First you have a *lead*. Leads can come in by any number of routes. Adverts, inquiries. Mostly it's done by cold-calling. Lots of people sitting in a room dialling phone numbers at random and trying to convince whoever answers that they need double glazing."

He stared at her and blinked.

"Most people will tell you to fuck off, but a percentage will fall for it, and they're the ones who get a visit from the sales force. A nice smiling boy or girl in a good suit who won't leave your house until you've signed a contract."

Ben thought about it. "This is nothing like selling double glazing," he said finally.

"It is," she said, trying her latte. "A bit."

He smiled. "How many visits have the *sales force* made now?"

Despite herself, she smiled too. "Twelve," she said. Only four of which were actually, in her opinion, of any use.

"Hm," he said. "Time's up." He held his phone up for her to see.

She squinted at the screen, which was showing the familiar shot of the assembly chamber. It was built like a shallow amphitheatre, concentric rows of pale wooden desks in an austere modern style mounting up to a wall of smoked glass which curved along the back wall to accommodate the press gallery. Normally, proceedings in the chamber were austere and not terribly well-attended, but today it was heaving with people, many of them hugging and cheering and throwing documents in the air, although almost as many were sitting stony-faced at their desks, and down at the front several men were trading punches while several others tried to pull them apart and at the dais at the centre of the amphitheatre a man wearing a grey robe trimmed with gold over his business suit was standing at a lectern banging a gavel in a hopeless attempt to regain order. Outside the café, Alice could hear the sound of car horns and people singing and shouting.

"Welcome to the Independent Republic of North Rhine," Ben said.

2.

SHE WAS DEAD. Missing presumed dead, anyway, according to the news. The Estonian authorities had come up with a fiendishly-involved scenario to explain the events of her disappearance, which involved her having an affair with Harry, Rob coming to the writers' house to confront the lovers, killing them and disposing of her body, before killing a neighbour who had come to investigate the noise and then finally killing himself. The Embassy had released a statement describing her as an invaluable member of the Diplomatic Service who would be sorely missed by her colleagues. In the following eighteen months or so, there had been a lot of coming and going at the Embassy. Meg and Antonia had been posted elsewhere. Tim had taken early retirement. Nicky had returned to Scotland, where she had made an unsuccessful run for the Assembly before taking up a number of non-executive directorships.

It was, of course, a ridiculous scenario. The Estonian police were not idiots, which begged the question of why they had bothered with it in the first place. But in its way, it was no less ridiculous a scenario than what had actually happened, which had involved being picked up off the beach by a stealth hydrofoil and taken down the coast to Sopot, and from there a long road journey under false papers to a safe house in Belgrade, where she had spent a period in the company of several trainers before being sent out again into the world to work as a Coureur. She was, in her way, an ideal operative. She had no identity, no nationality. She was, officially, at least, dead. She had been counselled not to try to contact her family or friends, which was hardly a stretch. She was a blank space.

She had been unable to discover what had happened to her life, and Victoria, who professed to being none the wiser herself, cautioned against digging too deeply, lest she alert whoever had been responsible. Nobody but the tabloid news audience really believed the official story. Everyone who actually knew what had gone on knew that she was probably still alive, even if they might not know how she had managed to spirit herself out of the situation. Victoria's best guess was that her role, whatever it had been, was over now, and as the years passed it all started to take on the aspect of a fading nightmare.

Meanwhile, there was a new life.

"We can't just suborn everyone and hope for the best," Victoria told her, "we don't have the resources. We have to be selective, wait for opportunities to present themselves."

The *raison d'être* of *Les Coureurs des Bois* was quite simple. In these days of new borders, new nations, it was quite often impossible for ordinary mail and courier firms to carry things across frontiers. Any firm wanting to stay within the law of these new national entities would inevitably come to a complete stop amid a blizzard of visas and new regulations. It was sometimes possible to route mail around emergent polities, but getting it in and out could prove tricky.

Which was where *Les Coureurs* came in, offering safe and discreet movement of documents, secrets, parcels, packages and sometimes even people *anywhere* in Europe.

Obviously, this required resources, particularly of the human kind; and, as with any other organisation, recruitment was always something of a chore. The trick was recruiting assets where they would be of most use. Suppose you wanted to move something considered illegal from Republic A to Polity B. All kinds of on-the-ground contacts were required, but recruiting them *after* Republic A and Polity B had seceded from their parent nation – let's say for argument's sake Greater Germany – could be difficult because one of the first things emergent polities did was to set up border and counterintelligence agencies of monstrous paranoia, which limited operations.

The obvious thing was to recruit your assets *before* Republic A and Polity B even existed, when you could just swan in and out of Greater Germany to your heart's content and only have to worry about Greater German counterintelligence, which was already busy keeping an eye on the many fracturing nations of Europe.

Fortunately, nations – with a few exceptions – did not just suddenly appear overnight like a rather embarrassing rash. It was the work of a few moments to scan the news sites and identify the states and regional units and cities and counties and territories which were gearing themselves up for nationhood.

For North Rhine-Westphalia, the process had begun almost eight months ago with a series of motions in the regional assembly, followed by exploratory talks with the UN and the Greater German Parliament in Berlin, followed by an advisory plebiscite, followed by a final vote in the assembly. And for all that time *Les Coureurs* had been working quietly in cities like Dortmund and Essen and Dusseldorf, searching out what they called *gladio*, agents in place, useful assets for when North Rhine-Westphalia put up border fencing.

"We've already identified a bunch of people who might be willing to work with us," Victoria said. "We've made an initial approach and what I'd like you to do is facetime them. Sit them down, have a chat, make a judgement about whether they'll be any use."

"You want me to do an HR assessment," Alice said.

"Kind of, but it's more involved than that. Some of the people on the list are walk-ins, people who've contacted *us*, and walk-ins can be trouble. Some of them are batshit crazy, which is not necessarily a bad thing but we need to know what *kind* of batshit crazy they are in order to deploy them effectively." She paused, thinking. "And sometimes the BfV likes to run dangles against us, just for fun." When Alice looked blank, she said, "Greater German counterintelligence. They don't like us. Well, *nobody* likes us, really, but mostly we rub along. The BfV like to play, though."

"You think some of the walk-ins could be plants."

"I'll be surprised if they're not *all* plants, it's a great opportunity for everybody to get someone on the inside and they'd be inept not to try. And the BfV are *not* inept, whatever else they are. No." She shook her head. "You'll have to use your own judgement. If someone smells wrong to you, we'll drop them; it's not worth the hassle."

"But if they know that we know they're sending volunteers to us, what's the point in doing it in the first place?"

Victoria smiled. "It's all a game," she said. "It's all just a game."

THE LID BLEW off Dortmund at a little after ten o'clock that evening. Borussia had been due to play an important European Cup match against Real Madrid and the city council, fearing trouble in the fevered atmosphere of Independence and the general unbearable weather, chose to cancel it at a few hours' notice. This occasioned a number of lawsuits from the club and their opponents and from UEFA, but by the time these had been served the city had other things to worry about.

Heading back to the hotel, Alice noticed a change in the atmosphere in the city. There seemed to be many parties in the restaurants they passed, and people out on the streets singing and cheering and waving the flag of the newly-minted Republic, but there were also sullen angry groups confronting the flag-wavers. She didn't see any fighting, but there was a lot of shouting. Independence, unsurprisingly, was not uniformly popular. Things had already been tense in the city, what with the heat and the anticipation of the final vote of the assembly, but now it felt as if someone had turned the tension up to eleven, and she was happy when they got back to the hotel – they had to ring the night bell because the staff had locked the front doors and they didn't unlock them until Alice had swiped her phone against the reader beside the entrance – and she could put the news on and try to get a handle on things. Meanwhile, outside, as with any catastrophe, a series of unfortunate events was playing out.

Madrid fans flying in for the match were corralled at the airport, put on specially-chartered flights, and sent home again. Some of them made their extreme displeasure about this clear to the riot police sent to control the situation, but there was little violence.

Things did not go quite as well at the main station, where a similar operation to turn back fans – both local and visiting – was overwhelmed by a tidal wave of bodies, who burst out into the plaza, ran across the ring road, and fanned out through the city centre.

Meanwhile, an ad-hoc march by anti-independence demonstrators was coming the other way, assailed by Dortmunders of a pro-independence frame of mind with beer cans and glasses and bits of al fresco furniture from cafés. The two groups ran head-on into the stampede of angry football fans coming from the station.

By midnight, the police had completely lost control.

THE MANAGEMENT OF the hotel had warned them to stay in their rooms and keep away from the windows, but Ben wanted to see what was going on, so they stood out on the balcony looking down on the road and the tricky intersection a little further along. The hot damp air was full of the sound of sirens and chanting and the smell of burning.

"Well, it's all kicking off a bit," Alice said into the phone, having finally managed to make a connection – mobile services and internet kept dropping out.

"I'm watching it on the news," Victoria's voice said. "Are you safe?"

Alice looked at Ben. "Are we safe?" she asked. He shrugged. "Ben thinks so," she told Victoria. "How does it look on the news? We can't see much from here." The hotel's television system had gone down about an hour earlier and nobody knew when, or even if, it would ever come back.

"It does look a bit lively," Victoria said. "I'm afraid you'll have to do the best you can; there's no way we can get support to you right now, even if we had anything handy."

"They're not going to help us," Alice told Ben. He shrugged again. "Ben thinks you're utterly fucking useless," she said to Victoria. "We're in the middle of a fucking civil war." The sound of glass breaking came up from the street and she got up on tippy-toe and looked over the parapet, but she couldn't see where it had come from.

"It's probably not *that* bad," Victoria mused. "The news said it's just football fans."

A dull *thud* echoed over the city centre and up into the sky. "Yes," Alice said. "That's probably all it is."

"Just sit tight where you are," Victoria told her. "Riots don't tend to last very long; people get tired of being angry eventually."

"Oh, we're admitting it's a *riot*, are we?"

"Don't be snarky, there's a good girl. If we could jump the two of you out of there we would, but things are a little *non-linear* there right now."

Alice took the phone from her ear and stared at it. She felt Ben nudge her, and when she looked where he was pointing she saw that the little multi-storey carpark diagonally opposite the hotel had begun to belch smoke and flame from all its windows, "Yes," she said. "Non-linear."

"What?" Victoria's voice came tinnily from the phone. "Didn't catch that."

Alice put the phone to her ear again. "This is fun," she said. "For quite a low value of fun."

"Short on lulz," Ben agreed amiably, as if he was watching a golf match.

A crowd of people, maybe a hundred strong, came running flat-out up the road, past the hotel, and disappeared in the direction of the railway station. They moved in a determined and eerie silence, only their feet on the asphalt making any noise.

"Seriously," said Alice.

All of a sudden there was shouting from directly below them, on the pavement in front of the hotel, followed by an almighty crash. A big cheer went up, followed by more shouting, and then screams. Ben touched her elbow.

"Got to go now," she told Victoria. "Catch you later." She hung up and put the phone in her pocket.

Ben had told her to assemble a go-bag from her luggage, and it sat on the bed, a cheap nylon tote-bag with a change of clothes and underwear, basic toiletries, and her pad. She went over to the desk, opened a drawer, and took out her passport and wallet. Stitched inside the wallet was an Estonian national identity card with her photograph and biometric data but a name not her own on it. Victoria had told her it would connect her to a small line of credit at Eestibank, one of the new financial start-ups in Tallinn, with a name rather cheekily almost identical to the Estonian National Bank's. She had been cautioned against using the ID to try and claim asylum at the Estonian Consulate, for obvious reasons.

Ben had tipped the room's armchair over on its side and was pulling up on one of its legs while pinning the opposite one down with his foot.

"You can't break up the furniture," Alice told him, horrified at the vandalism.

He gave her a long-suffering look and said, "Dude."

Fair point. "Okay," she said, and he heaved up and the chair leg snapped jaggedly off. He handed it to her and set about breaking off the other leg. She waved it a couple of times and it felt disappointingly light, as clubs went.

"Okay," he said, now similarly armed. He went over to the door and put his ear to it. He listened for a few moments and then opened it a crack and looked out into the corridor. "Go."

They walked down the corridor towards the lifts, but before they got there Ben nudged her towards an emergency door. He opened it a little and listened again, then pulled it open all the way, revealing a concrete landing and stairs leading up and down. As she stepped through, Alice glanced back at the lifts and saw that one of them was coming up from the lobby.

Instead of leading her down the stairs, Ben went up, cautioning her to be quiet, At the next landing, he opened the door but before going through he paused, listening. Alice listened too, and heard steady careful footsteps, not rushing, on the stairs a couple of floors below them.

They pushed through the door and into the corridor, Ben locking up behind them. All the room doors here were closed, but Alice heard what sounded like furniture being piled up against the inside of one as they passed, which seemed inadvisable considering the essentially combustible nature of the situation outside.

At the far end of the corridor was a big window plastered with *Exit* and *Emergency* stickers. Ben took a moment to examine it before pulling down on its big chrome handle and opening it, admitting the smell of smoke and the sound of distant bangs and crashes and shouts echoing across the city.

A little below and just to the side of the window, what looked like a large orange life preserver was attached to the building by a stout bracket. Ben pushed it until it locked down into a horizontal position, then he pulled a cord and the entire bottom half of the orange doughnut dropped away into the darkness, carrying with it what looked like a huge fishnet stocking.

"Oh, for fuck's sake," Alice muttered, realising what it was and what she was going to have to do next.

Ben went first, stepping out onto the big plastic ring and then slipping into the hole at the centre and disappearing. The fishnet stocking began threshing back and forth as he climbed down the inside of the emergency chute. Alice dawdled for a few moments, suddenly unwilling to leave the hotel whatever was happening, but then she took a deep breath, stuffed the chair leg into her tote, and climbed into the chute.

It was an absolute sod to traverse; the netting clung disconcertingly to her and the weave was barely large enough for her to poke the toes of her shoes through and the cord hurt her fingers, but she managed to drop two feet, four, ten. She'd got down as far as the first floor when she heard a scuffle below her, then a couple of quick thuds followed by the sound of something falling, and she stopped, hanging inside the big string bag by her fingertips and toes, too terrified to carry on to the ground but quite unable to climb back up.

"Are you there?" Ben asked quietly from the ground. He sounded quite calm.

"Yes," she said. "I'm here." And she made her way down the last few feet until she was able to stand on solid ground again and lift the bottom half of the plastic ring up and over her head.

The emergency chute dropped down onto a little patch of grass beside the hotel. Most of the lights were out, but there were enough for her to see bushes to one side, and a pair of booted feet sticking out from them. As she watched, the feet slid out of view, and then Ben's voice said, "Over here."

She pushed her way into the bushes and found Ben standing over the body of a stocky man dressed in black clothing and wearing a black ski mask. The front of the mask shone wetly in the light from the windows and liquid was puddling under his head and soaking into the soil.

"I don't think these are rioters," Ben said in a voice which was barely a whisper.

"No shit," Alice murmured, looking at the webbing harness strapped to the man's chest, onto which numerous mysterious objects were snapped. She found herself focusing on the sheaf of cable ties hanging from his belt. "Who is he?"

"No phone, no ID," said Ben. "He had these, though." He held up two automatic pistols and offered one to her.

"I don't do guns," she said.

"You do tonight. Just try not to shoot me."

Alice took one of the pistols. It was much lighter than she'd expected, like a plastic toy almost.

"Let's go before they come back downstairs," Ben said, pushing through the bushes away from the hotel. Alice slipped the gun into a pocket of her jacket and followed.

They emerged from the bushes onto a little street, beyond which the embankment of the railway rose against the night sky. A little further along, the road curved and passed under the railway, but there was the sound of many voices in the underpass and they all sounded tense and angry, so they climbed the embankment, crossed the tracks, and slipped and slithered down the other side.

Immediately there was a sense of something different. They were in an area of poorly-maintained social housing, blocks badged with graffiti, shop windows covered with anti-riot mesh. *Bad part of town*, Alice thought. Lots of people on the street, but few Northern European faces; a lot of people who looked as if they might come from the same general part of the world as Ben. Which was fine for him; he could fit in here, despite his expensive business suit.

They passed a group of people who were having a party in the middle of the road. Someone had set up a barbecue and a boombox was blasting out old Europop hits. The smell of burning meat drifted across the scene. The group, holding beers and passing spliffs between them, watched incuriously as Alice and Ben passed by, while an ancient Hasselhof song echoed up into the night.

Further on, they came across half a dozen cars which had all been overturned and set alight earlier in the evening and now sat charred and smoking in a great puddle of firefighting foam. A group of men carrying machetes ran towards them and she sensed Ben tense up beside her, but the men ran by without paying them any attention at all. Behind them, back towards the city centre, was the sound of more explosions. It occurred to Alice that it had been quite some time since she had last heard sirens. She wondered whether the emergency services had stopped seeing the point of using them, or if they had simply given up and withdrawn.

All of a sudden, Ben swerved into an entryway at the base of an apartment block, grabbing her arm and pulling her with him. They flattened themselves into a service doorway and a minute or so later two figures passed by on the street. They were carrying rifles and dressed like the man outside the hotel.

When they'd gone, Ben peeled out of the doorway and headed deeper into the entranceway. Alice followed, and found herself stepping cautiously out into a big courtyard at the heart of the housing block. By the lights of the windows all around she saw a space covered with scrubby weeds and bushes, from which the rusted remains of a children's adventure playground rose like the skeletal remains of a tiny lost city.

Keeping to the edge of the open space, below window height, they worked their way round to the other side, where there was another entranceway. Ben went first, checked the street outside, then beckoned.

In this way, for the rest of the night, they moved from building to building, through badly-tended little parks and along rubbish-strewn alleyways behind blocks of shops. Alice, whose grasp of the city was confined to the centre, was entirely lost, but Ben seemed to be moving with a purpose so she was happy to follow, and the noise of the riot seemed to be growing fainter and fainter behind them anyway, which was the main thing. They saw more groups of people, some of them partying, some of them armed, some of them just standing on street corners looking lost, but nobody threatened them, and they didn't see any more of the black-clad men.

By the time the sun came up, they were walking through Lünen. It looked as if there had been trouble here too – shop windows smashed and cars burned out – but it didn't seem to have been so bad and the streets were deserted now.

Alice was tired and her feet hurt and there was a pain in her shoulder where she thought she'd pulled a muscle going down the emergency chute. Her clothes were dirty and she smelled of smoke. On the other hand, she wasn't dead, so that was a promising start to the day.

"Who do you think they were?" she asked. There was no need to explain who she meant.

Ben shrugged. "Does it matter?"

"It might, in the short term." And probably in the medium and long terms, too.

Ben made a rude noise. "Contractors," he said. "Probably working for the BfV, but maybe also for a local agency." He thought about it. "And then again, maybe not. We should still be cautious."

Well, that went without saying. She'd already ditched the English passport she'd been travelling on and torn open her wallet to get at the Estonian ID; there was a rather sketchy legend to go with it, but she doubted any figures of authority they encountered in North Rhine over the next few days would bother to check too closely.

"We need to find somewhere to clean up and change our clothes," she said.

"Not yet," he told her.

She glared at him.

"I suspect we will stand out less here if we look as if we have survived major social unrest," he pointed out.

Fair point. "What now, then?"

'What now' turned out to be a walk to the central bus station, where Ben sat her down in a café two streets away and then vanished to scope the place out. Alice ordered an espresso and tried to look as if she didn't have a handgun and a broken-off chair leg in her bag. The waitress, seeing her generally dishevelled state, asked if she had been in Dortmund the night before, and by the time Ben came back they were deep in conversation about the waitress's niece, who lived near the city centre and from whom she had not heard since the morning of the previous day. Ben was all charm and smiles as he sat down with Alice and ordered an Americano, and when the waitress had gone to the bar he said, "Twenty minutes."

"Plenty of time for a coffee, then," she said.

The next stage of their dustoff from Dortmund involved a bus journey to Münster, which was just long enough for Alice to fall asleep and then wake up feeling achy and groggy with a horrible taste in her mouth. Ben, on the other hand, looked fresh as a daisy.

It appeared that the people of Münster had either slept through Independence, were one hundred percent in favour of it, or simply did not care, because the area around the bus station was free from signs of social unrest and crowds of people were just getting on with their day.

"*Now* we look out of place," Alice said, shouldering her tote.

"It's not so hot here," Ben murmured, looking about him.

Was that all it was? Just a combination of oppressive heat and humidity and a series of unfortunate coincidences? Alice suspected that History, if it ever bothered to record the events of last night, would see things slightly differently. "Anyway," she said, "I'm not going another kilometre until I've at least changed my knickers and brushed my teeth. And if we can find a bacon sandwich as well that will just about make my day."

3.

"WE DON'T KNOW who it was," said Victoria.

"Well, that's just great," Alice said. "I'm going to be looking over my shoulder for the rest of my life."

"They don't know who you are," Victoria told her. "They were after the legend, not you. You'll be fine so long as you don't go back to Greater Germany for a while."

"*That'll* be a chore." They were sitting on a bench in St James's Park in London, watching children hurling bread at the ducks in defiance of prominent signs telling them not to. It was such a le Carré sort of meet that Alice had almost giggled when she read Victoria's text message. "So, it could have been something to do with Tallinn."

Victoria shook her head. "That's all over," she said.

"For you, maybe."

"This chap Fram," Victoria said. "He actually offered you something?"

Alice nodded and sipped from her bottle of water. It was a bright warm day, but it was at least fifteen degrees cooler than Dortmund had been. The memory of the damp heat pressing in on all sides was fading now, but she kept waking up suddenly in the night knowing she had been dreaming of the man Ben had killed outside the hotel.

Victoria shook her head in wonderment. "Amazing," she said. "I would almost have been tempted to take it, just to see what it was."

"He thought we were spies," Alice said. "It was like offering official secrets to someone interviewing you for a job as a postman. He was trouble."

"You're right, of course, but there are levels and levels."

"You think I *should* have taken it?"

Victoria shook her head. "Chances are you'd have been arrested there and then if it was counterintelligence who were after you. No, you absolutely did the right thing." She sat back and stretched her legs out in front of her. "I just wonder if it's not worth sending someone else in to have a chat with him, try to scope out what he's got."

Alice said, "He's that important?" then thought better of it. She was only allowed to know certain bits of the jigsaw, for operational purposes. "Doesn't matter. Never mind."

"The BfV are getting a bit *keen* lately, anyway," Victoria said. "Too many bits of Greater Germany are going autonomous; they can't keep up and that's making them angry. I don't want to sour things for us there any more than I have to."

Europe as a whole was awash with intelligence agencies great and small as bits continued to calve off the former European project. And that was before you considered the Americans and the Russians and the Chinese and the gods only knew who else moving in to pick up product while the place was in chaos. Greater Germany was having to deal with threats from both outside and inside its borders, and while Alice could understand that this might make the BfV grumpy, it did not excuse them from trying to kidnap and/or kill her. If indeed it had been them.

Victoria took out her phone, looked at the screen for a few moments, thumbed a short message, then put it away again. "Come on," she said, getting up. "I'm tired of sitting here watching kids throw bread at ducks."

They walked out of the park and onto the top of The Mall. The road had been closed off to traffic for almost a decade now, and Londoners and tourists alike were shuffling through the security gates at Admiralty Arch.

"Have you noticed how London's becoming *subdivided*?" Victoria asked as they waited to pass through the scanners. "Physically, I mean, not just socially and economically."

Alice's visits to London since the catastrophe in Estonia had been few and far between. She'd never visited much, even before she took up the posting in Tallinn. "It's the bombs," she said. "And the other stuff."

"It wouldn't take much to fence off the whole of St James's Park and put a hardened security perimeter around Buckingham Palace."

"Maybe the King would declare independence."

Victoria laughed. "Christ knows he's wealthier than some emergent nations."

Getting around London, on foot and by car, had been getting trickier and trickier for almost a century now, but the security measures had arrived by increments, dealing with each perceived threat as it emerged. It was like boiling a frog; if you did it gradually enough the frog never noticed until it was too late.

There must have been an alert on or something, because instead of just walking everyone through the scanning gates the officers in charge were searching bags too. "Enjoy our job do we, sweetie?" Victoria asked the officer who rummaged through hers, and received a sour I-would-arrest-you-but-the-paperwork-would-be-a-faff look in return. Alice just smiled and let her bag be searched.

Not all the security measures were so onerous. Trafalgar Square had been bus-only since the van bomb in Whitehall some years previously, and for Alice it was joyfully unbusy despite the crowds walking about. She remembered a school trip down here to the National Gallery; the traffic going around the Square had terrified her.

They wandered up The Strand a little way, past the shattered façade of Charing Cross Station, too badly damaged to repair and all but hidden behind fencing and hoardings until someone could come up with the money to do something with the site. Alice wondered if there was some point in walking her around London's most recent terrorist outrages, and what it was.

Victoria paused and looked at another message on her phone, then turned off The Strand and led the way up a side street into Covent Garden. "Did you ever see *Frenzy*?" she asked.

"What?" said Alice.

"*Frenzy*. The Hitchcock film."

Alice, whose experience of Hitchcock began and ended with an utterly terrifying viewing of *Psycho* when she was eight, shook her head.

"It's actually a really funny film," Victoria went on. "There's a huge amount of comedy in Hitchcock, nobody really appreciates that. But it was filmed round here, just before the old fruit and veg market closed down. It's really weird to see it now." She stopped and looked around the plaza in front of St Paul's Church, where a crowd had gathered to watch a street performer juggling with chainsaws. "How on earth do you practise something like that?" she said. "I mean, it's fine with them turned off but you've got to turn them on at some point." She looked around the crowd, then turned and walked along the ranks of stalls in the colonnade.

"So what's the plan now?" Alice asked.

"Hm?" Victoria looked at her. "Plan?"

"For me. What do I do now?"

"Oh. Yes, we have to find something for you to do, don't we." They emerged from the colonnade near the Royal Opera House, and Alice suddenly sensed the presence of someone moving very close to them. She half-turned and caught a glimpse of a brown-haired young man moving away into the crowds of tourists with something in his right hand. "Hey," she said. "Did that guy just take something from your bag?"

Victoria stopped and unslung her bag from her shoulder and checked. She hadn't bothered zipping the bag up after the security check at Admiralty Arch. "Nope," she said. "Nothing's missing." And she smiled, the way people smile when everything's right with the world.

LOW COUNTRIES

1.

SOMEONE HAD ONCE told her that the distinctive curved gables of the older buildings in Amsterdam were actually modelled on the perukes worn at the court of Louis XIV. She didn't know whether that was true or not, but now all she could think of as she walked through Dam Square or along Prinzengracht was that the city was being presided over by tens of thousands of bewigged judges.

She'd always like Amsterdam, anyway, but it had taken her a long time and a lot of travelling to work out why. Firstly, it was because it wasn't a Catholic country. She wasn't remotely religious herself – her father would never have stood for that – but she found a weird, febrile atmosphere in countries where the Church was dominant.

But mostly, she had come to realise, it was the brick. The Amsterdammers loved to build in brick, made of clay dredged up from the rivers; the Rijksmuseum looked like some mighty edifice from the Industrial Revolution. After half a lifetime wandering a Continent built of stone and concrete or faced with painted plaster or stucco, there was something genuinely comforting about a city made of brick. She was sad that she wouldn't be here for longer, but she had been told that this was just a milk run, basically a piece of stringer business that needed taking care of.

"That's what I was told about Dortmund," Ben said. "And look how that turned out."

Dortmund had been... how long, now? Ten years? They hadn't seen each other since then, and she found herself staring, looking for the marks of passing years, but he seemed as quiet and watchful and capable as ever. He was, she realised, going to reach middle age as a man of considerable gravity and handsomeness. Today he was wearing jeans and a black T-shirt and a dark green hoodie, and carrying a small rucksack slung over one shoulder. Alice had gone for a pair of culottes and a blouse, but she'd put a cardie on before leaving the hotel because although the sun was strong today it was chilly in the shade.

"How've you been?" she asked. It had been some surprise to come down to breakfast at the hotel this morning and find him sitting there. For a few moments she hadn't known what to do – did she pretend they didn't know each other? – but then he'd looked up and smiled broadly and she'd gone over to sit with him and receive the rest of her instructions.

"Fine," he said. "Busy, as always. Yourself?"

"Not so bad, thanks." Although in truth she wasn't so busy these days. Situations had dried up a little after Dortmund, as if the events there had tainted her in some indefinable way. She kept meaning to ask Victoria about it, but their contacts were far and few between now; she got what Situations there were via dead drops or message strings on anonymised bulletin boards.

"Busy is good," he said. "Stops us thinking too much."

The hotel was small and quiet and quite expensive, ten minutes' walk or so from the Rijksmuseum. They'd left separately, met up at one of the pedestrian crossings at the Weteringcircuit, and walked quite casually towards the museum in the midmorning sunshine.

Amsterdam was a quiet, haunted place. The Low Countries had been hit hard by the Xian Flu and for a long time, even after the pandemic had burned itself out, very few tourists had come here. The trade still hadn't recovered in any meaningful way; Alice hadn't seen many foreigners here in the few days since she'd arrived. It made her and Ben stand out in a way that would have been impossible a couple of decades ago, and she found herself constantly scoping out her surroundings, assessing the people who passed by on their bikes and scooters. In Dortmund the atmosphere had been so amped-up that she had felt almost invisible; here everything was so quiet that she felt as if she was holding a big sign over her head reading I AM HERE DOING SPYING.

Except she wasn't. *Les Coureurs*, as Victoria had been at pains to point out, shied away from espionage. Espionage was something governments did. *Les Coureurs* just delivered mail. Although there were times, Victoria had grudgingly admitted, when the boundaries between the two did blur somewhat. They both employed the same basic infrastructures, and a Coureur could never be *quite* sure that what she was carrying was utterly innocent and blameless, or something more nefarious. The important thing, Victoria said, was the spirit of Schengen, of the brief period when Europe's border controls had mostly ceased to exist. *Les Coureurs des Bois* had quite simply refused to accept that that moment in European history had come to an end.

They passed through the colonnade under the museum and out onto the Museumplein. Once upon a time, the big AMSTERDAM sign would have been covered with tourists having their photographs taken clambering over one or other of the letters, but now there was hardly anyone about. A little further away, riggers were setting up a stage for an outdoor concert, and as they walked around that they saw a big crowd of people down by the Van Gogh Museum. Many of them were holding banners and chanting something which the breeze would have rendered incomprehensible, even if it had been in English.

"Student protest," Ben said genially. "Always protesting something, students."

It was not immediately apparent what the students were protesting about. Alice's Dutch was limited to half a dozen words and phrases, and none of these appeared on any of the banners and placards. Ben was of the opinion that it was something to do with a local politician. Whatever it was, a lot of people were angry about it; the crowd was several hundred strong.

Alice and Ben skirted the crowd and wandered down to the Stedelijk Museum. There was a big café/restaurant place next door, and they went in and ordered beer and *bitterballen*. The place was half empty. The Netherlands had borne the brunt of the Xian Flu, and unlike, say, England, they had somehow not quite bounced back. Alice couldn't remember how many people they had lost but she knew it was a large percentage of the fifty million or so who had died in Europe during the pandemic. There was a reflective, slightly haunted feeling about Amsterdam which grew even worse once you were out in the countryside. Out there, entire villages sat completely deserted. Some of them had been demolished and landscaped, others mothballed under a coating of spray-on plastic, waiting for the population to recover. Driving through them was a spooky experience.

Their beer and snacks arrived. Alice took a *bitterball* from its stainless steel basket, dipped it in the little bowl of mayonnaise, and popped it in her mouth. The outside was crunchy breadcrumbs; the inside was basically savoury lava. She took a swig of Amstel.

"You have to let them cool down a little," Ben said with a smile.

"I know," she said. "I always forget."

A woman came over, pulled out the chair beside Ben, and sat down. Alice and Ben ignored her. There were plenty of unoccupied tables, but people had a right to sit where they wanted. Although the woman, middle-aged with spectacles and a touch of grey in her hair, was quite well-dressed, Alice suspected they were about to be panhandled.

But the woman said nothing. She sat where she was, rummaging in the depths of an outlandishly large cloth shoulder bag, until a waiter came over. She looked at him, then at the *bitterballen* and beers. "I'll have those and one of those," she told him in English. She had a strong West Country accent. She returned to mining her shoulder bag. Ben and Alice exchanged glances.

The woman was still rummaging when her order arrived. She raised her head momentarily and squinted at her beer and food as if she had forgotten ordering them, then she nodded and went back to her bag.

"Look," Alice said finally, putting a hand in her pocket and coming up with a few crumpled guilder notes, "this is all the change I have. Maybe you could go somewhere else, eh?"

The woman looked at her, at the cash. "That's very kind of you," she said, "but I'm all right for money at the moment."

"Oh," said Alice, suddenly faintly embarrassed.

"No," the woman said, going back to searching her bag. "What I *really* want is to claim political asylum. Ah." She had finally found what she was looking for, a little slip of paper. She held it up and read, "I used to date the Rokeby Venus."

"It's DORTMUND ALL over again," Alice said.

"But without the rioting," Ben pointed out.

"A milk run," she muttered. "Are you sure about this?"

"It's a real contact string," he said. "I've used it myself."

Alice rubbed her face. "That doesn't mean anything," she said. "Anyone can get hold of a contact string." They were back at the hotel, in her room. The woman had excused herself to use the bathroom. "What are we going to do?"

Ben opened his mouth to reply, but at that moment the bathroom door opened and the woman emerged. "I'm sorry," she said. "I should have introduced myself. My name's Elsie Purnell."

"Tristan," Ben said smoothly. "And this is Isolde."

Elsie Purnell narrowed her eyes at him to let him know what she thought of that. Alice was tempted to do the same. Instead, she said, "You know we can't grant you asylum, Elsie? You need a government for that."

"Oh, no," Elsie said, going over to the room's armchair and sitting down. "You're exactly the right people. *Les Coureurs des Bois.*" She struggled a little to pronounce the name.

"I'm at a complete loss," Alice told her. "I'm sorry."

"I need you to pass a message to the people who run your organisation," Elsie told them. She leaned over and dipped a hand into her bag, which was sitting on the floor beside the chair. She straightened up and held out a long white envelope.

"That could take... *days*..." Alice said.

Elsie sat back and dropped the envelope in her lap. "You do deliver post, don't you?"

"Yes, but..." She looked to Ben for some kind of help, but he was watching Elsie. Alice shrugged helplessly. It was ridiculous. It was like her turning herself in to the BBC and asking for asylum.

"This is our job," Ben said to no one in particular. "Deliver the Package."

"We need to discuss this," Alice said to Elsie. "You can wait here, but we might be a while."

"That's all right," Elsie said, reaching into the bag again and coming up with a battered old paper copy of *Doctor Zhivago*. "I've got a book."

THEY WENT ALONG the street to Café Kale, ordered two espressos, and sat outside watching the traffic and the trams go by.

"Do you think it was wise to just leave her there?" asked Ben.

"If she wants to do a runner that's fine by me," Alice said. She dropped a sugar cube into her coffee. "What are we going to do?"

"I don't see this as any different from any other job we've done," he told her. "We've both moved people before."

Not terribly often, in Alice's case, but she wasn't about to admit that. "Yes, but that was from one place to another. We've never taken in a political refugee before. We don't even know what she's a political refugee *from*." She flashed on Fram, sitting in the restaurant in Dortmund and sliding the memory stick across the table towards her. "Suppose she's a dangle."

"A what?"

"A provocation. Something to give the authorities a pretext for picking us up."

"I was given to understand that the Dutch were reasonably well-disposed towards us, as much as anyone is," he mused. "Although circumstances can always change." He shrugged. "She's our Package. We move her."

"Move her *where*, though?" she insisted. "We can't take her to Coureur HQ because there isn't one; the best we can do is hand her over to someone higher up, and I don't see any reason why we shouldn't do that here. She doesn't seem worried about wandering around Amsterdam in the open."

Ben frowned as he pondered these variables. "First things first," he said finally. "She wants us to pass on a message, so we will do that. After that, it's entirely possible that decisions will be taken out of our hands."

"Did you know this was going to happen?"

He shook his head. "All I knew was that I was making a pickup at that restaurant. I wasn't told what it would be. I wasn't even told you would be here."

"You weren't?"

"It's been a day full of surprises."

Alice checked the clock on her phone. "And it's not even lunchtime yet."

"WHAT YOU HAVE to understand is that this is a brand new situation for us," Alice said. "We've never had anyone come to us asking for asylum before." Of course, she didn't know whether this was true or not; perhaps it happened to other Coureurs all the time. What she really meant was that it had never happened to *her* before, which was the pertinent point here.

Elsie digested this information. "You don't inspire a lot of confidence," she said. "If you don't mind me saying."

"We'll pass your message on," Ben told her. "Until we get a reply, you're under our protection, like any other Package. May I ask where you're staying at the moment?"

"I'm at an hotel near Amsterdam-Zuid station. It's not far on the bus."

Ben nodded. "Okay. We're going to check out of here, then one of us will go with you while you check out of your hotel, then we're going to find somewhere else to stay."

"You're making all this up as you go along, aren't you?" Elsie said.

"It's what we usually do," said Ben.

2.

THE WINDOW OF Alice's room looked out on a canal. Not one of the main ones; more of a side-street in the world of canals. Houseboats were moored along the opposite side. It was too narrow for the big tourist boats to pass down, but occasionally smaller ones chugged past with half a dozen passengers, sometimes picnicking with wine and cheese and bread as they went. Now and again a pedalo laboured by, the occupants' knees pumping as they paddled along. When there were no boats, a family of moorhens bobbed on the water, and once she had seen a swan gliding along. She remembered the old gag: serene on top but paddling like mad underneath. She felt like that, too, apart from the serene on top bit.

Her room was at the back of the apartment Ben had found for them, across the road from their original hotel and a hundred metres or so further up towards the Rijksmuseum. Ben's reasoning was that it would attract less attention to just move across the road than have the three of them trailing around the city on public transport, and Alice hadn't argued.

The apartment was two bedrooms, a living room, kitchen and bathroom. She had one room, Elsie the other. Ben slept on the couch in the living room. For the first couple of days they had subsisted on curries from the Thai takeaway a couple of doors down, but Alice had decided that it felt too much like confinement so she'd gone up the road to the Albert Heijn and bought some groceries and cooked them a proper meal, and ever since she had cooked the evening meal. She found it calming, a little pantomime of domesticity. What Elsie thought about it was anybody's guess, but she didn't complain about the food.

Ben had made the drop, copied the contents of the envelope and passed it on to whoever was tasked to pick it up. Five days later there was still no word. Ben didn't seem particularly worried, but Alice was beginning to get twitchy and Elsie seemed increasingly bemused by the whole thing.

"You'd think," she said out loud one morning, "there would be a little more *urgency* about all this."

Privately, Alice agreed, but it was unprofessional to trash one's employers in front of a client, so she tried to stay upbeat about the whole thing, in public at least. Ben had gone back to check the drop the following day, had returned to the apartment with the news that it had been emptied and a mark left to indicate that receipt had been taken of its contents.

"Could they just have forgotten about us?" she asked Ben one evening, while she was cooking and Elsie was taking a shower.

"I'm sure everything will be fine," he said, and she turned on him, vegetable knife in hand.

"Don't you *dare* patronise me," she snapped.

"I wasn't aware I was," he said with his usual supernatural calm. "I apologise."

"Don't pat me on the head and tell me everything's going to be fine," she said, wagging the knife at him. "I asked you a question."

He didn't look at the knife, kept his eyes on hers. "I doubt very much whether we've been forgotten," he said.

She listened to make sure the shower was still running in the bathroom. "It's been nine days," she said more quietly. "What the fuck is going on?"

"I don't know," he said, still not looking at the knife.

"I'm going to call Victoria."

"Victoria is unavailable," he said. When he saw the look on her face, he added, "I tried."

She put the knife down on the chopping board and crossed her arms across her chest. "And you were going to tell me this when exactly?"

"There seemed no point in bothering you with it. It hardly changes anything."

She ran through a mental checklist of possible replies, but realised that almost all of them would end up with her ranting at him. "Don't do that again, please," she said finally, turning back to the worktop and picking up the knife. "Keep me in the loop or I'll just sod off and let you take care of this on your own."

"Understood," he said, although she had the impression that the prospect didn't bother him in the slightest.

AFTER THE FIRST couple of days cooped up in the apartment, Alice had started to feel the walls closing in on her. It reminded her too much of the days she had spent hiding out in Tallinn. Elsie seemed happy to spend time with her Pasternak, and Ben was immune to boredom, but Alice found herself pacing from room to room without quite being aware she was doing it. After watching her for a while, Ben suggested they all go for a walk, and ever since they'd gone out once a day, usually up to the Vondelpark, Alice and Elsie walking together, Ben trailing them at a short distance.

Like practically every other open space in Europe, the park was full of parakeets, in spite of periodic culls. They shrieked from tree to tree overhead, bullied other birds for food and generally made a nuisance of themselves. The first couple of times, Elsie had stared at them as if not quite believing what she was seeing.

"I'm sorry this is taking so long," Alice said, the morning after losing her temper with Ben.

"It does seem a little unhurried, considering," Elsie told her, stepping out of the way to avoid being trampled by an approaching dog walker being towed along by at least a dozen assorted dogs.

"I don't know what's going on," said Alice. "It's possible that your request is so… um, *unusual* that structures are having to be put in place to deal with it before my superiors can go forward with your proposal."

Elsie glanced at her. "Sometimes," she said, "I have no idea what you're saying."

"Okay."

"All the words are English, but, I don't know, you put them in a strange order."

"Right."

They walked on for a while, chatting about the weather or the birds or the trees, and then, all of a sudden, Elsie said, "Aren't you the slightest little bit curious about why I'm asking for asylum?"

There was an unwritten rule – they were all unwritten – *you do not open the Package*. It was the same contract of trust you entered into when you sent something by a conventional courier or via the Post Office. They didn't open your mail, and you carried on using them.

Alice said, "It would be unprofessional to ask."

"You're quite sweet, you know," Elsie said. "How old are you?" Alice told her, and she said, "You look older."

"Thank you."

"I have a daughter almost your age. I had to leave her behind."

"I'm sorry." It was clearly a lie; Elsie would have to have been in her seventies to have a daughter her age.

"I didn't see a lot of her while she was growing up. I was away a lot of the time; her father's parents looked after her."

Baffled as to quite where this was going, Alice said, "That must have been difficult for you all."

"They don't know about her," Elsie said. "The people I ran away from. I didn't want them to have anything to do with her."

This was dangerous territory, as far as Alice was concerned; *opening the Package* territory. "I think it's best I don't know about this," she said.

"Oh, but I want you to know. I want you to know how important this is. I'm a spy. A deep-cover operative."

It would have been frankly embarrassing to stick her fingers in her ears and go "la-la-la" so she couldn't hear anything, but Alice had suspected something like this anyway, something espionagy, industrial or otherwise, and her sense of impending doom about this whole situation only deepened. "This may be why it's taking so long for my superiors to get back to us," she said.

And then Elsie opened her mouth and said something so utterly ridiculous that despite herself Alice had to ask her to explain, and for the next half an hour, while they walked around the Vondelpark and Ben followed them out of earshot, Elsie told her a story which was impossible to believe.

LATER, AFTER DINNER, Ben asked quietly what they had been talking about.

"This and that," she said, concentrating on rinsing the plates before she put them in the dishwasher. "She wants to go clothes shopping, if that's okay."

"That's not a problem," he said. She'd never quite trusted him, but now he seemed to be standing way too close to her, calm and half-smiling as if he was remembering a joke from a long time ago.

"She wants to know how much longer she'll be stuck here."

"Don't we all?" Ben said, although to be honest he looked as if he could spend the rest of his life in this apartment and not let it bother him.

"Isn't there *anything* we can do?"

"Not while Victoria's out of contact, no."

"Don't you know anyone else you can ask?"

He shook his head. "May I help?"

"You can wash that frying pan on the cooker, if you feel like it." She opened the dishwasher, put the plates and cutlery in, closed the door and straightened up. "But don't worry about it; I can do it."

"It's only fair," he said. "You cooked."

"There's no such thing as *fair*," she told him, and as he carried the frying pan over to the sink he glanced at her for a moment. *Keep an eye on the boy*, Elsie had told her. *He's a killer. I know the look. I used to know a girl like him. Eleanor. She died in Germany, we think, but we were never certain. She could hurt people all day and never break a sweat. Sometimes she did it for fun.*

IF ELSIE WAS at all surprised to hear that she wanted to go shopping, she didn't show it, and the three of them spent a leisurely morning wandering around the clothes shops within walking distance of the apartment. When they got back, Kaunas was sitting in the living room reading a magazine. He must have had the key code because there was no sign of how he had managed to get in.

"Excellent," he said with as much geniality as Kaunas ever mustered. "This must be our asylum seeker."

Alice and Elsie stood by the door, shopping bags in hand. Ben went into the kitchen; Alice heard him filling the coffeemaker. Elsie said, "Is this good news, or bad news?"

"Oh, good news." Kaunas got up and came over and shook Elsie's hand. "You're leaving today. I'm Kaunas, by the way."

"Hello," Elsie said guardedly. "Why has this taken so long, might I ask?"

"There was a lot of discussion," he told her. "We've never been approached by an asylum seeker before; taking you in has certain... implications. We almost turned you away. Hello." This last to Alice.

"Hi," said Alice. It was the first time she'd seen him since the night she'd left Estonia. He didn't seem much older, particularly, just... harder.

"So," he said. "If you'd like to pack, we'll be on our way."

"Now?" Elsie sounded surprised.

"Sure. Why not?"

"All right. Well." She looked at Alice. "I'll just be a few moments, then."

When Elsie had gone into her room, Kaunas said, "You're looking well."

"Thank you," Alice said, trying to fight a sense of dread that was forming around her heart.

"This has taken much longer than it should," he told her. "You could have been doing something useful rather than sitting here."

She supposed this was the closest she was going to get to an apology. "I *was* doing something useful," she said. "I was keeping her safe."

He smiled. "Yes. Of course. You'll tidy up here after we're gone?" He was looking at her when he said it, but she had the uncomfortable sense that he was actually speaking to Ben, who was standing in the kitchen doorway.

"Sure," she said.

Elsie emerged from the bedroom, shoulder bag in one hand, small suitcase in the other. She looked scruffy and vulnerable, like photos Alice had seen of refugees from the Blitz. "Well," she said. "Thank you for everything. You've been very kind."

"Our pleasure," Ben said.

She put her bags down and came over and gave Alice a firm hug. "You take care," she murmured.

"You too," Alice said.

Elsie stepped back. "All right," she said. She slung her bag over her shoulder, picked up her suitcase, and looked at Kaunas. "Shall we then?"

"I'll see you out," Alice said.

They went downstairs to the front door, and Alice stood on the doorstep watching them walk up the street towards the centre of town. When they were lost in the flow of pedestrians, she stepped outside, pulled the door shut behind her, and set off in the opposite direction at a fast walk.

A tram was trundling along the middle of the road towards her. She crossed over to the stop just as it arrived, stepped aboard, and tapped her phone against the ticket reader. As the tram passed the apartment building, she saw Ben standing on the pavement outside.

YEARS AGO, SHE would have been completely helpless. Years ago, she *had* been completely helpless. She was different now, though. Now she was completely self-contained and capable. Now she had experience and training and resources.

She rode the tram a couple of stops, then got off and hopped on a bus that took her out to Amstelveen. She shopped quickly in the little mall; a new coat and a new phone. She dismantled her old phone and dumped the pieces in a bin.

Amstelveen was more or less right underneath one of the flight paths in and out of Schiphol, but she wasn't going anywhere near the airport. With the new phone synced to one of her private bank accounts, she got a bus south towards Utrecht, settled back in her seat and started to download a new identity from a data cache no one knew she had. She'd had the ID made up privately not long after the fiasco in Dortmund, when she decided she never wanted to be in a situation like that again without at least one means of changing her identity. It wasn't particularly robust, and there were countries which wouldn't accept epassports, but it should get her around the Low Countries without too much trouble.

The bus dropped her not far from Utrecht station, and she shopped again. A change of clothes, cosmetics, a bag to carry it all in. Forty minutes later she was sitting on a train bound for Antwerp.

THERE WAS, ON the face of it, no reason for her to do what she was doing. Elsie's mad story was just that, a mad story. Except there had been something *wrong*, a change of atmosphere so subtle that she almost missed it, after that walk in the Vondelpark. She wouldn't have noticed it at all, back in her days at the Embassy, but her senses were different now. Elsie had sensed something, too, a sinking feeling that she had made a mistake, that she had trusted the wrong people. That was why she had told Alice the mad story in the first place, to see what would happen. She hadn't cared about what would happen to Alice, particularly, because if she was right it meant she was finished too.

One thing she had learned was that there was nothing to fear from travel, from being in a new, unfamiliar place. The world was mostly very ordinary, and full of very ordinary people going about ordinary lives. There was nothing to fear from these things. *You pass through the world like a ghost*, one of the trainers had told her. *Or like a cosmic particle, depending on your worldview.* In other words, the vast majority of the world did not care about you. The worst thing you could do was start behaving as if it did. That could only serve to attract attention.

Four months after leaving Amsterdam, she was in Venice. The newly-reconstituted city-state had recently built a wall around itself. A decorative wall, meant chiefly to please tourists, but a wall nevertheless. She was on her fifth new set of documents, a paper passport that identified her as a citizen of Ireland, and she had rented a small apartment in Mestre.

She was sitting in a bar one afternoon, lunching on *rixoto col tastasal*, when something on the big paperscreen stuck to the far wall caught her attention. The screen usually showed football matches, and repeats of football matches, or programmes about football matches, but today it seemed to be tuned to a news channel. It was showing a press conference of some kind. A man she vaguely recognised as Italy's Prime Minister was standing at a dais reading a statement, and a ticker scrolling across the bottom of the screen was summarising the main points. Her Italian was shaky, but every now and again a word came up that she recognised, and it was enough to make her take out her phone and call up an English-language news browser.

I'm from an invisible country, Elsie had told her, quietly and matter-of-factly, that day in the Vondelpark, *a country that doesn't exist. It's called the* Community *and we've been spying on you for hundreds of years. We're very good at it. But I don't want to do it any more. I've had enough. I want to rest.*

A mad story. But here it was. The Community was all over the news. People who until today probably thought they knew better were using the words 'pocket universe' and 'topologically superimposed' as if they actually understood them. There was footage of a pudgy, amiable-looking man in a tweed suit and a starchy collar signing a whole bunch of treaties with various European mucky-mucks. She spotted the English Prime Minister and the Scottish First Minister, a rather unpleasant little man named Flynn who had been Minister of Tourism when she'd been in the Diplomatic Service. "How does this news affect us?" one anchor asked a studio guest. Well, quite.

It was with her for the next couple of months as she travelled. It was on the news all the time, there was almost nothing else. Even the War On Terror seemed to have evaporated, although in Alençon she saw the aftermath of a truck bombing and knew that it had not. Documentaries about the Community; it looked rather nice, if a little twee. One of their films – a police thriller – did the rounds, and it was awful, like watching a really bad Ealing comedy.

It was under her feet, too, wherever she went. The sense that it occupied the same space as the cities and towns and countries she passed through, that it was there at the same *time*. All those people she had seen in the documentaries, right here beside her, separated by... what? Some unimaginable twist of space-time? The scientists interviewed on the news channels could not explain it, although they tried hard. She remembered Elsie saying *We've been spying on you for hundreds of years*.

All this went on around her as she travelled, this new geopolitical reality. The world changed. Spring became Summer, and Summer became Autumn and there was a new chill in the air and there was nowhere else to go, so in the end she went home.

PART THREE

FEIERABEND

CITY OF WINDS

1.

THERE WAS A statue of Stalin in the car park of the big out-of-town shopping centre, but it was a fake, a prop left behind from the filming of a science fiction drama a year or so earlier and never, somehow, removed by the production company. It was forty feet tall and featured the old monster in his *Generalissimo*'s uniform, pointing off in the general direction of the Caspian Sea. Instead of being torn down by an angry mob, or lovingly maintained by those with a misplaced nostalgia for the certainties of Soviet times, the statue had simply begun to accrete a layer of graffiti, and now appeared to be covered in the guano of paint-eating birds.

"Gives me the fucking creeps, if I'm going to be honest with you," said Pais.

"Why didn't the film company take it away?" asked Rupert.

"They went bust. No one knows who it belongs to now; the city's afraid to take it away in case the new owner turns up and sues."

Rupert sighed and tried to squirm into a more comfortable position in the tiny leather seat. The car was big and low-slung, with many aerodynamic features, but there was only room inside for two people. One didn't sit in it so much as wear it.

There were many places in Europe where a car like this, over half a million Swiss francs' worth of high-end designer engineering and arrogance, would have seemed hopelessly out of place. But this was not one of those places. Looking out through the steeply-raked tinted windscreen, Rupert could see a car park packed with supercars, both vintage and new. There was a great deal of money here.

Pais was wearing quite a lot of it. He was eighteen, with shoulder-length black hair and pale skin and a spirited attempt at a moustache fuzzing his upper lip. He was wearing an expensive grey suit and a cream silk open-necked shirt, and his wrists were weighed down by gold chains and an antique watch the size of a dustbin lid. Stalin was as much a figure of myth to him as Jesus and Santa Claus.

"I've got something else for you," he said.

"I didn't come here for something else," Rupert pointed out.

"No, I have that too. But there's something else. I'm not sure what it is."

"If you're not sure what it is, I'm not interested," Rupert said.

Pais seemed uncharacteristically thoughtful. "I'll give you this one for free, as you're such a good customer."

Rupert snorted. Until a month or so ago, neither of them had known the other existed.

"I know what you think of us," Pais said, *you* meaning Western Europeans. "You think we're all crazy, drunk on oil."

Rupert didn't comment, although he could have cited seeing two women conducting a duel with swords in a local park the previous day as evidence that things were not quite the same here as anywhere else.

"And maybe you're right," Pais allowed. "And who could blame us?" He made a rude noise. "But that doesn't mean order has completely broken down. Order is very important."

"I agree."

Pais looked across at him. "Ach, you don't care. Why should you?"

"No," Rupert said. "I agree that order is very important."

Pais looked at him a moment longer, then returned his gaze to the defaced statue. He took out his phone. "Let's do this, then I'll take you to lunch."

Rupert took out his own phone. He was still not entirely used to it, and it took him a couple of tries to establish contact with the bank and make the transfer. Pais watched as the money arrived in the escrow account.

"All right," he said, putting away his phone and starting the engine. "Let's eat."

BAKU WAS FULL of statues of strongmen whose names most people didn't even know. Some of them were gilded, some were white marble, some were mounted on plinths that rotated so that the hero's face followed the course of the sun across the sky. Some were in traditional garb, others in sober suits, still others on horseback. None of these statues had been defaced – in fact they were lovingly maintained – because they belonged to wealthy, powerful families, and no one wanted to lose a hand, or worse, for the sake of a moment's recreational tagging.

It was summer here, but it was not hot. The winds scoured the Absheron Peninsula all year round, the cold northern *khazri* and the warm southern *gilavar*. It was said the wind could drive a man out of his mind, if he stayed here long enough, although Rupert thought other factors were at play as well. The city's architecture was a wild mix of styles both ancient and modern, seemingly without much thought to urban planning. It was as if the world's architects had come here with their most absurd designs, the ones no other city in the world was mad enough to allow, and found an enthusiastic welcome.

"Wilhelm Dancy," Pais said, between the starter and the main course.

"What?" said Rupert.

"That's their man," said Pais. "A poet, apparently."

"I'm sorry?"

"They call themselves a *book club* – no, wait – a *reading group*. The Wilhelm Dancy Reading Group."

Rupert was already baffled. He had never been in a restaurant like this. The dining room was enormous and austere, with wooden floors and tall windows, but it only had a dozen or so tables, spaced yards apart. Each table had only two place settings, and the chinaware and cutlery were plain and unadorned. Within this huge space, black-clad waiters moved soundlessly, conscious that they were attending to some of the wealthiest diners on the face of the planet. The food was some bizarre iteration of *nouvelle cuisine* – not Rupert's favourite to begin with. His starter had consisted of two tiny cubes of *foi gras*, four postage-stamp-sized squares of almost transparently-thin wholemeal toast, a barely-detectable smear of something that tasted distantly fruity, and a single leaf of watercress which he assumed had been added for satirical effect. There were no prices on the menu, which in his experience was always a bad sign.

"I don't see why you think I'd be interested in a book club," he said.

"*Reading Group.*"

"Reading Group."

"They're looking for the same thing you are, pretty much. But in bigger quantities."

Rupert raised an eyebrow.

"I'm not dealing with them," Pais added. "But I know a guy who was. He says they're really spooky. No sense of humour at all."

Rupert looked around the dining room again, suddenly uncomfortable that the conversation had taken this turn in public. He said, "My own sense of humour is running a little thin, I have to admit."

Pais – he was named after a newspaper his father had seen while on holiday in Spain – gave Rupert a long, calculating look. "I know where you're from," he said.

That seemed unlikely in the extreme. "I'm from Somerset." In the years before the Community had made itself known, his accent would have sparked no curiosity at all; these days, he and Rudi had agreed that it was less trouble to claim he was from the West Country. He was impressed that Pais, whose English was good but not perfect, had spotted it.

"Sure," Pais said.

Rupert said, "I don't know what you're playing at, but I can always take the money out of escrow and go somewhere else."

"You can," Pais said.

"And I can spread the word about what a total arse you are."

Pais's face fell. "Hey," he said. "Don't be like that. We're friends, right?"

Rupert gave him a level look.

"Just a bit of banter, yeah?" Pais told him. "Lighten the mood a little."

Far away, on the other side of the dining room, Rupert spotted one of the waiters beginning the long trek towards their table with their main courses. He'd ordered quail, and he wondered whether lightening the mood wasn't a bad idea after all.

THE STREETS OF the city were choked with horrifically-expensive cars. This was Rupert's third visit here in as many years, and he still wasn't used to that. He'd seen one Lamborghini outside a hotel which had appeared to be made of solid gold. Baku rang with the sound of powerful, revving engines of vehicles which, because of the volume of traffic, could not move at more than five kilometres an hour.

Guns were also popular. Guns and kidnapping. Kidnapping, whether for ransom or for political ends, was something of a national sport in Baku, and many foreign governments advised their citizens to hire a personal bodyguard when visiting. The rest advised their citizens not to go there at all.

This latter piece of advice was broadly ignored. The reason for this lay about sixty miles from the city and several thousand feet beneath the bed of the Caspian Sea, where almost a decade ago vast new oil reserves had been discovered. Oil Rocks, the almost-moribund oil drilling city which had been growing out into the sea since the middle of the previous century, and which suddenly found itself sitting virtually on top of this enormous source of wealth, had promptly, in the spirit of the age, pronounced itself a sovereign nation. This was followed in short order by Baku's declaration of independence and a brief and almost bloodless conflict which had ended in Oil Rocks becoming a distant *canton* of the former Azerbaijani capital.

Baku had fed well in the ensuing years, insulated from the spate of droughts and crop failures and increasingly desperate and repressive governments which had devastated the economy of Azerbaijan. Now, like a comfortably sated vampire, it was settling down to enjoy its wealth.

It was, of course, not enjoying it in isolation. Oil Rocks had been drifting into decay and disuse for decades until the new oil strike; now it was a bustling metropolis of more than five thousand people, a network of platforms and bridges built out into the Caspian Sea and inhabited by a population of oilmen and oilwomen who hewed to no nationality save that of their company. They worked week-long shifts making sure the oil kept flowing, and on Saturday nights they came into Baku, and then the city became really dangerous.

Rupert had taken a room in a modest *pension* in the Inner City, down a side street that was at least too narrow for most traffic. He hadn't hired a bodyguard, on the grounds that there was a statistical probability that anyone he did hire would be connected in some way with the kidnapping gangs. Anonymity had kept him safe in the past; there was no reason why it shouldn't do so now.

There was also the thing that a bodyguard would have to go everywhere with him, and information about stuff like that could be sold. Baku had almost as many intelligence outfits as it had supercars, and that was before you started trying to count the cohorts of individual creeps, ghouls, crooks and gentleman adventurers the place attracted. There were days when you visited the café at the end of the street and you just knew that everyone there was a spy, or thought of themselves as a spy, or wanted to be a spy.

Pais's father was a spy – a real spy, a former field operative with Azerbaijan's foreign intelligence service who had crossed the aisle when Baku became independent and now worked in counterespionage, where, presumably, he was kept quite busy. Rupert had spent a lot of time doing his homework before he even set foot in Baku, and he'd made his choice with care. By any normal standards, Pais was a criminal, but he was a criminal with deep and solid connections, and the scope for Rupert to damage him, should the wheels come off the transaction, was really quite remarkable. Similarly, if Rupert were to displease Pais he presumed some fragment of State Security would be tasked to take care of him. And in this way they were both kept honest. Although in this context *honest* was a fairly fluid term.

He left the *pension* in the evening, just out for a stroll to a little restaurant he had discovered. The main street was crowded with cars and people, and he found it easy to submerge himself in the bustle, carried along by the press of pedestrians. He was wearing nondescript clothes – a good suit and shirt and a light overcoat – which would have identified him as towards the lower end of the income scale, perhaps a guest-worker, although anywhere else in Europe he would have looked like a well-off businessman embarking on an evening out.

The restaurant was busy – it was a Friday evening and the weekend was just gathering its momentum – but he'd booked a quiet table tucked away in a corner at the back, and when he seated himself he found he was concealed from the door and windows by a wall of security men sitting watching a table full of large, noisy diners.

He'd found himself quite taken with Azerbaijani food. Years ago, just after crossing into England from the Campus, he had not been particularly discerning about what he ate, and where. The fact that there was food at all had been enough, and he had set out to, in Rudi's words, 'eat his way around Europe'. These days, he was a bit more picky. It was strange to think that his palate had become so jaded.

This evening, he ordered *toyug plov*, a dish where the components – rice, chicken and eggs – were served on separate plates. After lunch – which had been, after all, more of an *impression* of lunch rather than an actual meal as he understood it – it was gratifying to have large amounts of everything brought to his table.

Finishing his meal, he ordered *shekerbura* for dessert, with coffee, and while he waited for them to be served he got up and visited the lavatory down two flights of stairs in the basement of the restaurant, opposite the kitchen. Instead of returning to his table, he walked down the short corridor to a door at the end and pushed it open. The door led to a steep set of steps up to the loading bay at the back of the restaurant. He crossed the bay to the entryway on the far side, passed through, and out onto the crowded street beyond.

A hundred metres or so down the street there was a little clothes shop. He'd spent some time over the past few days casually checking it out as he familiarised himself with the neighbourhood, and it only took him five minutes to buy a new coat – something slightly heavier and shabbier than the one he'd left behind in the restaurant. He left the shop with the coat in a carrier bag, but as soon as he got the chance he ducked into an archway, tore off the labels and tags, and put it on.

He took an indirect, meandering route to the bus station, checking to make sure he wasn't being tailed, and an hour or so later he was crossing the border at Saray on a French passport. He spoke pretty good French by now – certainly good enough to pass muster with the border guards out here. On the other side of the border he took another bus into Saray itself, where there was a room booked in his French identity at an anonymous and rather grim business hotel on the edge of town. The youth at the front desk barely looked at him when he asked for his key.

The room was dirty and smelled of tobacco and people with questionable personal hygiene, but that was all right because Rupert spent less than fifteen minutes there. On the way into Baku he had stopped here overnight and left a travelling bag in the wardrobe. He changed out of his suit and into jeans and a sweatshirt, and left again. The boy at the front desk paid almost no attention as he checked out.

He took a bus to the railway station at Sumqayit, arriving just in time for the last train of the day, a rattling little local which would take him as far as Shamakhi and the early morning express to Yerevan. From Yerevan there would be another express to Erzurum, and another four trains after that before he even reached Ankara. And when he did get to Ankara there was still the journey to Istanbul and then the long, nitpicking business of working his way up through the Balkans, across Hungary and Austria and the Czech Republic to Prague. A journey of more than a week. He still found the distances involved a little dizzying – he had grown up in a world just over two hundred miles across – but there was no way he was ever going to set foot on an aeroplane.

His phone buzzed as the train pulled out of Sumqayit, a short text message informing him that the delivery had been made and verified. He sent the codes which would release the money in the escrow account and then he settled down to get some sleep as the darkened countryside went by outside and Europe crept ever closer.

2.

"INTERESTING PROPOSAL, BY the way," Snell said after the soup course had been cleared away.

"You read it, then?" said Rupert.

"Oh yes." Snell folded his napkin and placed it on the table in front of him. "Very expertly presented, I thought. Highly professional."

"It should be. We spent enough on it."

"Ah," Snell smiled ruefully. "One must speculate to accumulate, don't the English say?"

"Yes," Rupert said. "Yes, they do."

Snell was a short, narrow man in a beautifully-cut tweed suit. "I showed it to a couple of my fellow board-members," he said. "I hope you don't mind."

Rupert shook his head. "They would see it anyway, if we went ahead."

"They were very positive about it. Quite keen, in fact."

Rupert didn't doubt. He said, "When do you think we'll have a decision?"

"Ah, well." Snell picked up his napkin and replaced it in his lap as the waiter brought the main course – roast beef for him, a steak and kidney pudding for Rupert. "There will have to be a full meeting of the Board, and those can be tricky to schedule."

"Of course," Rupert said, looking at his pudding, sitting stodgy and malevolent in a little pool of gravy and flanked by small piles of boiled potatoes and green beans. He felt a sudden pang of nostalgia for Azerbaijani *plov*.

Not that anyone here would have eaten it. Apart from a rash of fast-food franchises and coffee shops and a baffling fashion for Italian *trattorias*, contact with Europe had left the Community's cuisine almost entirely untouched. There was not a single curry house in the entire country; it was, at best, an unnerving place to be a member of an ethnic minority.

And Władysław was a hotbed of cosmopolitanism compared to Stanhurst, Ernshire's county town. Here there was not even a Caffé Nero. What there *was* was a little inn with private dining rooms, just the thing for discreet business meetings where one or both parties might be cautious about being seen in the big city.

"Are you not hungry, old chap?" Snell asked.

"Ravenous, actually," Rupert said, picking up his knife and fork and managing a wan grin.

"Excellent," said Snell, tucking in. "The beef's terribly good."

Rupert made an incision in his pudding. The suet crust was dense; it was like cutting into a wetsuit. He said, "I had a lathe brought over, for you to look at."

Snell beamed. "You did? That's good."

"It was good of you to help with the licence."

Snell waved it away and continued eating. For most of the people of the Community, computers might as well have been boxes full of sorcery. The Directorate had weighed up them up and seen only the threat of unrest and sedition; there was no end to the damage a single malcontent could do with a computer and a printer. And as for 3D printers... oh no, none of *those* were coming across the border.

There was much which was proscribed – temporarily, the President assured everyone, pending the moment the Presiding Authority judged that the populace was ready for mobile phones or virtual reality glasses. Although a French telecoms firm had discreetly installed a mobile network in Władysław and Stanhurst, for the Directorate's sole use, and cell coverage was being extended, bit by bit, across the country.

There were grey areas, chiefly in medical technology – an area where the Community lagged terrifyingly behind its European neighbour – and design and manufacture. Much of the equipment in these fields was computer-controlled, and to import any of it a firm needed special licences. Which was where Snell came in. A former member of the Presiding Authority, he was ideally-placed to put in a good word for people wanting to bring computer-controlled equipment into the Community. This of course had no bearing at all on the number of executive directorships he had been offered by manufacturing firms on both sides of the border.

"Where is it?" Snell asked. "The lathe?"

"At the station here." Rupert finally put some of his pudding in his mouth and chewed. Quite how anyone could extract almost all the taste and simple pleasure from steak and kidney was beyond him. "It's locked in one of the warehouses on Goods Way."

"Under guard, I hope."

"That was among the terms of the licence, if I recall correctly." Snell had wangled a temporary licence to import a single machine for demonstration purposes.

"Indeed." Snell had cleared his plate, and looked sadly at the mutilated pile of food sitting on Rupert's. "Thought you were hungry," he said.

"I thought perhaps you and some of your fellow board members might like to come over to the warehouse and see the machine in action this afternoon," Rupert said. "I have to go back to London in the evening and it would be a terrible faff to get an operator over here for a demonstration."

Snell thought about it while a waiter came and cleared their plates away, giving Rupert the briefest and most professional of hard stares as he left. When he'd gone, Snell said, "I don't see why not. We might not be able to get the whole Board together but I can see who I can round up." He dabbed his lips with his napkin. "Tell you what, order coffee and brandy and I'll pop downstairs and make a few phone calls. They keep a phone in a quiet little room here, for discreet discussions."

"I can see why you suggested we meet here," Rupert said appreciatively.

Snell got up from the table. "Right," he said. "This shouldn't take long."

After he'd gone, the waiter returned and Rupert ordered coffee and brandy. While he waited, he went over to the window and looked down into the street. It was market day in Stanhurst, and he looked down on a sea of hats and old-fashioned clothes bustling along between the stalls which had overspilled the Market Square. He remembered a time when he had dressed like that.

The waiter came back with a tray bearing a coffee pot, two cups, jugs of cream and milk, and a bowl of white sugar, alongside two snifters of brandy. He placed everything on the table and left again. Rupert stood by the window, counting to twenty.

At twenty, he went back to the table, opened his briefcase, and took out a small, very heavy cylinder. It was painted white and threaded at both ends, because until a couple of hours ago it had been attached to the lathe he'd had delivered yesterday. The customs men who had inspected the machine hadn't the first idea what was meant to be there and what was a later addition, but to be fair Rupert doubted most customs men in Europe would have been able to tell that the cylinder wasn't part of the original design.

Taking the cylinder in both hands, he twisted hard, unscrewing until it came apart. The thing he had bought in Baku sat cupped in the hollow lower half. It was the size of a grain of salt, and to make it easier to keep track of it was coated in a thick layer of nacreous plastic material so that it looked like a small pearl.

He tipped the pearl into one of the brandy glasses and watched as it dissolved completely in the alcohol. Then he quickly screwed the two halves of the cylinder together again and returned it to the briefcase, and a couple of minutes later he was standing by the window with his own glass in his hand, when Snell returned.

"I managed to get four of the Board together," he said. "They'll meet us at the station."

Rupert smiled and raised his glass in salute, and Snell picked his up off the table and swirled the brandy around. "To cooperation," he said.

"Cooperation," Rupert echoed, and he watched Snell take a long, satisfying drink.

STANHURST RAILWAY STATION sat in the middle of the town, fronted by a long, pretty building with white-painted canopies hung with baskets of flowering plants. Beyond this, green-liveried local trains sat at their platforms in clouds of steam and smoke. Goods Way ran down one side of the station, past the platforms, a tidy district of goods sheds and warehouses. The lathe had been delivered to one of these, and Rupert had spent a number of hours the previous day uncrating the thing and setting it up.

It sat in the middle of the brick floor like a peculiar abstract sculpture, illuminated by sunlight slanting in through the windows high up in the warehouse's walls. It seemed utterly out of place, as if it had come here from some far technologically-advanced future.

Actually, it was basically a piece of junk. Rupert had picked it up cheap because it was almost thirty years old and there were machines half its size that could do twice as much, but the board members walking around it peering at various tools and screens didn't know that.

They also didn't know that the firm he represented didn't exist. He'd spent almost a year setting it up and backstopping its legend, but he barely needed to have bothered; the Community was so eager to get its hands on European technology that Snell's Board had hardly made the effort to check him out. In European terms this was a catastrophic failure of due diligence, but here it was just the way things were done. The important thing was that his face fitted, he knew what he was talking about, and he seemed to be a decent chap. So much business was done this way in the Community that it was faintly baffling that anything got done at all; the Presiding Authority was acutely aware that it exposed them to all manner of sharks from the other side of the border, very few of whom could be described as decent chaps, but it was a hard habit to break. It was the good old-fashioned way that things had always been done.

Of course, once the deal had been agreed there would be more scrutiny, and then Snell's company would discover that there was nothing but fog and mirages on the other side, but by then it wouldn't matter.

Rupert switched the machine on, and the board members nodded appreciatively as its screens booted up and he walked them through the various menus.

"It'll take pretty much any stock," he told them, locking a fist-sized cube of aluminium into the jig at the heart of the device. "It's got over a thousand onboard patterns and it's the work of a couple of minutes to load custom ones. Forty-two separate tools, self-selecting, and with each machine we deliver another two hundred."

He pointed at the cutting head – he'd spent a long time with the manual to make sure he knew where everything was. "Again, you can swap them out in a minute or so, it's quite straightforward." He consulted the touch-menu on one of the screens, chose several options, then closed the shield that prevented the impulsive from sticking their hands into the whirling heart of the machine while it was operating.

The lathe started to make a quiet, high-pitched whirring sound, and one of its screens displayed a countdown, impressively fast because he'd selected the option to see it in tenths of a second. While it worked, he recited bits of the manual that he'd memorised because they sounded impressive, and Snell and the board members nodded in a sort of distant and patricianly impressed way. The situation was quite hard to decode, in a social sense, because, although he had presented himself as a successful businessman, as far as the Community people were concerned he was still Trade, not much better than a door-to-door salesman. He had to keep reminding himself that they were in charge here, not him, and he had to keep reminding himself not to punch anyone.

After a few minutes, the countdown reached zero and the lathe started to make a quiet beeping noise. Rupert lifted the shield, reached in, and took out a small aluminium goblet. "You can turn out two hundred of these a day with one machine," he told his audience, handing the goblet to Snell. "More complex forms take longer, of course, and some materials are harder or more brittle and need different handling. But you get the idea."

Indeed they did, as the goblet was passed round. Mass production had never really caught on in the Community, for some reason; the entire country was a huge cottage industry. The prospect of being able to produce two hundred – or four hundred, or eight hundred, depending on how many lathes they were running – identical items a day had intriguing possibilities.

"Under the terms of our licence we have to take the machine home after seven days," Rupert told them. "So what I'm going to do is leave it here – the warehouse is paid for until the end of the month – and you can pop in and experiment with it. The manual's here –" he held up a four-inch-thick ring binder of printed pages "–

and it's all pretty much self-explanatory. Thank you for your time, gentlemen."

There was a great deal of polite handshaking. Some of the board members looked impressed with the demonstration, others less so, it didn't really matter. Rupert left them to poke at the lathe some more, and walked to the door with Snell.

"I thought that went awfully well," Snell told him.

"I hope it gave you some idea of what the lathe can do," Rupert said.

"Oh, it did, dear chap," Snell told him. "It did. What time are you going back to London?"

"I'm on the half past five train."

Snell checked his watch. "Excellent," he said. "Time for drinks at my club, then."

"I can't, I'm afraid," Rupert told him. "I have another meeting." He had no intention of spending any more time with Snell.

Snell's face fell. "I didn't realise you were dealing with someone else. That's really not on, you know. I thought we had an understanding."

"Oh, it doesn't affect our understanding," Rupert said, with just enough lightness to unsettle Snell. "It's another matter altogether."

"Perhaps we could… discuss it," Snell mused. "I may be able to help."

The Community was always hustling, always trying to find an advantage, always wanting to come out on top. That was one of the things Europe had never really got its head around. The Community always wanted to be in charge.

"Honestly," Rupert said, "it has nothing to do with our business, and I doubt you'd be able to help. It's nothing. But I should go; I don't want to be late."

Snell looked downcast, "Well, if you're sure…"

"I'm certain." Rupert put out his hand, and when Snell put out his own hand he gave it the lightest of shakes. "I'll be back next Tuesday. Until then, please experiment with the machine, and if you have any questions, don't hesitate to get in touch." And leaving Snell slightly bemused and discomfited, he nodded a polite goodbye and turned and walked away.

*   *   *

TWO HOURS LATER, he was alighting from a train at Jackson's Halt.
Dusk was beginning to settle on the great quiet of the countryside,
and from the platform he could see a great vista of fields and
woodlands that seemed, on the very edge of visibility, to merge
with the horizon. He left the station and began to trudge down the
narrow road leading to the village.

Snell and his friends would play around with the lathe for the
next few days, happily producing little knickknacks for their wives
and lovers and wooden toys for their children and grandchildren,
all the while discussing how they could use machines like this
to their maximum monetary advantage. They'd lease, say, ten
machines, and in the first month of operation they'd make enough
to pay the lease for the entire year. After that, almost everything
was profit. The disappointment they were going to feel when they
discovered that he, his company, and all his machines save the one
in the warehouse, only existed on paper would be, he imagined,
quite considerable.

At some point in the next few days an internal countdown would
reach zero and the machine's wifi would attempt to make contact
with the nearest mobile phone cell, presumably in the station. The
lathe would unobtrusively transmit a package into the system, and
shortly thereafter the Directorate's private mobile phone network
would cease to exist. The hacker who had designed the package
had assured him that it would take weeks, if not months, to get it
working again. It was a fairly childish bit of vandalism, he knew,
but the opportunity had been too good to miss.

A mile or so from the station, he turned off the road and onto a
farm track, and a hundred yards or so along the track he climbed
a stile into a field. It was almost dark now, only a faint transparent
paleness in the cloudless sky to the west. A quarter-moon was just
peeking above a copse of trees on the other side of the field. Venus
was a bright spark low down in the sky, and higher up was Jupiter,
or maybe Saturn. Were they the same planets here as in Europe? Was
that the same Moon? It had always bothered him, somehow, like
a subcritical but nagging toothache. How could a pocket universe

have the same stars and planets as its neighbour? Had the Whitton-Whytes remapped the sky as well as the land?

He walked along the edge of the field until he reached the other side, then slipped through a gap in a hedge into the neighbouring one. He did this three more times, until he was deep in the countryside, far from the roads and any habitation. At one corner of the next field was a little wood. He switched on a little torch and stepped between the trees.

There was no path in the wood, and the light of the torch didn't pick out any freshly broken twigs or disturbed ground litter since he had last passed this way. He moved forward one step, a step to the left, forward, two steps to the left. A long time ago – in another life, it seemed now – he had known someone, a refugee from the Community. They'd travelled for a while in Europe, until she had become too ill, and then he had stayed with her at a clinic in Switzerland, and together, as she faded, they had watched the Community take its first steps onto the world stage. Not long before she died, she told him that the little dissident group to which she had belonged had once come into possession – for a very short time – of a map of border crossings. It had been useless because most of the crossings had either been closed decades before, or were being guarded, but there was supposed to be one which had been overlooked when the borders were sealed. It wasn't guarded because on later maps it was listed as closed. Everyone had forgotten about it. Her group had never got the chance to check it out – there was a feeling that it was a trap to lure those tender souls who felt that life in the Community had just become too much to bear – but she described it to him with all the detail of someone who has memorised the face of a lover they will never see again, the way he had been memorising hers.

Later – some years later – he thought about the crossing. This was when travel between Europe and the Community had become no more problematical than travel between any modern polities. There were, perhaps, fewer routes in and out of the Community, but really all you needed to do was get a visa and take a train, or get a bus out to one of the crossings and walk. So, armed with a set of false documents, he'd done that, and he'd spent a quiet week or so sightseeing like any visiting European. And then he'd spent a day as someone else, as the person he had been once, when he had worked for the Directorate, and he'd come out here undercover and found that the crossing was not only still open, but unguarded.

Two steps forward, one to the right, and there it was, the smell of pollution on the air and the low rumble of traffic in the distance. His very own private back door into and out of the Community.

He emerged from the trees on the edge of a modern housing estate. He walked unhurriedly past its quiet Closes and Avenues and out onto the main road. A few hundred yards away, hidden in a cutting, the M25 curved away from Gerrards Cross. He suddenly felt very tired. Too many borders, too much distance. He walked to a bus stop and waited for a bus to Uxbridge.

LA COMPLAINTE DU COUREUR DE BOIS

1.

AT AROUND HALF past five on a fresh Spring morning, a man walked through the streets of Kraków, Poland's ancient capital. He was wearing jeans and a long grey coat with its collar turned up, and he walked with a cane. He took his time, not hurrying. A casual observer might have said he was enjoying the morning air, pausing now and again to look in shop windows. The casual observer might have deduced that he had not a care in the world, although this deduction would only have been partly incorrect.

The man walked along Floria ska, one of the streets leading off the Rynek, the city's market square, and here the casual observer might have noted that he was a native Krakowian because he nodded hello to the shopkeepers and delivery men as he passed, and received greetings in return. In this, the casual observer would also have been only partly incorrect.

About halfway along Floria ska, the man stopped at a door between two shopfronts. The door was of solid oak, studded with square nailheads, promising perhaps some rustic or vaguely mediaeval experience within, and there was a little canopy above it, its original deep blue colour bleached by the years and the weather and the pollution until it was a delicate shade of teal. Mounted beside the door was a brass plate the size of a postcard. Etched on the plate in an elegant looping script were the words *Restauracja Max*. The man with the cane had lately considered replacing it with something lettered in Comic Sans, which suited his mood these days. The plate was smudged with fingerprints, brought up by a misting of dew, and he shook his head. He'd never been able to understand why people felt the need to poke and prod at the name of the restaurant, although the motivations of people were a continual mystery to him and he thought he really ought to be used to that by now.

He took his phone from his coat pocket and touched it to the door, heard the bolt withdraw. He turned and waved to the cameras glued to the buildings across the street, because his life really was that ridiculous these days, then pushed his way through the door and out of sight.

Beyond the door was a short corridor leading to a wide staircase, at the bottom of which was the maître d's lectern, its shelves neatly piled with printed menus in faux leather folders which Rudi thought were mildly tacky but which Max, the restaurant's late owner, had refused to replace. He paused at the lectern and took one of the folders, flipped it open and ran his eye down the menu, noting that the changes he had made the night before had been printed out. He put the menu back on its shelf and stepped out into the restaurant proper.

He still had a lot to do here. The restaurant, warm and snug and cosy, had thirty tables, places for a hundred diners. If you turned the main lights up you'd notice that not all the tables and chairs quite matched – Max had tended to source his furniture and fittings at restaurant bankruptcy sales – and the paintwork and wallpaper were looking a bit shabby. The carpet was starting to become worn; one of the bullet points on Rudi's to-do list involved taking up the carpet and replacing it with wooden flooring. On the wall nearest him, one of the light sconces was of a slightly different design to the others. He stood looking at it for a while before limping across the dining room and pushing through the swing-door into the kitchen.

Here, there was also much to be done. The gas ranges and ovens were fabulous things, built at a time when things were expected to last by people who understood restaurant cooking on a very deep level, but the fridges needed replacing and much of the other equipment, though still serviceable, was battered and well-used. Rudi glanced up at the kitchen's air conditioning system, which in all honesty would have looked dangerously outdated in the Eighteenth Century and which had been a continuing bone of contention between himself and Max. One of his earliest thoughts, when everything had settled down in his mind, had been that he was now free to have the damn thing excised and something modern – and, more importantly, functioning – installed in its place.

Over the past four months or so he'd had a bunch of tradespeople in to look at the work which needed to be done, and they had promised him that everything could be completed within the week-long window when the aircon was being replaced and the kitchen was unusable. Money was hardly an issue – he could afford to have the entire street demolished and rebuilt and barely notice the outlay, which gave him a weird feeling – but there remained the question of quite how far to go. He knew of restaurants which had actually gone bust because they'd misjudged a refurb; the chef, the food, everything else remained unchanged, but the new decor drove customers away, it was irrational but there it was. Customers were a conservative lot, by and large; you could lose regulars just by taking a dish off the menu. Rudi was inclined to stamp his own personality on the business, but Restauracja Max was like a comfortable old shoe; it was tricky to judge, and so he had been putting it off. They were just coming into their busiest time of the year, anyway; there was no point shutting the restaurant now. Maybe wait until just after New Year.

He sighed and switched on the coffeemaker, then he took off his coat, hung it in the cupboard off the corridor at the rear of the kitchen. When he returned, Kasia, one of his sous-chefs, was just arriving, bright-eyed and bushy-tailed and ready for the day. She was about eighteen and made him feel old and tired. They nodded hello. Kasia switched on the radio; a panel of men was discussing the implications of the disappearance of the Line for relations between Europe and the Community. Kasia flipped through the channels until she found a station playing classical music.

There was a banging on the door to the courtyard at the back of the building. Rudi unlocked and unbolted it and found Tomek, the restaurant's meat supplier, standing outside with his brother, surrounded by plastic crates.

"Morning, Chef," said Tomek.

"Morning, Tomek," said Rudi. "Morning, Rafal." Rafal didn't reply; he'd suffered some kind of head injury as a boy and now, in middle age, his face was as smooth and unconcerned as a child's. He was, though, immensely strong; Rudi had seen him, as a bet arranged by his brother, carry two full kegs of beer the length of Floria ska fifteen times before he dropped them. "I'm not in the mood this morning."

Tomek put on an expression of innocent surprise. "Don't know what you mean, Chef."

Max and Tomek had spent years trying to swindle each other; it had begun as something of a game, but by the time Max dropped dead in a supermarket while shopping with his wife it had evolved into a full-on battle of wills. As far as Rudi was concerned, that game was now over, but Tomek still seemed to be carrying a lot of momentum, despite the fact that Max had left the field of play for ever. Rudi's insistence on everything being correct and above board appeared to annoy Tomek, and Rafal was the physical expression of that annoyance. Rudi, who had survived attempts at intimidation by much scarier people than Tomek and Rafal, sighed inwardly as he stepped aside to let the two brothers carry the crates into the kitchen.

Where he made the two men stand to one side as, armed with a copy of his order, he went through the delivery crate by crate and item by item while the rest of the kitchen crew turned up in ones and twos and rolled their eyes mildly at the scene.

In the end, everything turned out to be in order. Rudi paid a smirking Tomek in cash, and made sure he got a receipt, and the brothers left. Rudi watched them go, then turned to his crew – who were all standing there staring at him – and said, "What?"

"You need a holiday," Gwen had told him a couple of weeks before over lunch at a restaurant in Kazimierz. "You look terrible."

"Thank you," he said.

"Seriously. You're going to make yourself ill." She was living in Zakopane at the moment, having split with Seth sometime in the past few months. Rudi had made sure everyone was well provided for and she never had to work again, but she was keeping busy copy-editing academic papers written by people for whom English was a second – sometimes a very distant second – language. She was in town to consult with a client at the Jagiellonian University. "What's wrong?"

That was easy to ask; not, perhaps, so easy to answer. On the face of it, there was nothing wrong. He finally had his own restaurant, and even if he had inherited it he'd put enough of his own blood, sweat and tears into the place down the years to feel he'd earned it. He was wealthy beyond most people's dreams of avarice, even if, once again, he had inherited it and was going to have to work out what to do with it sooner or later. He was the uncrowned and unrecognised master of a small but significant percentage of Europe's organised crime... well, maybe best not to think about *that*...

He shrugged. "Whiny ungrateful man is whiny and ungrateful."

She looked at him for a few moments, then rummaged in her bag. "There's something I wanted to ask you about," she said, taking out a little square cardboard box, not more than five centimetres on a side. "This was in my postbox yesterday." She put the box on the table and pushed it across to him.

The box was grey and unmarked. Rudi picked it up and turned it over in his hands, then gently lifted off the lid. Inside, in a little nest of grey tissue paper, was a wristwatch. It was an old-style wind-up watch with a worn leather strap, probably quite cheap when it was manufactured but now something of a rarity.

"I didn't order a watch," Gwen was saying. "And if I did, I wouldn't order *this* one. There was no address on it, nothing at all. Someone just opened my postbox and put it in just like that. I had a quiet word with the post office and they say I haven't had any parcels for eight months."

Rudi took the watch from the box and sat watching its second hand tick unhurriedly around the dial. There were two little buttons on the side which allowed the wearer to use it as a stopwatch.

"So what I was wondering," Gwen said, "is whether this is just someone's idea of a joke, or if it's something I ought to be worrying about."

He turned the watch over. There was engraving on the back. He said, "I can check it out, if you like, but I don't think it's anything to worry about."

"Well, *someone* put it there."

"Security cameras?" he asked.

"The building manager says the cameras in the lobby were down for maintenance for about an hour yesterday morning; software update. And the doors have only logged residents in and out since the weekend."

"Perhaps one of your neighbours is an admirer." He saw the look on her face. "Sorry."

"I can deal with a fucking stalker," she told him.

"Yes," he said. "Of course. Have you mentioned it to the police?" She snorted, and he added, "The Polish police are pretty good with harassment cases these days; it wasn't always like that."

She looked levelly at him. "This *feels* like something to do with..." She searched for the right word, gave up.

He put the watch back into the box, replaced the lid. "I'll ask around," he told her, putting the box down beside his plate.

"*Is* it something to do with...?"

"I don't know yet," he said reasonably, taking up his knife and fork again. "Your *schnitzel* is getting cold, by the way."

After lunch, they stood on the pavement outside the restaurant and Gwen gave him a vigorous hug. "You take care, okay?" she said. "If there's anything I can do, you know where I am."

"Sure," he said, returning the hug.

"And let me know if you find out anything about the watch, yeah?"

He felt the box bulking out his jacket pocket. "Will do."

He was not depressed. He was not – although the possibility had crossed his mind – suffering from post-traumatic stress. What he chiefly was, he had come to realise, was angry. Not at any one specific thing, more a concretion of gripes, set to a low simmer. He was angry with the Community. He was angry with Crispin. He was angry with his father – this had always been true, but it had lately taken on a novel twist. He was angry with the EU Police, whom he surmised were keeping the restaurant and his flat under surveillance although there was no way to be certain; modern cameras were tiny and camouflaged, and his one contact with EUPol had been working for Crispin, or for Molson, or for both. He was angry with his father's inheritance and the burden that had laid upon him. He was angry with the Coureurs, angry that he had wound up being the closest thing they had to a coordinating intelligence. He was angry with the Whitton-Whytes and the mathematicians of the Sarkisian Collective, and he had recently found himself nursing a festering resentment for the Treaty of Versailles. It was a big anger and it contained multitudes, and it was there all the time. In normal circumstances he might have confided in his therapist or his priest, but none of the circumstances of his life were normal, and this also made him angry. Anyway, he wasn't remotely religious, and even if he had been, the thought of confiding any of the details of his life to the Catholic Church brought him out in a cold sweat.

Lunchtime service completed without any serious problems, Rudi took a cup of coffee and a sandwich into the office to sort out some paperwork. The office was really just a cupboard under the stairs, a poky little slope-ceilinged room almost filled by a desk and two chairs and a couple of filing cabinets. He sat down and stared at the filing cabinets for a while, then he leaned down and unlocked the bottom drawer of the desk. He lifted out a pile of old invoices dating back to when Max was still alive, and from underneath them he took the box Gwen had given him.

He put the watch on the desk in front of him and sighed. There had been no need to look at the back; he'd known there would be engraving there, and he'd known it would be a date and the words *To Jan, Manager Of The Year*. He found that the watch also made him angry.

2.

ONE EVENING, A week or so later, one of the customers asked if they could meet the chef. This was not unusual, and Rudi normally went out into the dining room for a couple of minutes for a chat, although recently it had begun to feel like a chore and he had found himself asking Andrzej, his maître d', to convey his apologies, claiming insane busyness.

Tonight, though, Andrzej didn't budge from the door to the restaurant. "The gentleman was very insistent, Chef," he said. "Wouldn't take no for an answer."

"What did he have?" Rudi asked.

"The venison," said Andrzej. "*Rosół* for his starter, poached pears for dessert."

Well, there couldn't be any complaints about *that*, although you could never be entirely certain. "Do we know him?"

Andrzej shook his head. "Never saw him before, Chef. He's English, though."

"Where's he sitting?"

"Table twelve."

Rudi went over to the door, put his shoulder against it, and opened it a crack. Service was coming to an end and there were only a handful of diners still in the restaurant. At table twelve, a tall man in a good suit was raising a brandy snifter to his lips. Rudi took off his apron, tossed it onto a worktop, and went out into the dining room.

As he approached table twelve, the customer smiled broadly and half-stood, extending his hand. "My dear boy," he said in English. "Delighted to meet you." He had a strong West Country accent.

Rudi shook his hand. "What brings you to Kraków?" he asked.

The customer sat down again. "Sit down," he said good-naturedly. "You have time to sit, surely?"

Rudi pulled out a chair opposite the customer and sat. He caught Andrzej's eye and the maître d' vanished back into the kitchen.

"I've never been here before," said the customer. "It's a lovely city. And the food is, of course, excellent." His suit wasn't just good, it was magnificent. He was elegant almost to the point of loucheness.

"What do you want?" Rudi asked.

The customer looked a little disappointed. "I was in the area and thought I ought to drop in. Time we finally met, don't you agree?"

Rudi looked around the restaurant, but none of the remaining customers presented as bodyguards, particularly. He presumed they were somewhere nearby; it seemed unlikely that the head of the Community's security service would be wandering around Europe without any protection at all, but then again anything was possible.

He said, "Well, now we've met."

"To be fair," Michael said, "I have reason to dislike you too."

Andrzej emerged from the kitchen with a small tray on which sat two cups of coffee, a little jug of milk, a sugar bowl, and a small plate of amaretti. He came over and placed it on the table, then went over to deal with one of the other customers.

"So, I don't like you and you don't like me," Rudi said when he'd gone. "Which brings me back to my original question."

Michael took one of the coffees, dropped a sugar cube into it, added a splash of milk, and stirred. "Ambrose is in Prague, signing some damn intelligence sharing agreement or other, I've lost track," he said. "I got bored."

"Oh, please." He'd heard somewhere that the Community's amiable and entirely pliable President was visiting the Czech Republic, but that sort of thing wasn't front page news any more, it was easy to miss. "If it's intelligence sharing you probably drafted it."

Michael smiled and raised his cup in salute. He took a sip. "Oh, that's very nice," he said. "Could you let me have a couple of packets before I go? I'd be happy to pay."

Rudi took the other cup, loaded it with sugar, took out a tin of small cigars and lit one. He didn't bother offering the tin to Michael.

"Cross-border cooperation," Michael said. "Always tricky."

"It must be an absolute grind," Rudi agreed. Prague and Władysław, the Community's capital city, occupied roughly the same space; they were riddled with little border crossings, and the Czechs were finding their patience thoroughly tried by the hordes of intelligence operatives – both professional and amateur – flocking to the city looking for adventure. There had been, Rudi remembered now, some deaths. "Why does Ruston have to be there to sign it?"

"Ceremonial," said Michael. "All the important work was done and agreed upon weeks ago, but Ambrose thought it would demonstrate our goodwill if he turned up and put pen to paper, smooth some feathers." He took another sip of coffee, returned his cup to its saucer. "He likes it here, anyway. We let him go where he wants, within reason. Keeps him happy." He smiled at Rudi. "Anyway. How are you?"

"How am *I*?"

"You seem to have dropped off the radar somewhat recently."

Rudi blinked at him. "I'm sorry," he said. "I find it hard to believe that you were worried about me."

"You were quite a considerable thorn in our side, once upon a time," Michael told him. "Now, all of a sudden, nothing." He picked up his cup again. "I was curious. And as I said, I was in the area."

"I have a restaurant to run," Rudi pointed out. "As you see."

"Yes. Yes." Michael smiled again and looked around the dining room. "Yes. And really very excellent it is, too. How is it going, by the way?"

Rudi stared at him.

Michael took one of the biscuits, examined it for a moment, then dunked it in his coffee and popped it in his mouth and chewed contentedly. "Have you heard," he asked after a few moments, "from Crispin?"

Rudi, who fully expected to be long dead before Crispin next emerged from the bolthole the Sarkisian Collective had built for him, shook his head.

"How about Andrew?"

Rudi shook his head again, although he had a strong suspicion that Molson would be visiting Europe periodically, doing whatever it was he did. "I thought he worked for you," he said, more for devilment than for conversation's sake.

"Andrew has always had something of a *freelance* disposition."

Michael probably had very little idea just how much of an understatement this was. "I haven't heard from either of them," Rudi told him. "I haven't heard from anyone. I'm retired. I run a restaurant now."

Michael raised an eyebrow.

Rudi said, "Do you still run the English intelligence services, by the way?" He said it conversationally, but he said it loudly enough for a couple at a nearby table to glance over at them.

Michael gave him a level look. "We don't run the English intelligence services," he said in a quieter voice.

Rudi raised an eyebrow.

Michael said, "We prevented a catastrophe. Us. You. Our... friends in England. Our friend from the Campus. Please don't tell me it wasn't worth it."

Rudi noted that Michael had omitted Crispin from this jolly band of Musketeers. He tapped a centimetre or so of ash from his cigar into the ashtray and drank some more coffee. He still had a nagging doubt whether the catastrophe had been prevented, or just deferred. The Community still had the original Xian Flu virus, and there were always those nuclear weapons. The progressive faction in the Presiding Authority for whom Ambrose Ruston was a figurehead wasn't going to last for ever, and it wasn't all that progressive to begin with. He wondered what, if any, measures the Directorate was taking to secure the status quo, but it seemed indelicate to ask.

Michael said, "Everything looks lovely, doesn't it? The Community and Europe are friends, we have a seat on the United Nations Security Council. The King of England was in Władysław last month. Imagine that."

Rudi could imagine the security concerns, at least. He winced slightly. "You must have been busy."

"It's not all lovely though, is it," Michael said.

Rudi thought about it for a while, then he shook his head.

"And if you and I can see it, so can others."

"We do have a certain... perspective, to be fair," Rudi said. "But I take your point."

Michael reached into his pocket, took out an envelope, and placed it on the table beside the coffeepot. Then he sat back and looked at Rudi.

Suddenly conscious of what had happened the last time someone had done this to him, Rudi stared at the envelope for a while. With a sigh, he picked it up, lifted the flap, and looked inside. History, he believed, tended to repeat itself first as tragedy, then as farce, but it was often difficult to tell which was which. He removed the envelope's contents and put them on the tablecloth in front of him, several printed colour photographs.

The top photograph was a panoramic view out across some huge open space filled with greenery. Far away, a wall of stepped terraces lined with doors and windows mounted up out of sight. Off to the right on one of the terraces, a group of people were caught in furious motion.

The next few images zoomed in by degrees on the group, and it became obvious that there were actually two groups here, one in modern clothes and one whose dress was subtly old-fashioned and formal. The group in modern clothes was roughly half-and-half men and women, while the other group was all male and seemed to be somewhat older than their counterparts. Right in the middle of the group, someone had been caught in the moment of falling, a bulky man whose pose suggested a puppet whose strings had been cut.

The final couple of shots centred on someone behind and just to the right of the falling man. This was an older man, perhaps in his seventies, and he was standing in front of an open doorway, seemingly in the act of toppling backward, mouth open in an expression of surprise. The very last photograph, grainy and blown-up almost to the limits of usability, framed the face of the old man, and behind him, almost hidden in the darkness of the doorway, Rudi could just make out another face, floating like a phantom, a younger face, almost Mediterranean in aspect.

Rudi rearranged the photos in order, put them in front of him, and gave Michael a hard stare.

Michael moistened his lips and said, "All the surveillance cameras in Mirny went down for about five minutes around the time of the assassination. Except the one that took those." He nodded at the little stack of photos. "That one had already been taken off the system for maintenance. The technician who was working on it was running some sort of diagnostic test, and it took those images."

"Who died?" Rudi said in a level voice.

"Chap named Penrose. An architect. We were at university together, actually. Nice man; wouldn't hurt a fly."

Rudi shuffled through the photos until he had the penultimate one again, the man falling backward into the open doorway. "No one saw it happen?"

"It was chaos, you can see that. All it took was a moment. Security did their jobs; they got our people and the Mirny delegation to safety, gave poor Penrose first aid, but it was too late for him of course. By the time anyone noticed Mundt was gone..." He shrugged.

Rudi sighed. He had been sleeping a lot better, these past couple of years or so, in the knowledge that Herr Professor Mundt was safely dead.

"There was another surveillance breakdown, about an hour later," Michael said. "Just for a few minutes. We're guessing that's when they moved him."

That must have taken some cool, sitting there at the scene for an hour while all the madness was going on outside. Rudi grunted.

"After that, we don't know," Michael went on. "Mirny was in lockdown. We're presuming they put Mundt somewhere safe until the heat died down and then just walked him out, perhaps under sedation, perhaps not – we don't know to what extent he was a willing participant."

"He certainly *looks* surprised," Rudi mused, looking at the photograph. "And you thought it was best if everyone thought he was dead while you tried to find him. And you haven't been able to find him."

Michael said, "We know he tried to contact *Les Coureurs* before. When he was in Dresden."

"You think this was a Coureur operation?"

"It has a certain... craziness about it..."

It did, apart from the bit about carrying out an assassination in order to cover up a jump. That was maybe too crazy, even for Coureurs. On the other hand, Mundt was a prize worth having. "I wouldn't know about it, even if it was," said Rudi.

Michael sighed.

"That's not how it works," Rudi told him. "And if you knew anything about the Coureurs, you'd know that." He looked at the final photo, feeling a familiar sinking sensation. He had never met Mundt, never seen his face before. "You should have told me about this earlier," he said. "When it became evident that you couldn't find him."

Michael let the slur pass. "We needed to be sure you were not involved yourself," he pointed out. "And you and I have not been the closest of friends."

Rudi put the photos back in the envelope, put the envelope on the table, and clasped his hands on top of it. "I'm a chef, not a private detective," he told Michael. "And even if I were, I would be pointing out to you that more than two years have passed and the trail has gone cold. Mundt could be anywhere."

"Professor Mundt was a bit of a *disappointment* to us, really," Michael said. "Uncooperative."

Rudi tipped his head to one side. He'd assumed Mundt had handed his research over to the Directorate at the earliest opportunity. "But you tried to make him... cooperative..."

"The Professor is old, and not in the very best of health," said Michael. "We decided that coercion might be counterproductive. He has no family in Europe, no one he values particularly. We thought it might be better if we just appealed to his better nature."

Rudi thought about that, suddenly seeing the scale of the catastrophe which had overtaken the Directorate. "You decided to be *nice* to him and hope he'd give you what you wanted."

"Blunt force trauma is not always the best way to achieve things."

Mundt's original research had led him to an absurdly low-tech way of manipulating the topology of spaces so that they connected somehow with other, more distant, spaces. The same technique could be used to open and close border crossings between Europe and the Community. The many nations of Europe were still coming to terms with the prospect of the Community driving a nuclear weapon across the border any time they felt sufficiently threatened, but Mundt levelled the playing field – he made a European first strike possible.

"Our contacts in the English Security Services haven't heard any chatter about him," Michael went on, "which is hardly surprising. What you have to keep in mind is that Mundt's discovery doesn't just threaten our security; it threatens everyone's. Any rogue state, any jihadist, could use it to deliver a bomb or worse anywhere in the world and nobody would be able to stop them. So please, if you're about to tell me it isn't your problem, don't."

"It's been *two years*, Michael," Rudi said again. "It would have been hard enough to find him immediately after he was snatched."

Michael smiled at him, then finished his coffee and dabbed his lips with his napkin. "Excellent meal," he said, standing and holding out his hand. "Genuinely."

Rudi sat where he was.

"Oh, one more thing," Michael said, as if it had suddenly occurred to him. "I'd like to speak to our friend from the Campus."

"I'm not a private detective, and I don't reunite old friends." Although *friends* was perhaps stretching things too far when describing Michael and Rupert.

"He's been making mischief," Michael said, his face suddenly quite serious. "On my turf."

"Are you sure it was him?" There was no end to the adventurers and bravos who fancied a little intelligence-gathering in the Community. Most were so comically inept as to be harmless; the Directorate gave them a couple of hard days in a cell and then sent them back to be dealt with by their respective countries. Some, though, had caused real problems, stuff that had actually stirred diplomats into action.

"Someone died," said Michael. "Painfully, and horribly, and over a long period of time. If you see our friend, tell him I want a word, there's a good chap."

"I'm not a messaging service either. Find him yourself."

Michael gave him a long, level look. "I'm sure we'll be in touch in due course," he said. "About one thing or another." And he walked off across the restaurant towards the door.

LATER THAT AFTERNOON, Rudi took a train out to Skawina, and a cab from the station to a bank on the other side of town. The manager received him in his office, and completed a formal identity check before leading him to a lift discreetly hidden away at the rear of the foyer, for the convenience of his shyer customers.

Three floors below ground, the lift opened onto a featureless corridor ending in a vault door. The manager, keeping the smalltalk to a professional minimum, invited Rudi to type his half of the passcode into the touchpad on the door, and then stepped in to complete the sequence with his own string of numbers and figures.

There was a solid thump of bolts withdrawing, and the door swung inward on a hum of servos. Beyond was a room whose walls, floor to ceiling, were lined with little metal doors. Some of these doors were no larger than a letterbox, some were big enough that a Shetland pony could have stood in the space beyond, if it flexed its knees a little.

The two of them stopped before a column of smaller doors, and on one of them they performed a ritual of swiping key-cards, tapping in code numbers, and finally turning brass keys in twin locks. The door opened, and the manager nodded and withdrew to the corridor to wait.

Rudi reached in, grabbed the handle, and pulled out the safety-deposit box within. It was about a metre long, thirty centimetres wide, and ten centimetres deep. He carried it over to a curtained alcove at the back of the room, set it on a table, and used yet another brass key to open the lid.

He did not, out of habit, keep all his secrets in one deposit box. He had about a dozen, scattered all over Małopolska and Upper Silesia and several other countries. Some held paper passports from a number of nations in a number of names. Others had running money, bank bearer bonds in denominations of a hundred thousand Swiss francs apiece. He removed the contents of this particular box and laid them on the table. There was a little notebook, of some antiquity. There was a rather battered old books of timetables from the Great Western Railway in England. There was a rolled paper map.

He unrolled the map on the table and used the books and the end of the box to hold it down. Then he took a deep breath and looked at it.

He was angry about a great many things, many of them with great justification, but there was a single over-arching anger, a kind of ur-anger, and it centred on this map. The first time he'd seen it, he had missed its significance entirely, because it was all but meaningless without the other two items in the box. When he *had* realised what it meant, he had completely missed something else, because again he was missing a considerable part of the puzzle. And when he *had* that part, he had been too occupied to think about how it changed the meaning of the map. It wasn't his fault; he'd been trying to prevent a catastrophe. But he was incandescent with himself, because if he had known just how significant the map was, there were a number of things he would have done completely differently.

3.

"Is it him?"

Rupert tipped the photograph towards the light and squinted. "The last time I saw him was twenty-odd years ago," he said. "It certainly *looks* like him." He handed the photo back and Rudi returned it to the envelope. "Are you sure this isn't a fake?"

"Why bother?" Rudi sat back and looked around Bunkier. The bar was almost empty, its regulars off doing something else somewhere else and the tourists out enjoying the sunshine. As lunchtime came round, it would get busy, but for the moment all was peace and quiet.

"Michael enjoys playing games. It's been a while since you and he butted heads; maybe he's bored. Maybe he has an operation of his own going on."

That had actually crossed Rudi's mind. Get everyone thinking Mundt was alive, have them running around like headless chickens while the Directorate quietly got on with doing something quite different in the background. "He seemed quite genuine," he said.

"Well, yes. That's his job." He drank some beer. "What are you going to do?"

Rudi pouted. "I don't see that we have any choice. If there's even a chance that Mundt is running around..."

"It's been, what, two years? Two and a bit? He could be anywhere."

"Yes. I said that."

"Bloody cheeky, that," Rupert said with a scowl. "Coming here and expecting you to do his work for him. He knew you wouldn't just be able to ignore this."

"To be fair, I doubt he'd have come here if he'd been able to find the Professor himself."

Rupert picked up the other photos and sorted through them,

frowning. "He's got other problems, over there. A lot of English people are emigrating to the Community. *English* English people."

"Ah." For a certain type of English person, the Community was a wet-dream of Return, a place where tricky concepts like ethnic diversity and political correctness and sexual equality had never taken root, and gay rights were a misty fantasy. By any number of modern standards, it was an awful place, and that was probably why so many of the English wanted to move there.

"Some of them have been talking to the traditionalists," Rupert said. "Doing *politics*."

Rudi frowned. The thought of the English driving one of the ruling factions of the Community even further to the right was not a happy one. Contact with Europe had proved awkward in a lot of unforeseen ways.

Rupert put the photos back in their envelope. "You don't think this was a Coureur operation, do you?" he asked, handing it back.

"No, but I've put out feelers, just in case." The problem with the Coureurs was that they were deeply informal and massively compartmentalised. Nobody had an overview, nobody was running things. "I tried to contact Kaunas, but no luck so far."

"This is never going to be over, is it," said Rupert.

"Over?" Rudi raised his eyebrows. "I never expected it to be 'over'; I was happy to settle for armed hostilities not breaking out."

Rupert snorted.

"Have you been over there lately?"

Rupert raised an eyebrow.

"Michael seems to think you've been messing around on his patch. He says someone died."

Rupert shook his head. "He can't pass up an opportunity to stir things up. You know how he is."

Rudi looked at him a moment longer. "Well," he said, "he wants to talk to you about it, so maybe best to watch your back for a while, just in case."

Rupert had been watching his back since before he had left the Campus; it was hardly a stretch to carry on doing that. He was a little disappointed that it had taken Michael this long to get round to looking for him.

"Are you still in touch with the English Security Service, by the way?" Rudi asked.

"The English are involved in this?"

Rudi shrugged. "Michael says not, but who knows? But no, this is something else." He took the watch from his pocket. "This was delivered to me a few days ago by roundabout means. The last time I saw it, I'd just been kidnapped by MI5 or MI6, I'm still not entirely certain which."

Rupert took the watch and turned it over in his hands. "I've been trying to avoid them."

"I know, and I wouldn't ask if there were some other way of doing this. Someone obviously wants to talk; the least I can do is see what they want."

Rupert nodded and handed the watch back. "I'll put out a contact request, but after that you're on your own."

"Thank you."

"What about..." Rupert nodded at the envelope.

Rudi sat back and picked up his glass. "I think we need to send a message."

THE CROSSING

1.

ON THE FIVE hundred and seventy-third day, the Community blockaded the border again.

"Someone has been running contraband," the functionary told Meg.

"Like what?" she asked.

The functionary – she had never seen him before and had not bothered memorising his name because next week it would only be someone else – consulted the file in front of him for a few moments before saying, "I'm afraid I'm not at liberty to divulge that, Colonel."

She sighed inwardly while maintaining an image of cool professionalism, one of many skills the Army had taught her down the years. "So you can cut off our supply line but not tell us why?"

This conversation, or a version of it, had happened twenty-seven times now. The functionaries handled it in varying ways. Some were apologetic, some combative, some slickly diplomatic. This one, younger than most and a little awkward, seemed baffled by the question.

"Contraband, Colonel," he said again. "Our agreement expressly forbids a number of items. You can't expect us to just sit back and allow restricted materials across the border."

The 'number of items' ran to a list seventeen pages long, printed in a tiny, single-spaced font. It was some time since she had read it, but she recalled that the majority of the items seemed to have been included out of spite. She said, "This is intolerable," which was what she usually said at around this point in these conversations.

"We have actually been quite lenient," the functionary said. "Your government seems to find great entertainment in exploring the outer boundaries of our agreement." It was weird hearing diplomatic double-speak coming out of the mouth of someone who spoke like a character from *Poldark*; Meg still hadn't got used to it. "They're constantly trying to get stuff to you which is proscribed. You know it, I know it, they know it. Half the time I think they just do it for fun."

"I'M NOT IN control of what my superiors do," she told him.

"Nor am I, Colonel. The decision is out of my hands. Twenty days without supplies."

Meg glared at him. "I need to discuss this with my Consul."

"Ah." The functionary looked genuinely sad. "I'm afraid that won't be possible. Not at this precise moment."

"Why?"

"It seems there is an ongoing diplomatic incident."

"A what?"

"Everyone is working hard to resolve the situation," he told her. "But until it *is* resolved, all travel by foreign nationals has been banned."

"You can't keep me from consulting with my country's representatives," Meg said, barely keeping a lid on her anger. "This is a violation of our human rights."

"Yes, well," the functionary said, starting to put his documents back in his briefcase. "You'll recall that we are not yet actually signatories to any of your human rights acts."

Meg narrowed her eyes at him.

"I'm sure we'll get round to it," he said, snapping the briefcase closed. "In due course."

*　　*　　*

AFTERWARD, HER DRIVER, Sergeant Foy, took her back to Terminal Two. Foy was built along the same general lines as a large traffic bollard, and he had an evil sense of humour, but today he had the sense to keep a lid on it.

"Tell you what, Sergeant," she said after a couple of minutes. "Let's do a bit of a tour."

"Right you are, ma'am," said Foy.

Meg settled back in her seat and watched Heathrow pass by outside the window. Everything seemed in order. Aircraft were pulled up to their stands, doors locked and fuel tanks drained; there wasn't enough hangar space for all of them. Vehicles were drawn up in lines along the runways to prevent anyone attempting a landing, although the Community had no air force, or indeed aircraft. What they did have, she was assured, were surface-to-air missiles, a number of which were stationed around the perimeter in case anyone became frankly insane enough to try flying out of here.

Over on the north side, they drove down the short stretch of the Bath Road which had come here with the airport. In the early days, the hotels which lined the road had been full of displaced people – passengers, airport staff, office workers – but once the repatriations had started they began to empty. Now they were deserted apart from a skeleton staff of caretakers, the fuel for their emergency generators exhausted and their stocks of food used up. Meg kept patrols especially strong here; locals kept coming over the fence and stealing stuff. Not particularly important stuff – there was a lot of hotel furniture sitting in parlours and dining rooms in the surrounding towns and villages, as well as dining room china and cutlery, and over a period of several weeks some enterprising soul had stripped all the rooms on the first floor of the Radisson of their carpeting – but it was the principle of the thing.

It was impossible, of course, to secure the entire area properly. For the most part, the Community had respected the perimeter – the border, she supposed – but there was the ever-present danger that one day their patience would wear thin. It would be an act of war, but her whole career had been spent preparing for that eventuality, in one way or another.

The whole situation was impossible. Heathrow sat, over a thousand hectares of concrete and machinery and tempting technology, right in the middle of the county of Ernshire, far from any support and yet at the same time tantalisingly close. No one had yet been able to offer her a rational explanation for what had happened. The official English stance was that it was an act of terrorism committed by the owners of the Line – in this at least they and the Community were in general agreement – but as to *how* it had been done, and *why*, those things seemed still to be a mystery, at least officially.

She hadn't felt it happen – none of them had – but she thought she had *seen* it happen. She had been supervising a joint counterterrorism exercise at the airport. An old decommissioned 747 had been parked far from the terminals and a hijacking scenario enacted to test the readiness of the Army, police, airport security, and a number of other emergency services. The whole thing was scripted like an old-style disaster movie and things were just starting to get exciting – a detachment of SAS was preparing to storm the plane – when a flicker of motion caught the corner of her eye.

She'd been standing on the roof of a small building some distance from the action, where she could get an overview and listen in to the radio chatter of the various teams, and she'd blinked, and as her eyelids lifted again, in that fraction of a second, she'd seen something.

Scanning the area with binoculars didn't resolve the mystery. She looked out towards the perimeter of the airport and everything seemed serene, but she knew she'd seen something. She looked again, and still saw nothing, although this time she had the feeling that what she *was* seeing was not quite right. Out at the exercise, the SAS blokes were entering the Jumbo. The sound of flashbangs and gunfire – everyone using blanks, of course – came faintly to her over the breeze, and she should really have been paying attention to that, but some part of her brain said that this was more important.

She lowered the binoculars and took a deep breath, raised them to her eyes again, and looked out into the distance, and all of a sudden the picture sorted itself out in her head. She could no longer see traffic driving along the roads outside the airport. Or buildings beyond the fence. Everything in the near and middle ground was unchanged, but in the distance she could only see fields and trees, and the spire of a church. Closer to, there was a queue of aircraft waiting to taxi onto the nearest runway. It was a long queue, but the runway seemed to be clear. In fact, looking to the west, she could no longer see the lights of aircraft coming in to land. There were still vehicles moving about, and passengers deplaning, but there was a strange, sudden stillness, broken only by the racket being caused by her exercise.

Her radio squelched and a voice said, "Colonel Chapman?" It was not a voice she recognised, and it was not observing radio protocol.

She thumbed the transmit button. "Chapman. Who is this?"

"It's Roger Saunders," said the voice. "Senior control tower supervisor. We've got a problem."

The control tower was considerably taller than her vantage point; the view from the gallery would stretch for miles. "What is it?"

"I don't know, Colonel," said Saunders, more bemused than frightened. "London seems to be gone."

"Yes," said Tom Maxwell. "There is a bit of a spat going on in the capital at the moment. I'm sorry you've been dragged into it."

Meg looked around her office. "What kind of spat?" she said into the radio.

"One of their businessmen has died. They're saying it was murder."

"So? What does that have to do with us?"

"He appears to have died from radiation poisoning. We got him over the border to London for treatment, as a favour. St Thomas's think someone administered polonium to him." Maxwell was a diplomat with thirty years' experience of tough postings. He had been parachuted – almost literally – into the English Consulate in Stanhurst when the scale of what had happened became apparent. Without his support in those early days, Meg thought she would have lost control and never regained it.

"Did you say 'polonium'?"

"They're blaming us, of course. They're calling it a political assassination; the victim was a former member of the Presiding Authority."

"And you didn't think to mention this to me, Tom?"

"It's only blown up in the last eighteen hours or so, but yes, I should have given you a heads-up. I'm sorry."

Meg sighed. "Fucksake," she muttered.

"Things are a bit fraught out here, as you might imagine," Maxwell went on. "They've put a moratorium on travel for non-Community citizens. There's a line of trucks twenty miles long waiting to use the border crossing on the Easterby Road, the one that leads into France. All cross-border rail services cancelled. They're talking about sanctions."

'Fraught' probably didn't even begin to cover it. She said, "What are you going to do?"

"There's nothing we *can* do. Just try to manage the situation and wait for everything to calm down."

Meg got up from her desk and went over to the window. The office had once been part of a suite of meeting rooms in Terminal Two, a place where businessmen in transit could hammer out deals before flying off to their respective destinations. The window looked out onto a car park for airport vehicles, now sinking into darkness. Here and there, lights were starting to come on around the airport, but not many; there was an ocean of fuel for the emergency generators but it wouldn't last for ever, and one of the first things she'd done when the command of the place had been foisted on her was to turn off all nonessential systems and devices.

She said, "Did we kill this bloke, Tom? Just between you and me?"

"I couldn't tell you that even if we had, Meg," he said. The radio link was encrypted, but you could never be sure. "I suspect if we were to kill someone we wouldn't make it quite so obvious that we were responsible. FCO's seething."

Well, of course they were. But the Foreign and Commonwealth Office wouldn't necessarily be in the loop. "Kind of puts my troubles in perspective," she said. "I'm guessing there was no 'contraband'."

"Oh, I wouldn't be so certain of that. We've no end of wingnuts writing in with suggestions about how we can support you. One chap had a plan to smuggle tanks across the border."

"Good lord."

"On a slightly more realistic level, it's not beyond the realm of possibility that someone in the supply chain didn't find a way of hiding a case of automatic rifles or grenades in the latest run."

And lord knew they could use them; they were woefully short of weapons and ammunition. Not that they could put up much of a defence even if they had all the supplies they needed.

"But it's more likely to be about this thing," she said.

"I think so."

"Well, this is a situation just bursting at the seams with joy, isn't it."

"Yup."

"Okay, Tom. Well, thanks for that. Keep me informed, please."

"Will do. And Meg, please don't do anything to make things worse."

"I have no idea what you mean," she said, and broke the connection.

IN THE EARLY days, for all that they still had no idea what had happened and everyone was panicking, it had been a bit like a game. An hour or so after Meg noticed that the scenery beyond the airport had changed, an armoured personnel carrier had driven across the site and parked beside one of the aircraft standing at Terminal Two. Then it had just sat there, surrounded by police and airport security. Because it was a British armoured personnel carrier, albeit without any markings at all, someone alerted Meg.

The first news that something had happened was beginning to percolate across Heathrow. Drivers trying to get onto the M4 and local roads reported that the roads came to an abrupt end in fields or woodland. The Piccadilly Line stations were being evacuated because the number of people waiting for trains which did not arrive had caused dangerous overcrowding. Cut off from the National Grid and reliant on emergency power, large parts of the infrastructure were browning out. But for the most part no one realised that anything had happened.

She'd terminated the exercise and despatched the units under her command to various parts of the perimeter, and she was still receiving garbled and disbelieving sitreps when she arrived at Terminal Two and the besieged APC.

Keeping her distance, she used a megaphone to hail the vehicle, and a few moments later the rear hatch opened and half a dozen soldiers climbed out, dressed in vaguely old-fashioned uniforms and carrying bolt-action rifles. A distant connection suddenly closed in her brain, and she stared at the approaching soldiers and their vehicle with a growing dread.

Their leader was a tall, dreary-looking man in his forties, better-uniformed than the others but with unfamiliar insignia. He marched up to her and without bothering to salute said, "Name's Harrow. Fuck are you doing here?" He had a West Country accent, and Meg's feeling of dread just kept getting worse.

"Colonel Megan Chapman," she said. "Where is *here*, exactly?"

Harrow looked down his nose at her. "Run and get your commanding officer, there's a good girl." Beside her, Megan heard Sergeant Foy groan ever so slightly.

The British Army had come on in leaps and bounds as far as equality was concerned, but Meg had still had to put up with entirely too much of this kind of bullshit during her career. "I *am* in command," she snapped. "What's your rank? Gods help you if you're anything below a Brigadier."

Harrow sketched a languid salute. "Major Harrow." He looked past her to where the Commissioner of the Metropolitan Police, who had been observing the exercise, was standing among a small group of anti-terror officers. The Commissioner's uniform was an impressive landscape of braid and service medal ribbons. "I say," Harrow called. "You there. Are you in charge?"

"*I'm* in charge, Major," Meg said. "And you're under arrest. Sergeant?" This last to Sergeant Foy, who moved with surprising grace for such a bulky man and was moments later standing nonchalantly with Harrow in a chokehold. The other soldiers who had emerged from the APC seemed unwilling to come to his aid, possibly due to the sudden appearance of two dozen SAS blokes from behind a fuel truck. They weren't to know that the SAS weapons were loaded with blanks, and it probably wouldn't have mattered if they had. A hard man was a hard man, no matter which universe you were in. The SAS blokes actually *growled* at them, and that was enough for weapons to be laid on the concrete and hands to be raised in the air.

The carrier's engine started up, at which point several counter-terror officers jumped into the open hatch. There was a lot of shouting, then the engine shut off again.

Meg walked over to Sergeant Foy. Harrow had struggled briefly, but now he was starting to sag in the Sergeant's embrace. She bent over and tipped her head to one side so he could see her properly. "Your move, Major," she said, but he had passed out.

SHE HELD A meeting of team leaders in one of the conference suites, told them what the situation was regarding supplies and the wider diplomatic shitstorm. Everyone was annoyed and grumpy, but they'd all shown a remarkable degree of professionalism considering what they'd had to face and she knew she could rely on them. Her ADC, Lieutenant Warren, took notes, and when the meeting broke up she said, "Any other business, Peter? Please say no."

Warren grinned sadly and turned back several pages in his notebook. If there was one thing Heathrow did not lack, it was notebooks and pens. "The Civilian Authority are asking for a meeting," he said. "Mr Lamb has been in and out of the office all day."

Meg winced. "Noted. Make him an appointment. I'll see him in the morning. Anything else?"

"Looks like we had another incursion. Patrol found a hole in the fence over on the west side; seems to have been cut deliberately."

The patrol's report would be waiting in her in-tray. She could read it later.

"The patrol swept the area and found nothing," Warren read on. "They wired up the hole and posted a guard on it. Sergeant Grey's of the opinion that it was kids."

Local kids were becoming the bane of her life, standing outside the fence and throwing eggs at passing patrols. Her people had orders to shoot only as a very last resort, but if children were starting to break into the site it was only a matter of time before someone got hurt. "Draft a letter to the local Squire," she said. "Strongest possible terms. Copies to all the police stations in the area. For all the good it'll do."

Warren nodded and made a note. Then he sat there not quite clearing his throat, and after a moment she said, "What's up, Peter?"

Warren thought about it – she got the sense that he *had* been thinking about it a lot, and she suddenly knew, with a sinking heart, what was coming. "It's my wife, ma'am," he started. Then he thought about it some more. "It's been almost two years."

"You're thinking about putting in for repatriation," she said.

He nodded and sat there looking miserable. "I'm sorry, ma'am."

"You've been an exemplary officer, Peter," she said in a kindly tone that hid how tired she felt. "I couldn't have asked for a better ADC. Put your papers in. I'll see they're processed as soon as possible, although in the present situation I can't promise when you'll be able to go." Warren nodded with a sort of ashamed gratitude. He didn't want to go, but she couldn't blame him. She looked at her watch. "It's getting late," she said. "Go and get yourself some dinner and I'll see you in the morning."

"Yes, ma'am."

After Warren had gone, she went to the window and stared out into the darkness beyond her reflection. When things had settled down, England and the Community had come up with a programme of repatriation to return the people trapped here to their homes. According to Tom Maxwell, there was an identical programme on the other side of the border, where the area of the Community displaced by Heathrow had turned up. A surprising number of the military, police and emergency personnel had chosen to stay here, and an even more surprising number of civilians. Clearly it was one of the great dreams of modern people to live in an airport, who knew?

The problem with repatriation was that it only worked one way. Under the agreement signed by the English government, there were to be no replacements for personnel who went home, and no one who crossed the border would be allowed to return. After the initial rush of homeward bound refugees, there had been a slow but steady trickle of people suddenly having second thoughts and asking to be allowed back into England. The service personnel had all done a wonderful job, but eventually too many of them would leave and her little kingdom would become unsustainable.

And then what? She'd be forced to hand the place over to the Community? She'd watch Hell freeze over first.

* * *

AN HOUR OR so after the circus with Major Harrow, another APC came trundling across the grass and the runways. This time Meg was sure; the MoD had been selling – bartering, really – a whole raft of nonlethal military equipment to the Community, the majority of it obsolete. These carriers were twenty or thirty years old, had been mothballed out of active service before she ever joined the Army. She could come up with only two explanations for their presence here. Either the Community had invaded England, or she and the rest of Heathrow were in the Community. Neither of these possibilities made any sense at all.

The APC pulled up alongside the first, and Meg and the SAS detachment went out to meet it. After some moments, the rear hatch opened and a single figure climbed out. The figure stood by the rear of the carrier for a few moments, looking around, then it straightened its uniform and walked towards them.

This one was older than Harrow. His hair was oiled back and he had a little David Niven-style moustache. He stopped in front of them and said, "Colonel Rothery, Second Ernshire Light Infantry."

"Colonel Megan Chapman, First Battalion Grenadier Guards." They looked at each other for a few moments, then Rothery put out his hand and Megan shook it.

"Look," said Rothery, "I don't know who you are or what's happening here, but first I need to know about my men."

Harrow and the soldiers who had arrived with him were currently sitting in the cells in one of Heathrow's police posts. Megan said, "They're safe. They haven't been harmed."

Rothery was clearly having as much of an issue speaking to a woman soldier, let alone one the same rank as him, as Harrow, but at least he was making an effort. He said, "I don't understand…"

"You're from Ernshire?" Meg asked.

"We're *in* Ernshire," Rothery said. He looked about him, at a loss for words. "At least…"

"Perhaps we should go inside," Meg suggested. "Is anyone else in the carrier?"

"Only the driver," Rothery said, and he went up in her estimation.

She turned to the commander of the SAS detachment. "Major, would you escort the driver... somewhere he can have a cup of tea and a bite to eat? There must be a staff canteen here somewhere. He's not to be harmed, abused, intimidated or growled at. Don't go into the public areas of the airport with him."

The Major nodded. "Ma'am."

A thought occurred to her. "See if a couple of your blokes can find some civvies in that wardrobe van," she said. A busload of film extras had been brought in to play passengers in the exercise scenario, and with them had come wardrobe and makeup trucks. "Get them to have a wander around the airport and see what's going on. See if they can find a member of staff who'll take them landside for a shufti as well."

The Major saluted and was gone.

"Right, Colonel," Meg said to Rothery. "Shall we see if we can find a quiet corner and try to work out what the fuck is going on?" And the look that briefly crossed his face taught her the second lesson about the Community that she had learned that afternoon. They didn't like hearing women swear. Well, fuck that.

RONALD LAMB HAD been on his way back to Minneapolis when Heathrow was somehow shoehorned into the Community. At the very moment two sections of worlds became superimposed on each other, like a cut-and-paste job in a particularly simple-minded image processing program, he had been sitting in the departure lounge in Terminal Five, nodding hello to the airline's gate agent because they knew each other, saw each other a couple of times a week. Moreover, the gate agent knew that Ronald Lamb was a US air marshal, and that he was carrying – and had a permit to carry – a sidearm.

In the aftermath of what the inhabitants of Heathrow later came to refer to as The Switch, the airport came under military control, because apparently there had been soldiers at the airport at the time and their commanding officer outranked everyone else in the place. This had rubbed Ronald Lamb up the wrong way for several reasons, but chiefly because he thoroughly disliked being told what to do. He was basically his own boss, on his own for hours at a time while in transit, reliant only on his own wits. He did not like the idea of becoming someone else's subordinate.

In the chaos of those first days and weeks, Ronald started chatting to some of the other refugees, and he found enough who were of a similar mind to advance the idea of what eventually became the Civilian Authority, an elected group – democracy was very important to Ronald – which would represent the needs of the civilians at the airport to the military. He had been elected head of the Authority because no one either dared or could be bothered to stand against him. Because he had been elected to represent The People, he liked to think of himself as President – it had been his idea to declare Heathrow a separate nation within Ernshire, a move both London and Władysław were trying to strangle at birth. Meg did not think of Ronald as President of anything. She was in charge because she had all the guns, and until the English government told her otherwise that was the way things were going to stay.

"I understand the Community are blockading our supplies again," Ronald told her.

"They say they've found contraband."

"And you believe them?"

Meg shrugged. "It doesn't matter whether I believe them or not, Mr Lamb. It wouldn't change anything." Ronald preferred to be addressed as 'Mr Chairman'; winding him up was petty and childish but it was one of the few genuine pleasures she had left.

"I find that disappointing, Colonel."

Meg looked down and shuffled some papers on her desk. "Yes, well, life is just one long disappointment, isn't it."

Ronald had lost weight over the past two years – all of them had; Meg had instituted a system of rationing because, though there was a colossal amount of food at Heathrow, it would not last forever. He'd been a big, beefy man with wispy blonde hair when The Switch happened. Now he was just tall and jowly. He said, "The medical supplies qualify as humanitarian aid. They can't block those."

"Of course they can. I can't stop them, Mr Lamb." Heathrow was a literal cornucopia; pretty much anything anyone could ever need was there in large amounts. The problem was that it all belonged to other people. There was tens of millions of pounds' worth of merchandise in the duty-free outlets alone, and there had been a heated debate in the early days, much to Meg's angry disbelief, about whether using any of it counted as looting. To Meg it was a no-brainer; she had a lot of people to look after and she needed those resources. To the retailers it was a vast amount of stock that they would quite like to get back one day, somehow; it was their property and if someone took it without paying that was stealing.

It still hadn't been resolved to Meg's satisfaction. The food franchises had enthusiastically agreed that the refugees use their stock – it was good publicity and the food would only go to waste otherwise – but some of the others had dug their heels in. Meg had ordered all the retail outlets shuttered and guarded by their staff, although a lot of stuff had gone in the interim. That sweater and jacket Ronald was wearing looked like they'd come from one of the Boss stores.

She said, "Mr Lamb, I'm rather busy at the moment. Could you please get to the point?"

"Someone's going to die if we don't get those medical supplies," he said.

Well, she couldn't argue with that. She'd been surprised how quickly they'd run out of even basic over-the-counter medicines like painkillers; more serious stuff like antibiotics was in very short supply and the emergency treatment centres at the airport weren't equipped for large-scale medical emergencies. By a miracle, they'd had no serious injuries, but last year two burst appendixes and a tonsillectomy had had to go to hospital in Stanhurst, which had been a logistical nightmare and only put them further in the Community's debt.

"The people have begun questioning your handling of the situation," Roland went on.

"'The people' meaning you and your friends on the Authority."

He let the insult bounce off him. "Not at all. We held an informal poll and your approval rating is through the floor. You're letting the Community walk all over us and we're not sure how much longer we can allow that to continue."

"Oh?" Meg sat back in her chair and clasped her hands in her lap.

"You're not?"

"You've done your best, Colonel," he said, "but you're tired. The people are thinking maybe it's time you stepped down and let someone else take up the burden."

He wasn't stupid enough to want the position for himself – he knew it was a no-win situation – but she didn't doubt he had someone pliable in mind. Meg swallowed several possible replies, a number of them involving Roland's arrest, and said, "Well, thank you for the heads-up, Mr Lamb. I'll take that under advisement, but you should know that I work for the English government and they're the only ones who can fire me. And until they do I think I'll keep trying to do my best."

He gave her a long, level look, a half-smile on his lips that she wanted to plant her fist on. Finally he nodded and stood up. "I'll see myself out, Colonel. Good day."

After he'd gone, Warren came in from the outer office and found Meg sitting with her head tilted back, staring at the ceiling. "Ma'am?" he said.

"You know, I might put my own papers in, Peter," she said after a few moments, and she was only half-joking.

JACOB ROTHERY TURNED out, certainly by the standards of the officials she was to meet later, to be quite a decent man. He was a career soldier, like her, and although she could see it was a stretch for him he treated her with the respect of a fellow officer. He filled her in on the situation from his side; Heathrow had suddenly appeared out of nowhere in a place where there had only been fields and woods and little villages. From his point of view it was a fiercely dangerous incursion, and he doubted the Presiding Authority would see it any differently.

"This could lead to war, you know," he told her in a small windowless room they had found.

"It's not our fault," she protested. "Not so far as I'm aware, anyway."

"I think the most important thing right now is for no one to panic," he said.

"Gods, yes." Meg thought of the thousands of people now trapped in the airport, unable to go home. She thought of the Community's forces, bewildered and terrified by the event. She thought of what would happen when the two collided. There was no way to control it.

"I've spoken to you, and I'll speak with my commanding officers," Rothery said. "They'll speak to the Presiding Authority and no doubt the Presiding Authority will make a great deal of noise in your government's direction. These next few days are going to be very bumpy, but everyone needs to keep their heads."

"I can't let your forces onto the airport until we've sorted out some kind of understanding," she told him. "If they try they'll be met with force."

He nodded. "Understood. By the same token, I can't let any of your people out to just wander around the countryside."

"Yes," she said. "All right. So that's the first thing. What else?"

"Major Harrow and his men."

"That was a misunderstanding," she said. "I was... unprofessional."

"I suspect if there was any unprofessionalism it was all on Major Harrow's side. I'll make sure there are no repercussions for you."

"Thank you."

"We got off to a bad start, but understandably so, considering the circumstances. If there are going to be hostilities, I'd like to think they were for a better reason than Major Harrow's ego."

"I'd like to think there aren't going to be hostilities at all," she said. It occurred to her that this was the way things had been decided for centuries; not by diplomats and generals sitting around tables but by two squaddies in a windowless room knowing that if they fuck up many people are going to die.

There was a beeping sound, and Rothery said, "Excuse me, please," and took a bulky radio from his pocket. He thumbed a switch and said, "Yes?"

"Major Barnett, sir," said the radio. "There's someone here says he's from the English Consulate."

"Well, that didn't take long," Rothery said. "You'll have asked for his identification?"

"It all looks above board to me, sir."

"Very well." Rothery looked at Meg. "What do you want to do? Go to him or have him come here?"

Rothery had trusted her, had come almost alone. It had been an act of almost absurd bravery; she supposed she owed him the same level of trust. "We'll take your car, Colonel," she said.

They drove out to the perimeter fence, where a section had been cut down to allow vehicles through. On the other side was nothing but farmland as far as she could see, broken up by stands of trees and solid-looking stone-built houses in the distance. She suspected it was going to take a long time to get her head around this.

Beyond the fence, a large number of vehicles and soldiers were gathered. None of them raised their weapon as she and Rothery left the APC, which she thought was a heartening sign.

Among the group of soldiers nearest to the hole in the fence – officers, she was starting to recognise their insignia – was a dark-haired man in his thirties, wearing a suit and looking flustered. He stepped forward and said, "Hello, I'm James Corcoran, English Consul based in Stanhurst. Could you tell me what's going on, please?"

"Colonel Chapman," she said, shaking his hand. "I was hoping you could tell *me*."

Corcoran looked around the group of soldiers. None of them seemed particularly angry, but they all looked twitchy. "Perhaps we could go somewhere more private and discuss this?"

Meg looked at Rothery, who nodded fractionally, and she beckoned Corcoran to follow her onto the airport and several metres along the fence away from the Community soldiers.

"So," Corcoran said when he thought they were out of earshot. "What's... *this*...?"

"I don't know," she said. "We were running an exercise and then all of a sudden we were here. This *is* the Community?"

"Yes, it is, and all kinds of stuff is kicking off. They've closed the borders, no one's getting in or out. They've declared an alert that's only a notch or two below martial law, the Embassy is frankly having a meltdown."

"I need to talk to London."

Corcoran shook his head. "You can't radio or phone in or out. We tried laying a landline across the border but that didn't work. The only way to communicate with the outside world is by diplomatic bag."

"The Embassy needs to get a courier across the border with a message telling London what's happened."

Corcoran was nodding enthusiastically. "Yes, yes, that's being worked on, and my report will go in the bag as well. Have you had any casualties?"

"Not yet so far as I know, but things are going to get a bit unsettled soon."

"Right. I've had no official steer from the Embassy because they still don't know precisely what's happened, but I'd suggest you do what you can to secure the area and keep everyone calm and in one place until we both get word from our superiors."

"Colonel Rothery and I have decided there will be calm," she told him.

"Good," he said. "Good. Is there anything you need?"

"For the moment, I'll settle for someone telling me what's going on. We can worry about everything else later."

"That could take a little while." Corcoran looked out across the vast expanse of concrete towards the distant terminal buildings and shook his head in wonderment. "Well, I didn't expect this when I woke up this morning."

MEG WAS OF the opinion that everyone had got lucky that day almost two years ago. On a personal and professional level she had been lucky that, when she had made an announcement about the situation over the airport public address system, there hadn't been a riot. There were isolated, sporadic disturbances by passengers and members of the public, but police and airport security – themselves traumatised by the news of what had happened – defused them with what she thought was outstanding professionalism.

On a wider level, they had been lucky that England and the Community hadn't started shooting at each other. Couriers had gone to and fro across the border, carrying messages from their respective Embassies, and shortly afterward diplomats made the same journeys and eventually things cooled down and the border crossings were reopened and things returned to normal. Ish.

She had received many visitors in the first few weeks – bureaucrats, representatives of the Ministry of Defence, high-level intelligence officers, the English Ambassador and representatives of the various embassies of those passengers who had been caught in transit. She still got sealed pouches with briefings and instructions, but it had been quite a while since anyone had bothered to come in person.

Her immediate instructions were to secure the airport, its inhabitants, and the enormous amount of machinery, fuel, aircraft and vehicles. The bonded warehouses were to be sealed and to remain sealed until arrangements could be made to transport their contents back to England, although a large consignment of weapons and ammunition – the paperwork and end-user certificates suggested it was bound for Turkey, for reasons which were not dwelled upon – was released into her care. The thinking seemed to be, in those early days, that Heathrow was still English territory, no matter where it was, and nothing much had changed since then.

Shortly after cross-border travel resumed, Tom Maxwell took over at the Consulate, and things began to settle down. There was some excitement when the repatriation programme was finalised, but again that eventually became simply commonplace. It was amazing how you could get used to something as huge and impossible and ridiculous as finding yourself trapped in an airport which had been abruptly transported to a neighbouring universe. It was by no means the worst posting she'd ever had – she'd done two tours in Syria, one of them in Damascus itself – but its open-ended nature wore at everyone. Efforts, she was assured, were being made to find a solution which would allow everyone to go home, but so far nothing had happened. She couldn't blame Warren, or any of her personnel, for wanting to leave.

In the afternoon, when her anger at Ronald Lamb had finally reduced to a simmer, she changed into civvies and went for a walk around the public areas of Terminal Two. If she went out in uniform it was more than likely that someone would recognise her and try to engage her in conversation about some damn thing, but putting on plain clothes was as good as making herself invisible. People tended to see the uniform rather than the person.

She'd tried, as much as possible to keep the civilians out of the private areas of the airport, the warrens of corridors and rooms and storage spaces that passengers never usually saw. She wasn't worried about them breaking things or stealing stuff, particularly, but there were just too many ways for people to hurt themselves and then lie there for hours on end in some out-of-the-way and rarely visited area.

She had, though, opened the doors and passageways between landside and airside and let the passengers mingle with people who had been waiting in Arrivals. That particular distinction, she had decided, had disappeared the moment Heathrow arrived in the Community.

They'd never even tried to do a head count. A year or so after The Switch, she'd received a document from FCO which estimated that there had been a little over a hundred thousand people at the airport when it had been moved. That had seemed a lot to her, but she assumed they had access to airline records and other sources, and it turned out, once the first wave of repatriations ended, that slightly less than fifty thousand had chosen to return. The best guess now, after several return operations, was that about twenty-eight thousand people were still at Heathrow, of whom maybe two thirds were civilians. The Community wanted them all to go home; even if they took every item of value with them from the shops and warehouses, there was no way they could get the aircraft back across the border, and as soon as the last of them got on the bus for Władysław and the train to England the Community's technicians would be all over the airport looking for useful technology. There was still some debate, in Whitehall, about how to tackle this.

From Tom Maxwell, she got the impression that things had gone no better with the area of Ernshire which had erupted in Heathrow's place. Apparently almost all the farmers and villagers and landowners there had decided to stay in England. The Community had accused the English of holding their citizens hostage, so the English had, in the presence of the Community's Ambassador to the Court of King James, taken down the fencing surrounding the anomalous farmland and woods and villages. At which point fully half the displaced citizens had simply walked off looking for a new life and adventures. Most of them came back after a few days, tired and hungry but full of excited stories about the new world they had found themselves in. A few were still in the wind; one had somehow managed to get over the border into Scotland and finally walked into a police station in Wick and asked for a lift back to London.

It was a near-fiasco, no matter which side of the border you were on. It was a miracle they had done as well as they had.

Twenty-eight thousand was a lot of people, but it was a big airport and Meg liked to keep them busy, so Terminal Two this afternoon was deceptively quiet. Walking through the departure lounges, Meg saw a few people sitting around chatting or reading, but pretty much everyone else was out somewhere. She did a tour of the retail outlets, making sure their shutters were undisturbed, then walked up the dead escalator and through Security control and emerged on the landside part of the terminal. Here too there was retail – newsagents, chemists, some fast food and coffee franchises – but not so much. She saw people sitting in one of the coffee outlets, and after a few moments she turned back and went in for a coffee herself.

She sat in a corner with an Americano and idly watched the other customers. One of them was an attractive woman in her early forties, with curly brown hair, and she was engrossed in a sudoku magazine. There was something wrong with her, something that had caught Meg's eye as she passed and made her come back for a better look.

It was nothing she could put her finger on. The woman just looked wrong, out of place. Maybe it was her clothes, maybe it was her hairdo. Maybe the people who had been here for almost two years had picked up some indefinable patina that the woman lacked. But she looked as if she didn't belong. It went without saying that the Community's security services had infiltrated the airport in the early, chaotic days of The Switch, and Meg didn't doubt that there were still deep-cover operatives here, but the woman seemed too obviously *fresh* for an infiltration specialist.

Meg got up and started to walk over to the other woman's table. She'd got about halfway when there was a distant *boom* and everything seemed to rattle fractionally. The other woman looked up from her magazine, saw Meg standing there, and smiled at her. Not the uncertain smile of someone being approached by a stranger. More a smile of apology, of sympathy. The noise of another explosion rolled across the terminal, and another, and now the other people in the coffee shop were standing and wondering what the fuck was going on. The only person still sitting was the curly-haired woman. She didn't break eye contact with Meg. She tipped her head to one side.

Meg turned on her heels and started to run back towards airside, her radio beeping in her pocket. She glanced over her shoulder one last time at the coffee shop, but the curly-haired woman was gone.

2.

AROUND THE END of the second year, Costas began to plan how he would kill Anton.

He didn't mean to go through with it – not in the beginning, anyway – it was more of a thought experiment, something to stave off the boredom. Costas had a lively imagination, and he liked to let it off the leash every now and again for some exercise.

Anton was a tall, pale, ascetic man with swept-back hair and the scars of a serious adolescent brush with acne on his cheeks and forehead. He was neat and tidy, always in full uniform while on duty, even though Costas was the only other person within a hundred kilometres. He reminded Costas a little of the android Michael Fassbender had played in those old *Alien* movies. Prim. Composed. Tightly-wound.

Costas himself was rather less than tightly-wound. He suspected that if Anton were to find a word for him, it would be *slovenly*. Well, fuck him.

Here he came now, uniform scrupulously-pressed and clean, cap on head, rifle slung over his shoulder, making his way from the road to the southbound blockhouse. Costas watched him from an upstairs window and pictured crosshairs superimposed on his forehead.

He heard the door open and close, heard Anton putting his rifle back in the gun safe and locking it. "I'm back!"

"Up here!" Costas called.

Footsteps on the stairs. Anton stepped into the doorway. "What are you doing?"

Costas held up his binoculars and gestured towards the road.

"Anything?" Anton asked.

Costas deadpanned him. It had been over a week since a vehicle had used the crossing. He had begun to believe the world had forgotten they existed.

IN THEORY, THE Line still kept a presence in Europe in the form of an Embassy in Belgium, a small anonymous building in a village just outside Brussels. But the building was shuttered and the doorbell went unanswered. The Line had taken itself into a pocket universe, there to settle a new world. Or something. It had become impossible to winnow truth from fiction in the news.

What seemed inarguable was that all the Line's citizens and rolling stock had vanished, seemingly overnight, while simultaneously a corporation headquartered in the Bahamas had begun recruiting a very large number of security staff around the Continent.

Costas had been a bit down on his luck that year. He'd managed to get a job working nights at a laundry in Milan, and a room in a guesthouse which he shared with a large and solemn and mostly-drunk Ukrainian man who spoke no English, Greek, or come to that Italian either. They mostly communicated via nods and grunts. It was hardly the ideal situation Costas had envisaged when, after four years of trying, he had finally received his visa. He'd lost track of the number of temporary jobs he'd had, and the fear of deportation had become a constant nagging ache. He was acutely aware – you only had to follow the media for a couple of days – that Greeks were just one step up from refugees as far as Northern Europe was concerned. The only purpose of Greece, its economy and political system on their knees, was as a firewall against immigration, and the only purpose of its people was as cheap, easily-replaceable labour.

Even so, the link his sister in Athens sent him didn't at first sight appear to be a solution.

"It's a job, Costas," she told him over the phone. "It pays ten times what you're making now, and it comes with accommodation and citizenship of the Line."

"I don't see how *that* helps," he said. He supposed the Line still existed as a vague entity, but as a functioning nation it had blown away on the breeze.

"It's *citizenship*, you fool," she said, and he could almost feel her anger emanating from the phone. "It's not just a *visa*, or a *work permit*. It's *citizenship*. If you have *citizenship* you have *residence*, and if you have *residence* you can apply for the rest of us to join you."

The rest of us was his sister, her drunken shiftless husband, and their son, who seemed to have stepped out of a movie about demonic possession. It was hardly an attractive prospect. But he clicked on the link anyway, and filled in the form and did an interview via a conference space, and eight months later, somewhat to his surprise, he received word that he was to present himself at a certain office building in Turin. He was to bring one suitcase of personal items, nothing else, but that was hardly a problem; his meagre belongings barely filled a large carrier bag.

In Turin, he found himself in a room with twenty other men of around his age. They were of numerous nationalities – Italians, Turks, Greeks, Albanians – but they all had one thing in common; they all had a single suitcase.

Thirty hours later, Costas was carrying his suitcase across the Arrivals area at Novosibirsk airport, and the following day a minivan dropped him outside a concrete blockhouse out in the middle of the countryside, kilometres from any habitation. A couple of hundred metres away, a high fence seemed to run off into infinity in either direction, unbroken save here, where what probably passed for a main road in this benighted place pierced it.

The Line ran from the Iberian Peninsula to what had once been Russia's Pacific coast, twin railway lines many thousands of kilometres long enclosed by high fences. In places it was almost a kilometre wide, in others it narrowed down to a few tens of metres. It crossed rivers and skirted inland seas and went over or under or around mountain ranges, and in doing so it cut through uncounted thousands of pre-existing roads. Had it not been for a system of tunnels, bridges and level crossings, the Line would have literally divided Europe.

The majority of the crossings were automated, run from a central control room somewhere in Belgium, but human crews had always been needed as a backup. Now, in the wake of the Line's disappearance, it needed caretaker staff, people to guard and maintain the infrastructure in case it was needed again, and people to man the level crossings.

Which placed Costas here, somewhere deep in the forests of Sibir, standing beside the world's longest railway line and watching a tall, painfully-neat Austrian wearing the uniform of the Line coming towards him from the blockhouse. He silently cursed his sister and went forward to meet his new colleague.

Costas cooked, because Anton could not. There were many things Anton could not do. He could not cook. He could not lift heavy weights. He could not go outside in snowy weather, or in the rain. He could not do the cleaning because detergents brought him out in a rash. What he could do was operate computers. Anton was a wizard when you put him in front of a keyboard, which made him the obvious choice to run the crossing. As the gates never closed and they got, even when it was busy, no more than five vehicles a day passing through, this left him plenty of time to lounge about reading or shining his boots or snoring, while Costas got on with all the other work.

It was Costas's opinion that Anton had never done a day's honest work in his life before, but it turned out that he had actually worked at the Line Consulate in Pozna more than a decade previously, and had lost his job – and his citizenship – because someone had broken in and stolen something. This job was the first step towards unblotting his copybook and eventually joining his former colleagues... wherever they had gone, rumours abounded.

Had Costas liked Anton, this might have been quite a sad little story, but as it was he did not, and he couldn't have cared less about Anton's attempts to rejoin the Line. He had signed on for a five-year contract and he suspected he was going to spend all of it right here with this almost-useless and appallingly prissy man.

Dinner that night was elk stew. One of the locals – it was a loose term; he lived fifty kilometres away – did some poaching on one or other of the wildlife preserves dotted around the area, and every now and again he passed through in his whistling wreck of a gas-turbine-powered truck and dropped off a haunch of something or other. Anton professed himself unable to even look at raw meat, although he was more than happy to tuck into the finished product.

"The wolves are back again," he said between spoonfuls of stew.

"The wolves never went away," Costas grunted.

"It's not our job to cull them," Anton grumped. "We're not here to control the local animal population."

"We are if you don't want to be eaten the next time you go out to fix something at night," Costas pointed out. Which was never going to happen anyway, because going outside at night was something else Anton could not do. "How many did you see?"

"Three. Out in the woods on the other side of the tracks. They didn't seem to want to approach me."

Well, Costas couldn't fault them for that. He said, "We have to do something about them, Anton."

"Like what?"

"I don't know. Do I look like an expert on wolves?"

"We should report it to Turin," Anton said. "Perhaps they will know what to do."

Costas had not encountered anyone, in his brief visit to Turin, who looked like an expert on wolves. "I'll talk to Dima, next time he passes through."

"The poacher?" Anton glanced down at his half-empty bowl of stew.

"He *lives* in this fucking wilderness, Anton. He'll know what to do. Or someone we can call."

Anton looked unconvinced. He didn't like Dima, although this did not extend to the meat Dima provided. "We should go through official channels."

Costas snorted. "*Official channels* can barely keep us supplied with toilet paper. You think they're going to drag all the way out here to deal with some *wolves*?"

"They have a duty of care to their employees," Anton went on doggedly. "Suppose we're killed? Who will care for the crossing then?"

Costas had no illusions about that. They were expendable. Southern Europe was awash with economic migrants; if anything happened to him and Anton, someone else would just be hired in their place. Maybe it had already happened. Maybe they weren't the first crossing keepers out here, maybe somewhere out there in the woods there were a couple of rough graves. Maybe more than two.

"Fine," he said. "Put it in the report, we'll see who's right." As if Anton would do anything else.

Sometimes, at night, if the weather was warm, Costas took a chair out onto the loading dock beside the blockhouse and sat looking out across his little kingdom. There were lights, in the Line. Great blue-white lamps set on thirty-metre poles spaced about a hundred metres apart. The lights, and the fence, ran away to the west as far as the eye could see, and Costas imagined a line of light that crossed the whole of Europe and finally, at the very end, illuminated some lucky bastard watching a crossing on Portugal's Atlantic coast.

East, the fence carried on for ten or fifteen kilometres, then climbed the steep slope of a range of wooded hills, protecting the place where the Line entered a tunnel. The road – on the maps, it didn't appear to actually lead *from* anywhere *to* anywhere, it was just *there* – ran parallel to the fence for some kilometres, then made an abrupt turn and crossed the Line north-to-south. There were enormous gates in the fence which opened inward – and similar gates on the opposite fence. When they were fully open the opposing gates locked together and formed a tunnel of wire almost a hundred and fifty metres long, The gates had been open when Costas arrived, and they had remained open ever since.

There was no way to tell if there was anyone, or anything, inside the fence. The mesh was so dense that it was like looking through fog. Costas occasionally went down and stood right up against it, his face pressed to the wire, trying to see the other side, but all he was able to make out were vague shapes that could have been machinery or low buildings. He had considered climbing one of the trees near the blockhouse and trying to look over the fence, but in the end had decided it wasn't worth the effort. Two sets of track, of a gauge unknown anywhere else in Europe and probably in the world, crossed the road, and that was all he really needed to know.

They were guarding a railway line.

There were two blockhouses, squat brutalist structures like little postmodern ziggurats. One was on one side of the fence, beside the southbound carriageway of the road, and one was on the other, beside the northbound. He and Anton were required to maintain both of them, but they lived in the northbound one. There was a big communal room on the ground floor, with a kitchen and a cheap entertainment set, and half a dozen bedrooms on the second floor. The roof sprouted an array of dishes and aerials. A smaller room off the main one housed all manner of screens and terminals and devices for observing and operating the gates in the event of a failure of the automatic systems. In the event of a catastrophic failure, there were protocols in place to open and close the gates manually, but Costas didn't like to think about that.

"Costas, there are no wolves here," Dima said a week or so later. "There was a sickness. They all died. Killed my dog, too. Fucking good dog." He waved a hand to indicate the general area. "You've noticed maybe I have no dog? That's why." He shook his head and said, "Fucking good dog," again.

"We've seen them," Costas protested.

"I don't know what *that* guy saw," he said – they shared the same low opinion of Anton – "but you, my friend," Dima soft-landed a hand on Costas's shoulder, "I think you have been out here in the forest for too long."

Dima was a large, loud man in a filthy camouflage suit and a battered and ancient baseball cap whose logo had, in some distant past, been torn off, leaving a barely-paler octagon on the faded fabric. He had a hunting rifle with an extremely good optical scope slung over one shoulder, and ex-NATO combat boots on his feet. Most of his face was hidden by a great black beard shot through with grey, which parted when he spoke to reveal a mouth full of ruined teeth.

Nominally, he was the Mayor of the area, or whatever they called it round here. Costas could only speculate in wonder what the other candidates had been like. He'd turned up a couple of days after

Costas arrived and solemnly presented each of them with a bear claw, drilled through at one end and strung on a leather thong. Costas had wondered if this was some obscure joke, but he wore his anyway. He later found Anton's in the garbage.

Anyway, Dima was a good person to know, above and beyond the meat he kept bringing them. He was also head of the local militia, some flavour of Orthodox preacher, a botanist, and the regional correspondent for a number of news sites. In addition, he owned a hotel and a chain of grocery stores.

"So, Costas my friend," he said, "I got to ask you, have you seen any strangers about?"

Costas looked around them. "You're kidding, right?" Dima's was the first human face he had seen, apart from Anton's, in two days.

Dima looked grave. "You sure about that?"

"We had a car through here the day before yesterday. Old man Golovkin and his fucking Hummer. He almost drove off the road."

"Golovkin drinks too much," Dima allowed, which was quite a statement – as far as Costas could ascertain the only entertainment out here was drinking, driving like a lunatic, or shooting things. "But nobody else?"

"No. Why?"

Dima considered it for a moment. "Got some guys in town," he said, meaning the regional administrative centre almost a hundred kilometres away, a place whose name Costas could not pronounce. "New guys. *Professional* guys, if you take my meaning."

Costas did not.

"I'm thinking maybe they're juju men."

"What?"

"Juju men," Dima repeated. "Like in *Tinker, Tailor, Soldier, Spy*, you never read that?"

Costas shook his head.

"Well, you see anything unusual, you let me know, yeah?"

"Sure," Costas said, nonplussed.

After Dima had gone, Costas went back into the blockhouse. Anton was sitting in the control room, cycling through the hundreds of cameras stationed up and down their section of the fences. "I'm looking for wolves," he said when Costas came in.

After his conversation with Dima, Costas was no longer sure *what* he had seen a couple of months ago. It had been dark, and it had been Anton who had said it was wolves. "Forget about the fucking wolves," he said. "Have you seen any *people* on these things?" He gestured at the big paperscreen on the wall above the consoles, its image tiled into a mosaic of camera views.

"People?" Anton sounded baffled. "No."

"Dima was asking. He says there are strangers in town."

"Strangers?"

"Juju men, he said."

"What, like witch doctors?" Anton swivelled his chair to look at his colleague. "What would witch doctors be doing out here?"

Costas regarded Anton soberly. *One punch to the throat*, he thought, *destroy his windpipe, take his body deep into the woods and bury him.* He said, "I don't think that was what he meant."

Anton was starting to look panicked. "We should report it."

Costas shrugged. "It's just Dima. You know what he's like."

"I heard people have been cutting through the fences, getting in and stealing stuff."

That would hardly be a surprise. The scrap value of the fencing alone must be astronomical. For a while, the Line's reputation and the sudden and baffling nature of its disappearance had kept scavengers away, but that wasn't going to last for ever. "Can you not do anything without asking Mummy about it first, actually?" he asked. "Report it, don't report it, I don't care. Just keep an eye out."

"Right." Anton turned back to the screen.

Costas went back outside and stood on the loading dock, staring at the slick grey metal barrier of the fence . He didn't seriously think anyone was coming to rob the Line. And even if they did, so what? He wasn't about to get between someone and a couple of kilometres of trackside cabling or a few sections of rail. They were replaceable; he was not.

IN THE EVENT, nothing happened. Not that day, nor the next, nor the one after that. Anton sat in the control room staring at the camera feeds, and saw nothing. Not even a wolf. Eventually Costas forgot about Dima's juju men.

"We still haven't decided what to do about the wolves," Anton said one evening over dinner.

"There are no wolves," Costas said. "All the wolves around here are dead. We imagined it."

"I know what I saw."

Costas sighed and looked at his plate. Tonight's dinner was a spaghetti carbonara made with a bag of minced venison he'd found in the freezer. He couldn't be bothered to make the effort to cook anything else. "Dima said there was a sickness," he said as if explaining it to a five-year-old. "All the wolves died. And his dog."

"Maybe they escaped from one of the reserves."

Costas looked at Anton and opened his mouth to say something, and at that moment they heard the engine of a car out on the road. It sounded like a larger and better-maintained engine than most of the vehicles round here carried, but that wasn't the unusual thing about it. What was unusual was that it wasn't alone. While he stared at Anton, Costas counted the sound of three, maybe four vehicles coming up the road towards them. He got up and went over to the window, and saw several sets of headlights in the distance.

"What?" said Anton. "What is it?"

"Get in the control room," Costas said. He pressed the button that dropped the shutters over the windows and doors, then went over and opened the gun locker. Inside were three shotguns and two rifles. He took one of the shotguns and a box of shells and followed Anton, loading the gun as he went.

On the screen, four SUVs were coming up the road towards them. They were identical, black, and looked brand-new as they passed in and out of the illumination from the light poles inside the fence. Anton zoomed one of the cameras to try and look into the cars, but the windows were not only tinted but mirrored. That last little detail was the one that convinced Costas they were in trouble. He reached over Anton's shoulder and grabbed a loose-leaf binder from the shelf above the consoles. He opened it, flipped through the pages, found the one he was looking for, and ran a finger down the list of numbers. He picked up the phone handset from the desk and dialled quickly.

After a few moments, Anton swivelled his chair to look at him. "They're not answering," Costas said.

"Perhaps they went home for the night," Anton said. Costas glared at him, hung up, dialled again, Same thing. He consulted the list again and tried another number. Then another.

"Right," he said. He dropped the phone and binder on the desk and went over to a little plastic box mounted on the wall. He flipped the cover up, revealing a fat red button. His briefing, in Turin, had not taken very long, and most of it had been taken up by stating and restating the instruction that he was not to press this button except in the direst of emergencies. He put his thumb on it and drove it home, heard Anton gasp a little behind him.

Nothing happened. No alarms, no flashing lights, no sign that the button had done anything at all. Hopefully, many thousands of kilometres away, someone was being alerted that something was in the process of going terribly wrong out in the wilds of Sibir.

"Costas," Anton said.

He turned from the button. Anton was watching the screen again. He'd cancelled all but one of the camera views, and expanded this one to fill the screen. It showed the four SUVs. They had pulled up and stopped on the other side of the road, a few metres from the crossing. No one seemed in a particular hurry to get out of them.

"What are they doing?" Anton said, and then every console on the desk lit up. "Fuck," Anton said in an awed tone of voice.

"Why is it doing that?" Costas asked, but he was distracted by something on the screen. Outside, lights mounted along the top of the fence had come on and started to blink. "What's happening?"

"There's a train coming," Anton said.

"That's impossible." And yet, as he watched, the gates seemed to stir themselves from a long slumber. They jerked and shuddered, as if testing their strength, and then started to swing smoothly closed. "Fuck," said Costas.

It only took a couple of minutes for the gates to close, and then the fence seemed completely blank and everything became still and quiet again, apart from the flashing lights. Still the cars sat impassive at the side of the road.

Anton was reading the monitors. "Something's coming," he said.

He switched to another camera, tiled its view beside the one of the crossing. The new camera was mounted on a pole not far from where the Line ran into the tunnel. The pole wasn't tall enough to actually see over the fence, but after a few moments a great cloud of what seemed to be smoke or steam billowed up from the other side, illuminated from within by a powerful light. The cloud began to move westward towards them.

"Maintenance engine," Anton said, deciphering serial numbers on one of the screens. "They're clearing the track."

After almost two years of disuse, the track must be littered with debris. Anton switched from camera to camera, following the maintenance vehicle's progress until it reached the crossing and passed on without slowing down, leaving a great mist of vapour in the air behind it. Still, the people in the cars waited.

More lines of text appeared on Anton's monitors. "Three-car train," he said. "Locomotives front and rear." On one camera, another set of lights emerged from the tunnel. Again, Anton followed its progress until it began to slow and finally pulled to a halt actually on the crossing. Costas imagined he could actually feel the vibration of its fusion-powered engines through the soles of his boots.

And then everything was still again, wreathed in vapour in a great pool of light far out in the hinterland of Siberia. No one moved, nothing happened.

"Maybe they're picking somebody up," Anton said.

Costas didn't say anything. The thought which had been going through his mind ever since the maintenance loco had arrived was that whatever this was, it was all happening in the middle of nowhere, in the middle of the night. He had a suspicion that the road had been blocked in both directions, a kilometre or so in either direction, on the off chance that someone passed by. It was as clandestine as it was probably possible to be, considering you were talking about trains. And he and Anton were the only witnesses.

Abruptly, the passenger doors of the SUV opened and four men stepped out. They were all wearing suits and they were all carrying assault rifles, and their faces were bulky with image-amplifiers. They moved quickly but without hurry to the fence and took up position.

There was a smaller gate in the middle of the main left-hand gate. It swung open, and several more armed men emerged, and then a group of unarmed men and women in casual clothes. The gate closed behind them, and they all climbed into the SUVs, which made quick, expert turns in the middle of the road and drove back the way they had come.

After a couple of minutes, the train started to reverse up the track towards the tunnel, and shortly afterward the maintenance engine passed by again, and a minute or so after it had gone the gates of the crossing started to open again. When they were fully open and locked, the blinking lights on the fence suddenly went dark.

Costas and Anton stayed where they were for a long time, but eventually Costas went to the front door and raised the shutters and went outside.

There was a faint smell of steam and chemicals on the night air, but apart from that there was no sign that anything had happened here tonight. Costas walked out into the middle of the road and looked in the direction the cars had gone. He couldn't hear their engines, but he could hear, far away on the edge of audibility, the sound of a wolf howling.

3.

JUST OUTSIDE BRUGES, there was a hotel with no name. Housed in a fine old building set in a hundred hectares or so of parkland, it did not advertise its presence. For generations, it had belonged to an aristocratic family. During the Second World War the Wehrmacht had used it as a field headquarters, and the US Army as a hospital. In the 1950s, it had been, for a period, a sanatorium. And then, quietly and without any fuss, it had disappeared. It was not to be found on any map or satellite photo or official document. The perimeter of the estate, thickly wooded, hid the house from view. Every now and again, historians or architecture students would turn up at the front gate – oddly hard to find down several twisty, narrow lanes – to be met by a polite man at a sentry kiosk who informed them that the house itself, alas, had fallen into ruin and been demolished at the turn of the century and the site was being used by the Defence Ministry. The airspace above it was restricted, and drones, passing overhead either innocently or with intent, were shot down. The house was *resistant*. It turned back enquiry.

It was a place where the leaders of warring nations went to discuss how catastrophe could be avoided, or encouraged. Billionaire businessmen thrashed out takeover deals that could alter the geopolitics of entire regions. It was deniable, neutral ground, a place where the real business of the world could take place, far from the public eye.

Its owner arrived early one afternoon with a group of aides. He was slightly-built and of medium height, and he had long auburn hair bound in a ponytail, and if there was a look of annoyance on his face it was because he had expected never to see this place again.

The little group passed straight through the foyer – there was, of course, no check-in procedure – and took a lift to the top floor, which comprised a single suite of rooms. The hotel's owner led the way down a richly-carpeted corridor to a door at the end, opened it.

The room beyond was furnished – very nicely – as a sitting room. Its tall windows looked out on the parkland surrounding the house, and there was a coal fire – in defiance of Flemish environmental regulations – burning in the grate to take an edge off the unseasonal chill in the air. Arranged by the fireplace were three comfortable armchairs, complete with side tables. Sitting in one of the chairs, smoking a small cigar, was an unremarkable man with grey in his hair.

"This is a non-smoking place, you know," Crispin told him.

"Then you should report me to the authorities," Rudi said. He didn't get up to shake hands.

Crispin thought about it, then he said to the other members of his group, "Okay, guys, go find yourselves some lunch. I'll have a club sandwich and a coffee." He looked at Rudi. "You?"

"I ate in town."

"Very wise. The food here's terrible but we can't find a good chef. They can't cope with all the NDAs; chefs hate to be cut off from publicity. You want a job?"

"I have a job."

"Mm." Crispin stepped into the room as his colleagues withdrew – all but one, a tall, raffishly-handsome man in his mid-to-late thirties with fair hair and an amused smile on his face. He closed the door behind them, and they walked over and sat down in the armchairs by the fire. Molson and Rudi exchanged nods of greeting.

"So," Rudi said when they were settled, "I expect you're wondering why I asked you here today."

"I should have got you to drag your ass all the way out to Sibir," Crispin told him. "*That* trip would've wiped the smile off your face."

"It took you long enough."

"You're lucky I didn't just send an attorney to see what you wanted." Crispin took a packet of cigarettes from his jacket pocket, lit one, and sat back in his chair. "Okay. Now I'd like you to explain how blowing up a half dozen airplanes at Heathrow is in any way supposed to help anyone. And don't insult my intelligence by denying it, please. I have people there and they spotted that girl of yours, and she wouldn't have been there alone."

Actually, Gwen had turned out to have a talent for demolitions, but Crispin was right; she hadn't been there without support. Rudi said, "You weren't answering your phone." Out of the corner of his eye, he saw Molson smile.

"Not funny," Crispin told him. "Not funny at all. Now there's a full-scale diplomatic incident over there and I'll have to lean on people to defuse it."

"And she's not 'my' girl," Rudi added.

"Whatever. Okay, you got my attention. Well done, I'll leave you a forwarding address this time. What's going on?"

Rudi took an envelope from his pocket, removed a wad of photos, and handed them over. Crispin looked through them once, then again, this time handing them one by one to Molson. "What am I looking at here?"

Rudi was watching Molson. As he reached the final photograph, a brief and very faint expression of pain crossed his face. Rudi said, "They didn't tell you?"

Molson shook his head. "No." He shuffled the photos, handed them back to Rudi. "No, they didn't."

This in itself was interesting. If the Directorate, for whatever reasons, had stopped trusting Molson, it was going to make it all the more difficult for him to operate in the Community.

"Hello?" Crispin said, raising his hand. "Hi. I'm still here and I still don't know what the fuck this is all about."

"Herr Professor Mundt is not dead," Rudi told him.

Crispin closed his eyes and pulled a face as if someone had just driven a spike into the top of his head. "Gah," he said. He opened his eyes and made a gimme gesture. Rudi gave him the photos again and he went through them one more time. "So," he said, "who's got him?"

One of the great things about dealing with Crispin and Molson, Rudi found, was that he didn't have to explain stuff to them. "Someone who's not averse to carrying out a murder in order to cover up a kidnapping," he said.

"Someone with brass balls," Crispin mused. "I heard about that business in Mirny." He had, of course, heard about it from Molson, who had heard about it from Michael, who had not been telling him the absolute truth. "Any sign they've been using him?"

Rudi shook his head. "Not that I can tell, no."

Crispin looked at the final photo again, held it up to the light and tilted it this way and that, looking at the face behind Mundt's. "And this guy?"

"Unknown."

"It's been two years, right?"

"About that, yes." Crispin could be forgiven for being a little shaky about the date; as far as he was concerned, it was only a couple of weeks since he and Rudi had last seen each other.

Crispin flicked his cigarette end into the fire. "Well," he said, "we can't have *that*."

"The Community have been trying to find him, but they don't have the resources in Europe," Rudi said. "They came to me because they think I do. But I don't, not for something like this."

Crispin nodded. "What do you want?"

"I want to play with your toy in Dresden."

Crispin nodded again. "Yeah, I figured." He stared into the fire for a while. "Okay. Done."

"The people who have him aren't going to give him up without a struggle."

"You can hire your own hoodlums; Christ knows you've got enough money. What are you going to do if you find him?"

"I haven't decided yet. Do you want him?"

Crispin made a rude noise. "I've got my own Professor."

"How is Professor Charpentier, by the way?"

"That guy is just pissed off *all the time*. I'm tempted to give him back to you."

"No you're not."

Crispin chuckled. "No," he said. "I'm not." He sighed. "Right, so that's sorted. Keep me in the loop on this, okay? I'll give you a contact number; we can't keep on communicating via international incidents. One of my people will be in touch with permissions for Dresden." He glanced at Molson. "What about you?"

Molson had been deep in thought ever since he had seen the photos. "The fact he hasn't been used is suggestive," he said. "He may well be dead. He did have a heart condition."

"That would be unfortunate for whoever went to all that trouble to snatch him, obviously, but I'm not going to be sure this time until I see the old bastard's corpse, and identification DNA. Also," he turned to Rudi, "I want a full go-to on whoever took him."

"That goes without saying." They had always suspected there was another player out there somewhere. Opinions differed on who they might be, and they had proved elusive.

"Okay, then." Crispin nodded to himself. "Anything else?"

"I wouldn't mind a quick word in private," Rudi said.

If Molson was hurt by this, he gave no sign. Crispin said to him, "It's okay, Andrew. I'll catch up with you downstairs. Let's go to Paris, yeah? We might as well have a decent meal while we're here."

When Molson was gone and the door was safely closed again, Crispin said, "You ought to give that guy a break."

Rudi was still some way up the road from resolving his feelings about Molson manipulating him. "I'll take that on advisement."

"Hm. So, say what you have to say, I'm starting to get hungry."

Rudi got up and went over to one of the windows and stood with his hands in his pockets, looking out over the parkland. "Some years ago, I was involved in a... caper, I can't really call it anything else, to steal something from a Line Consulate."

"Yeah," Crispin said, "I remember that. I had the whole staff of that place redeployed to the most godawful places I could think of."

"It was completely off-piste, unofficial. I still don't know the whole story because the person who actually stole the material is dead." He turned from the window. "Was that you, by the way?"

Crispin shook his head. "Guy was away on his toes; we couldn't find him. He was good."

"Not good enough, in the end."

"If you're expecting me to apologise for you being interrogated, you can forget it."

"I was tortured," Rudi said evenly.

"Interrogated, tortured. I know you were just a patsy, but you were still involved."

Rudi waved it away. "Doesn't matter any more. Anyway, eventually I got the material back." He saw the look on Crispin's face and he added, "I'm not going to tell you how, and I'm not going to tell you where it is now. It stopped being important when the Community made itself known to the wider world anyway, right?"

"You can say that," Crispin muttered. "It wasn't stolen from you."

"The person who stole the material called it *proofs*. Proofs of the existence of the Community. An old train timetable, an encrypted notebook, and a map of the Line – and yes, I know you know what was taken, but let me do this step by step, okay?"

Crispin made an 'after you' gesture.

"The map was the thing that did it for me," Rudi went on. "The thing that made everything click together. The notebook was decrypted by then, and it was... oh, I don't know, I thought it was *fiction*. And then I had a closer look at the map and I realised there were branches coming off the Line that didn't seem to lead anywhere, but they were marked with the names of towns in the notebook. That's when I suddenly realised what I had."

Crispin was sitting very still all of a sudden.

"I didn't know about you, of course, back then," Rudi went on, coming back to the fire and sitting in his armchair. "I just thought the Line and the Community were connected somehow. But there was too much other stuff going on, so I parked the idea, and as the years went by it sort of faded away into the background." He lit another cigar. "But after that business a couple of years ago, it suddenly occurred to me to wonder. If you and the Community had been poking at each other for over a century, blowing things up and generally being dickish towards each other, why were there branch lines into the Community?"

There was a knock on the door. A waiter entered with a tray on which were Crispin's club sandwich and coffee. He put the tray on the table beside Crispin's chair and left. "That took a long time!" Crispin shouted after him. "Tell the kitchen someone's going to be looking for another job!" He looked at Rudi. "Yeah, okay. Carry on showing your working-out."

Rudi smiled. "I went out and had a look at some of the branches last year. Some of them are really quite long, aren't they, for branches. And very straight. And they're all dead ends. No border crossings, not even a set of buffers. Just a set of rails running right up to the fence."

Crispin pouted.

"Mundt told Rupert he'd discovered the spatial tunnelling thing by accident; he spun him a story about it being a hobby, something that had started because he was interested in how topology affects human perception. And from the spatial tunnelling, he spun off a way to open and close the border between Europe and the Community. But that was a lie, wasn't it. It was the other way round. Mundt was working for you the whole time, trying to open the border at those branch lines. It was the spatial tunnelling that was the spinoff."

Crispin sighed. "I will give him credit," he said, "he is very sly."

"The map that was taken from the Consulate in Pozna. It's an *invasion* map, isn't it."

Crispin folded his hands in his lap and dropped his chin onto his chest and looked into the fire for so long that Rudi thought he'd nodded off. Then he said, "A Line train can top two hundred kilometres an hour, on the straight, with a long enough run-up. And they're carrying fusion tokamaks. So no, not really an invasion."

Despite himself, despite everything he had been through over the past decade or so, Rudi felt a thrill of horror. Everyone had seen, in no uncertain terms, what an exploding Line locomotive was like. "You're kidding."

"We'd have solved that problem, if we'd had to. Totally dislocated their stiff upper lips. They'd never have seen us coming."

Rudi sat back in his chair and looked into the fire. "Good lord," he said.

"Oh, come on," Crispin chided. "They nuked their own territory and let a pandemic loose over here. It's not like they're Switzerland or something."

"You didn't tell Mundt about this, did you?"

Crispin grunted. "Hell no. He was just doing proof-of-concept stuff, really far-out abstract mathematics. We were never going to let him out in the field and find out what it was for, but then he decided to erase all his work and make a run for it."

"And you couldn't find him, so you needed someone else to do the work for you."

Crispin nodded. "Andrew told me the story about the Sarkisian Collective and your dad and the trust fund and we figured that if any of the Sarkisians were left, they'd do instead. Then when we had Charpentier we realised we didn't need to bomb the Community; we could just erase it."

Rudi took a few moments to process all this, fitting the bits together in his head. "Okay. But if you'd lost Mundt and his research, and you didn't have Charpentier yet, how did you pull off the thing with the Realm?" A square mile of the Community had, in similar fashion to Heathrow, erupted into Luxembourg a year or so before the Heathrow Event.

"We didn't."

"You didn't."

Crispin shook his head. "It suited us to let people think it was us, but it wasn't."

Rudi said with exaggerated calm, "Have you any idea *who* it was?"

"Nope."

Rudi counted to ten. Then he did it again. "Do you not think," he said quietly, "that you could have told me there was someone *else* out there who could do that?"

"It wasn't your problem. We're still looking for them. Maybe it's the same guys who have Mundt. Maybe you and I are working opposite ends of the same problem." He nodded at the little pile of photographs on the table beside him. "Maybe this guy's our way in."

Rudi rubbed his face. "Jesus Maria," he muttered.

4.

IT WAS A LONG time since he'd visited London, and the last time he had hardly been in sightseeing mode anyway. Nothing much seemed to have changed. The place was still bustling, the shopping streets crowded. Of all the European capitals he had seen, London was the one which seemed to have recovered most from the Xian Flu.

From the Eurostar terminal at St Pancras, he caught a Northern Line train up to Highgate, and then a bus to Muswell Hill. It was a nice day, and a fresh breeze was blowing across the heights overlooking central London as he walked unhurriedly along the Broadway, checking out the shops. There was a nice-looking deli which he made a note to visit later.

At the end of the Broadway, by the roundabout, there was a coffee shop. He went in, ordered an espresso, and went over and sat down at a table.

"Hello," said the woman who was already sitting there.

"Hello," he said. He reached into his pocket, took out the watch, and put it on the table.

The woman smiled. Two years into retirement, the former Director-General of the English Security Services seemed to be enjoying life. She looked fit and tanned, as if she'd just returned from a walking holiday somewhere sunny.

"Thank you for coming," she said. "And I appreciate the courtesy of your meeting me here, on our territory."

"Except it's not *really* your territory, is it."

She smiled again. "Well, it was. One grows attached to these things." She picked up the croissant which sat on a plate in front of her and broke off a piece. "You're a hard man to contact."

"That doesn't seem to stop people trying," Rudi said. "But I'll try to organise some kind of Bat Signal for future occasions."

She chuckled. "Perhaps the image of a huge Serrano ham projected on the clouds."

That sounded about right. "Does your successor work for the Directorate as well?"

"No." She shook her head. "No, she's English through and through. *British*, I should say. Very keen on Reunification. We tried to influence the selection process, but in the end it was in the hands of the Joint Intelligence Committee."

"Are you telling me there are politicians here who cannot be corrupted?"

She laughed. "I know, hard to believe, isn't it? Still, no doubt we'll adjust to the new situation and muddle through somehow. One always does. You look tired, if you don't mind me saying."

Rudi sipped his coffee. "I've been doing a lot of travelling." He put his cup back on its saucer. "So, will you be going home now?"

"No, I've done my time. I'm retired on both sides of the border. I get to choose where I go, and I've chosen to stay here."

"And the Directorate will let you do that?"

"They're not monsters."

"Yes they are. When it suits them." The D-G had spent decades as a deep-penetration operative within the Security Services. If she had gone native, he could hardly blame her.

She sat and looked at him.

"All right," he said, nudging the watch with a finger. "I'm here." It had not escaped his notice that she had done what he had done to Crispin, only without the danger of causing a war. "What do you want?"

She looked at him a few moments longer, then said, "We'd quite like to speak with your friend Rupert."

"'We' being...?"

"There was an internal audit last year, it turned up an anomaly that we'd like to resolve."

"He's unlikely to want to help you sort out administrative matters."

"He might be interested in this one. It's about Araminta Delahunty."

Rudi considered going through the whole I'm-retired-I'm-just-a-chef routine again, but he didn't have the energy. "Araminta Delahunty died when the Community destroyed the Campus," he said, "She's been dead more than twenty years."

"Yes, we know."

"So?"

The D-G put the bit of croissant back on the plate. "In the course of the audit someone was tasked with going through our file on Rafe Delahunty, just to tidy up any loose ends. The file has the very highest security classification, so we didn't just let an intern loose on it. It was someone very thorough. What we were especially interested in were any failures in the vetting processes Rafe went through when he left university, seeing as he was working with live viruses. Somehow he slipped through the net, and we wanted to find out how, and improve our procedures so it wouldn't happen again."

This sounded reasonable, considering Rafe had taken himself off to the Community and offered to create a biological superweapon for them.

"Anyway, our officer found the original vetting documents and he noticed a discrepancy. The background check listed all his family members, and it turns out that Araminta died when she was six years old, during the Xian Flu."

Rudi sat very still and gave the D-G a hard stare.

"The people who did the original vetting even suggested that Rafe's interest in viruses stemmed from losing his sister at such a young age. He had a personal investment in finding a cure."

"Except it wasn't a cure he was looking for."

"No. Anyway, we went back through everything we had on the Araminta Delahunty who visited the Campus – and it was quite a lot."

"And you discovered that she didn't exist."

"Oh, but she *did*." The D-G beamed at the thought of it. "It's one of the best legends I've ever seen. It's backstopped for *decades*, the level of detail is breathtaking. It's a work of art."

The D-G smiled at him, picked up the piece of croissant again, and this time popped it in her mouth.

"Excellent," he muttered.

"We know there's always been someone else involved in all this," she said. "We know it, you know it, Crispin knows it. This is proof that they were meddling in the Campus, and probably in the Community too. Suppose they were after Rafe's superflu to use for themselves. They lost one operative when Araminta was killed; that doesn't mean they've given up."

Rudi thought of the conversation he'd had with Crispin a few days ago, of the unknown creators of the Realm. Eventually, he thought, he was going to discover that every living thing on Earth was involved in some conspiracy or other.

"You told the Directorate, of course."

The D-G looked abashed. "Well…" she said.

Rudi raised an eyebrow. "Have we had a falling out?"

"A difference of opinion."

This in itself was interesting. "About what?"

"Can't say," she told him. "Sorry." And that was the price of his cooperation; the admission that a schism had appeared between the Community's security service and its clandestine assets in England. Rudi wondered just how far it extended.

He said, "How can Rupert help?"

"He spent a lot of time with Araminta. He was the last person to see her alive, as far as we know. She may have told him something, given him a clue to who she was working for. Something he might not have registered at the time."

"It was a very long time ago."

"I know, but you'd be surprised what people remember."

He sipped some more coffee. It was going cold. "What's in it for you? Rafe and Araminta are both dead, Rafe's superflu and all his research were destroyed in the Campus."

"We'd like to identify her principals." There it was again, 'we'. Not 'we the Directorate' or 'we the English Security Services'.

He said, "If you're gearing yourselves up to go rogue, please don't. Whatever's going on in the world right now, far too many people are mixed up in it already. And if you're telling me all this in order to get me involved, forget it. My to-do list is already extensive enough, thank you."

The D-G looked sadly at him. "All we want to do is speak with Rupert. His debriefing was a scandal. He did it by post."

Rudi smiled at the memory. "You could hardly blame him."

"We'd ask him ourselves, but he seems genuinely uncontactable."

"Yes," Rudi said. "I must ask him how he does that." He scratched his head. "Have you considered the possibility that she was working for Crispin? Araminta?"

She nodded. "It doesn't scan. The Line... the EU... whatever you want to call them, they were already carrying out proscribed research in the Campus through the Science Faculty. Their people probably bumped shoulders with Rafe on occasion; they had no need to put in another operative. In fact, what she most resembles is a Coureur, because all she really did was jump Rupert out." The D-G raised an eyebrow.

Rudi shook his head. "I told you, I'm not getting mixed up in this. I'll ask Rupert about it when I see him, and then it's up to him whether he contacts you. But that's all I'm doing. The rest of it, you sort it out, if you really are that way inclined." Although if Araminta *did* turn out to have been a Coureur, this whole thing was just going to come back and sink its teeth into his leg at some point along the way.

They finished their coffees and went outside. It had clouded over a little, and the breeze had strengthened. He said, "Reunification. Is that a thing? I thought the English government had ruled it out."

"Oh, it never went away," said the D-G. "It was always sort of simmering underneath everything else, but there was a lot of anger on both sides. It could happen, if they found a way to do it without either side looking weak and rubbish."

"That's interesting."

"Isn't it? It's not going to happen any time soon, maybe not in our lifetimes, maybe never. But it's becoming increasingly possible."

Rudi tipped his head to one side and looked at the D-G, wondering what was going on behind that calm, capable façade. He shook her hand. "Whatever you're thinking of doing, just be careful who you make friends with."

"That's good advice," she said, smiling.

"Yes. I wish someone had told me that a very long time ago."

St Kat's was gone. Not just closed, or repurposed as something else. The entire building was gone, the site surrounded by high hoardings covered in KEEP OUT signs.

"It burned down six years ago, lovely," a passerby told him when he asked. "They had to knock it down, it was so badly damaged. Did you know someone there?"

Rupert looked at the hoardings. "Once upon a time," he said.

"Place was a death-trap, I heard," she said. "The bloke who ran the place went to prison, but the people who owned it got away scot-free. Those sort always do, don't they."

"Yes," Rupert said. "I suppose they do."

"You look like a nice man," she said. "Could you lend me a tenner for a cup of tea?"

He looked at her and belatedly realised he had inadvertently spoken to a bag lady. She was in her late fifties and better-dressed than most of the homeless he'd seen in England and on the Continent, but there was dirt under her fingernails and worked into the wrinkles around her eyes, her grey hair had a weird, greasy, untamed texture to it, and the heels of her shoes were catastrophically worn down. What he had mistaken for two bags of shopping were actually full of clothes, clean and neatly folded but the stuff you might find in a charity shop. He dug in his pocket and came up with two ten-pound coins and handed them over.

She took them without saying thank you, stuffed them into her coat pocket, picked up her bags, and started to walk away, but after a few paces she stopped and turned. "Are you lost?" she asked.

All the time… "No, I'm fine, thanks. It's just been some time since I was last here."

She nodded. "You'll see some changes, then," she said, and she walked off.

HE DIDN'T, THOUGH. He supposed that was because the last time he was in Nottingham everything had been new and strange and frightening and he'd been too confused to notice very much about his surroundings. His memory of the three days he'd been here seemed almost hallucinatory. The most concrete thing he remembered, the homeless shelter where he'd stayed, was gone.

In place of the terrifying parade of images, there was a fairly ordinary Midlands town. The people, who had once seemed incomprehensible and exotic, were perfectly normal. The buildings were, on the whole, nothing out of the ordinary but he remembered staring at them open-mouthed. He barely even noticed traffic now.

He walked for a while, trying to retrace his memories, and in time found himself standing on the banks of a wide, slow-moving and rather grubby-looking river. There was a housing estate on the opposite side, and closer to, right on the bank, was a newish concrete building that looked like some kind of pumping house or water treatment centre. As near as he could judge, it was either right on top of, or just beside, the tributary he had canoed along to escape from the Campus, the tributary he had been unable to find in order to return. Presumably, the building housed some sort of monitoring station installed by the English Security Services. The tributary might well still be there, he had no idea, the road to his lost home. If Baines, his handler, had been telling the truth, it would be tens of thousands of years before anyone could live there again, if ever.

Standing there on the other side of the river, a tubby man in his early sixties in jeans and a black sweater and a NATO surplus combat jacket, he found that he didn't feel anything much. Oddly weightless, hollowed out, but no great yearning or feeling of loss. He'd internalised all those things so long ago that he didn't even notice them any more. It took a real effort to remember the Professor of Intelligence whose biggest problem was that the heating in his Residence had packed up. Except that had not been his biggest problem.

He walked back into town and caught a tram out to the University, and here there *were* resonances. Walking onto the campus, some of the buildings looked eerily familiar – there was one that could have been a twin of the Admin building he had once known – and there was even a section of the University the students called 'Science City'. He wondered how much of this was ghosts, how much of it had bled through somehow with clandestine visitors from England and the Community and Europe, everyone who had abused and used and manipulated his people down the years.

Following a road up the curve of a steep hill, he found himself approaching a brand-new library building, a great glass and composite cube that seemed to be wearing much of its internal structure on the outside. He followed a crowd of students through the doors, waited politely at the main desk while one of the librarians dealt with someone's query, and then asked for Doctor West.

The librarian turned to a young woman who had been rummaging through a box of books balanced on a chair behind the desk. "Foz?" she said. "Chap to see you."

The young woman looked round, momentarily confused, then smiled. She had purple hair and ear-rings that looked as if they had once done service holding up a set of curtains. "Professor Henson?"

"Yes. Hello." He had thought it unwise to introduce himself by the name he'd gone by for so long, Rupert of Hentzau.

"You're early." She came over and shook hands across the desk. "I wasn't expecting you until this afternoon."

"My other business didn't take as long as I thought it would," he told her. "So I thought I'd come over anyway. I hope you don't mind."

"No!" She was full of good humour. "No, I was just sorting some stuff out for my students. If you give me a minute or two I'll be right with you."

"Of course. I'm not in a rush."

He wandered a little while West finished whatever it was she was doing. There was a little café area over in one corner, and another area with seating where students and lecturers were reading printed newspapers and magazines. He supposed he ought to feel at home here – it was, after all, the environment in which he had been brought up by his English Lecturer parents – but he didn't. He didn't feel anything, really. It was just another place, one more in a long line of places he'd seen since he left the Campus. The world was very big and very amazing, but that was all it was in the end, just a lot of places.

He felt a hand touch his elbow. "Professor?"

It was such a long time since anyone had called him that that he almost didn't respond. He turned and found West standing behind him smiling, an armful of books clutched to her chest. "Shall we…?"

It was lunchtime, and the place was crowded with students, sitting outside eating sandwiches or chatting with friends or just going from place to place. Everyone here seemed happy and well-fed. No one was forming escape committees or fishing in a dead lake in the forlorn hope that something – anything – edible would take the bait. Nobody was wearing worn-out old clothes, and if they were it was a fashion choice, not out of desperate necessity. In the last, terrible days, there had been cases of rickets on the Campus.

"I'm sorry," West said as they walked, "you were a little vague on the phone. Have you come far?"

The Campus and Nottingham occupied roughly the same point in space, but in superimposed universes. They were impossibly close and impossibly distant. "Quite a way," he said.

"Well, I hope you find something interesting in the archive."

"I'm sure I will."

"He wrote about Nottingham University, you know."

"Yes." He looked about him, smiling. "I can see how the place might have inspired him."

"You've never been here before?"

"Once, but it was a long time ago."

West's office was in a new building overlooking a long sloping grassy hill dotted with trees. She dumped her books on her desk, collected a key card, and led him further down a corridor to a door marked *WILHELM DANCY ARCHIVE*. She unlocked the door and swung it open for him. "Here we are, then," she said.

HE HAD BEEN born, according to the few online sources Rupert had been able to discover, in 1968 in Halle, when Halle was still in East Germany. His father was an Englishman who had... well, *defected* was too strong a word, he had simply moved there in the mid-Sixties to teach at the local university, met a local girl, and never left. Wilhelm – and later his younger sister Hannelore – had what passed for a normal childhood in the East. He didn't show any especial aptitude for anything at school, but while he was at university, around the time of the fall of the Berlin Wall, he had suddenly begun to produce poetry.

It wasn't a huge amount of poetry – he only ever published three collections – and to Rupert's eye it wasn't even particularly good, but for some reason it had struck a spark in Britain, as it was then. Dancy's work attracted a hard core of young political thinkers eager to parse his portraits of life behind the Iron Curtain. Partly it was the scarcity of his work – his first collection was assembled from poems smuggled page by page out to the West – partly it was a sense that Dancy spoke to some inadequacy within them. It was a turbulent time, and to the Wilhelm Dancy Reading Group it seemed that his work was offering them a path through to a better time of History.

Quite how they had evolved into a charitable foundation providing medical imaging machines for hospitals in Azerbaijan was not immediately obvious.

THE ARCHIVE WAS not large. It was housed in a room no bigger than a suburban living room. Two of the walls were lined with shelves; the third had a window that looked out onto a flower bed planted with a great mass of spiky-leaved bushes. In the middle of the room was a table and a couple of chairs. And that was it. Rupert stood by the table and looked at the shelves, lined with cardboard file boxes. Well, this was what happened when you spent too long on the internet...

He wasn't entirely sure why he'd looked up the Reading Group that first time, except he'd been bored on one of the legs of his long train journey back to Europe, and Pais's mention of them had made him curious. Maybe they could be useful, maybe they should be avoided; it was better to find out which.

There were only a few mentions of the group, and not that many more of Dancy himself; he went through them in an hour or so, and he was about to give up and go to the dining car to see if there was anything edible for dinner, when he happened upon a page of Dancy's poetry, scanned from one of his collections and posted on a website by some fan almost fifty years before. According to Rudi, nothing ever went away on the internet.

The half-dozen or so poems were nothing special. Stuff about growing up in East Germany, political references Rupert lacked the cultural background to unpick. But the final poem on the site was called 'Science City', and when he saw the title he felt a moment's thrill of familiarity and disorientation.

It turned out that 'Science City' was a later poem, written after Dancy had moved to England in the wake of the collapse of the Iron Curtain. He'd taught, for a brief time, at the University of Nottingham, and the poem was his reaction to the city and English academic life. It was stultifyingly dull. Rupert shut down his phone's browser and went to have something to eat.

It was only days later, settling into his hotel room in Ankara for the evening's layover before his next train west, that something nagged at him. He stood in the middle of the room, listening to the sounds of traffic from the busy street four floors below, trying to work out what it was.

He went and sat on the bed, took out his phone, called up the browser, and went through its history until he found the page of poems he'd been looking at. Near the end of 'Science City', there was a line about 'chaining my bike to the DNA'. A metaphor, no doubt, for Dancy's English heritage and his commitment to life in the West, but something about it bothered Rupert, something which had taken a long time to surface and make connections, a half-buried memory. He googled *bicycles* and *chains*, and *DNA*. The first image to come up in the DNA search was of the molecule itself

– Rupert had seen images like this on science shows, but he only had the vaguest grasp of its importance or how it did whatever it was supposed to do. The molecule looked like a spiral staircase made of wire and billiard balls, and he sat back and blinked. There had been a sculpture very like this outside the Science Faculty building in the Campus. He had a sudden memory of chaining his own bicycle to it.

None of which meant anything, of course. The world was more or less constructed of coincidence. Dancy had chosen a rather heavy-footed image to express how he felt about his new life in England, and it just happened to resemble an experience Rupert had had in a pocket universe. He didn't doubt that if he rattled through the entire canon of English language poetry he would find numerous similar examples, scraps of shared experience and images which appeared to address him personally. It was only the circumstances in which he had first heard of Wilhelm Dancy that made it stand out.

He came back to it the following day, on the train to Istanbul. Again, he was bored, and his mind just seemed to settle on Wilhelm Dancy and his peculiar fan club. Judging by what he could assemble from online sources, the Reading Group had first come together in London. Someone had scanned yellowing pamphlets in which they had discussed Dancy's work with occasional bad humour. Reading through them, Rupert thought he could detect a core group around seven-strong, and then beyond them perhaps thirty more who seemed to pop in and out of discussions when they felt like it or were sufficiently exercised by the topic.

The numbers waxed and waned down the years, people seemed to drop out, presumably because mortality or some other aspect of life had got in the way, or because they had simply lost interest. But although the names changed, there were always seven central members of the group

It seemed ridiculous to Rupert. The entire extent of Wilhelm Dancy's published work could not have been more than fifty poems. There were only a certain number of ways one could disassemble and critique a poem, and yet these people did it over and over again, for years. By the time Wilhelm Dancy died, of liver cancer, a few days short of the Millennium, Rupert estimated that the Reading Group was more than two hundred strong.

And still they went on, into the era of the internet, with discussion boards and chatrooms, turning the same old poems over and over in their hands and producing no new insights. And then, as if finally realising that they had extracted every last drop of sustenance from Dancy's work, the numbers began to fall away. By the time of the Xian Flu and something that was vaguely referred to as The Dancy Bequest, there were probably no more than fifty people still taking part in discussions and chats. Then everything went dark, the discussions stopped, as he might have expected. The Plague Year, the year the Community had released a flu pandemic which his own people, in the Science Faculty, had created. Either it was an accident or it was not – in an absolute sense, it didn't matter. Many millions had died. No one was certain precisely how many, even now. But a few months before the discussion boards and chatrooms fell silent, mirroring the silence that had been drawn across Europe, someone, in the course of dissecting, for the thousandth time, a poem called 'Charlottenberg', wrote, 'Jesus, this is an old one. I first saw this poem back when I used to date the Rokeby Venus'.

"THE BEQUEST?" WEST said. "Yeah, they got a lot of money. A *lot* of money. No one knows from who – the donors made the bequest on the condition that they remained anonymous – but it paid for this place and for the maintenance of the archive. Probably well into the next century."

"This place?" Rupert asked, looking round the room.

"This department. The Reading Group endowed the department."

"Oh," said Rupert.

"Anyway," West said, "I'm afraid I have a Faculty meeting in a couple of minutes. Will you be okay on your own?"

"Yes," Rupert said, wondering who could have given the Reading Group so much money that they could go on to pay for an entire university department, albeit quite a small one. "Yes, I'll be fine."

West pointed at a filing cabinet. "Gloves in the top drawer," she said. "I'll have to ask you to wear them when you're handling the documents. Some of them are a bit fragile."

"Yes, of course." Rupert smiled at her. "Don't worry. I can cope."

She chuckled. "I'm sure you can. Right. I'll be back in a couple of hours then."

When West had gone, Rupert opened the filing cabinet and found a box of white gloves, slim as surgeons' gloves but made of cotton. He took a pair and wandered along the shelves, reading the labels on the file boxes. The archive was smaller than he had expected, but he supposed the rest of it was online, in the form of thousands of pages of chat and discussion. He took down a box at random – it was labelled *Stonehaven* – and took it to the table and sat down, but instead of putting on the gloves and opening it, he took out his phone and opened those last few posts again.

He'd deliberately factored in a few days' break in Istanbul before he caught the express to Prague. He was tired and he'd travelled too far in one swallow and he needed to feel the pavement under his feet for a while. What he wound up doing instead was drifting from internet café to internet café, using anonymisers Rudi had given him the addresses of to go back through the gigabytes of posts and chats and discussions the Reading Group had produced down the years, and it dawned on him that not everyone was using these spaces to talk about Wilhelm Dancy and his poetry. Some of the traffic – quite a lot of it, he thought – was messages, hidden in plain sight. Little turns of phrase, sentences which seemed unnecessarily awkward even by the standards of the internet, significant only to those who knew their real meaning. He had, he thought, stumbled across an intelligence network. An intelligence network which used – not once, but several times, over the years – a recognition string he had first heard twenty years ago in the Community.

Stonehaven was material referring to Dancy's visit to the north of Scotland, near the end of his life. There were printed copies of the poems he had written there – only a couple – a printed précis of what he had done, a couple of yellowed and brittle cuttings from a local newspaper, trapped in little plastic wallets, with brief stories about the Famous Poet doing a reading at some civic hall or other. He put the lid back on the box and returned it to its place on the shelf.

The Reading Group resurfaced a year or so after the Xian Flu, but now it was different. It had become a charitable foundation. In the chaos following the pandemic and the subsequent dissolution of the EU, it set out into the East, visiting hospitals in far-flung places and endowing new medical equipment to replace devices which in some cases were more than fifty years old. Everywhere it went, it left behind shiny new operating theatres, anaesthesiology suites. It brought in modern medical imagers, took away outdated x-ray machines. It was good work, and if it was carried out even partly on the back of the Bequest, then the Bequest must have been large indeed.

Another box was labelled *Charlottenberg*. Rupert brought it over to the table. Here was much more material, all of it pertaining to Dancy's two years in Berlin immediately before the Wall came down. He read the printed account of Dancy's brushes with authority, the rumours of his involvement with the Stasi – although by that time in East Germany a large percentage of the population was involved with the Stasi in some form or other, however tenuously.

Right at the bottom of the box was a little black and white photograph, not much larger than a credit card. It was possibly the only surviving photograph of Wilhelm Dancy, a man who had protected his privacy with some care. He was standing outside a rather grim Soviet-era office building in Berlin, and behind him was a group of ten or twelve people, mostly quite young, dressed in casual clothes. Wilhelm Dancy was wearing a suit and tie and looked quite uncomfortable in them. He was tall and handsome and his fair hair was worn in a quite ridiculous-looking mullet which must have marked him out as a dangerous subversive to East Germany's security services. He was looking straight into the camera and squinting a little against the sunlight, and he was Andrew Molson.

Rupert looked down at the photograph quite calmly. He looked at Molson, he looked at the faces of the other people. He lost all sense of time. He barely noticed when West came back from her meeting, saw him sitting there, and quietly left again. He only came back to himself when he became aware that his phone was ringing.

He picked it up off the table, looked at the caller ID, pressed the 'answer' icon and said, "Hello?" He listened. "I'm in England. Where are you?" Listened again. "What are you doing there?" Listened for quite a long time. "All right. No, it's not far from here,

I think. I'll meet you there. There's something you should know, anyway."

He hung up and went to put the phone in his pocket, but he stopped, stood up, and, stooping over the table, took several photographs of the photo of Wilhelm Dancy. He turned it over and took photographs of the writing on the back, too.

THE WITCH
OF SAAREMAA

1.

SOMETIMES, IN THE Summer evenings, local boys – and it was mostly boys, she'd noticed – sneaked up to her door and rang the bell as a dare and then ran away. It had at first scared the living daylights out of her, and then annoyed her, although she had never made a fuss about it. These days, it didn't bother her too much; it was only childish bravado, and there were far worse things in the world.

It hadn't happened for a while, anyway. She thought maybe the last generation of kids had grown out of it and the next was still a little too young. It helped that she knew all their parents, too; there were only a couple of hundred families in the village.

Maybe things would have been different if she'd decided to live in Kuressaare; she would have been more anonymous there, but there were too many people and she'd felt that she had been among people enough for a while. She wanted peace and quiet, she wanted to be able to observe the normal ebb and flow of everyday life, she wanted to be able to recognise the people around her and note when any strangers turned up. During the tourist season, the island's population swelled appreciably, and most of the visitors came to Kuressaare. The village on the edge of which she lived still got tourists – it was impossible to avoid them completely – but not many; there wasn't much here for them to see, apart from a little folklore museum and some restaurants and shops.

She kept herself to herself, pottered around the garden, worked on the house. It had been quite dilapidated when she first came here – its previous owner, a little old lady, had not done a lot of maintenance on it. It was still sound, but run-down. All the electrics had needed replacing – several of the light switches crackled alarmingly when you switched them on – and for that there had been Kristjan the local handyman. When the roof needed repairing there was also Kristjan. Via Kristjan, the villagers, curious about their new neighbour, learned that she was an *artist*, a painter of landscapes, not famous but doing well enough. There was a lover in her past, a broken heart, and she had come here to recover herself, to heal and perhaps rediscover her Muse.

And she did paint, for the first time since she was at school, and it turned out she wasn't bad, after a few false starts. Good enough to be able to sell her stuff through a gallery in Kuressaare and attract the attention of a couple of local media sites who wanted to do lifestyle pieces, which forced her to remind the gallery owner that she was in seclusion and it might be for the best, if he wanted to continue to receive commission on her sales, to make sure she stayed that way. Crazy Old Recluse Lady. She discovered she rather liked that.

She'd cut her hair short and dyed it black, got rid of her contact lenses and adopted a big, old-fashioned pair of spectacles, but despite this, and in spite of having lost quite a lot of weight down the years, she looked at herself in the mirror and didn't feel she looked nearly different *enough*, and in the early days there was the constant fear that she would bump into someone she had once known. It had never happened, though. Saaremaa was one of Estonia's most popular tourist destinations – during the summer there was always some Festival or other going on in Kuressaare – but for the most part they did not come out here, and after a time it was easy for her to spot unfamiliar faces. It also helped, of course, that she was dead.

These days, she found, she woke early and went to bed late. She ate a sensible breakfast, read for a while or listened to one of the local audio channels, and if it was Friday she checked her messages

– there was no need to do it more often because the gallery were the only people who had her contact details – then put on a T-shirt and a pair of dungarees and took a mug of coffee into her studio.

The studio was a weird sort of shed-thing the little old lady who previously owned the house had built alongside the main building. Quite what it was originally meant to be was anyone's guess – when she'd bought the house it had been full of junk, including several old petrol-driven lawnmowers rusted beyond salvation – but it had a good light, once it was cleared and cleaned up, and it was dry and cosy and once she'd decided to take the painting seriously it had seemed the obvious place to do it rather than in the house.

She didn't work from life. That, in the early days, had turned out to be the main stumbling block rather than any fault in her technique. She'd soldiered on, standing at her easel in a field somewhere or on a hill or in a wood, and everything she painted was terrible, almost unspeakable. It wasn't until she tried working from a photograph that she produced anything remotely worthwhile. She didn't know why it was like that, it just was and there was nothing she could do about it. A couple of years ago she'd tried taking the easel out again and it was like she'd forgotten everything she'd learned about painting. It was a blind spot, some weird circuit in her head.

So these days she wandered around the island with an antique digital camera she'd found in a junk shop. It had taken her days to find the associated software online, and another day or so to convince her pad not to turn its nose up and refuse to work when she tried loading it. She could have used her pad to take photos, but she liked the quality of image she got from the old camera, the laughingly low pixel-count. She was thinking of getting hold of an old analogue camera and trying that, if she could find anyone who still manufactured and processed film.

The latest project was a country scene. A field not far away, bounded on one side by a drystone wall, on two others by lines of trees and juniper bushes, and on the fourth looking out into the distance towards the Gulf of Riga. She had dozens of photos, blown up and printed and stuck to old whiteboards arranged in a semicircle in front of the easel. The photos had been taken over a period of several days, to show changes in the light and the weather.

When she'd got round to printing them she'd discovered that in two of them, taken a couple of days apart, the same tourist was walking across the middle distance, a man with a rucksack slung over his shoulder and a walking stick in his hand. She didn't usually paint people – she wound up making them look lumpy and deformed – but she'd put the tourist into the painting that stood two-thirds finished on the easel. A couple of brush strokes, no more, and there he was, a tiny figure lost in a huge landscape with the whole world behind him. She thought she detected a certain determination in the way she'd painted him.

She worked on the painting for a few hours, then heated up some of the chicken soup she'd made the previous day and sat in the kitchen eating it with a couple of thick slices of homemade bread while she listened to the audio channels again. She mostly did audio these days; most of the news sites seemed horrible and it was impossible to tell who was trying to outdo whom in sensationalism. The local audio news, with its interviews with visiting musicians or writers and its folk music and its ten-minute-long weather forecasts, was soothing by comparison. Once a week, on Friday – Friday had somehow become her day for engaging with the outside world – she did a quick scan through half a dozen of the less batshit-crazy rolling news channels, and that was usually enough for her. The most recent news involved a diplomatic incident of some kind between the English and the Community. She'd watched it for five minutes, then turned it off.

After lunch she usually did another couple of hours' work, then, if the weather was okay, she took her camera and went out for a wander, scouting for new subjects. Even after all this time, she was still finding odd corners and perspectives she hadn't seen before. Saaremaa covered about two and a half thousand square kilometres; she thought it unlikely that she was going to run out of things to paint.

Today was a nice day, bright and breezy, and in her old ex-Army greatcoat and big floppy hat she stomped along quite happily for several kilometres. She'd looked at herself in the mirror when she bought the coat and hat, and found she quite liked this look. She looked as if she had been assembled from several jumble sales, which was how she felt some days.

She was contentedly taking shots of one vista when she noticed movement in the far distance. It was gone almost as soon as she noticed it, but when she looked at her most recent photographs and zoomed in she saw a little figure against a stand of trees, walking unhurriedly away from her, rucksack over its shoulder and cane in hand. In the final shots, the figure was gone.

It was probably nothing to worry about. The paranoia of her early days on the island had given way to a more pragmatic acceptance of coincidence and happenstance. The tourist was probably renting a cottage in the area; it was hardly surprising that she would see him while out walking. But when she got home later, she locked the door behind her, and when she went to bed she armed the house's security system for the first time in what seemed a very long time.

SHE DIDN'T SEE the tourist out on his wanderings again; discreet enquiries turned up the information that he was a writer from Tallinn who had been renting one of the big houses on the far side of the village for a month, presumably while he wrestled with some particularly intractable manuscript. But he was gone now, back to the city, and in the following days she forgot about him, although she still set the security system – she'd got sloppy, thought she was safe, and that was not a good place to be in.

She finished the painting, hung it on the back wall of the studio for a few days so she could get used to it. Once upon a time, she had sent the gallery everything she produced, but these days she was more picky. There were some works she liked too little – or too much – to allow out of the house, but there was a sort of mellow commercial median where she was prepared to let paintings go. This one wasn't bad. Certainly not bad enough not to sell. She'd done much worse.

She left the painting where it was and went back into the house, where she found a large blond man wearing what looked like a jumpsuit made entirely of old rags sitting in the kitchen.

They looked at each other for some seconds, him sitting at the kitchen table, her standing in the doorway, and the only thought that would go through her mind was that she had spent a quite

considerable amount of money on the alarm system and this man
had walked right through it as if it hadn't been there.

He didn't move from the chair. He smiled and said, "Hello," in
heavily-accented English. He seemed quite amiable.

Without quite taking her eyes off him, she glanced down the
hallway and saw another large blond man – not related, but
certainly the same body type – standing by the front door. Equally
calm, equally amiable.

"How the fuck did you get in here?" she said.

"I don't speak Estonian, I'm afraid," he told her, standing slowly.
"A gentleman I sometimes do little odd-jobs for would like to speak
with you. Please don't panic. You won't be harmed."

For a moment, she almost gave up. In some hidden-away corner
of her heart, it seemed that she had always known this moment
was coming. There was nowhere to run to, no way to fight it. But
she suddenly found herself connected to a bottomless well of anger
which she had not suspected was still there. Anger at Rob, at Selina,
at Polsloe, at the situation in Tallinn which had ultimately led her
here, at the way her life had been hijacked and bent out of shape,
at the two Estonians and their fucking pretty skull. She screamed
and flew at the blond man and saw a gratifying moment of surprise
on his face.

It was a bit like a fly attacking the Eiger, but she got a couple of
punches off before everything went black.

2.

"I'm sorry," Alice said.

"You wouldn't have been human if you hadn't tried," Rudi said
equably.

"Did I hurt him?"

"Not really, no."

She folded her hands in her lap and looked at him. They were
sitting in the living room of a small but comfortably-furnished
apartment... somewhere, she had no idea where, but she had a
feeling it wasn't Estonia. Looking out of the windows, she could see

the rooftops and apartment blocks of a northern European town, but no landmarks.

"You really wouldn't have been harmed, you know," he told her. "My friends look a bit scary – I suppose they are when they want to be – but they really are quite gentle when you get to know them."

"Who are you?"

"I just want to ask you a few questions," he said. "Then you can go. You can go back to Saaremaa, if you want, although I should advise you that your house is under surveillance."

"What?"

He put his hand in his pocket, brought it out holding an object not much larger than a sugar cube. He put it on the coffee table and Alice watched as it started to vanish.

"Mimetic coating," he said. "You can stick them anywhere and they just sit there for years and years, transmitting images. There are about thirty surrounding your house."

"I don't believe you."

He shrugged. "You can check for yourself, when you get back. I'll give you the number of a security firm who'll do a sweep for you." He nodded at the almost-invisible object. "You'll need someone professional; your average specialist would miss them."

"You work for them, don't you."

He gave that one some thought. "Well, it depends on who you mean by 'them'. If we're talking Illuminati, the Secret Rulers Of The World, then no, I don't work for them, although we have met. If we're talking the people who sent you into Dortmund, then again, no, I don't work for them."

"Where am I?"

He smiled at her. "You think I won't tell you, don't you. But actually there's no reason why you shouldn't know; you'd find out in about two minutes if you did manage to get out of here. We're in Lviv."

"*What*?" she said. "Are you crazy? What the hell are we doing here?"

"We have to be *somewhere*," he said. "It's perfectly safe."

She snorted and said, "Ukraine. Safe."

"The surveillance on your house complicated things," he said. "I couldn't just walk up and knock on the door. If I'd tried to talk to you in the street you'd just have taken off and there's no way I could catch you." He nodded at his cane, leaning against the arm of his chair. "So we have a day's window, maybe two. A friend of mine is staying at your house, pretending to be you. She doesn't look much like you, but if she wears your coat and hat she ought to be able to fool the cameras when she goes out."

Somehow, that made her angriest of all. Not being sedated and kidnapped and smuggled across Europe to a city that was constantly on the verge of civil war, but the thought of someone else wearing her coat and hat. She said, "Fuck you."

He sighed and rubbed his face. "Look," he said. Then he stopped and looked towards the window, thinking. He looked at her and said, "I've gone about this all wrong, and I'm sorry."

"If you're looking for sympathy, you're looking in the wrong place."

He got up and limped over to the window and looked down into the street. "Really," he said. "I am. I've never liked this thick-ear stuff; it just makes people angry and it's usually counterproductive. But I've been working on this for more than a year and I was already two years behind when I started and I can't shake the awful feeling that I'm very short of time. I got desperate."

He seemed, to her horror, absolutely sincere. Who the hell were these people? "I'm still not going to tell you anything," she said.

He thought about it, then said, "Well, I'll tell you things, then. Then you can go home."

Back in the mists of time, she had had a couple of training sessions about interrogation techniques. None of them had covered anything remotely like this situation.

He came back to the chair and sat heavily. "Well, to start with, I'm sorry to tell you that you're not a Coureur."

She narrowed her eyes at him.

"*I'm* a Coureur," he told her. "Or I was. I'm retired. That's not going very well, by the way."

"Bull," she said, "shit."

He shook his head. "I'm sorry, but it's not. I've spoken with the man who called himself Fram, so there's no point in denying what happened in Dortmund."

She didn't say anything.

"It's quite hard to find out about Coureur operations," Rudi went on. "Everyone thinks – because it's natural to, I suppose – that *Les Coureurs* have an organisation, a structure of some kind, but that's not the case. They're actually a large number of independent groups, all working towards a similar end – to move things from one place to another. No one's running it, no one has an overview. No one set it up, really, although you'll sometimes hear Coureurs talking about 'Founding Fathers'. As far as I can work out, the whole thing sort of spontaneously combusted around the time European borders started going back up post-Schengen."

Anything she said or did, she thought, would be tacit acceptance, so she just sat there looking at him.

"The Coureurs in Dortmund were quite annoyed when they found out someone was running a recruiting operation on their turf," he said. "It was a fractious time, as I'm sure you recall; they didn't need someone else coming in and stirring the pot. Eventually one of their stringers decided to try and find out what was going on, and as far as *she* could discover, the recruiting operation was not a Coureur one. She couldn't find out where the Situation had come from; it seemed to have simply erupted out of nowhere." He looked down at his hands, clasped in his lap. "And that's where things ended, really. She dug around for a bit and then she decided there was a smell of *espionage* about the whole thing, something governmental, and she dropped it."

"Why should I believe any of that?" said Alice.

"Apart from it being the truth?"

"It doesn't even work as fiction, let alone as truth."

"Well, that's the thing about truth," he said.

"I don't have to sit here and listen to this," she said. "And I don't have to answer any of your questions."

"Of course you don't. I told you, you can go home any time you want."

"Why would I want to, if what you say's true and my home is surrounded by cameras?"

"Ah, well," he said. "The only way you'll know for sure is if you go back and check to see if they're there. And by then it may be too late."

"You could have put them there yourself."

He looked slightly abashed. "Well, actually, I did. Some of them, anyway."

Alice gave him a hard stare.

"That's how we found the others," he said. "We realised we were picking up feeds from cameras that weren't on our network."

That at least had a ring of truth about it; no one would bother to make up a ridiculous little detail like that. She said, "You have a very unusual way of doing things, if you don't mind my saying."

He shrugged. "Life is often absurd. Mine is, anyway. I'd like to say you get used to it, but you don't quite, really." He seemed to come to a decision. "Look, let me tell you what all this is about and then, if you still want to go, I'll get my friends to take you back to Saaremaa or wherever else you want to go."

"I probably won't believe it."

"I wouldn't blame you."

Alice thought for a moment. "All right. Surprise me."

Rudi took a few seconds to compose his thoughts. "More than twenty years ago, there was a man called Mundt. He was working for the people who own the Line, trying to develop a method of opening border crossings into the Community." He saw the look on her face. "I promise you this is all true. I really wish it wasn't because my life would have been a lot simpler."

"Okay," she said noncommittally.

"So, Mundt. *Professor* Mundt. He not only worked out how to manipulate border crossings, but he also found a way to travel more or less instantaneously between two points in space."

"Like a wormhole."

"Well, no, that's not how I understand it, insofar as I understand it at all. But that doesn't matter. What *does* matter is that simply by knowing these two things, Professor Mundt became one of the most dangerous men in the world. Imagine a jihadi group able to place bombs anywhere they wanted from half the world away. And that's before we get to him giving Europe a first-strike capability against the Community. He's basically a weapon of mass destruction."

"What's the Line got to do with all this?"

He sighed. "Don't worry about the Line; that will only complicate things."

Things already sounded complicated enough. "Okay."

"For a little while, the Professor was in the hands of the Coureurs. Then, for quite a long time, the Community had him. Then, about three years ago, he was murdered."

"And everyone breathed a sigh of relief."

"Exactly. Exactly that. But last year someone told me that the Professor wasn't dead; he'd been abducted by... well, we don't know who. But we do know that this man was involved." He took a photograph from his jacket pocket and passed it over, and Alice found herself looking at Ben's face, grainy and not terribly distinct, but recognisably Ben, even after all this time.

"Yes," Rudi said, seeing her reaction. "You do know him, don't you."

She gave the photo back.

"So," he went on. "Here is this weapon of mass destruction, in the hands of who knows what batshit crazy organisation, and that has made a lot of people very nervous. People who were already quite nervous enough to start with. One of them was responsible for the Xian Flu and another was behind the Heathrow Event, to give you an idea of the kind of people we're talking about." He shrugged. "And they've asked me to find him." He sat back in his chair and looked at her and waited for her to sort everything out in her head. He thought she was lucky; at least she had someone to explain it to her. He'd never had that luxury.

"*Responsible* for the Xian Flu?" she said eventually.

"That, also, is going to have to wait until another day. They also have nuclear weapons, though. Just to give you an idea what the stakes are."

She thought about that for a while, too. "What will you do with him?" she asked. "If you find him?"

Which was not a question he had expected, although he had been giving it a lot of thought himself. "I don't know," he told her. "I really don't."

"You'd have to kill him," she said. "If what you say is true he's not safe with anyone. You'd have to kill him."

He shook his head. "I'm not going to kill him." Although he had not ruled out arranging circumstances so that someone else did it. "But you're right, he's not safe anywhere. If it didn't sound egotistical I'd say the only person he's safe with is me, and I don't want him. I have a restaurant to run."

"And you think Ben will lead you to the people who have this Professor, and I'll lead you to Ben."

"Ben," he said. "Is that what he calls himself? Well, *Ben* has done a *lot* of travelling, down the years. I know someone who has… well, let's call them *resources*. And he used these resources to break into a lot of border control databases around Europe and look for anyone who matched that image we have of Ben. And he pops up quite a lot, under a lot of different names. It turns out that one of my friends who jumped you out of Saaremaa has actually met him, you know. He says he's pretty sure Ben hired him and a few of his colleagues to smash up my restaurant twenty-odd years ago. Imagine that. Small world."

"I wasn't jumped," she reminded him. "I was drugged and kidnapped."

"Anyway. Once we could place *Ben* in a certain country or a certain city, it was a matter of breaking into traffic control cameras and street surveillance systems and then just going through their footage for clues. The thing about the Surveillance State is that it doesn't work very well; cameras break down, recognition algorithms give false positives or false negatives. But it works just *well enough*, if you have enough processing power, to spot you and Ben together in Dortmund and in Amsterdam."

"And when you couldn't find Ben you decided to look for me," she said, a cold sensation in the pit of her stomach.

"Don't worry," he said, as if reading her mind. "Very few people in the world have the capability to process that much data in any meaningful timeframe – the NSA, some corporations, maybe – and none of them has the inclination. And you *are* dead. No one's looking for you."

"Yes," she said. "Murdered by my jealous husband. Who also murdered my lover and an innocent bystander and then killed himself."

"It's a terrible story," he agreed. "It's an insult to the Estonian police."

"You think they know what really happened?"

"I think they know whatever they were told. It was an embarrassment to your government; they flew two detectives over from Scotland and they wrapped up the case in a few days and presented a report to the Estonians, who never bothered to question it. Everyone just wanted it to go away."

She put her hands to her face and rubbed hard. "Do you know what happened? In Tallinn?"

"No," he said. "I don't. But I believe you've been the victim of a terrible con-trick. Whoever did this destroyed your life."

"It wasn't much of a life," she told him. "I was glad to be rid of it, to be honest."

"Did you never," he asked delicately, "try to find out yourself what had happened?"

She'd thought about it, down the years – there was no way not to – but in the end she'd decided there was no point. It had happened; she couldn't change that. "It happened to someone else," she said. "You wouldn't understand."

"Actually, I would." He clasped his hands. "It must be quite a thing, to be able to make peace with something like that. I couldn't do it."

"I didn't make *peace*," she said. "I... put it away. It wasn't important any more." She looked at him. "So that's how you found me? Just by going through traffic camera footage?"

"It's a bit more complicated than that, but yes, basically. You can do pretty much anything, if you have the right tools. Fortunately, as I said, very few people have the right tools. Otherwise the world would be a terrible place." He thought about it. "More terrible."

She was silent for a very long time. Finally, she said, "If I tell you what I know, will you find out what happened to me, and why?"

"I'll try," he said. "I can't promise anything."

After all these years of being self-contained, it felt a lot like stepping off a precipice. "Okay," she said. And she told him everything. Rob, Tallinn, the Embassy, Bodfish, the skull, Dortmund, Amsterdam, all the other Situations she'd been involved with. She talked round Polsloe – even now her instinct was to protect him – but she told him everything else, and he listened patiently and politely and only interrupted her when he thought a point was not clear. She saw him wince a little when she described the two Estonians who had brought the skull to the Embassy, and a look of quite surprising anger momentarily crossed his face when she mentioned Kaunas.

It took her most of the afternoon to tell her story. At some point one of the big blond men came in with an absurdly dainty tray of coffee and sandwiches.

When she'd finished, she said, "So, does it all make sense now?"

He poured them both the last of the coffee, dropped sugar into his cup, and sat back. "Some of it does," he said. "Some of it just seems more complicated."

She snorted. "You should have lived through it."

He nodded. "Yes, I know how that feels," he said absently, stirring his coffee. He looked at her. "Thank you," he said. "I'll make arrangements to get you out of here as soon as possible."

"Where would I go?" she asked. "Someone's watching my house."

"Anywhere you want to."

She leaned forward in the chair and rested her elbows on her knees. "I took control," she told him. "Again and again and again. I did a runner from the safe flat in Tallinn and they were there waiting for me at Käsmu. I ran away in Amsterdam and you turned up on Saaremaa. There's always someone ahead of me."

Rudi felt his heart break. Alice's life had been so comprehensively broken down and rebuilt and then broken down and rebuilt again that there was nothing left. She had been constructed out of chaos by people who did not care about her, only about the next step in the game, and he supposed that, yes, he was one of those people. He'd been doing something like this for years, and while he'd always tried to be conscious of the collateral damage, he had not always been aware quite how far or how devastatingly it had extended.

He said, "Once this is over, no one will ever trouble you again. I promise."

She snorted, and he felt the weight of the water on the dam she had constructed against the indignities of her life. Her crappy job, her dickhead employers, her bully of a husband, the impossible surges and reverses of the years since she had left Estonia. It must have felt to her like a punishment meted out by the Furies, except the Furies cared about their victims and the people who had done this did not. Alice was only a fulcrum, a tool. Her life had been wrecked, not just once but again and again, simply because she was the right tool for the job. Or perhaps not even the right tool. Just the one closest to hand.

"I promise," he said again. He drank some coffee. "I am interested in the skull, though," he mused. "For a lot of different reasons. Can you remember anything else about it?"

"I can do better than that," she said. "I took pictures. I wasn't entirely stupid back then."

"You weren't stupid at all," he told her. "You were just given no choice. I'd quite like to see these photographs."

"Well, for that we'll have to go to Pärnu."

"Pardon me?"

"We'd have to go to Estonia anyway," she told him. "I want my hat and coat back."

3.

IN PÄRNU, THE weather was bright and crisp. The city centre, almost cut off from the mainland by the curve of the river, was full of people on bicycles and electric scooters. There were no direct flights from Lviv, so they had found themselves having to fly to Tallinn and then catch an onward internal flight. A pretty woman with curly brunette hair was waiting for them at the gate for the Pärnu flight. She had a rucksack with her, which she handed over to Alice. "I brought your hat and coat and some other things," she said apologetically. Alice dug her hat out of the rucksack, shook it a few times to dewrinkle it, and sighed.

Pärnubank was a low, modern building not far from Munamäe Park. Alice and Rudi went in together; Gwen waited across the road in a café. Five minutes of presenting ID and swapping authorisation codes left Rudi and Alice in the bank's safety deposit vault looking down into a small strongbox. There wasn't much in there – some IDs and passports, a wad of Swiss francs held together with an elastic band, and an old hardback copy of *A Tale of Two Cities*.

Alice took the book from the box, flexed it open and shook it, and a little plastic-wrapped package fell out.

"This is a copy," she told him, unwrapping the package. "The original's somewhere else."

Good tradecraft. He approved.

Inside the package was a little SIM card. She opened the back of her phone and swapped cards. "I didn't even realise I had this until quite a long time later," she told him. "I left my phone in the flat, but I'd been swapping cards back and forth for days because... well, I'd been swapping cards, and I'd just lost track of which one was in my phone." She swiped and tapped menus, opened a photograph, and held the phone out to him. "Here. This is it. I photographed it before I took it to the University. Just in case."

Rudi looked at the photo, the eerie carnelian eyes seeming to shine with a light of their own. He swiped to the next image, and the next, and the next. He stopped briefly at one which showed a pattern of marks on the back of the skull, then swiped on. "This is excellent stuff," he said, but he was frowning as he said it.

"What's wrong?" asked Alice.

He sighed. "Well," he said, "it was a long time ago, but I think I've seen this thing before."

WADLOPEN

1.

"THEY'RE CALLED *WULFRUNIANS*," said Rupert.

"What?" said Rudi.

Rupert held up a leaflet he'd found on the room's desk. *Wolverhampton And Area*, it said, over a rather dated-looking photograph of a church. "*Wulfrunians*."

"Oh." There had been some discussion, over dinner the previous evening, about what the city's inhabitants were called. It hadn't been much of a discussion, but then it hadn't been much of a dinner.

Rupert dropped the leaflet on top of a little pile of similar leaflets, all advertising the apparently quite considerable attractions of the West Midlands. "This has all the makings of a fiasco," he said. He didn't add 'even by our standards,' but he might as well have done.

Rudi sighed. "Yes," he said. "I know."

Rupert got up from the desk, went over to the window, and peered through the thick net curtain into the car park below. They had booked into the cheapest, most anonymous hotel Rudi had been able to find, and there had been quite a lot of competition in that area. They'd taken three twin rooms; Gwen was babysitting Alice, and Seth was sharing with Rupert, as much to keep Gwen and Seth apart as anything else. All they'd done last night was stare stonily at each other.

Alice, who was a professional – if not perhaps quite in the field she had thought – looked mystified at becoming attached to this circus, even though she'd insisted on coming along. The sensible, operational, thing to do would have been to park her somewhere safe – Rudi had a sense that whatever part she'd played in this business down the years was over now anyway – but he wanted to keep her in sight, just in case. If nothing else she would help establish his bona fides, although he had also entertained a brief fantasy where he was able to swap her for Mundt.

"So," Rupert said.

"So," Rudi said. He was still processing Rupert's tale of the Wilhelm Dancy Reading Group, not least his account of where he'd heard of them in the first place. He'd detected a certain amount of *elision*, there. "Oh, the former Director-General of the English Security Services wants a word."

"Oh?"

"She says it's something about Araminta Delahunty."

"Araminta's dead."

"Yes, well, she still wants to talk with you about it."

"Hell will freeze over first."

"Actually, I think there's something odd going on there. I think Michael tasked her and her cell to kill you because of that chap who died in the Community." He waited for Rupert to provide a name, just in case, but nothing happened. "I think she's decided not to kill you, for whatever reasons, and that has truly pissed Michael off. I think she and a number of other Community deep penetration operatives are about to set up shop on their own."

Rupert thought about it. "Interesting. But none of my business."

"It might be, one day. They could cause trouble. Did you ever meet her? The D-G?"

Rupert shook his head. "I only ever saw Baines and Bevan and the clinic staff and a few debriefers. They kept me insulated from everyone else."

"Right. She's good, anyway. Better at this than I am."

"It might be a kindness," Rupert said, "if the next time you saw Michael you made it clear to him that I had nothing to do with killing anyone in the Community."

Rudi looked at him. "I get the feeling you don't care too much, either way."

Rupert grunted. "What *are* we doing here, anyway?"

Rudi looked at him a few moments longer, then went over to the room's rickety built-in wardrobe and took out a bulky attaché case.

"We've always been looking at trains and tunnels and roads and paths when we think of the border crossings between Europe and the Community," he said, laying the case on the bed. "But the Whitton-Whytes began building Ernshire before railways really took off in this country. They would have had to move people and materials back and forth across the border, and they could have done some of that overland, but not all of it. Some of it would have been just too heavy. So how did they do it?"

"Rivers," Rupert said, thinking of the tributary between the Campus and Nottingham.

"Canals." Rudi started to go through the sequence of combinations and key-swipes that prevented the case from flash-burning its contents. "The Whitton-Whytes were creating Ernshire during the great period of canal-building in England. The Staffordshire and Worcestershire Canal was built by James Brindley, who was basically the father of the British canal system," he said. "It was completed in 1771, the year after General Herbert Whitton-Whyte began his Alternative Survey, and there is some apocryphal evidence that Brindley and Whitton-Whyte were acquainted." He opened the case and started to leaf through a sheaf of printed documents. "The canal was part of a larger network that links one side of the country to the other, from the Bristol Channel to the North Sea, via the River Trent. Really quite an engineering feat." He took a photograph from the sheaf of documents and held it out. "And this is a map of it."

Rupert took the photo and looked at it. "It's not much of a map," he mused.

"That's what was engraved on the back of the skull."

Rupert looked at the pattern of marks again and shook his head. "I still don't see it."

"Crispin let Lev have an hour's very strictly supervised access to Dresden-Neustadt," Rudi said. "He wasn't keen, after all the time we spent using it to locate Ben and Alice, but I talked him into it. The Machine does pattern recognition really well, apparently. It came up with six possible matches for that design." He perched on the corner of the room's desk. "And only one makes any sense, because only one shows the border crossing between the Campus and Nottingham."

Rupert looked at him, then at the photo, then at Rudi again. "Are you sure?"

"The Machine is sure. Well, it's also sure that it's a pre-Inca calendar and a chart of pulsars as seen from the Southern Hemisphere, among other things." He shrugged. "But what are the chances?"

"If you asked the Machine about this, Crispin has it too now, you know," Rupert pointed out.

"Yes, I know. It's unavoidable, it could conceivably work out in our favour, and frankly I'm running out of fucks to give."

Rupert thought about it some more. "Well, this is very interesting, but what does it have to do with us being *here*, particularly?"

2.

PETE WAS DOWN below, doing some routine maintenance on Behemoth, when Angie called, "Someone to see you!"

Muttering to himself, Pete levered himself out of the engine space – it was about time they had the boat in dry dock again and gave her a proper service, but he'd been putting it off because the summer season had been busier than usual this year – and went topside, wiping his hands on a rag.

A couple were standing on the towpath, talking to Angie. He was a tall, slim Afro-Caribbean lad with a little grey in his hair, she was shorter and younger. Both well-dressed. He looked faintly awkward, and her body language reminded Pete of Angie's when they'd had a fight.

"Afternoon," he said. "I'd shake hands, but..." He held up his hands to show them why they wouldn't want to. "What can I do for you?"

"We're looking for a boat," said the young woman. "Are you for hire?"

Pete glanced at Angie, who shrugged. He said, "Yeah. Just yourselves, is it?"

"Party of five," the woman said.

"Team-building exercise," the man said, and Pete thought he detected a look of distaste crossing the woman's face.

"We're not a party boat, you know," he warned. They'd had a group of paintballers, the year before last. There had been drinking, things had been broken. It had taken a while to get the paint off of everything.

"We're not in the mood to party," the woman said. "Really."

Pete made a show of giving it some thought, even though he'd already decided. "All right," he said. "We can do the paperwork now, if that's okay with you?"

It was. They sat in the cabin and the woman took care of everything. She and the man sat side by side, but she made an effort not to touch him, and as they left and walked away down the towpath, Pete heard her say to him, "Fucking cockwomble."

"What do you reckon?" Pete asked Angie.

"I reckon," she told him, "I never saw two people who needed team-building more than them."

THEY WERE BACK first thing the next morning with their friends, two older men – one of whom walked with a stick – and a woman wearing a long olive-green coat and a floppy hat. They were the unlikeliest bunch of team builders Pete had ever seen. Most of the corporate hires they had looked roughly the same, similar age, similar demographic, similar way of speaking. This group looked as if it had been assembled from people picked off the street at random.

Pete took them on the tour of the boat, explaining how everything worked and where everything was and what to do in the event of a fire or a sinking or a collision, but only the two older men seemed to be paying any attention, and one of them seemed to be off with the fairies half the time. The younger couple were doing their best to stay as far apart as they could in the cramped surroundings, and the older woman had taken off her hat and coat, revealing jet-black dyed hair and clothes that looked as if they had come from a charity shop, and was looking around as if she couldn't quite believe where she was.

The induction over, Pete went back to the cockpit and started the engine. Angie cast off fore and aft, and he steered them out of the basin. Behemoth was ticking over nicely, as it always did. It was a marvellous engine, just needed a little TLC every now and again.

They'd been on their way for a couple of minutes when the one with the stick came to the cockpit. "Hello," he said.

"Hiya," Pete said. "Settling in all right?"

"Very well thank you," the other man told him. He had a very faint accent, nothing Pete could place. He stood watching the buildings on either side of the canal go by for a little while, then he said, "I wonder if I could ask you to do something for us."

"Sure."

The man with the stick took a folded slip of paper from his pocket. "I wonder if you could take us to these coordinates?"

Pete raised an eyebrow.

"It's part of our exercise," the man assured him. "It's nothing nefarious or anything, we just have to navigate from one place to another for a couple of days, then we can go home."

"Sounds a rum sort of exercise, really," Pete mused.

"I agree, but if we don't do as we're told Human Resources will get upset and there will be memos and reports and personal reviews and everyone will be unhappy."

Pete thought about it. "Where did you say you worked again?"

"London. It's a new PR startup. Very keen."

Pete took the piece of paper, looked at the GPS coordinates on it, put it in his pocket. "It's your hire, mate," he said. "But if I was in your position I'd be looking for somewhere less stupid to work. No offence."

The man with the cane smiled brightly. "None taken. I know exactly what you mean."

*   *   *

THERE WERE TWENTY-one locks between the Gas Street Basin in the middle of Wolverhampton and Aldersley Junction, where the Birmingham Main Line Canal joined the Staffordshire and Worcestershire. It was only a few kilometres, but it took them quite a while to navigate the lock system because they had to wait for each individual one to cycle and allow other traffic through before they could proceed. Seth seemed eager to help out, possibly to prove that he was not actually the 'festering dicksplash' that Gwen had called him as they checked out of the hotel this morning, possibly just to get out of her way, and he moved back and forth along the boat, helping to open and close the lock gates.

"I wouldn't have asked you if there had been anyone else," Rudi told him at one point, almost halfway through the locks.

Seth looked at him and shrugged. "Happy to help out," he said. "You know that."

Rudi lowered his voice a fraction. "Pardon me for prying," he said, "but what on earth did you *do*?"

For a moment, he thought Seth was going to answer, but he shook his head. "Better you don't know," he said.

"Okay. But look, this is probably going to be tricky, so I'd appreciate it if the two of you didn't start punching each other at an inopportune moment."

"You should mention that to her," Seth told him, making his way towards the bow. "She's the one who does the punching."

Rudi watched him inching along the running board down the side of the boat and wondered if his first instinct, to bring Kerenyi and a couple of his Hungarians with him, hadn't been the right one.

Down in the passenger cabin, Alice and Gwen were sitting at the dining table chatting, and Rupert was examining the tiny shower cubicle. As Rudi went by he said, "You know, if we wind up in the Campus this is going to be a boat full of very unhappy people."

"It's not exactly a ship of joy as it is," Rudi told him.

Rupert snorted. "Ship of fools, more like."

Rudi grinned. "It's going to be fine," he said. "I wouldn't have brought anyone with me if I wasn't sure."

"You only have the word of Crispin's machine that it'll work at all."

"Well, if it doesn't the worst that will have happened is that we'll have had a nice boating holiday and we'll have to go away and think of something else."

Rupert made a rude noise.

Rudi went and sat with Gwen and Alice. "So," he said. "Here we are."

"Gwen's been telling me what you did at Heathrow," Alice said. "Are you *completely* crazy?"

Gwen, who had developed a somewhat disturbing fondness for explosions, was inordinately proud of what she'd done at Heathrow. He said, "It was a calculated risk. I needed to get someone's attention. No one was hurt, and the English are going to blow up all the aircraft at Heathrow when they leave anyway, to stop the Community getting their hands on them." It had also been a reminder to everyone that he was tired of having his life messed around with, but he didn't think that part of the message had got through. Somehow, it never did. He took a breath and said, "I should apologise to you, Alice."

"It's a bit late for that now I'm here, isn't it?" she said.

"No," he said. "Well, yes, I should apologise for *this* too, but what I should *really* apologise for is that I think there is an overwhelming certainty that my father was one of the men who brought the skull to you."

She thought about that. "The goth?"

"No, that was Juhan, his sidekick."

She narrowed her eyes at him for a few moments, then shook her head. "No," she said, "I don't see a likeness."

Which he supposed was some comfort. "They probably didn't steal the thing in the first place – that would have been too much trouble for my father – and I don't know to what extent they were involved with everything else that happened to you in Tallinn, but on behalf of my family, I should apologise to you."

She thought about it for a while, then nodded. "And the whole thing was just about the map on the back of the skull?"

"I don't think so, no," he said, partly because no one likes to hear that their life has been utterly fucked up because of something quite trivial. "Things are never that simple. That thing about a turf war sounds about right, although I could only guess at who was involved, and why. Whatever happened back then, it appears to have been something quite significant because a number of different groups were involved, and when it was over you were going in one direction and the skull was going in the other." Towards its eventual rendezvous with him in Barcelona.

"It might be less risky if we went looking for Kaunas," Gwen said.

He shook his head. "Kaunas doesn't want to be found and I can't ask Crispin for the use of the Machine again, he was annoyed enough when we used it to process the map. Even if we did find Kaunas, he wouldn't tell us the truth. He's like my father; he works for everyone."

"How risky is this going to be?" asked Alice.

Rudi glanced at Rupert, who was leaning up against the galley sink with his arms crossed, following the conversation. "Not risky at all," he said. "I hope."

FINALLY CLEARING THE flight of locks, *Grace Mercy* turned west on the Staffordshire and Worcestershire Canal. Rudi sat on the cabin roof and watched the buildings on either side of the canal go by. Old warehouses, newer business parks and light industrial estates. Some kids on bicycles rode along the towpath for a little while, keeping pace and shouting abuse at them before speeding up and disappearing into the distance.

Rupert came up and sat on the roof with him. "Do you remember that old contact string?" he asked. "The one about the Rokeby Venus?"

Rudi nodded.

"Did you come up with that on your own, or did you see it somewhere?"

"It was something my father used to say. If he'd been doing something for a long time he'd say, 'I've been doing this since I used to date the Rokeby Venus.' He thought it was funny, but nobody knew what he was talking about. I had to look it up in the end, and even then it still wasn't funny. Why?"

"I think you ought to consider the possibility that your father was associated somehow with the Reading Group," said Rupert, and he explained how he'd seen the phrase on one of the Group's message boards.

Rudi thought about it. "I suppose it explains some things, anyway," he said finally. "I did wonder how you got hold of it in the Community, but of course it was given to you by Molson, AKA Wilhelm Dancy." He shrugged. "As for my father working for them? O the shock, O the surprise."

Rupert glanced casually back along the roof. He could just see Pete's head as he stood at the tiller, and beyond him the canal. "You know we're being followed, don't you," he said.

"I know there's another boat behind us, but that's hardly suspicious," said Rudi.

"Hm," said Rupert. They were silent for a little while, then he said, "I can guess what you're planning to do."

"That's a neat trick; I barely have much of an idea myself."

"Trying to reason with people hardly ever works, you know. You're not going to be able to just *talk* these people into giving you Mundt."

"I can try." Although if he wasn't back in Wolverhampton in three days to stop it, Crispin and Michael would receive a message telling them exactly where he was going and inviting them to come in all guns blazing. He might have been naively confident about the power of reason, but he wasn't stupid.

Gradually, the buildings on either side became fewer and fewer. They reached a place where the canal seemed to curve to the right, but they carried straight on. The sound of traffic and aircraft faded away. Bushes appeared on the banks, then trees. Between gaps in the trees, they could see a great stretch of grassland running away to the horizon on both sides of the canal.

"Well," Rupert said.

The boat chugged patiently on, hour after hour. The canal went on before them into some vastly distant vanishing point. Alice and Gwen stayed in the cabin; Seth came up and sat in the bow of the boat. No one seemed particularly keen on conversation, so Rudi went and sat in the cockpit. Pete was still taking his turn on the tiller, although as far as Rudi could see the boat would carry on for ever in a straight line without any human guidance.

Angie brought them mugs of tea, strong and black and treacly with sugar. "If you want milk you're out of luck," she told Rudi.

He smiled as he took the mug. "No, that's lovely, thank you," he said, although the first sip made his teeth cringe.

When Angie had gone back below, Rudi asked, "Do you have any weapons on board?"

Pete looked at him. "There's a baseball bat in one of the cupboards," he said. "Just in case. What would we want weapons for?"

Rudi thought about it. "Pirates?"

Pete chortled. "You've never been on a narrow boat before, have you."

"I was on a barge on the Danube once."

"Oh aye? What was that like?"

Rudi looked about him. "Bigger," he said. In the distance behind him, he could see the other boat, the one that had followed them up out of the locks from Wolverhampton.

Pete grunted. "Always fancied a trip on the Rhine," he mused. "Ange wouldn't have it, of course. 'We live all our bloody lives on a boat, you daft sod; why would I want to spend my holidays on one?'" He chuckled and shook his head. "Must be quite something, the Rhine."

"Yes," said Rudi, thinking of the Rhine and the Danube and the Ruhr and where they might lead, if you only had the right charts. "Yes, it really is."

The day grew warmer. Seth took off his jacket, bundled it up as a pillow, and stretched out on the cabin roof. Below decks, Angie and Gwen and Alice were gathered around the little dining table; the sound of raucous laughter occasionally drifted up through the hatchway. Rupert pottered about, unable to settle.

At one point, he came and stood in the cockpit and said, "Is this going to take much longer? We didn't bring any food."

Rudi glanced at Pete, who pouted. "You tell me, lads," he said. "It's your hire. Guests usually bring their own provisions." When the other two men didn't respond, he said, "I daresay Ange could do you all a fry-up, if you asked nicely."

Rupert, who was not about to ask the fierce little woman anything, nicely or otherwise, grunted and went away again.

"Team-building exercise, you say?" Pete said when he'd gone.

"Yes," Rudi said.

"Hm."

Late in the afternoon, Rudi thought he smelled cooking in the air. A few minutes later, he saw a little dark shape ahead of them on the canal. Rupert, who had been sitting in the prow chatting to Seth, came back along the boat to the cockpit and said, "We've got company."

Rudi squinted into the distance. "I think we're the company," he said.

The boat ahead of them was another narrow boat, this one riding low in the water as if heavily-laden, chugging along slowly. As they caught up, Rudi saw the name *Lucie Rose* painted on the stern. The man at the tiller exchanged a wave and some words with Pete. By now, standing on the cabin roof, he could smell cooking meat, and see what appeared to be a large group of people on the bank some distance ahead. Seth, who had been standing up in the prow like a slightly disconsolate figurehead ever since spotting the other boat, turned to look back.

They reached a place where the canal widened until it was broad enough for two or perhaps three boats to pass abreast, and here several more narrow boats and cabin cruisers were moored by the bank. As Pete steered their boat in to the side, Rudi saw that some building work had been done here. The bank had been shored up with brickwork, and a concrete quayside poured. A little further back from the bank, there were a number of brick sheds with steeply-pitched roofs that almost touched the ground, and in front of these a barbecue appeared to be going on among a group of small marquees.

Pete throttled back the engine and began to steer the boat towards the bank. Rudi smiled at him and said, "Journey's end?"

"Team-building exercise," Pete said. "You'll feel right at home."

As Pete tied up the boat to bollards on the quayside, Rudi saw that it actually *was* a barbecue. About thirty people were standing around picnic tables laden with plates of burgers, sausages, buns, bowls of salad, packs of beer and bottles of wine. Some of them looked round incuriously to look at the newcomers, but most of them were chatting amiably. None of them seemed dangerous; they were mostly middle-aged river people like Pete and Angie, but Rudi saw a few children running about playing tag or wandering around with hot dogs clasped in their fists. As Rudi and the others approached, a tall woman holding a glass of white wine came towards them, smiling.

"Hi," she said. "I'm Rachel. Are you lost?"

"Usually," Rudi said, shaking her hand.

She laughed. "That's okay, I know who you're here to see."

"You do?"

"Yes. Just you two, mind," she said, nodding at Rupert. Then she looked over his shoulder and shouted, "Casey! Casey, get away from there!" at a small child who was pretending to walk the high wire along the edge of the quayside. "Alex? Take care of her, will you? She's going to fall in." As a younger man went to rescue the child, Rachel smiled at Rudi again. "Kids, eh? Want to come this way?"

Rudi turned to the others, who, faintly embarrassingly, had gathered in a group behind him like a bunch of schoolchildren on an outing. "You might as well get yourselves something to eat," he told them.

"What's going on?" asked Gwen.

"I actually have no idea," he said. "But the food smells good." He looked at Rachel. "Just us?"

"Just the two older gentlemen," Rachel said, with the tone of someone repeating an instruction.

Rudi and Rupert exchanged glances. "Hard to argue with that," Rupert murmured. "We're certainly *older*."

Rachel led them along the quayside, down the line of boats. Rudi counted seventeen narrow boats and three cabin cruisers. He had no idea whether this was an impressive number or not, but it certainly seemed like a lot. About half the narrow boats were sitting lower in the water than the others, tarpaulins draped over what would have been their forward cabins. Through a gap in the line of sheds, he caught sight of a narrow road curving away out of sight in the high grass. Looking back, he saw the boat which had followed them from Wolverhampton mooring up behind *Grace Mercy*.

There was a small cabin cruiser moored at the front of the line of boats. A man was standing on the roof, an assault rifle slung over his shoulder, and Rudi had seen enough images of him over the past few months to recognise him as Ben. Rachel motioned them to climb on board. Rudi went first, and found that the door to its cabin was open. He looked inside and saw a brown-haired woman sitting at the cabin's dining table. Sitting opposite her on a bench seat beside the boat's galley was Herr Professor Mundt. Neither of them looked in the least bit alarmed or tense.

The woman smiled at him. "Hey," she said cheerfully. "You made it. Come on in."

It would be nice, Rudi thought, to be one step ahead for a change. He wondered how that would feel. Everyone else seemed to enjoy it. He walked down the steps into the cabin. "We've met before," he said.

Victoria didn't stop smiling. "You have a good memory."

"It was a memorable time. Did you return the skull to its rightful owners, in the end?"

She didn't answer. Instead she looked at Rupert, who was coming wearily down the steps as if fearful of what he was going to find. "Wotcher, Rupe," she said amiably. "'Sup?"

Rupert stood at the bottom of the steps and looked at her for a long time. "Hello, Araminta," he said finally.

Rudi looked at him, then at Victoria, then at Mundt, then back to Victoria. "Is anyone *else* going to come back from the dead?" he asked testily, but he asked it in a quiet voice, just in case his father was waiting to spring from a cupboard.

Victoria made a show of thinking about it. She shook her head. "Nope, that's about it. Unless you know better."

Rudi sat down heavily beside Mundt and glanced out of the window. Another narrow boat was chugging past, low in the water, its wake rocking them gently. "How many do you have?" he asked.

"Sixteen." They engaged in a staring contest for a few moments, then she grinned. "Look on the bright side; at least we have them, not some utterly batshit bunch of jihadis."

"Oh thank the gods," Rudi deadpanned. "Now I can sleep soundly."

"How many what?" Rupert asked.

Victoria and Rudi exchanged glances. Rudi said, "You can take the radioactive source out of an old hospital x-ray machine, pack high explosive around it, and make a bomb. Not a nuclear weapon, but equally you wouldn't want one going off in your town."

Rupert raised an eyebrow, which Rudi thought was an admirably restrained response, considering the circumstances.

"We have a lot to talk about," Victoria told them.

"Oh, I'd say," Rupert murmured.

There was a sound of footsteps on deck, and a moment later a voice from the hatchway said, "Well, the gang's all here," and Andrew Molson came down the steps. Rudi finally decided there was no point trying to understand any of this; it was time he just gave up and went with the flow.

"Hi, Stephen," said Victoria, and Rudi realised there was actually a family resemblance and that he knew which family it was. All of a sudden, he saw the picture in the puzzle.

"Oh, *bastard*," he said.

IF THIS WERE a mellow entertainment, a lightly-exciting thriller perhaps, this scene with the four of them sitting around the boat's cramped dining table would have seemed wildly contrived. But real life doesn't care about cliché. Real life is so impossibly complex and full of the caprices of real people that coincidences do happen, and sometimes a signal does emerge from the noise. Professor Mundt went for a walk, accompanied by Ben. Everyone agreed that it would be careless to lose him again.

"Shall I start?" Rudi said when no one spoke up. "Okay. Well, I'm *very* angry."

Rupert and Victoria paid no attention. They were looking calmly at each other from opposite sides of the table. She reached out and put her hand over his, where it rested on the tabletop. The look on her face was heartbreaking.

"You're the Whitton-Whytes, aren't you," said Rudi.

"Last of the vintage," said Molson. "Well done."

"I'm so sorry, Rupe," Victoria said.

"I thought you were dead," he told her, and his voice was level. "All these years I thought you were dead."

"I had a pickup arranged," she said. "All we had to do was wait for them, but you never came back."

"What the fuck is going on, please?" Rudi asked Molson.

"Victoria and I have a difference of opinion," Molson said. He thought about it. "Actually, that's not quite fair. It's more a difference of perspective." He thought about it some more. "Perhaps even just a difference of body language."

Rudi glared at him.

"I needed you out of there," Victoria was saying. "I needed to stop Rafe Delahunty; he'd have wound up killing everyone on Earth."

"You needed Mundt as well," Rupert said.

"Yes, well, he was a bonus. I didn't expect you to fucking lose him, though, you muppet."

Rudi looked at Molson. "Let's go outside," he said.

Molson glanced at Victoria and nodded. "Yes. I could do with stretching my legs a bit."

After they'd gone, Victoria said, "Well, that was done with wit and subtlety."

"You're lucky he didn't punch somebody," said Rupert.

She glanced towards the hatchway. "Really? He's never struck me as being a violent man."

"Unlike me?"

"You?" She looked at him and smiled. "He's a good man," she said, waving in the direction Rudi and Molson had gone. "Always trying to do the right thing, never stopping, no matter what gets in his way. Just puts his head down and keeps plodding along. But he'd go a long way out of his way to avoid hurting people. You're different. You're a good man, too, but you're violent when you have to be, and you don't obsess about it. That's quite unusual."

"I saw you in the photograph," he told her. "At the Dancy Archive. Berlin." Her face had been right at the back of the little group of people behind Wilhelm Dancy, her name among those written on the back of the photo. 'Hannelore Dancy'.

She smiled. "Andrew and me," she said. "We were playing poets. It was hard to be a poet in East Germany unless you were working for the State, but that was what made it fun." She stopped smiling and shrugged. "That was when things *were* fun."

He blinked slowly at her.

She said, "I first heard about Rafe, oh, years ago. He was digging around the Community conspiracy nuts in London. I was digging through them too, which is how I heard about him. Rafe was something less rare than you. He was a bad man and he had a bad idea. He wanted to go to the Community and offer his services as their pet plague specialist. I figured the obvious place to find him was the Campus – it was the place where the Community and the EU were both doing proscribed research."

"But he was in the Community instead."

She nodded. "He set up a lab in the Campus, but he wasn't going to live there."

"I can hardly blame him."

"No." Victoria looked sad.

"What were you going to do when you found him?"

"What? Oh, I was going to kill him. That was always going to happen. Kill him and destroy his research so the Community couldn't use it."

"Does that make you a good person or a bad one?" he asked.

"He was developing a strain of flu that made the Xian Flu look like a bit of a sniffle, Rupe," she said evenly. "And he was doing it for money. Don't get all high and mighty with me. I know what you did to Snell, so don't pretend you're on the side of the angels." When he looked blankly at her, she said, "I sent Ben to have a chat to the hoodlum who sold you the polonium. He sang his little heart out."

Rupert found himself wondering what had happened to Pais, found himself unable to care very much. He said, "Snell deserved it."

"No one deserves to die like that, Rupe. He had a wife and kids."

"So did quite a lot of the people he killed in the Campus."

"*Rafe* killed those people. With his fucking flu virus and his frankly shonky containment procedures. Everyone in the Campus was already dead, and if it had got out everyone in the Community would be dead and probably most of the rest of the world too. That virus was an extinction-level event and Snell stopped it."

"He killed over a hundred thousand people," Rupert said. "I liked some of them."

"He signed a piece of paper."

"He pushed the button." It had, in the end, proved impractical to revenge himself on the entire Community for the destruction of his home. He'd settled for the man who had given the order. "And please don't lecture me; you haven't been building bombs as a hobby."

She shook her head. "What the hell made you kill him like that, anyway?"

"I read about it in a book," he said. "It seemed appropriate."

"Well, if he'd just quietly fallen under a tram or something you might have got away with it. As it is, you may as well be wearing a sign around your neck saying 'I DID IT'. The Directorate are coming after you, Rupe."

"They have to find me first."

She sighed. "Well, I might be able to help you with that."

"Do YOU THINK she's telling the truth?" Molson said. "About the bombs?"

Rudi glanced at him. "It's *your* literary fan club that's been going round the East for more than two decades collecting old x-ray machines," he said.

"The Reading Group was Victoria's little joke," Molson said. "Not mine. I thought they were a bit creepy, to be honest. I didn't realise she'd weaponised them until it was too late."

"*Wilhelm Dancy...?*"

Molson looked about him, searching for the words. Finally, he said, "I was bored. It was the Eighties." He shrugged. "It was fun, for a while. Although East Germany wasn't really *fun*. Interesting, more than anything."

Rudi tried to imagine what it would be like to spend a few years as an East German poet just because it was *interesting*. He said,

"She has sixteen dirty bombs. She has Mundt, so she has access to the Community and the Dominions, and he can open doorways into any piece of infrastructure in the world. Nowhere's safe from her."

Molson sighed.

"I suppose it would be redundant to ask why you didn't stop her," Rudi said.

"We haven't seen each other in... oh, years," said Molson. "I just saw where she'd been, the effects of things she'd done. And really, we do both want the same thing. We both want peace between Europe and the Community."

"You just differ on the details of how to achieve it."

"Victoria has a certain directness of spirit."

Rudi put his hands in his pockets and looked about him. "This isn't the Community, is it," he said. "This is somewhere else."

Molson nodded. "It was the first thing we ever built. Nobody knows about it. *I* didn't know how to get in; I had to follow you."

"Because Victoria had the map and she wouldn't share."

Molson smiled sadly.

"How far does it go?"

"Oh, I don't know. There was a story that if you go far enough down the canal it eventually comes back in a circle, but no one's ever done that. I've only been here once before, when I was a boy. My father brought me."

"Captain Charles."

"We spent the day fishing," Molson said. "It was a nice day. A couple of years before he died."

"Did James Brindley ever come here?"

Molson smiled. "Here? No, but I believe he was invited to visit Ernshire once, although that was long before my time. I understand he refused to believe it. He thought it was some kind of trick." He looked thoughtful. "What do you think we should do?"

"About what?" Rudi said.

Molson deadpanned him.

"Yes." Rudi scratched his head.

"Suppose she bombs the Dominions. Crispin will just have Charpentier write completely new landscapes over Europe *and* the Community."

"It would certainly bring lasting peace."

Molson shook his head.

"We could always kill her."

Molson looked at him. "You don't mean that."

"No. No, I don't."

Molson started walking again, and after a moment Rudi followed. What had the Whitton-Whytes built here? A landscape entirely their own, not to be shared with anyone? The most secret of all their secrets? It was rather pleasant, as supervillains' lairs went.

"Everything was fine until the Flu," Molson said. "We were living in the Community, popping over to Europe every now and again for a look. We were at the Versailles Peace Conference, you know; I remember seeing the Sarkisian Collective, all these *very* serious young Frenchmen with their umbrellas and their mad plan to build a world. I was the one who suggested to Crispin's people that they took the Sarkisians seriously. I wanted to see how they were going to do it – I didn't find out till later that Roland Sarkisian was a distant relative and he'd come into possession of the Treatise. After that..." He shrugged. "We moved into a cottage on the estate, near the House By The Sea, as you keep insisting on calling it."

"Does he know who you are?" Rudi asked. "Crispin?"

Molson shook his head. "I suppose we meddled a *bit*, but not very much." He waved a hand to indicate the canal, the Community, all the nested universes. "This was our *inheritance*. We were *responsible* for it." He stopped and stared off into the vast distance. "And then the Flu happened and it became obvious that someone had to do something, otherwise the Community and Europe would eventually be at war. Victoria got very Avenging Angel."

"And it was your inheritance."

Molson let it go. "We thought we could make it less dangerous," he said. "Lay some groundwork, set some conditions, whisper in the right ears, nudge things along. It seemed reasonably straightforward."

"Until you discovered it wasn't."

"It's like driving a car," Molson said. "Once you've started the engine and pulled out into traffic, you can't just let go of the steering wheel."

"And eventually you start to argue between yourselves about the best route to take."

Molson nodded.

"But you're not *driving* a *car*, are you," Rudi said, a little more loudly than he had intended.

"Well, quite," said Molson after a few moments.

They walked on a little further in silence.

"Who's the other player?" Rudi asked.

"Beg pardon?"

"Don't be cute," Rudi said. "It's not just you and Victoria and me and Crispin and the Community."

"From a certain perspective, all those things are the same," Molson pointed out. "But no, you're right. There is another party. They're very sly and they have a very light touch, but they're there. They've been *dabbling* for a long time." He pulled up a stalk of grass, looked at it for a moment, then put it in his mouth. "There was a Whitton-Whyte on the *Mayflower*," he said.

Rudi thought about that for a long while. "Oh, *fantastic*," he said finally.

"He was one of the crew, travelling incognito," Molson said. "Bit of a black sheep, really. We know he reached the Plymouth Colony because Edward Winslow mentions him briefly, but after that we don't know."

Rudi could have cared less about Edward Winslow, whoever he was. "Your fucking family," he said.

"Quite."

"What do they want?"

Molson shrugged.

What Rudi chiefly wanted to do was get back on the boat, return to Europe, and hope this mess would just go away. He said, "I had to use Crispin's computers to make sense of the map. He'll know where we are."

"He's always known," Molson said. "He had the skull for a little while, once upon a time; he'll have run it through the Machine ages ago. I wouldn't worry about that; if he wanted to be here he would be."

"I had it myself, once," Rudi said, remembering watching Tómas photographing the skull. Tómas's principals, and probably the Vatican as well, he realised, also had the map. He saw the look on Molson's face. "Long story," he said.

"In all honesty," Molson said, "I'm a bit weary of long stories."

Rudi watched swifts darting and shrilling in the sky overhead. He wondered where they nested, and then he wondered if they migrated, and if so, where to. "Me too," he said.

BACK ON THE boat, Rupert and Victoria were sitting in the same places, but the atmosphere in the cabin seemed calm enough. Nothing appeared to be broken, anyway. Rudi slid into his seat beside Rupert and said, "There's someone here to whom you owe an apology."

Victoria actually gave a little laugh and clapped her hands together. "You brought *Alice*!" she said.

"I don't want to know what happened in Tallinn, because I already have too much to think about, but you owe her an explanation."

Victoria subsided. "Yes. Yes, I do."

"I would, though, like somebody to explain the skull to me. Anyone?"

The Whitton-Whytes – he might as well start thinking of them like that – looked at each other. "We lost everything, you know," Victoria said. "The family. We wouldn't stop drawing bloody maps and eventually it ruined us. We had an estate in Nottinghamshire, a big house in London. All gone. The skull was in the house in London, it sat in a glass case for years and years and years and nobody bothered to look at it because it had always sat there. When the family went bankrupt I suppose it was sold along with everything else, and down the years it was sold again and again and again, until it turned up in Estonia. And then I found this old letter that mentioned it and said there was a map on the back."

Rudi looked at Molson, who just shrugged. *Not my circus, not my monkeys.*

"I don't know what was going through your father's head when he took it to the Embassy," she went on. "Maybe he thought he could make more money from them than I was paying him. After that…" She shook her head. "We tried to get it back but it was off in the wind. Christ only knows how it wound up in the hands of those Basque muppets."

Rudi thought about it. At some point he was going to have to process the sheer amount of damage his father had caused to so many people with a single simple act of venality, but right now he had bigger things to worry about. "All right," he said. "So, the Americans."

She looked at him, then at Molson, then at him again. "We don't know anything about them," she said finally. "Except that they've been there for three hundred years and they've recently been poking around in Europe. We need to be ready for them and all Europe and the Community have been doing is dicking about trying to prove who has the bigger balls."

"There might be nothing to worry about," he said.

"They tried to kill you to get their hands on the stuff your father left you," she pointed out. "Not because of the money, although Christ knows a billion dollars is always useful, but because they knew it would lead them to the remaining Sarkisians. That implies all kinds of things."

It certainly did. For one thing, it suggested that they had been doing more than just 'poking around'. "My father worked for you, didn't he," he said. "Not the Community."

She snorted. "Me *and* the Community. Sly little bastard."

"Something didn't seem quite right," he said. "Charpentier said they worked for the Community, helping them secure the borders. But if that were true, the Community wouldn't have needed Mundt – they'd already have known everything they needed to know."

"The Sarkisians were dangerous," she said, "for reasons you know very well. They needed putting somewhere safe."

"With you."

Victoria sighed. "And they *were* safe. And then Roland Sarkisian offered your father a *lot* of money to help him get away from us."

The little corner of his mind where Rudi kept a running tally of his father's various evils wondered idly what had happened to that money; certainly it had never raised its head while he and Ivari were growing up motherless in a succession of poky flats.

He said, "I'm sorry to labour this point, but if the Sarkisians were in your possession, and doing research on the Community's borders, why do *you* need the Professor?"

"Because the research they let us see was incomplete. Just like the Professor's research that Stephen gave to the English media was incomplete. It didn't work. It was useless. Worse than useless because we didn't know how much of it was kosher and how much they'd just made up off the top of their heads." She saw the look on his face. "These were not stupid people; they knew that once we had everything they'd just become a liability. They kept stringing us along until they were ready to skip town."

"So," Rudi said. "You have the map, you have someone to open the borders for you, you claim to have a number of dirty bombs and a fleet of boats to take them anywhere you want. What now?"

She let the *claim* bit pass. "I want the borders between the Community and Europe opened. In perpetuity. I want proper *détente*. A real Union, not just a piece of paper covering up a mess of politicking. Something that means something. I want them to be ready for whatever the Americans are planning."

That was going to be quite a *détente*, considering there was no such thing as 'Europe', just an ever-expanding roster of countries. "You know, people don't generally respond well to threats."

"They'll respond well to this one."

This was probably true; everyone was already tiptoeing around in case Crispin suddenly got the urge to rewrite some landscape again. "You could just tell them about the Americans, let them make up their own minds."

"You know what happens then," Victoria said, shaking her head. "People will try to break in. There will be provocations, things will get out of control."

"You seem awfully certain that the Americans pose a threat."

"There's some speculation that they were responsible for the Realm," she said. She looked at Rudi and Molson. "Which was an act of war all on its own. Oh, yeah, it was harmless enough and nobody got hurt, but it was a warning, to anyone who was smart enough to read it. They'd have to have had detailed topographies of both the areas they were transposing, to pull that trick, which means they're in Europe *and* the Community." She nodded at Rudi. "You think about that for a minute or two."

"And I'm sitting here listening to all this because...?" But he already knew the answer.

"Someone has to deliver the message," she said. "Someone Crispin and the Community and the Europeans will listen to."

"You'll forgive me if I'm a little weary of being everyone's messenger boy."

"Isn't that just what you are, though, *Coureur*? You've done it before for Crispin; you can do it now for me."

He sighed. "They'll want proof."

"I'll get you proof," said Rupert. Everyone looked at him as if he had suddenly appeared in their midst in a puff of smoke. He looked bashful. "We were talking, while the two of you were outside. This place has a border with the American Community; Professor Mundt will open a crossing and I'll go over and take a look."

Rudi thought about it. "I should go with you," he said.

Rupert shook his head. "Not this time. Maybe later, when we have some idea who they are and what they want."

They engaged in a staring match, which Rudi as usual lost. "Well," he said. He looked at Victoria. "What about the Professor?"

"He stays here."

"Unacceptable, sorry."

"Listen," she said, "this place borders on *everywhere*, but it's useless without him. I can't threaten people if I don't have anything to threaten them *with*."

"That actually sounds like not such a bad result," he told her.

She shook her head. "Not going to happen."

He thought about it. "It's not beyond Crispin to start erasing choice bits of the Community until you give Mundt up, you know."

"That's a game of chicken he's not going to win."

"Come to that, he could just get Professor Charpentier to erase *this* place."

She shook her head. "Detailed topographies," she said. "He'd need proper surveys, and he's not going to get those."

Obviously, the world and everything in it had been stupid since the dawn of time. It was just that, every now and again, there seemed to be a surge in stupid and there was nothing anyone could do about it except hang on and hope things would get better soon.

"So," Victoria said briskly. "We're all agreed, then?"

Rudi thought about it. "No," he said finally. "I've had enough of this. *Rudi go here, Rudi go there, Rudi do this, Rudi do that.* I'm sick of it." He looked round the table. They were all looking at him as if he'd lost his mind. "Okay," he said a little ruefully. "Rant over, but you get the general idea. I came here to ask you to turn Professor Mundt over to me, not carry notes about for everyone. Send a postcard or something."

She gave him a long, level stare, and he got a momentary sense of how she must see him, as an asset, a piece to be moved around a board. "All right," she said. "Shall we eat?"

"About fucking time," Rupert muttered.

AS AFTERNOON TURNED to evening, the sun began to settle towards the far horizon and lights started to come on along the quayside, strung up on poles and along the edges of the marquees. Citronella candles were lit against swarms of midges. Some of the river people took out guitars and fiddles and, to Rudi's horror, started singing sea shanties.

He found himself gravitating, by default, towards the barbecues, and shortly after that he was cooking burgers and sausages and chicken drumsticks and handing them out on paper plates to whoever went past. Which was obviously what one did when one had tracked a supervillain down to their secret headquarters and exposed their evil plan for world domination.

Rupert came over, accepted a hotdog with all the trimmings. "I was starving," he said round a mouthful of food.

Rudi looked at him. "Are you going to be all right?"

Rupert washed down his hotdog with a swallow of beer from a plastic cup. "It's what I do, right?"

"It's what *I* do."

"You have a restaurant to run."

"Also some errands."

Rupert shook his head. "Go home, cook food. Molson's coming with me; we'll be fine."

Over at the quayside, Alice came up out of *Grace Mercy*'s hatch and stepped ashore, a glass of wine in her hand. Victoria followed her, and they stood by the boat, talking. Alice threw her wine at Victoria, then slapped her across the face, then stomped away. Rudi knew how she felt. Victoria – and he supposed Molson as well – had been driving him and Rupert around like old ponies for quite a large part of their lives, assessing them for their usefulness, placing them in situations where they thought it would do the most good.

"What are you going to do about her?"

Rudi sighed. "Resettle her. Give her some money, hope she lives happily ever after. And yes, I'm aware it's not enough, but I don't have anything else."

Rupert took another bite of his hotdog, another swallow of beer. "So," he said, "this has been a shining failure."

"We found Mundt," Rudi pointed out.

"Good luck trying to explain that to Crispin and Michael."

Rudi took up a pair of tongs and turned the burgers and sausages on the barbecue. He waved smoke away from his face and looked away, and saw Seth and Gwen sitting side by side in deckchairs over on the edge of the party. Seth looked utterly bereft, and Gwen looked incandescent, but at least they were talking. "Spreading sunshine and happiness wherever I go," he muttered.

"What was that?"

Rudi shook his head. "Nothing."

"Are you really not going to tell Crispin about all this?"

Rudi shrugged. He'd been thinking about it, trying to fit all the angles together. Crispin didn't know where he was, but he knew the map on the back of the skull was significant. When Victoria conveyed her threat to him it would only be a matter of time before he decided to come here and have a look. Mundt would close the border crossings, Charpentier would open them again, Mundt would close them again. It would all get messy very quickly. It might be for the best, after all, if Crispin heard the news from someone rational. "I don't know," he said.

Rachel came up and said, "You look like you're having a nice time but we're going to be leaving soon. We'd like to get back onto the Staffordshire and Worcestershire before it's properly dark."

Rudi nodded. "I'll go and round everyone up."

"Excellent. We're over there." She pointed at a rather raffish-looking cabin cruiser moored a little way along the quay.

"Okay. Thank you."

Rachel left, and Rudi sighed and looked at the barbecue. He tapped one of the other cooks on the shoulder and handed over the tongs, and the man clapped him on the shoulder heartily enough to dislocate it.

He walked round in front of the barbecue and held out his hand, and Rupert shook it. There seemed, all of a sudden, nothing and everything to say, so he just compromised and nodded and turned and walked away to see if he could find Alice.

UNLIKE THE CANALS of England, there was no speed limit here, and Rachel and Alex's boat was impressively nippy. The light was fading in the sky behind them as they approached the border. The little girl, Casey, was asleep in one of the bunks in the cabin; Gwen and Seth were sitting in the prow of the boat, still talking. Alice was at the dining table, a mug of tea in front of her.

Rudi looked at her as he went by, but she just shook her head tiredly and he carried on towards the hatch leading to the cockpit. To one side of the steps there was a pile of toys and cloth animals and water pistols and alphabet blocks, even a couple of books printed on brightly-coloured felt. He approved of such analogue child-rearing tools. He picked up one of the little books and flapped through it, read the story of a big blue cat who had many adventures and experienced many sadnesses but finally found peace and happiness because he'd learned that people were, on the whole, kind and good. The author was a realist, though; the cat was still alone at the end of the book.

He bent down to replace the book on the pile, and noticed, poking out from under a crumpled blanket, what looked like a wad of paper. He pulled it out – there was most of a ream there, and turned his back to the light in the cabin while he leafed through it.

The document looked, to his admittedly untutored eye, well cared-for but undeniably old, and otherwise it fitted the only description he had of it, a thick wad of papers covered in mathematical notations in many different hands. It might, conceivably, even be the original, the paper looked old enough. What it was undoubtedly not, by now, was the only copy. The little girl had been busy with it, diligently attempting to conceal the arcane mathematics beneath crayon drawings of animals and houses and people. She showed some talent. Her horses were pretty good. Or maybe they were dogs.

Which left the eternal question: What to do now? Was it a test? A bribe? Was someone waiting to see what he would do with it? Should he take it and use it on his own account – always assuming Lev could make head or tail of it? Did someone expect him to start writing and rewriting universes? That momentarily didn't sound so bad. A universe without beefburgers had a certain appeal. He was tired of games like this, but it was only recently that he had noticed just *how* tired.

He laid the pile of papers back on the blanket, turned away, and walked up the steps out of the cabin. Halfway up, he stopped, turned, went back and picked it up again.

He carried the sheaf of papers up into the cockpit, where Alex and Rachel were sitting at the boat's controls, and with a strong backhand throw he flung the Treatise out over the canal. The dozens of pages fluttered suddenly like a flight of birds in the failing light before falling to the surface of the water and disappearing into the churning wake of the boat.

Fuck you. As a message, it may have lacked tact, but for the moment it was all he felt inclined to send.

He stood there for a while, watching the pages of the Whitton-Whytes' miracle disappear. As he'd told Rupert, things were never *over*. They just went on and on, and all you could do was hold on for the ride. You couldn't do the best for everyone, but that didn't mean you shouldn't try.

"Oi," said Alex. "Was that our Casey's drawings?"

He scowled and turned to the couple, feeling suddenly awkward and embarrassed. "Yes," he admitted.

"What the hell did you want to do something like that for?" asked Rachel. "She was really proud of those. She'll be heartbroken."

Rudi opened his mouth. Closed it again. There was nothing,

nothing at all, he could say which would not make things worse. He felt his shoulders starting to hunch up.

"I wouldn't come into *your* house and start throwing stuff away," Alex told him. "You can bloody well apologise to her when she wakes up."

"You're lucky we're not chucking you out and making you walk," said Rachel.

He nodded and turned and went back into the cabin.

"You okay?" Gwen asked when she saw his face.

He looked at the little galley kitchen, decided Alex and Rachel might not be too well-disposed towards him using it right now. "One of those days," he said.

ACKNOWLEDGEMENTS

AND HERE WE are, finally. End of the Line. It's been a wild ride; I certainly had no idea, when I finished *Autumn*, that it would take us so far or involve quite so many books, but now it's done.

Thanks to:

Peter Haynes for the canals
Caroline, for the level crossings and everything, really
Drags, for Bodfish; it's my dearest wish that someone somewhere names a band after them
Rachel, for the Falt Skreen Teevies and the Bendi Falt Skreen Teevies
Elchien, for Amsterdam
Alice, for pointing out what was wrong with the map
Bente, who was there
Nik, Louis, Krista and Kaisa, for Estonia

And thank you, everyone else who came along for the ride; Rudi abides.